Hindsight

CRISPR, the Last Word in WMD

L. A. Jaworski

WestBow Press books may be ordered through booksellers or by contacting:

WestBow Press
A Division of Thomas Nelson & Zondervan
1663 Liberty Drive
Bloomington, IN 47403
www.westbowpress.com
1 (866) 928-1240

ISBN: 978-1-9736-7390-3 (sc)
ISBN: 978-1-9736-7391-0 (hc)
ISBN: 978-1-9736-7369-9 (e)

Library of Congress Control Number: 2019913452

Print information available on the last page.

WestBow Press rev. date: 11/14/2019

Prologue...

Displaced by Technology, Humanities Sunset—Daniel placed the paper on the table. He finished his morning coffee, milk, two sugars. *The Rag* was a local nondescript newspaper. Circular really. The author, Jenny Pendleton, was no better. Yet, it was the insight and conclusion that interested Daniel. Internal projections put the number closer to 38%, not 27%. Ms. Pendleton's conclusions were correct. Overpopulation... the proverbial *it is what it is* cliché.

The issues identified by Ms. Pendleton were mainstream economic reality...headline fodder for the talking heads...political WMD's for the president. Daniel was chief economist for the Federal Reserve Bank of St. Louis. He knew his duty. He agreed something need be done but what? No one had successfully put the genie back inside the bottle. Daniel doubted Ms. Pendleton held the answers. He trusted his instincts and acted accordingly.

Chapter One

An archeological finding from the University of Calgary determined that humans have relied on cereal grains for over 100,000 years...rice, wheat, and corn...a staple dietary crop.

Argentina
Pampas and Mesopotamia Regions

Alberto looked at his fields from the kitchen window. Not close, but close enough. Close enough for Alberto to set his morning coffee down and have a look-see.

It was the first week in November. Alberto suspected there was a problem. He stepped from the kitchen and crossed the porch. The screen door clanging shut was barely audible over the crunching gravel beneath his feet. Alberto was deliberate; his actions had purpose. The sounds a distraction from the problem that loomed before him.

The crops were not coming up. Sprouts should be visible. No late frost or blight reported. Yet there was most definitely a problem. Alberto dropped to one knee. He reached into the ground. Who says farmers don't get dirty? What he pulled up was unsettling. He stood up and looked down the field. He started to walk. Periodically he stopped to check the row. He stepped across rows while he walked and checked neighboring rows. They were all the same. He continued this procedure while he retrieved his cell phone and called his neighboring farmers. He ordered them all back into their fields. Each one was provided instructions, report back to him immediately. Time is money. If he could get replanted in ten days, there would be a crop to harvest. If not, it would be a long winter.

The calls came in one by one. Everyone was reporting the same thing. Some more extensive than others. *Meeting tonight in town at the hall. Eight o'clock*, the text message read. Alberto stared off into the distance, the Andes clearly visible. Two more calls to make…the first call was to the local botanist at the University in Rosario. The second was to the Minister of Agro-industry, Alberto's cousin José.

~~~

"José speaking."

"José, it's Alberto."

"Alberto, how are you?"

"Not good. We have a meeting scheduled tonight at eight o'clock. I have called the University in Rosario and spoke with the botanist, Angelina Montero. She will be here tomorrow. I think you should be as well." José hesitated before questioning his older cousin. José had the job that Alberto did not want.

"What seems to be the problem?"

"I honestly do not know. My fields and those of my neighbors and their neighbors are ruined. I will have to replant and by extension so will everyone else."

"They can't be saved?"

"No, they cannot. I'm more worried about the soil and a barren field than I am a poor season."

"I'll see you tomorrow at ten," José said.

"She'll be here at nine," Alberto responded.

"Nine, it is." The call ended. José did not want to but knew that he must. He stood up and walked down to the president's office. Bad news never gets better with age.

Alberto's thoughts returned to the evenings meeting and the establishment of a plan.

~~~

Jesus Maria, Argentina

Alberto arrived at 6:45 p.m. Neighboring farmers began to arrive by 7:15. By 7:50, there was a packed house. Standing room only to the event nobody wanted to attend. The average Argentinean's farm is over 400 acres. More times than not, the farmer's children choose city life over the family farm. The Quinterro's enjoyed farming. Their farm grew by acquisition. It seemed to work for them.

At 8:00, Alberto took the stage and everyone sat down. "Okay, let's get started. You all know why we are here. Tomorrow morning, I will be meeting with Ms. Montero from the University in Rosario. José will also be present." Everyone knew the Quinterro family and most knew José personally.

"I see many of you brought samples. Mine are on the table over there." Alberto motioned with a wave of his arm. "I expect Ms. Montero and José by nine o'clock tomorrow. If you haven't brought samples but wish to do so, please provide the seed used, fertilizer, disease suppressant, and when you planted. Any questions so far?" Alberto asked.

Alberto was all business. Everyone in the room knew he had their best interest at heart with his own.

"My fear is the soil, not a poor season. Whatever this is, it struck quickly and effectively. I personally estimate an 83 percent destruction of all cereal grains planted on Quinterro land. If affected, some of my fruit trees and grapevines will be showing stress soon. For those of you that have similar crop selection, let's stay in touch. This is not the time to be competitive, parsimonious. Assuming this is isolated blight, we may have to burn our fields to destroy whatever it is. If that is the case, then this season is likely over now." People began to stir and mumble. Many, if not most, were not financially sound. The Quinterro's and a select few could survive. A lost season was the difference between one and done for the majority.

"Quiet, please," Alberto said. The mumbling died down. "Let's think about it. If it is a spore, we cannot take the chance that it's still in the soil to destroy newly planted crops. Water could spread the spore… and wind. If we burn the field, we lose the topsoil and will be forced to fertilize. We'll plant alfalfa or a similar crop to stave off soil erosion. That's my thought process. We'll know more tomorrow. For now, does anyone have any questions for me? Anything I'm not considering?"

The room fell silent, there were no questions for Alberto. There were no items missed or what ifs not considered. It was a bad situation that could get substantially worse.

~~~

The Argentinian agriculture industry contributes 5 percent to the country's gross domestic product, GDP. GDP is the national output of goods and services valued at market prices. Five percent may seem immaterial, but the ripple effect is staggering. The agriculture industry employs over 13 percent of the nation's workforce. That is 1.4 million people. The likelihood of those jobs being absorbed elsewhere in the economy is zero. Food costs would skyrocket, adding to hyperinflation that the country might never recover from. The previous economic crisis was still fresh in the minds of the average Argentinean.

Alberto was neither a biologist nor a botanist. He was a farmer. However, he was an educated farmer. He knew there were over 100,000 different kinds of fungi. Most were beneficial to the soil through decomposition; however, there were roughly 8,000 types of fungi that were deadly to plants. Damping off was one such kind.

Damping off attacks seedlings before they break through the soil. It has been known to strike seedlings that are an inch or so tall. The fungus rots the stem at the soil line and can destroy an infected seedling overnight.

Alberto was looking at various samples under the microscope and concerned. Damping off requires that the soil the seedlings are placed in be saturated. Excessively moist. The soil on his fields was not overly moist. If this were a new strain, it could create problems for future crops. He looked at several more samples before calling it a night at 2:47 a.m. Morning would arrive soon enough.

~~~

Alberto woke at 6 a.m.—late. There was a time when he was up at 4:30 a.m. every morning, but those days were long gone. He walked to the kitchen. Remembering his cell phone on the nightstand, he retraced his steps. At fifty-seven, he did not have to worry about many illnesses, but he was becoming forgetful. He laughed. Returning to the kitchen, Consuelo was making his breakfast. "Good mornings" were exchanged before Alberto took a seat at the breakfast table outside.

He checked his text messages. None of the neighboring farmers' fields had a high level of soil saturation. While finishing his second cup of coffee, three vehicles pulled into the turnaround at the end of the driveway. More samples for the botanist. Fifteen more were to be received by the time Ms. Montero and José were to arrive.

José was early, eight o'clock. Consuelo showed him to the breakfast table. Alberto and José were deep in conversation when Consuelo showed Ms. Montero to the table.

Angelina Montero was thirty-four years of age. She was new to the university. She was considered extremely intelligent and had written many articles on terrorists' use of the food chain. A weapon of mass destruction. The fact that she was five feet nine inches tall, shapely with shoulder-length coal black hair that glistened in the sun, only added to her overall beauty.

Introductions were made. Alberto dove right into the problem. "Ms. Montero..."

"Angelina . . . please."

"Angelina, José and I were discussing your academic credentials just now. We were also discussing your views on terrorists' use of the food chain as a potential weapon. I am not saying that this is the case here nor am I now discounting it. I will say that it is something I never considered."

"Okay," Angelina said. She was not yet certain why she was here other than the fact that Alberto Quinterro called.

"Angelina, every year we check the soil that we farm. We have over four thousand five hundred acres of farmland and take over three hundred soil samples. This farmland is the richest most fertile soil in the world. True black gold. That is, up until this time yesterday." Alberto paused because he wanted her to grasp what he was about to say.

"I have lost over 80 percent of my crop. Wheat, corn, soybeans . . . gone. My neighbors have all lost percentages close to that. Their neighbors and their neighbors' neighbors have lost similar percentages. My fruit crops have not yet been affected but I will need to check them daily. Again, my neighbors will be doing the same and their neighbors. On the table behind me, are marked samples from twenty-three neighboring farms. The farthest one from this farm is over two hundred miles away." Pause for effect and a sip of coffee. "We have all been hit. We have all been affected." Alberto's voice tailed off. The impact of what had happened was starting to sink in.

Angelina thought for the longest time. She had always believed that the cereal grain portion of the food chain was a likely terrorist's target, or at least it should be in her opinion. Cereal grains are a primary source of carbohydrates and proteins. They are not simply for human consumption either. Most cattle and other types of livestock are corn fed. The pros and cons aside, it is still a fact. But Angelina had always queried what would happen if the cereal grain supply chain were disrupted.

"Just so I understand you, you're saying that your farm and every farm between here and 200-plus miles have been affected by a disease? And that that disease has wiped out approximately 80 percent of the crops planted?" Angelina raised an eyebrow and moved forward in her chair. She placed her hands on the table before moving further to stand up.

"Yes, Angelina, that is exactly what I am saying," Alberto responded. She stood up from the breakfast table and walked over to the table that held the samples. She grabbed a bag at random and looked at the contents. Each bag had an index written directly on the bag or on a Post-it Note. The index included the date planted, seed used, fertilizer, and disease suppressant and insecticide. This would be useful data but likely useless in finding a solution. She looked at two or three more bags before asking to look at some fields.

The first fields viewed were Quinterro's. Angelina took 100 sample bags with her. They drove across several of the fields. "Was it like this yesterday?" Angelina asked.

"No," Alberto said before adding, "This field was still green yesterday. Now it looks dead. The disease has consumed everything." Alberto shook his head. "Whatever it is, it is fast acting."

They continued to walk across the fields. They noticed a few dead crows in the field, a mouse or two. Angelina took them for further testing. Once she'd filled her sample bags from various points on the field and compass, they drove to three other farms and did the same thing. By the end of the day, they had exhausted the sample bags but had a fairly accurate geographic coverage.

"Any suggestions?" José asked.

"None yet," Angelina said.

"Should they replant?" José asked. "This is not the time to be overly cautious. A complete loss of crops will make the economic crisis of 2000 look like a day at the beach." José was not trying to pressure her. The situation was minacious and needed no help from him.

"My guess would be no to replanting, the disease may have a dormancy characteristic. Remember, most fungi do not make their own food; they live off their host. In this case, they have consumed the host. If there's a dormancy characteristic, then replanting won't do anything to help."

"Do fungi generally have a dormancy characteristic?" José asked.

"Some do."

"So what makes you think this one does?" Alberto asked.

"The distribution's too widespread. To me it seems planned. Orchestrated. All crops affected. Arguably within the same time period. Too much of a coincidence for my thinking." Angelina sighed. "Besides, if this is manmade, and I'm not saying that it is, it's what I would have done were I to create such a fungus." Alberto and José looked despondent.

"Should they burn their fields?" José asked.

"Give me a couple of days," Angelina said.

"We don't have much time. I need to be back in the field; otherwise, I won't have any crop to harvest."

"Would you rather I tell you to return to the field and lose yet another crop? Give me a day, two tops. Call others in if you'd like; they'll tell you the same thing." She got into her car.

"Listen, I understand the situation," she began. "I was standing in line just like everyone else in 2000 to draw my allotment from the bank. Post a notice to all farmers affected. Have them send me soil and crop samples. Where possible, provide GPS coordinates, I would like to see the area affected. I'll be in touch," and she drove off.

Alberto and José stood in silence. The situation was bad and they both knew it. Neither was used to being asked to wait for answers. Both secretly hoped it was not what they thought. Secretly . . . neither wanting to verbalize what the other believed.

"I have to call the president," José said. He entered the house. Alberto followed. He drafted a group text message and sent it out. *Soil samples, crop samples, Angelina's address at the university, and above all else, do not say anything to anybody for at least forty-eight hours.* Alberto knew that that would never last.

Chapter Two

The United States is the largest export of cereal grains in the world and produced more food than the entire European Union combined.

St. Louis, Missouri

Work was work; Katie was reminded when she entered her office. Bail Prichard had had some success in creating a potentially deadly fungus. Small-scale testing would be required. "I am still looking at the end of the year. From there we could begin development of a fungicide," the email read.

Katie was burned out. Joseph's letter and package to her confirmed her fears. She was being frozen out but by whom or was it a group of whoms. It was her discovery…her research that would save the world. She sat motionless before exhaling and beginning her day.

~~~

National Security Agency

Larry continued to monitor local developments in Argentina. He was able to triangulate the location of the cell phone transmissions and focused his attention there. The area he was interested in was the northern portion of Argentina. It was the more densely populated part of the country. Yet there was no traditional evidence of a terrorist attack.
~~~

It was when Larry thought of it in a traditional sense that he began to think outside the box.

"Why must everything be a car bomb?" Larry said out loud. Another analyst happened to walk by.

"Excuse me."

"Sorry. I was just thinking out loud. I was asking myself must everything be a car bomb. At some point, terrorist will evolve into a higher form of terrorism. Evolution is not selective. Everything evolves or dies."

"Higher forms of terrorism may have us wanting the car bomb," the analyst said before walking away.

~~~

Buenos Aires, Argentina

José's phone call with the president went as expected. She informed the Minister of the Interior and the Minister of Science, who sent fifteen lab assistants to the University in Rosario to work with Dr. Montero. This was given top priority.

~~~

Countries are always at war. True warfare in modern terms is economic. But at the end of the day, it's all about trying to do the right thing. The president had consented to José's suggestion that he send an alert to several trading partners, a gesture of goodwill. The email went out to twenty-six recipients. There are 193 individual countries in the world today. Less than 15 percent qualifies one for doing the right thing. The email was short and sweet with confirmation that further information will be forthcoming.

Jonathan Livingston was a recipient of José's gesture. He read the email and initially paid it no mind; however, an hour later, he reread the email and forwarded a copy to Patrick with a query. "Please confirm through your overseas operation. Would your super-seed survive?" For the time being, Jonathan chose to forget the conversation he had had with Amged.

Upon receipt of Jonathan's email, Patrick was concerned. Not at the question but at the gaps in José's initial email to Jonathan and the other recipients. He forwarded the email to Amged with the note *Please follow up and advise.* Upon receipt, Amged simply smiled and held on to the email. He would later forward the email to Marshall, but first he placed a call to Sherrief and informed him of the outcome of Project Jericho. The call was intercepted and forwarded to the assigned desk analyst.

~~~

Larry received and analyzed the call for content and location. With that, he was better able to triangulate the cell phone to Central Illinois. The calls were simply too short in duration to afford a better and more accurate location fix. The Argentinian situation was easier. Seven messages simultaneously leaving an area create their own beacon. There was no question that something had happened. Unfortunately, Larry's lack of actual field experience did not afford him a gut instinct.

~~~

Dr. Montero had worked through the night and was greeted in the morning by fifteen lab technician/assistants. They were from the Ministry of Science. She was thankful for their support. Space and equipment were at a premium; they came prepared. Given the relatively rural nature of Argentina and its developing country classification, previous administrations had purchased several mobile labs. These labs were equipped with powerful microscopes, portable computers that could be networked together, and one portable electronic microscope. One being better than none.

After an entire night of research, Dr. Montero was more comfortable explaining to the technicians what her expectations were. Given the long night of analyzing plant and soil samples, she was beginning to formulate a hypothesis.

While the lab technicians continued the task directed, Dr. Montero took a quick nap. She would discuss the results of their research and hers with José when she had time. That is to say, after she woke.

~~~

Tabuk, Saudi Arabia

Sherrief sat outside his residence and looked to the sky for answers. He was not alarmed that Project Jericho had been discovered within a relatively short period of time. It was always going to be discovered. Of that, there was never a doubt. What troubled Sherrief was the delivery system. *How can we disburse Jericho to the true infidel and those usurper wannabes?*

Since 9/11, the United States had been more difficult to infiltrate. People were nosy into the affairs of others. There was a pre–World War II mentality: *Report aggressive drivers by texting *77, Report suspicious personal behavior, See Something Say Something.* The groundwork had been laid. Sherrief intended to build on it.

Sherrief and his operatives would not be able to purchase planes and fly them into the United States without being stopped. China either. They would also find it difficult to purchase several planes within the two countries for the intended purpose. Canada could be added to that list. Discreet multiple purchases were an option. Rental for this particular task was an option. Coordination would have to be perfect. But again, how to outfit the planes for crop dusting without someone or a group of someone's becoming suspicious?

Hakeem had joked about simply sprinkling the spores from the windows of the plane and trusting to the trade winds. That was a possibility but again not reliable. Air balloons were even discussed but again trusting to luck.

Sherrief sat there and stared at the sky, waiting for an answer. Call it divine intervention.

The sky was beautiful. It always seemed to be. Higher elevation brought one closer to the clouds. The air was crisp and clean. There was
~~~

no pollution here, this was not the West and Far East. *Men of the West and those who chose to follow them had no soul,* Sherrief thought.

The moon was out. The night sky was relatively clear. There was a light cloud shrouding the moon in a fine see-through veil. More mist than cloud really. Cirrus clouds, Sherrief thought. They are the clouds that are at 20,000+ feet. Tabuk was at 2,500 feet. There were times when he felt he could touch the clouds they seem so close. Sherrief placed his feet on the balcony ledge and leaned back in his chair. Something he would scold his children for doing. He sat back staring at the shroud, becoming mesmerized by it. He was missing something. He stayed in that position for several minutes before falling asleep.

~~~

Buenos Aires, Argentina

José was in his office early. He'd barely gotten any sleep. He had been in contact with his counterparts in Brazil, Paraguay, and Uruguay. These countries were not necessarily friendlies nor were they enemies. Again, it was the right thing to do.

Each country seemed to have been affected. Though on a much smaller scale. They were also less able to deal with the situation. *Developing country* is a relative term. Data should be forthcoming... sufficient to reflect the extent of the devastation. José was confident while he sipped his morning coffee. *What was the likelihood of this being a natural phenomenon?* He would hold off further exploration of that idea until he spoke with Dr. Montero.
~~~

Chapter Three

Argentina ranks number 2 in corn exports, 7th in wheat exports, and 15th in rice exports.

Rockville, Maryland

Jonathan woke earlier than normal. Being the Secretary of the Department of Agriculture was not demanding in today's technologically driven economy. However, it had possibilities, which were what was keeping Jonathan from a sound night's sleep. He recalled Amged's comment or conversation, depending upon one's point of view. Amged was pretty clear with his meaning being anything but vague: "A test area first, say Argentina." Coincidence? Jonathan was not that naïve to think so.

The question Jonathan had was twofold: *What's in it for me? And do I have the stomach for it?*

The answer to the first question was easy. *Money!* And a lot of it.

The answer to the second question was more difficult. That answer would require soul-searching, introspection, self-examination. Jonathan was no fool. He was in politics. He had skeletons in the closet and bodies buried out back. *This will take some time,* he thought.

~~~
~~~

St. Louis, Missouri

There was a buzz about the office Katie noticed. Maybe it was from the vacation. She felt more relaxed than in recent days. *Sun, sand, and good company can have that effect on people . . . even me.*

"So what's all the excitement about?" Katie was getting coffee in the break room. The lab technician looked at her before responding. *Back already*, Katie thought.

"There was some type of natural disaster or some such," the technician said with a wave of his hand, "in Argentina. Our super-seed is getting field tested . . . literally." The technician giggled at his own witticism.

"Disaster? Where?" Katie asked.

"Argentina someplace. Marshall has the details," the technician said before he left the break room. Katie leaned against the counter and sipped her coffee. She did not want to, but knew she must speak with Marshall. She had acted honestly and without regret. Marshall was the one who had frozen her out. She pushed off from the counter; she had been standing there with her arms crossed, holding a cup of coffee . . . *classic defensive stance.*

"Marshall," Katie knocked on his door before entering.

"Katie, come in." Marshall was warm and full of smiles. He was the old Marshall. "How was the vacation?"

"Good, thank you. Very much in need," Katie said before adding, "I hear our super-seed is getting field tested."

"Yes. There's been a situation in Argentina. It couldn't have worked out any better for us. Laboratory testing is one thing but actual field testing against a fungus should solidify our discovery . . . your discovery."

"I hadn't heard or read about a fungus."

"It just happened a few days ago, give the news agencies time," Marshall remarked. "Jonathan called Patrick, who told Amged, who called me."

"That's an extreme telephone grapevine. Any details?"

"None yet. They're currently gathering samples to determine how widespread the fungus is. From what I understand, it's extensive."

"Keep me in the loop, I'd be interested to know how the seed performs." Katie got up from the chair and returned to her office. Along the way, she made a detour back to the break room for more coffee. She thought about the situation and the likelihood of this being a "natural disaster." Although it had been a while and the conditions under which they had parted were not 100 percent amicable, Katie sent an email to Joseph. She kept it professional.

To: Dr. Joseph Patrick, University of Arkansas
From: Katie Pendleton
Subject: Argentina Super-seed Field Testing

Joseph:

Trust all is well.
I was wondering if you heard anything on the situation in Argentina. If you have any news involving the nature of the natural disaster, please let me know. I have some thoughts that may help improve the seed's resistance to potential known diseases.

Thank you,
Katie

She pressed Send before reaching for her cell phone. She sent a text message to Bail regarding the situation in Argentina. The text message was more personal than the email to Joseph but there was nothing she could do about that. *It is what it is*, she thought. She advised Bail that Amged and Patrick had been apprised of the situation by the Secretary of the Department of Agriculture, Jonathan Livingston. The disaster was very recent so there had been nothing reported in the news service. *I will keep you in the loop the best I can. Alternatively, see if you can find anything out on your own.*

Bail received Katie's text message and thought about calling her first but decided against it. He would speak with her tonight. He then sat back in his chair and thought about where he was on the research and what she had originally asked of him . . . *I said "known diseases."* Bail was a nonbeliever in coincidence. *Known diseases,* he mumbled. He thought about whom to call that may know somebody in Argentina that might be working on this. Twenty minutes later he placed his first call.

~~~

Buenos Aires, Argentina

It was after one o'clock when José spoke with Dr. Montero. "Hello." Fifth ring.

"Dr. Montero, José Quinterro here. How are you today?" José asked. It was his position to get the caller feeling at ease in a stressful situation.

"All things considered, fine. The lab technicians sent along with the equipment were appreciated. I had two colleagues from the University in Buenos Aires offer technical support on research. They'll stop by over the next couple of days."

"That's good news. It sounds like you have the manpower. If you need anything else, let me know immediately," José added. Pressure was not always focused.

"I certainly will." *The conversation was going to easy.*

"I mean it, Dr. Montero. You know what's at stake here." José let the statement's meaning condense the time into unbearable silence. The proverbial pregnant pause. The first one to speak loses.

Dr. Montero knew that she should have instantly said, *Yes, I do, thank you,* and quickly hung up, but she thought José was going to add something else. To hang up now would be wrong but the seconds were becoming uncomfortable. She caved. "Anything else?"

"Other than the obvious, Doctor, where do we stand?" José asked.

"Mr. Quinterro, I have reviewed either the samples themselves or the results from the samples. The spores from the fungus are highly resilient and destructive. I would guess the field's two hundred miles from your brother's fields are damaged now as your brother's were
~~~

yesterday. This fungus is very deadly, very aggressive . . . deadlier than any fungus I have ever seen. We are looking at a multiple-year loss in crop production."

"Multiple-year loss, Doctor!" José blurted out. Pressure. He was astonished at how easily it seemed to come from her lips.

"Yes, given the aggressive nature of the spore and the dormancy characteristic of spores. I don't believe we have a fungicide strong enough to kill this particular spore. If we do, the plant itself will perish and the microbial organisms within the soil that provide the basic nutrients for growth. Your brother's black gold."

"We'll find ourselves in a situation where we have to treat the topsoil with chemicals. Nitrogen, phosphate, etc., to try and restore the soil. This could take years to achieve."

"Is there no alternative?" José pleaded.

"Burning the field may provide a quicker turnaround on the soil, likely less destructive than a harsh chemical, but it will kill most, if not all, of the microbial organisms in the soil. We'd be out of the business of farming for three, maybe four seasons."

José expected a lost season. He was willing to stomach that type of bad news. But a multiple-year loss would be beyond devastation. "How will the people live?" he heard himself ask.

"I don't know, Mr. Quinterro." She could hear the compassion and fear in his voice. *There must be something.*

"Mr. Quinterro, can you provide me with non-diluted industrial-strength fungicides? I would like to test them against the spore. If you could get me samples of the top ten brands available for commercial and residential use. Five hundred gallons of each, please. In the meantime, I will be treating the spores with sulfur, lime sulfur, and Bordeaux mix."

"Household products, Doctor?" José asked questioningly.

"We have to try everything, Mr. Quinterro. Non-diluted, remember." Dr. Montero wanted to be thorough and aggressive. There was a lot at stake and she knew it. "Sulfur doesn't kill the spores but it does inhibit spore germination. My fear is damage to the plant. Lime sulfur can actually kill recently germinated spores and prevent growth. But again, what effect will this have on the plant being protected? Is the cure deadlier than the disease? Bordeaux mix is copper-based, which can affect the plant, but again, we need to try. Time is of the essence, when can I expect the samples?" she asked politely.

"Tomorrow morning first thing," José said, not sure which call he dreaded more—the president or his cousin Alberto. He thought about it, he would have to be present when he spoke with Alberto and the other farmers, the president's call won by default. He called the chemical companies before speaking with the president.

~~~

Alberto received a text from José. "Set up a meeting for tonight at eight. See you at seven." José reached for the phone and began placing his calls.

Forty-five minutes later, the president called a special meeting of her cabinet for tomorrow at one o'clock. "Dr. Montero, I would like to speak with you before our cabinet meeting. Please make yourself available at 12:30 p.m. Any questions?"

"No, Madame President," Dr. Montero said. She was uncertain what questions she could ask, so the call disconnected naturally. She returned her attention to the lab and designed a schedule to maximize lab hours. She wanted everyone present when the samples arrived. In the meantime, she began her experiments previously discussed with José.

~~~

José left for the Quinterro farm. He would like to have Dr. Montero present but understood her time was better spent in the lab.

On the way, his counterpart in Uruguay responded. Uruguayan agriculture accounts for 9 percent of the labor force and 17 percent of the GDP. Chief crops are wheat, corn, rice, and sugarcane. Early estimates were a 47 percent loss in crops planted. It was requested that samples be sent to their lab for analysis. Uruguayans were not adequately equipped. What could José say but yes. He provided his counterpart with Dr. Montero's address and index of information requested.

The remaining drive to the Big Q, was a two-plus-hour scenic journey on most days but not today. By this time of year, drivers should see the first signs of summer months ahead. Yet the fields remained barren. Within a few days' time, someone better have answers before people start asking difficult questions. They would be looking for answers from government officials, especially Madame President.

Alberto was sitting outside when he saw José turn into the driveway. He walked out to meet him in the turnabout. José looked awful. Bad news and pressure, stress had that effect on people.

"José, the news is worse than we thought, isn't it? Don't try to be a politician, give it to me straight," Alberto offered. He placed a hand on José's shoulder. He could feel the tension. There was a slight change in plan. "Let's have a drink first."

Alberto led José into the study, where they each grabbed a shot glass and went outside. A bottle of Jim Beam Black Label was in his other hand. He poured them both a shot and offered a toast . . ."to better times ahead."

"So how bad is it?" Alberto asked.

"Bad, Alberto. Multiple years bad." José regurgitated out what Dr. Montero had told him earlier in the day.

"And she has no solutions? No ideas?"

"Not at this time, Alberto. But let's be reasonable, it has been less than sixty hours since you first discovered the problem. She has identified aspects of the spore. She is currently running test using sulfur, lime sulfur, and Bordeaux mix."

"Busywork," Alberto interjected. Obviously frustrated.

"Yes, but necessary. This is an elimination scenario, Alberto, it is not simply a determination one." José was tired and tried not to show it in either his voice or temperament. "In the morning she will be conducting research using non-diluted industrial-strength fungicides. The top ten commercial and residential brands."

"That will destroy both the plants and the soil." Alberto stood up and paced along the porch. "The cure is worse than the disease."

"Her exact words," José responded.

"It will take time . . . three to four seasons to restore the soil." Alberto words trailed off after he spoke that sentence. Reflection. The Quinterro farm would survive but what about the other farms? "How many would survive . . . could survive? My country? How will the government maintain order? This could end badly, José." He looked at his cousin, who simply nodded his head in agreement. They were sitting in the reclining chairs looking out toward the mountains when Consuelo walked out onto the patio and reminded them of the meeting at eight o'clock. They left together. Alberto drove.

They arrived at the meeting a little before eight. If the first meeting was crowded, this one was standing room only. They were four to five people deep at the back of the hall and two deep on the side aisles. Alberto and José walked up to the podium and immediately called for silence. A hush fell upon the attendees.

José took the microphone and introduced himself to those who did not know him. "Thank you all for coming. I will start off by telling you what I do know, the reason why we are all here tonight. I will then tell you what options have been discussed. What we are doing. At the end, I will take questions. Please be respectful of everyone in this room and ask only those questions that pertain to everyone. No personal questions, please. Any question on this particular type of format before I proceed?" José looked around the room. He was not surprised by the turnout but he was surprised by the medley of faces. Some were deathly afraid while others were optimistically hopeful. Still others were every conceivable point between the polar opposites.

"Okay, then, let's begin. Dr. Montero at the University in Rosario has begun the arduous task of trying to determine what type of plant disease we are dealing with. After I initially informed the president of the situation, she dispatched over a dozen lab technicians along with mobile laboratories to assist Dr. Montero. She has also received additional assistance from professors at the University in Buenos Aires." José paused. Mentally he was fatigued and hoped that it did not show. He wanted to instill a sense of confidence that what was being done was all that could be done. That the government did care and that he cared personally.

"So what has Dr. Montero accomplished so far?" José began. The tone of his voice sounded confident. Not hopeful or somber. He wanted these individual farmers, each and every one of them, those that he did know and those that he did not know, to realize that he had a personal stake in this situation, that he was one of them.

"Dr. Montero and her staff have examined many of the samples provided. Soil and plant. From your samples, they have determined that the spore is an aggressive hybrid that is extremely hearty, destructive, and resilient." José paused again because of the next piece of information. It would be devastating to everyone in the room including the farmers financially strong, not just the Big Q.

"Dr. Montero believes that the spore is so deadly, so resilient, that we may be looking at a multiple-year loss of crops."

There was no way to sugarcoat such an economic impact. Everyone knew that the people in the room would be ruined financially were this to last beyond a single season. Many might not survive even one season. Only a handful of the farmers could survive multiple seasons. The government couldn't bail them out. This was not America. The government would be hard-pressed to feed her people and survive. The mumbling continued, José held up his hand, asking for quiet.

"So what can we do? Dr. Montero has asked for non-diluted fungicides both commercial and residential, for use in determining what can be done to kill the spore. Most of you know, non-diluted fungicides will likely kill the plant and soil at the same time. It is a fact that the spore must be killed . . . at all cost, at any cost. Chemical treatment to the soil will likely kill not only the spore but the soil. True Argentinean black gold is the microbial organisms in the soil. The soil would then have to be fertilized with replacement of the nitrates and phosphates lost from the chemicals. We would then try and grow alfalfa or clover. That's the three to four seasons." José looked out over the crowd.

"How about burning the field?" someone yelled out.

Everyone was in a hurry to get back into the fields. José understood this and he empathized with the farmers . . . big and small. He was, after all, a Quinterro.

"Burning the fields would require that the ground be saturated with a combustible material. There having been very little crop growth to speak of. Said material would then have to penetrate the ground to a predetermined depth to ensure destruction of the spore. The material would likely kill both the spore and the microbial organisms that make the Pampas and Mesopotamian Regions some of the most fertile soil in the world. Creating another scenario where the cure is as deadly as the disease." José paused, he had discussed this very issue with the president. She had the data, inconclusive.

Studies have been conducted on the use of fire and grazing (either singularly or in combination thereof) to promote pasture restoration versus simply letting a field rest its way to restoration. Unfortunately, the studies have been inconclusive to any effect other than a marginal one. José was content simply to state what he knew and hold off on any speculative decisions.

"I discussed that particular issue with Madame President. The results would likely be more harmful to the soil and therefore less effective. But again, we are looking at multiple seasons. Whatever we do, we need to be certain of two things: first, that the spore is killed and the fields are clean. Second, the level of damage to the soil is minimal."

"Anyone else affected?" an audience member asked.

"Unfortunately, yes. We are not alone. I heard from our neighbors in Uruguay. They have experienced the same type of spore related blight that has affected us. Currently they estimate 40 to 50 percent loss in crops planted for the season. They, however, are less equipped than we are. They're sending samples to Dr. Montero."

"How about the United States? Have they offered any help?" another gentleman asked.

"I sent an email out to several of my counterparts regarding what we have experienced. I did so to warn them. I have not heard back from anyone but I anticipate hearing something within the day. On a separate note, the president called an emergency cabinet meeting for tomorrow. I will know more then and will communicate what I can through Alberto." José then asked if there were any further questions. One or two more were asked and answered. The meeting began to break up into small groups and move out into the hallway and parking lot. José remained at the podium. Several old friends walked up to say hello. Some merely wanted to reaffirm José understood their personal suffering.

José overheard several conversations. Many of the smaller farmers were hoping for a bailout. Some form of government-backed initiative that would let them keep their farms. Personally, he did not see it happening. There were still several signs of financial concern in the marketplace from the 2000 financial crisis. With current whispers of yet another government default.

José tried never to question where someone else's money went. He knew that it was tough. A true struggle. Yet most local farmers barely made enough to survive. There never really seemed to be enough left to save. He knew Alberto was strong financially, some others were, but he would ask anyway.

Chapter Four

During the Great Depression, farm subsidies were created. The idea was to save the family farm and ensure a stable food supply. Today there are over 60 federal programs that help farmers with marketing, agricultural risk, price loss coverage, crop disaster, et cetera.

Central Illinois Corn & Soy
Decatur, Illinois

Patrick followed up with Amged on the situation in Argentina. "This may be a way for us to expand market share without much effort," Patrick said.

"I agree completely. I should have an answer later today from Juan Domingo. Juan is in charge of our local operation. He works directly with the co-ops and larger farms," Amged said. "I also forwarded the email to Marshall." He wanted Patrick to know that he had initiative.

"Okay. Good work. Let's stay on top of this." Patrick walked back to his office and other issues.

~~~

San Louise, Argentina
Population: 155,000

Juan Domingo read the email from Amged. He was not aware of any problems with the current crop. However, he was not going to argue
~~~

with corporate. He called several local co-ops before calling Alberto Quinterro. He was meeting with Alberto in the morning and would know more then.

~~~

Rosario, Argentina

Dr. Montero was up by five o'clock. She had taken a nap more than a night's sleep. It would have to do. There was work to be done.

As expected, the sulfur, lime sulfur, and Bordeaux mix was proving ineffective. More time would be required but that was more to say we gave it a shot versus expectation of a favorable outcome. The spore was simply too hearty.

A typical damping-off spore will die when microwaved for 15 to 30 seconds. This particular spore didn't seem to die. Its ability to regenerate was nothing short of amazing. Dr. Montero strongly believed this spore evolved with assistance. *Terroristic help*, she mumbled with an exhale.

~~~

Raul was a lab technician. Dr. Montero had sent him to the Quinterro farm to retrieve contaminated soil. The soil was to be complete with plants and active spores. She had apologized to Mr. Quinterro when she called, given the lateness of hour. "It's something I should have requested earlier."

"If it will help, I am more than willing," Alberto said. "May I ask what you will do with the soil?" Dr. Montero explained the experiments. Alberto listened attentively and offered careful suggestions.

Raul returned at the exact same time several of the commercial chemical companies were delivering the requested fungicides. The area was quickly becoming a hazardous zone.

There were seven experiments overall, two groups of three plus one. One experiment would be conducted outdoors while the second experiment, plus the one, would be conducted inside a makeshift greenhouse. There would be three aspects to the overall experiment except the stand-alone experiment. Each experiment would be conducted in greenhouse-style flats.

Experiment A would have the seed introduced into the contaminated soil with the fungicide introduced at a later time. Experiment B would have the seed and fungicide introduced into the contaminated soil at the same time. Experiment C would have the fungicide first introduced into the soil with the seed introduced at a predetermined time.

The six flats were labeled A, B, and C. Each flat had ten individual cells. Each cell was of equal size. The soil was placed in the flat and leveled off with a skew. Use of the flats allowed for easier and more reliable monitoring of the experiments. Time test results were set and adhered too. How quickly would the spore react with and without fungicide? Effectiveness of the fungicide was the finger crossing moment.

Raul had been on the road when Dr. Montero designed the experiments and explained the logic to the various lab technicians. His question was the same asked by many of them. "What is the difference between the six experiments plus the one?" Raul asked.

"The two groups of three are self-explanatory. The one stand-alone experiment will be conducted without the introduction of seeds. The stand-alone experiment will contain contaminated soil plus the introduction of the fungicide. We will be keeping the contaminated soil moist with the fungicide while checking the effectiveness. We will review the soil at established time intervals. If it works and destroys the spore, then we can try to modify the strength of the fungicide. Remember, we are also concerned about the organisms within the soil," she explained.

José Quinterro stopped by Dr. Montero's office on his drive back to Buenos Aires. He wanted a progress report. She showed him what was going on and discussed with him the experiments. While they were discussing the situation, the two professors from the University in Buenos Aires arrived. Both biologists, both unaware why they were summoned given Angelina's expertise in the area. One of the professors, Jesus Aguilar, had received his PhD in biology from the University of Illinois. He still had contacts in the United States.

"We may need them," José said, "provided they are qualified."

"*Sí*. Bail Prichard is a noted biologist specializing in cereal grains. He used to work for a food processor before choosing academia," Jesus said.

"Bail Prichard? Dr. Bail Prichard from Millikin University?" Dr. Montero asked.

"*Sí*," Jesus responded.

"He called me yesterday…left a message that I have to return," she said. They each stood there lost in their own thoughts.

"Why would he be calling you now?" José verbalized what they were all thinking, the statement being rhetorical.

"What's going on?" Jesus asked. Dr. Montero restarted her conversation for the group.

"Eighty-plus percent for us and fifty percent for Uruguay," Fernando Alvarez said in astonishment. "Those are amazing numbers and crippling from an economic point of view, but the design of your experiments, let's get started."

Dr. Alvarez was more of a practical biologist. He enjoyed getting his hands dirty and was not afraid to roll up his shirtsleeves.

"Thinking out loud, worst-case scenario, we can free-range our livestock. However, before doing so, we should field test the grasses where they will be grazing. That may lend us some insight into how to deal with the spore" Alvarez added.

"That's an excellent point and one I don't think anyone has considered," Jesus said before adding, "Fernando also teaches economics at the university."

"Introductory, but yes, I do."

"Okay," José said. "It sounds like you have everything under control. Please remember to call Dr. Prichard and then myself after you have spoken to him. I must return to Buenos Aires for the cabinet meeting. Good luck to us all."

"Uh, José," Dr. Montero said. She caught herself being informal, "Mr. Quinterro, if you could have the cattle ranchers send in soil and grass samples of their fields where they would free-range their cattle."

"Certainly, and I have always found it easier to work under stressful situations when the formalities are dropped. Please, call me José."

~~~

Tabuk, Saudi Arabia

Sherrief woke with renewed vigor. He could not ever recall being this alive, this fresh. He felt closer to Allah than ever before. And why not? He knew now that he was the chosen one. His dream foretold of his success and rise. The true leader. The Imam of the entire Islamic faith. The one caliph to unite and lead his people.

Dreams are voices of spirits past that provide true listeners with guidance. Sherrief was not only a true listener but a believer. It was why his dream was more of a vision. He was alone in the desert. The ever-changing sand dunes marking the passage of time. *The winds of change*, Sherrief thought. Past to present to the future yet to come. The individual grains of sand were the voices of his dream. Sherrief looked up into the sun and the heaven beyond. For a midday desert sun, it was unusually cool when the rain began to fall, continuing while the sand dunes took shape. They leveled off. The sand replaced by lush fields of green. Trees with tropical plants of all kinds. Birds and animals of all types carried the word of Sherrief's presence in the oasis which had once been a desert. And the people came, his people. And they asked, "How did you do this? How did you defeat the desert and restore us to our true and rightful self?"

"I made it rain. My brothers and sisters, I made it rain!"

Sherrief woke this morning with that sole thought resonating in his mind. "I will make it rain," he said with a smile.

Khadijah, was lying next to Sherrief. She woke at the sound of his voice. She asked about his smile and he told her of his dream, his vision. He told her how he'd stood alone in the oasis and watched it grow in a crowd of his united faith. His people...all three denominations of the Islamic faith coming together. The Sunnis, Shia, and Kharijites were no
~~~

longer warlike against each other. His word, his story, his vision over the nonbelievers of the East and the West, was what they'd come to hear. Khadijah looked at Sherrief and smiled. She gave thanks on the altar of her god.

Sherrief spent the next several days conducting research. He entrusted this research to no one other than himself.

~~~

Cloud seeding was developed in the early 1940s by scientists in the United States. The irony, Sherrief thought, was that their destruction should be at the accomplishment of their own hands. Early experiments proved less than successful. The difficulty was in the understanding of cloud structure and the use or type of seeding agent.

When we look at the sky, we all see clouds shaped like elephants turn into rabbits and then back again into something from our favorite childhood memory. That's because clouds are always in a state of flux. They're alive in a manner of speaking. The elephant that became a rabbit does so when it interacts with an air mass in its path. The elephant to rabbit cloud loses energy. Yet the cloud directly adjacent to the elephant maintains its shape. The air mass is identical to that of the cloud itself. Once scientists understood this randomness, they began to comprehend the nature and significance of cloud formation and weather in general.

Cloud formation is evaporation and transpiration . . . moist air rises in the form of water vapor. Water vapors then join with particles of dust to create a cloud.

Air can hold a certain amount of water based on the air temperature. A direct correlation exists. Calculable. Warm air holds more water vapor than cool air. When the temperature in the air drops to a certain level, a dew point, the water vapor begins to condense upon itself to form droplets. The understanding of dew point levels was a further breakthrough. The droplets form clouds . . . rain.

For water vapor to condense, a microscopic particle need be present. Cloud condensation nuclei become the center of droplets. Such nuclei form from sulfuric acid and ammonia. Trace elements found in air.
~~~

Ammonium sulfate, magnesium sulfate, dust particles and smoke are the nuclei water vapors require to condense around.

Where the air temperature is below 32° Celsius, water vapors form into ice or snow crystals. This process is called sublimation. Air temperature above 32° Celsius produces rain.

When the droplets of condensed water vapor become too heavy, they fall to the ground, rain or snow or a combination thereof. Droplets grow into raindrops through condensation of additional water vapors onto their surface and by combining with smaller droplets. The snow crystal behaves the same way. The falling snow crystals may collide together to form the six arms of a snowflake.

Sherrief sat back. He thought further about this. The time to act was now—of that there could be no doubt. No hesitation. The infidels would develop the fungicide to render his super-spore inactive. That was yet another certainty. Spring season for planting would be the time. With weather models having improved substantially over the years, a ten-day forecast would provide Sherrief with plenty of time to act.

Sherrief would spend his time in the lab developing a hygroscopic water-attracting agent that the spore would attach to like water vapor. Temperatures are historically greater than 32° Celsius, he was confident in the plan. Again, very few moving parts.

Chapter Five

United States arable land is 16.8%. China arable land is 14.6%. Argentina arable land is 14.3%. Saudi Arabia arable land is 1.2%.

Cabinet Meeting
Buenos Aires, Argentina

Madame President and José Quinterro met before the scheduled cabinet meeting to discuss the current situation. It was dire. There was no way to sugarcoat it.

"Have you heard anything from your counterparts?" the president asked. Her voice carried the understanding of stress. Why anyone would openly want the position was beyond José's ability to understand. Public life was a thankless job.

"Uruguay has experienced crop loss of 40 to 50 percent. Paraguay 70-plus percent. Brazil 30 percent," José said.

"That's assuming they are providing us with the correct figures. Suffice it to say we are not alone. How are they dealing with it?" she asked.

"Uruguay and Paraguay are sending us their samples. They are not in a position to properly evaluate the situation. Brazil has asked to speak with the researcher in charge. I thought that I would await your approval before giving the okay."

"And the American's?"

"Nothing directly, but indirectly, Juan Domingo called and met with Alberto this morning. Juan is in charge of Argentina's operations for Central Illinois Corn & Soy. He works out of the food-processing plant in San Luis."

"What did Alberto tell him?"

"Everything. I told Alberto to relay Uruguay's, Paraguay's, and Brazil's percentages plus our own. I did not see any sense in hiding the truth."

"I agree," the president said before permitting the Brazilians to speak with Dr. Montero. There was a small pause before the president used the intercom to have her secretary call Dr. Montero.

~~~

"Dr. Montero speaking."

"Yes, Dr. Montero, please hold for the president," her secretary said.

"Dr. Montero, I am here with José Quinterro, how are you today?"

"Fine, Madame President, thank you for asking," Dr. Montero said, there was a very slight pause.

"Well, I see no point in small talk, given the gravity of the situation. What, if anything, can you tell me?" she asked.

Dr. Montero quickly discussed the experiments she was working on but unfortunately the spore was highly resilient to current fungicides and combinations thereof. "I am sorry to say." At one point she admitted that they simply tossed live spores into a mixture of all ten fungicides and ended up with nothing to show for it but failure. The spore was resilient and acting like an engineered organism.

"Engineered?" the president responded...she and José leaned closer to the speakerphone.

"Yes, ma'am," Dr. Montero said. The president hesitated so José spoke.

"Dr. Montero, what makes you believe that the spore was engineered?"

"Its advanced evolutionary characteristics. It's easily several evolutionary cycles ahead of any known fungicide on the market or in research. Remember, we develop fungicides to combat know fungi
~~~

and are generally ahead of the disease, not behind." Again, there was a pause…time required for the information to be processed.

"Dr. Montero, for the time being, please keep that bit of information between you, José, and me," the president said while they spoke longer before disconnecting. The unspoken understanding, she would call again very soon.

José and the president stood up and walked to the room where they held their cabinet meetings. Three hours later, José was on the phone with Alberto. *"Burn the fields, Alberto. All of them."*

Generally speaking, burning a field is not necessarily a bad thing. The burnt corn stocks, soybean plants, and wheat fields would actually provide the field and soil with nutrients. Unfortunately, in this case, the seedlings were only an inch or two high. The fields would, therefore, have to be covered with hay, straw, or some substance before covering the field with gasoline, kerosene, or the like. Enough of an accelerant to seep into the ground four to six inches. The spores had to be killed.

"We don't want to have to do this twice," Alberto said to a packed house. The oil fields and refineries are partly government owned, thus the cost would be heavily subsidized. But in the end, it would still be expensive, each individual farm owner knew.

There were several murmurs from the crowd on burning the fields versus the use of chemicals. Alberto discussed the tests being conducted. "The current chemicals approved for commercial and residential use are being employed in the controlled tests. Under optimum conditions for the chemicals, they are proving ineffective and unsuccessful against the spore. Fire was successful. Both processes killed the microbial organisms within the soil that make the Pampas valley black gold. I personally believe that burning our fields is the best possible hope for success that we have. However, it is your farm, your decision to make."

It was a hard decision. Alberto knew that half of the people in the room would lose everything. Not just their farm but everything. Their lives and families would be ruined. Irreparably damaged and left with no one or nothing of consequence. He looked out upon the group assembled and sighed. It was time to conclude the meeting with the scheduling.

Alberto provided everyone with the telephone contact number for scheduling confirmation. He discussed in detail how this would work. He then opened the floor up for questions. There were only a few. First question from somewhere in the back showed the raw exposed nerves of the farmers.

"Who determined the schedule?"

"I did," Alberto said. "To those of you that do not know me personally, I apologize. I try and meet with everyone, time permitting. In furtherance of your question and my answer, understand that my name is last on the list. You will all have your fields treated before mine. For ground coverage to aid in the process, if anyone requires hay, straw, clover, or alfalfa, you need only ask. I have plenty and it's free of charge. If anyone else has extra hay or straw, now is not the time to forget your neighbor. To survive this, we are all going to have to stick together. Our voice is only loud if in mass." Alberto let that sink in before asking for further questions. Hearing none, he adjourned the meeting, and everyone drifted outside to find their way home. Even the shortest drive felt long.

~~~

San Luis, Argentina

Juan Domingo stared at the phone for what seemed like hours before finally placing the call to Amged. With no product, they would have to close the plant. Would it ever reopen? What would everyone do for jobs? Although the plant was extremely modern, it was still labor-intensive. The wet milling operation employed close to 1,500 people. Overall, 2,500. Most of them friends. Where will they go to find comparable work? What impact would this have on the overall economy? One that had barely survived the financial crisis in 2000. *My country will be ruined. Inflation will be . . .* Juan was thinking when the call was answered.
~~~

"Hello . . . hello . . . hello," Amged said. He could hear breathing so he knew someone was there.

"Yes, Amged, Juan here. Sorry, I was just thinking about our situation here. The ripple effect." *Tsunami would be more like it*, Amged thought.

"Juan, how bad is it?" He asked. Concerned . . . not excited.

"It is bad. Very bad," Juan said. His voice was somber, almost hollow. "We have lost everything. I understand they will be burning the fields, hoping to eradicate this demon spore. Uruguay, Paraguay, and Brazil are also affected. Not bad like us but still 30 percent to 70 percent crop loss," Juan said. He recited the percentages from memory.

After his conversation with Alberto Quinterro, Juan had felt overwhelmed by the information. That initial feeling gave way to numbness, which was followed by anger and then replaced with acceptance. Acceptance is a door that leads one to the room of survival. Not individual survival in this case but collective survival. The head of operations, Juan had learned to think of the greater overall picture rather than the micro, I or me. To him, the overall picture was focused on South America. He knew that for a time corporate would send raw material to the San Luis plant. Only for a time. Once they confirmed a new crop date, a new season date, they would shut the plant down. Economics. Juan understood. He would survive financially but most others would not.

The residual cost would have to be absorbed by someone somewhere. Consumers again foot the bill. A penny here, a dollar there, it all adds up. And not just for food items. Cereal grains and their oils are in everything. If Dr. Montero was correct and the effect could be for multiple seasons, then the ripples caused by the tossed stone would only intensify the further removed from the event horizon. *Despair*, Juan thought to himself. Yet another emotion to experience.

"What will corporate's position be?" Juan asked. He had to ask.

"Nothing has been discussed. I'll alert my people and see what can be done. We have some new seeds in research that we'll likely try out, given the opportunity," Amged said before adding, "Sorry. I didn't mean for that to sound the way it did. I trust you did not find my comment cavalier."

"No. I understand," Juan said. "When can I expect to hear back from you?"

"Later today."

Juan followed up the telephone call with an email, habit. He sent it off to a fairly large distribution list. Six people in total received the synopsis of their conversation. Juan had learned from the mistakes of others and found such memorialization of a call like this necessary. Decision-makers were on the list. There was nothing more for him to do other than wait.

~~~

Central Illinois

Loose lips sink ships and those unfortunate enough to be aboard. Jed was not willing to abandon ship when it was easier to remove those not part of the master plan. Following Sherrief's example, Jed began ensuring that those involved were necessary and integral moving parts. Those not involved required elimination. The fewer moving parts the more efficient the plan.

~~~

Rosario, Argentina

Dr. Montero had a break in the action after speaking with the president and José. She used the time to confirm the status of the experiments. She discussed her procedures with the lab technicians while she shared a cup of coffee with Jesus and Fernando. Collectively they called Dr. Prichard.

"Bail Prichard here," he said on the second ring.

"Dr. Prichard, Dr. Montero, returning your call. I have you on the speakerphone, I am sitting with Jesus Aguilar and Fernando Alvarez."

"Jesus, how are you, my old friend?"

"Bail, I am good, all things considered. Thank you."

"Dr. Alvarez, Dr. Montero," Dr. Prichard said by way of greeting. "All things considered . . . how are things?" Prichard asked.

"Your call was not a mere coincidence, was it?" Jesus responded.

"My friend, I wish that it were," Prichard said. "What are you dealing with?"

"A highly evolved, very resilient spore that currently is unaffected by any known fungicide, commercial or residential." Dr. Montero spoke while Jesus nodded deferment. She had an edge to her voice, Bail realized. One borne from skepticism, friend or foe.

"What type of spore?" Prichard asked. Again, Jesus nodded to Dr. Montero . . . *We can trust him.*

"It seems to be a hybrid, given its aggressive nature. We have lost close to 80 percent of our cereal grains. Uruguay 50 percent. Paraguay 70 percent. Brazil 30 percent," Dr. Montero said before stating the obvious. "You don't seem surprised. Why is that?" There was a pause. Prichard's turn.

"I'm sorry. Currently, I am not at liberty to say much but what I can tell you is that a former student of mine created a super-seed. They asked me to conduct some research on fungi that might likely be a threat to the seed. Apparently, someone else was conducting similar research."

"What can you tell us?" she asked.

"From what I understand, you're to receive an engineered super-seed," Prichard said before offering additional assistance. "Why don't you send me what you have and I will review it and see if I can point you in the right direction. I will speak with my employer on this project. Sound fair enough for the time being?"

"Sure," Dr. Montero said. They exchanged contact information, including email addresses.

She was reluctant, to be sure. Coincidence never sits well with anyone. Add to that this being her area of warning come true, it was safe to say Dr. Montero felt partially responsible.

The food chain was completely exposed to attack. She had repeatedly stated this to deaf ears. People think the water supply is vulnerable yet its impact is marginal when compared to an attack on the food chain. She pondered the "what if's" in her mind while she looked at Jesus and Fernando. "What's going on?" she asked.

"I do not know, but if Bail can help us, I know he will. He is an honest man," Jesus said of his old friend.

~~~

Bail reclined in his chair, while looking at the phone receiver. He reached for his cell phone and sent a quick text message to Katie . . . *There was a hybrid spore released in Argentina. It was and is very effective and very dangerous to current crops. They experienced a crop loss of 80 percent. Neighboring countries experienced crop loss varied: Uruguay 50 percent loss, Paraguay 70 percent loss, and Brazil 30 percent loss. I have spoken with the researchers in Argentina, a Dr. Montero and an old collegiate friend of mine, Jesus Fernando. I asked that they send me what they can. Please confirm that I can share information with them. I will keep you advised, Bail.*

~~~

St. Louis, Missouri

Katie received Bail's text message. So, there was a hybrid spore that had been created and released. She reached for the phone . . . hesitated . . . and then reached again. She hated to call Joseph but believed she must. Something was going on; of that she was now certain. She dialed Joseph's number from memory. *Too late now*, she thought when he answered.

"Marshall, I said I needed more time! Stop calling me!" Joseph's irritation was predictive.

Katie realized that because of their last conversation, there was no reason for her to call him. Thus, his caller ID would automatically trigger a Pavlovian response to Marshall, not Katie. *So old dogs can be taught new tricks, nice to know*, she thought.

"Joseph, it's me, Katie . . . what's going on? Why are you on edge?"

"Katie . . . sorry, I thought you were Marshall."

"Obviously."

"So how have you been? How was the vacation with your father?" Joseph started.

Woman scorned? We only slept together once? Maybe twice Katie thought . . . rocked his world.

"Joseph, let's keep this civil. I said before, what happened, happened. It's not healthy to harbor such feelings of resentment. We need to move on, move forward. I cherish the moments that we shared but that was all they were—moments. I'm sorry."

"Yeah, Katie, I'm sure you are. For me, it was more than that. For me, it was a future, commitment."

"Joseph, you're married. With children, in case you've forgotten."

"People get divorced, Katie. It happens all the time."

"Joseph, I called because I know something is going on with my research and I want to know what you know. Are you involved in any of this or not? If you can't discuss this in a civilized manner, then simply say so and we can end this call now." Katie questioned why she'd ever thought to call. She had had enough of his pining for her. She had done nothing to pique such a reaction.

"Sure, Katie. Civil," Joseph said. He wanted to say more. He wanted to hurt her; she had hurt him. City girl, country bumpkin, what was he thinking?

"No, Katie, I am not involved." There was an edge to his voice. Not malicious; it was more confrontational. Threatening . . . but a hollow threat. "Did Marshall have you call me? That coward!"

"No, he didn't. Why? Is Marshall involved?"

"Marshall's a fool, Katie . . . and so are you. This discovery is more than a simple seed of corn. It's a grain of sand in an entire desert field with grains of sand. In a few years I challenge you to find your grain within that desert or any desert for that matter. I don't know what's going on, but if somebody has created a disease that can destroy your seed, then they are smarter than me."

"Joseph, are you aware of anyone else that might have this research?" Katie questioned herself for asking. She should've known better.

"No. No, I am not. Remember, you have been working on this for fifteen years. I don't see how anyone could've figured out your understanding of the coding sequencing combination. It's random but not."

"If you hear of anyone or anything with this baseline research, please let me know. I would appreciate that, Joseph."

"Sure, Katie." Joseph was desperate for more time with her even if it is only voice time. Finally, Katie said, "Thank you," and hung up while Joseph held the receiver just a moment longer.

Katie sat back in her chair and swiveled around to look at the skyline of St. Louis. She had a nice spacious office that afforded her a panoramic view complete with the Arch, Busch Stadium, and the Mississippi River. She was glad Joseph was not involved although she was less certain of Marshall. Other than Katie, Marshall was the only one that had Katie's complete research paper. The coding sequence combination was not random. There was a certain symmetry to it. A beauty that captured the eye and imagination. Katie recognized that she was fortuitous. But what was the likelihood of someone else being equally so without help? She was still sitting there pondering the true definition of beauty (a rose, a sunset versus death, destruction) when Marshall knocked on her door.

"Katie, are you busy?" Marshall asked. She swiveled around in her chair. Marshall was already halfway to her desk.

"No. I was just thinking about something."

"Another breakthrough possibly? You had that same look on your face when you made your last discovery." They both individually reflected upon the moment. Marshall realizing Katie had greatness and Katie being naïve enough to believe in Santa Claus. Yet it worked for them, a team.

"I just wanted to let you know they'll be sending out the initial seeds to Argentina before the Thanksgiving holiday. This is really exciting."

Katie didn't hate him. He had earned the opportunity to make his fortune and bask in the glory that comes from years of hard work. It meant something to him. To her, the discovery had lost its luster. A virginity somehow tarnished with the ugliness of the other side. She knew that there was no way to remove the stain regardless how hard she tried.

"Any word on the type of disease?" Katie asked.

"Nothing concrete. They're testing, I believe." Marshall was still standing. Katie had not asked him to sit down.

"Marshall, have a seat." They talked for several more minutes. She realized at some point throughout the conversation that she missed their talks. They used to have them every night. They would discuss the day's research progress. Marshall was very encouraging of her work and support thereof. He had a great deal to do with her discovery. She likely could not have done it without him.

~~~

"That's what I want to do." Jenny was sitting at the bar with Lawrence. Mickey was behind the bar pouring drinks. They were watching CNN.

"Ya got any x'tra space up there in the mountains, lad?"

"For you, Mick, I'm sure we can find a spare bunk."

"I don't need m'ch, ya know."

"Really, Mick? You think it's that bad?" Jenny asked.

"Yeah, I do, lass. The territorial water issue is a big deal."

"I always thought that it was further than twelve nautical miles," Jenny said.

"It is, lass. Twelve nautical miles is fer da territorial waters. Th'n ther's da contiguous zone, which is 'nother twelve. But ya lik'ly think'n of da two hundred nautical miles which is da exclusive economic zone fer fish'n and now oil drill'n." Mick was a wealth of information; all he did was read newspapers and listen to the news.

"But why have a fight that no one can win?"

"'cause I think da Chinese b'lieve they have enough people. More of them will survive than us. I also b'lieve that read'n about something
~~~

is different than see'n it. I'm sorry, lass, maybe I'll be wrong aft'r all." Mickey turned back to the television report. Lawrence squeezed Jenny's hand. She looked at him and smiled. They returned to their conversation while the news media reported other world news.

Chapter Six

Satellite imagery revolution is ground based, not aerial. Soft copy, digital imprints, have been revolutionized with the addition of visible light imagery. Two dimensional images now become multidimensional. These envisions have both military and diplomatic application.

Presidential Meeting
Washington, D.C.

Jonathan received very few one-on-one conference meetings with the president, so when he was fortunate enough to have one scheduled, he maximized the time. The situation in Argentina provided Jonathan with unexpected exposure. Face time where Jonathan thought about testing the water.

"Matthew, we're certain that this wasn't an act of terrorism?" the president asked. Matthew Sheffield was the director of the NSC.

"Mr. President, we are certain of only two things. We intercepted several cell phone transmissions between Tabuk, Saudi Arabia, and the Pampas region of Argentina which included a subsequent call to the Central United States. Second, cereal grain crops in several South America countries have been destroyed in whole or in part. We now believe that the two events are linked, Mr. President." Matthew knew that the buck stopped with him and was not so proud forgo acceptance of responsibility.

"The cellular telephone activity occurred within the timeframe that would fit with the crop destruction. Enhanced satellite imagery provides us with a clear picture of the losses suffered in Uruguay and Brazil." Matthew produced the envisions previously discussed with Jonathan. "Paraguay and Argentina are deemed to be a complete loss, the fields have been burned in most cases or are in the process of being burned."

"What assets do we have in the area?" the president asked.

"None. We will be sending Larry Seabreeze down tomorrow. Larry has been following the cellular phone activity and previously believed a strike of some kind was in the works. Unfortunately, his concern fell upon deaf ears."

"Whose?" the president asked.

"Mine, sir," Matthew said. "There just wasn't enough direct evidence in my opinion. Plus the game has changed."

"Yes, it has Matthew, yes it has," the president said. Clearly, he was tired of the game and playing it. Jonathan noticed that his friend had aged several years since being in office. Several!

"Jonathan, I understand that you have some potential good news for the situation."

"Yes, Mr. President, I believe that I do." He expanded his role ever so slightly. *Why not?* he thought. Everyone else is a revisionist.

"Mr. President, several months ago I met with one of our larger food processing companies. We discuss many things when we meet. One such conversation is always the U.S. trade deficit and foreign ownership of said debt. In taking judicial notice of various roles of economics, mature developed economies are at a distinct disadvantage with underdeveloped and/or developing economies. We see this today with China and similar such countries. We no longer see it with Japan and the other developed economies. The only true advantage we have is research and development. So, we decided to focus time and effort into the development of an engineered seed for corn and other cereal grains. A super-seed, sir. This seed grows in half the time and produces twice the yield. Nothing on the market comes close. We just need your permission to export the seed to the area affected. If this seed is successful, we can single-handedly control the cereal grain food market overnight. It may not sound like much, Mr. President, but if we all remember our introduction to economics class, the trick is to find a happy medium between the productions of guns versus butter," Jonathan said.

The president was nodding his head. He looked over at Sheffield, who nodded concurrence. "Make it so, Jonathan," the president said, "and thank you for being on top of this."

A thank-you from the president is a homerun in anyone's book. Jonathan returned to his office, where he drafted the email and sent it out. The distribution list included the Ministries of Agriculture for Brazil and Paraguay and the Minister of Stockbreeding, Agriculture and Fishing for Uruguay. It also included José Quinterro and Patrick Livingston. The initial recipient was the U.S. president. The email was addressed to him. The actual presidential email address being used was a dump address for individuals...Jonathan being one such individual. The email was read by the president's chief of staff underlings for content.

~~~

Central Illinois Corn & Soy
Decatur, Illinois

Patrick Livingston received the email and smiled. He was always willing to help out a friend and more than happy to help out Jonathan. Jonathan had done a lot for Central Illinois Corn & Soy and, by extension Patrick. Payback was a part of business, a part of life. If you cannot help out your friends, then who can you help? Patrick forwarded the email to both Amged and Marshall. "Merry Christmas. We should be able to send out the first shipment of seed before Thanksgiving. Don't be surprised if they name a holiday after us . . . LOL."

~~~

Tabuk, Saudi Arabia

Sherrief had a brilliant mind and was well motivated. He was simply misguided and easily led astray. The psychology of the LSC syndrome (lucky sperm club) is well documented. How often do we read about spoiled little rich kids getting into all sorts of trouble? Often enough so that we believe they should be brutally punished. No compassion . . . and yet in the end most, if not all of us, are happy to see that the courts are reasonably lenient on them. We still envy them their jet-set lifestyle and endless supply of irresponsible action yet most of us would rather keep our own shoes rather than walk in theirs.

There exists a level of stress associated with their God-given talent. It wasn't anything that they earned; it was simply given to them. Things that are given can easily and readily be taking away. A singer's voice can be lost. An athlete can have a career-ending injury. An actor can simply lose their appeal. Somebody born into wealth can spend their entire life trying to prove their own worth . . . yet never succeed. Sherrief fell into the latter category.

Sherrief's discovery of the super-spore was a triumphant achievement. Unfortunately, he doubted whether or not he would've seen the coordinated logic to the coding sequence combination. Once shown to him, it was easy enough to follow but that is not the same feeling when discovering something on your own. Therein lay the problem. Self-worth assessment, still something to prove.

The spore worked and would be delivered to India, China, Vietnam, and the United States. Vietnam was decided upon simply because of location. No other reason. Again, nothing personal.

Sherrief was able to locate a family friend to assist in brokering a deal for four DC-9s. Pilots and crews would be the responsibility of the buyer. Each airplane would come with up-to-date maintenance records. The planes would be equipped with extra fuel tanks. Other equipment would either be purchased locally or shipped to the destination.

~~~
~~~

National Oceanic and Atmospheric Administration (NOAA)

The United States government began gathering information on weather in 1870 when the U.S. Public Weather Service was established. At the time, it was part of the Army Signal Service. By 1890, Congress organized the Weather Bureau under the Department of Agriculture. This lasted until 1941, when the Weather Bureau was transferred to the Department of Commerce. In 1965 the Weather Bureau became part of Environmental Science Services Administration before finding a more permanent home in NOAA with a new name in 1970. The National Weather Service (NWS) was transferred to NOAA; an agency within the Department of Commerce.

The National Weather Service headquarters is in Silver Springs, Maryland. A regional office exists in Kansas City, Missouri. Kansas City is home to the National Severe Storms Forecast Center. They are responsible for forecasting tornadoes and severe thunderstorms.

Weather reports are sent to the National Meteorological Center from all across the country. The NMC is a department within the NWS. The Washington, D.C., office houses the central computer complex, where the data is received and used to create models for weather forecasting.

Computer models used today are extremely accurate. Five- and ten-day forecasts are close to 70 percent accurate. This level of accuracy meant that the operatives in the United States would be in and out quickly. China's weather forecasting was equally reliable due to the pirating of the program several years earlier. Vietnam and India were less exact; however, it was decided to equip the DC-9 with both cloud-seeding atomizers and crop-dusting sprayers for those locations.

The DC-9s purchased for use in China and the United States would be fitted with extra fuel tanks. The atomizers would be placed along the length of the wings. They would not be fitted for crop-dusting sprayers.

Testing performed by Sherrief found that the spore attached nicely to particles of silver iodide and potassium chloride. But the true test would be in actual use. Would they attract water vapor and attach to it? Computer models were accurate, but nothing worked like an actual cloud. So Sherrief decided to make a cloud and test the probability of a silver iodide particle attaching to water vapor to produce a drop of rain. He would then do the same with a potassium chloride particle.

To create a cloud, Sherrief found two 2-liter plastic bottles, a match, masking tape, a flexible strip thermometer, and one silver iodide spore particle and one potassium chloride spore particle. Sherrief would be performing two separate experiments.

Once the 2-liter plastic bottle was thoroughly rinsed out and dried, Sherrief folded the strip thermometer together, and with the masking tape, made the letter D. He made certain that the numbers were clearly visible for easy reading before placing the strip thermometer inside the bottle. Sherrief capped the bottle and waited for two minutes before recording the temperature of both bottles. Remember, air holds moisture and warm air holds more moisture than cool air. To increase the temperature within the two 2-liter plastic bottles, Sherrief squeezed both bottles. Khadijah, Sherrief's wife, looked on for moral support. All great men of history needed a strong woman by their side. "Will this work?" she asked.

"In theory, yes, but I must see it for myself. I need to be certain that the water vapor will attach to the spore to deliver my *malak almawt*—my angel of death—from above."

After two minutes of squeezing both bottles, Sherrief checked the temperature. Both bottles recorded over a 2-degree increase in internal temperature. When he released his grip, both bottles popped back into shape.

Sherrief then poured three quarters of an inch of water into both bottles. He swirled the contents around to coat the sides, top, and bottom before pouring out any excess water. With the cap on, water vapors could be seen.

"It's a light mist," Khadijah said, clearly excited. Sherrief squeezed both bottles to create air pressure. "And now it is a dense cloud," Sherrief said. They watched the mist take shape and form a cloud.

Turning the bottles upside down, he removed their caps and placed the bottles over both atomizers and a match. The atomizer would be used on the plane. It would disburse both the silver iodide spore solution and the potassium chloride spore solution into the clouds. The match was used to aid in the experiment's visual effect, Sherrief told Khadijah.

Sherrief lit the match and immediately extinguished it. The smoke rose into the bottles with the spore particles being released from the atomizer. Sherrief placed the caps back on the bottles.

"Ooohhh," Khadijah said. "It's a cloud."

"Yes, it is. The water vapor has joined with our spore particles." Sherrief squeezed the bottles and the clouds disappeared. "Air pressure," he said to Khadijah. Leading her, they walked over to a hearty house plant. He looked at her and she nodded. Sherrief then released his hold on the bottle and the cloud returned. He then removed the cap and released the *angel of death*. When they returned from a passionate interlude, the plant was wilted and dying while their time was finally seeing the light of day.

~~~

St. Louis, Missouri

The story of the disaster in South America, in particular Argentina and surrounding countries, was mainstream news after Thanksgiving. The irony was not lost. Jenny felt she had gained every pound back (and then some) that she'd lost due to her daily gym visits.

The shipment of super-seed from the United States to South American countries affected was a very big deal. It received continuous television coverage. Jenny almost died, though, when Erin Brackfield of CNN mention her by name, Jenny Pendleton, and quoted her article, which was ran again in both the *St. Louis Post-Dispatch* and *The Rag*. Both lead stories. Both front page articles. Both above the fold.

Katie had informed Jenny of the super-seed shipment a few days before actually being shipped. The voyage was relatively long. The seed would leave Decatur by rail, where it would be delivered to Cairo, Illinois. From there it would be offloaded onto barges and taken down the Mississippi River to New Orleans for its final destination—Buenos
~~~

Aires, Argentina. Jenny spoke with Mack and Timothy, who saw the importance of the article. The U.S. playing white knight was a feel-good story which plays nicely for the holiday season.

The article would be a two-piece story. The first piece Jenny would co-write with the *Dispatch*'s Foreign Desk. The second piece would be all her.

Cause of the fungus devastation and failure of both commercial and residential fungicides to address the problem lend itself to mass speculation. Terrorist attack is the primary answer to every unexplained event. Historically, gods used to be blamed. Now it is terrorists.

The first article gave a detailed description of the problem and associated ripple effect. The Argentinean and Brazilian governments are stabilizing elements to developing countries. Trading partners the United States looks to provide stability in the region. Both countries have recent experience with economic and political unrest and would experience a destabilizing situation without immediate aid and assistance. Given the potential for worldwide exposure, the World Bank had begun looking into foreign aid for farmers affected by the biological fungi. The World Health Organization was also monitoring potential spread of the fungus. "And I quote the co-author of the article, Jenny Pendleton, *'There are short-term and long-term implications to this regional situation. With the world becoming smaller, not larger, it is incumbent upon all countries to help their neighbors. Countries like China, who consider themselves a world leader, should stop playing bully to nations in the South China Sea and start acting responsible. This is, after all the twenty-first century.'* Erin Brackfield, reporting for CNN . . . Xi Jinping, would you care to respond to Jenny Pendleton of the *St. Louis Post-Dispatch* and *The Rag* and/or to meet me at CNN? You know our numbers."

The second piece was scheduled to be run two weeks later and involved detailed interviews with Katie Pendleton; Marshall Feldman of Feldman & Company Biotech, Inc.; Chief Economist Dr. Daniel Gray of the Federal Reserve Bank; Patrick Jackson, vice president of Central Illinois Corn & Soy; and Cabinet Member and Secretary of

Agriculture Jonathan Livingston. A star-studded list of Who's Who. Question posited: *When is Science Unethical?*

~~~

"Twice the quantity of cereal grains in half the time," Katie said during her interview. "Think of the possibilities . . . no more hungry children . . . worldwide end to starvation . . . lower food costs . . . lower product cost on certain items. The list is longer still but I believe you see the point. You understand the benefits."

"Not all science is bad, Jenny. Splitting the atom did produce a nuclear bomb but it also saved lives and ended a war while simultaneously answering questions about our universe. Science does nothing wrong. We the people do the wrong. I am sure the caveman was unethical with the benefit of hindsight. Might made right then…now it's science and technology." Katie undoubtedly was piggybacking off Jenny's South China Sea comment.

~~~

Jenny was up early. Morning coffee and CNN news prior to her interview with Daniel. Youth aided her recovery. It had been a good night.

"Good morning, Robbi," Jenny said while entering Dr. Gray's office.

"Good morning, Jenny, how are you today?"

"Fine, thank you."

"Can I get you something to drink? Coffee? Tea? Water? Dr. Gray is running approximately fifteen minutes late."

"Is everything all right? Does he need to reschedule?"

"No, dear, were that the case, he would have contacted you directly."

"Okay, I'll have a cup of coffee, milk, two sugars." Robbi smiled and walked down the hall to the break room.

In Robbi's absence, Jenny perused magazines and newspapers lying around the office before seeing one of interest, Barron's. The newspaper was a day old but she skimmed through headlines reading bits and pieces of eye-catching articles. She was in the middle of one article when Robbi returned with her coffee. It was in a styrofoam cup complete with a lid, milk, and two sugars. She set her coffee down, when the *London Times* headline caught her eye: CHINA NOTICEABLY ABSENT FROM DEBT OFFERING. Jenny started to reach for the article when Dr. Gray walked in.

"Good morning, Jenny."

"Good morning, Dr. Gray. How are you?" the look on his face said it all. He saw; she'd noticed.

"Stress is a part of my life, my job, Jenny. Come, let's go into my office. Bring the *London Times* and your coffee." Dr. Gray walked into his office. They sat at the same table.

They were enjoying a nice conversation when Robbi buzzed Dr. Gray on the intercom. "Sorry to bother you, Dr. Gray, but Magne is on line two."

"Okay. Thank you, Robbi," Dr. Gray said. Jenny started to gather her things to leave. "No . . . no . . . please stay. This won't take that long."

"Magne, hello. How are you?" Dr. Gray asked, having placed the call on speakerphone.

"Daniel, I am fine, thank you." Magne left a slight pause, her's to lead. "So you are the only one that believes this to be a non-issue." Dr. Gray pointed to the article; Jenny nodded in understanding.

"Yes, I do see this as a non-issue. China needs us more than we need them. Within twenty years, manufacturing will start returning to America. Whether that is now or in twenty years, it will happen. We have lower, middle, and upper classes that are fully developed. We have a sophisticated banking system and infrastructure in place. They lack both. We can do what they can't. It may be hard but we can do it."

"I agree with you, which is why I will inform the president that China's absence is, in fact, a non-issue. Thank you, Daniel."

"China," Dr. Gray said. He looked at Jenny with a thought on his mind. A reflection of the conversation just ended. A wildcard being the new kid on the block. How would all this play out and did it have anything to do with what they were going to speak about . . . only time would tell.

"Where were we, Jenny?" Dr. Gray said. They resumed their discussion.

They spoke about the short-term and long-term effects of the disaster on the people of Argentina and the other countries affected. The macro and micro interplay of events. It was not just about the farmer although it was from the farmer's point of view. It was about the secretary at the local doctor's office and the office worker several towns over and the president of Argentina directly. The people in countries that tried to help them directly would be less affected but would still experience something. Each individual might feel the pain of the farmer at some point throughout the process but only slightly.

"The stone being tossed into the pond, Jenny, is the disaster. The kurr-plunk sound represents the size of the disaster. Those closest to the stone are affected first and hardest. In this case, the farmer is the first ripple. Farming represents 5 percent of Argentina's GDP but employs 15 percent of the workforce. The short-term effects for the farmer involve the immediate things of necessity. What do I have? What do I need? What will I do if not farming? How will I maintain my standard of living? Food, utilities, clothing for children, household necessities, repairs, et cetera. There may be savings for both short-term and long-term events but it is never enough. People start pinching pennies immediately. Jenny, I guarantee that the economic numbers for Argentina, Brazil, Paraguay, and Uruguay will be horrendous under the best of circumstances."

"So secretly we're glad it wasn't us." Jenny truly meant to ask it in question format.

"Secretly . . . yes." Dr. Gray paused . . . he was looking at something—just what, she wasn't certain.

"The U.S. economy could withstand such an impact; we have programs in place. We have marginal cereal grain food supply reserve. However the U.S. farmable, arable land is vast."

Dr. Gray began spewing forth numbers and percentages off the top of his head. Jenny was thankful that the interview was being recorded. There was no way she could have kept up without shorthand and the assistance of at least three scriveners so she did the next best thing, she sat back and listened.

". . . the lower forty-eight states alone total 1.9 billion acres of arable land. Of the 1.9 billion acres, 44.5 percent represents agricultural land. Yet only .3 percent is permanent crops. The U.S. has 16.8 percent arable land that could be made available for use given time and logistics. This is important when you consider that the United States has the largest arable landmass available. China is fourth. Yet the United States has 69 percent more arable land than China. We could use this excess supply to keep the food processing plants of those affected open and in business. It will reduce the true financial cost but you can see the effect of the second ripple. Argentina is now further indebted to us and to those other countries that will offer assistance."

"The third ripple will affect the financial institutions and manufacturers of the farming community. Existing bank loans will have to be renegotiated. Further loans may require the backing of the Argentinean government and the World Bank. Farmers looking to purchase new machinery, parts, and accessory equipment may delay. Jenny, this will cause the manufacturing sector to be affected and the financial markets...globally. How long after the farming sector before manufacturing output drops off? The wider the circle, the more people encompassed by the ripple. The more people affected, the greater the overall impact. Each ripple cripples both the government and the people's belief in the government. This crippling effect then becomes systemic. Food lines start to form. There's a run on the banks. People recognize cash is king. These visual effects cause a spiral effect to which there is no end."

If Jenny didn't feel bad before, she definitely did now. "How will they survive?" she seemed to have asked because Dr. Gray looked at her before answering.

"Adapt. People have an amazing ability to adapt and move forward. Other countries will supply aid to the area. But with the second round of aid comes a greater responsibility upon both the government affected and its people. Robber barons and carpetbaggers," Dr. Gray said. "Humanity's penchant for greed knows no limits."

"When does it end? When will a citizen of Argentina know that the end is here, near, or in reach?"

"When they see things become better for them, their family, and their friends. Time is the key. Time heals all wounds," Dr. Gray said. "Spiritual, personal, financial."

"So public sentiment plays a part in the financial markets?"

"Definitely. There are researchers that take monthly polls of public sentiment and belief in the economy, their job security, retirement, government, to name but a few of the topics that they track. We even subscribe to the Quinnipiac polls."

The interview lasted far longer than initially scheduled. Robbi interrupted with a knock on the door. "Sorry to interrupt, Dr. Gray, Jenny, but I was wondering if you would like for me to order you both something from the cafeteria."

"Dr. Gray, Robbi, I'm sorry I lost track of time," Jenny shouted.

"Apparently, so did I. Jenny, how about we finish this over a salad. I am afraid my favorite hot dog stand may not be up to your culinary standards."

Jenny laughed and said yes.

"Robbi, two salads, please. Chef salads at that."

After lunch, they resumed their interview. China being prevalent in world affairs, they addressed the South China Sea, China's noticeable absence from Treasury Offerings, Brexit, North Korea and financial disturbance in Europe. "There are always world economic issues to discuss, Jenny," Dr. Gray remarked before the interview came to a close.

Chapter Seven

Treasury Bonds are often deemed the safest investment in the world. Backed by the U.S. government, the yield curve moves inverse to the perceived economic future. A bidder's absence can be seen as our Trust in God finally standing alone.

Millikin University
Decatur, Illinois

Bail was shaking his head in disbelief. *Shame* might be a better word choice. Whatever it was, it was most certainly not pride. It had taken a considerable amount of time but he was able to isolate the altered sequencing for the dampening-off disease. The use of the word *altered* might be premature, but it was a strong consideration. He looked at the clock before placing the call.

The call came in at just before five o'clock. Dr. Montero was still at the lab. She had been working 24/7. The situation warranted nothing less. She looked at the caller ID display prior to answering.

"Dr. Prichard, Dr. Montero here. How are you today?"

"Good . . . thank you . . . and you?"

"Equally well. All things considered. However, I have a feeling you are about to ruin my day."

"How did your experiment turn out?" Prichard asked, knowing beforehand the answer.

"Not good. The first set of experiments was a failure. The second round proved no better. We even discovered that some spores, not many but some, survived our fire experiment. I have kept quiet at José's request for obvious reasons."

"Huh. That would fit with what I have discovered," Dr. Prichard said. He wasn't overly excited at his own statement, which was simply the way he was. He enjoyed his job and was passionate about it although that did not always translate.

"I will be emailing you the sequencing combination I discovered. *Uncovered* may be a better word choice. The sequencing is what I believe causes the damping-off disease to be so resilient. Take a look at it and discuss it with Jesus and Fernando. I'll send it to a colleague or two here, let's stay in touch."

"Okay. Thank you, Bail, and if we don't speak before, have a Merry Christmas and Happy New Year."

"Thank you, Angelina; you and your family and friends."

The call terminated. Dr. Prichard sent the email to Dr. Montero with a description of his findings and the likely next few steps that needed to be taken. He then sent the same email to Katie, requesting they sit down to discuss this further when she was home for the holidays.

~~~

St. Louis, Missouri

Katie received Bail's email; she reviewed his findings. It had taken some time but thankfully progress was being made. She agreed with his course of action and was in the middle of a thought when there was a knock on her door.

"Marshal, come in," Katie said. Marshall had the door open and was stepping into her office.

"Katie, sorry to bother you," he walked up to her desk and sat down in the visitor's chair.

"No, that's all right. I'm just reviewing some research documents." She minimized the screen. The background picture of her and Brad by the Black River came into view. Marshall noticed the new photo.
~~~

"Things going well?" he nodded at the photo.

"Yes, actually." She was starting to blush; she could feel her face getting warm.

"I'm sorry," Marshall said. "I don't mean to pry."

"No, that's all right. But yes, things are going well." And they were, Katie thought, so why be embarrassed. They were in love and both knew it.

"So to what do I owe this pleasure?" Katie asked.

"I just wanted to let you know they started planting your super-seed. We should know something after the new year." Marshall reached into the breast pocket of his suit jacket and produced another check. He was smiling when he slid the check across Katie's desk. She unfolded it and noticed in the folio section the notation *1 of 3*. She looked up at the amount and was shocked . . . THREE MILLION DOLLARS AND NO CENTS, all in capital letters, was typed underneath the PAY TO THE ORDER OF line.

Katie was stunned. "I just never consider the financial benefits of any of this."

"Katie, your research may have changed the financial lives of a few people but it has impacted the world on a much larger scale. At the risk of sounding condescending, I am very proud of you and what you have accomplished," Marshall looked at Katie, smiled and got up to leave.

"Thank you, Marshall," Katie said when he reached the door. Recognition can be a slow process.

Marshall smiled. He turned before saying, "You look happy in that picture, Katie. Merry Christmas to you, Brad, and your family." Marshall closed the door on his way out.

Katie looked at the picture and remembered the weekend. It was difficult not to have had a nice time. She realized she was happy with the relationship and her life. But after a few moments of daydreaming, she returned to work and the task at hand.

She revisited Bail's work and resolution of a small piece of the puzzle. She reflected on her breakthrough being an evolutionary acceleration, could one argue the same for the spore? Katie believed not. She typed in Joseph and his email address popped up. She would send him a cut and paste of Bail's work and progress. She would ask for his assistance and hoped he would provide it. She had the remaining cereal grains to research; otherwise, she would pursue a viable fungicide.

~~~

Pyongyang, North Korea

The United States has been shipping food to the people of North Korea for the past fifty years, primarily cereal grains. The gesture is one of goodwill. Payment is the coverage of expenses. So, when Kim Jong-un complained about the United States diverting a percentage of grain normally destined for North Korea, it came as a surprise to the State Department and Secretary of the Department of Agriculture. "No good deed goes unpunished," Jonathan was quoted. Kim Jong-un believed the super-seed should also be factored into humanitarian aid they receive. The State Department refused comment, so did the Secretary of the Department of Agriculture. The story died with no one to add fuel to the fire.

~~~

Chat-room Posting

Not every job posting uses Monster or Linkedin, some jobs are posted and accepted without a résumé. One's knowledge of the bulletin board was proof of qualification.

PART II

Between the holidays of Thanksgiving, Christmas, and New Year's, not much beyond an average day's work gets accomplished. There are a total of six days the vast majority of Americans have off. These holidays are generally enhanced by early dismissal the day before, which increases the total to approximately seven and a half days . . . let's say eight days. When Christmas and New Year's fall in the middle of the week, Wednesday or Thursday, that increases the possible vacation days closer to ten. Assuming a total number of days between Thanksgiving and New Year's is thirty-seven, days off are between 16 and 27 percent. A relatively material percentage when one doesn't even consider holiday lunches, water cooler conversation, extended break room coffees, etc. Katie's and Jenny's world were no less affected and may have been affected to a greater extent, given their proximity to the fire albeit still unknown.

Jenny's article was front-page news . . . below the fold for both the *Dispatch* and *The Rag*. Not a big deal from her standpoint. "Been there done that," she was overheard saying. Not in a conceited way for other articles were well written and deserving of position. Her article was well received and ran in both the *Washington Post* and the *New York Times*. First section for both, one week later.

Katie's time had been spent in close contact with several people on several fronts. Sequencing research for both wheat and soybeans had achieved significant breakthroughs. Genetic code had been solved with each requiring an exponentially fewer amount of research hours than previous cereal grain. There was a definite commonality to cereal grain sequencing. Actual tests were scheduled but computer simulations were producing amazing results. It was agreed she would proceed with the remaining cereal grains before looking at other high-volume food items.

Over the holidays, Katie had a chance to speak with Bail and review some of his work at Millikin University. The laboratory facilities were first rate; however, the electron microscope was first generation. Quality still but it had limitations. Thankfully, Champaign, Illinois, is only a thirty-minute car ride. The University of Illinois was more than willing to assist a fellow academic. So with Bail's research and Katie's laptop, they were able to make substantial progress within a relatively short period of time. Fourteen-hour days seemed like eight, but in the end, the news was less than ideal.

Conclusions arrived at would need verification; however, they were confident in their findings. They agreed not to mention anything to anybody until after the holidays. Secretly Katie knew she would tell Brad, no reason not to. She needed his support.

Katie and Bail were not alone, others were working during the holiday season. Our three biologists at the University in Rosario were hard at work. Bail had sent Dr. Montero a quick text message: *Good news bad news. Will call to discuss soon.* Fourteen-hour days were the norm. Progress was slow; hope was on the super-seed's ability to withstand the super-spore's aggressive nature.

Larry Seabreeze was also working in Argentina. His presence in country was classified. His actual date and point of entry were also classified. José Quinterro and Madame President were both aware that a U.S. operative from some agency would be in country but that was all they had been made aware of. Given the overall level of paranoia U.S. officials felt, post 9/11 life, they were desperate for a successful resolution of this issue. Yet one's plate is never full enough; the world stage saw continued country posturing for front page news.

China's continued absence from Treasury auctions did not have the effect Chinese officials hoped. U.S. markets were calm. Holiday trading had been lighter than normal but not a concern. Markets were behaving in an orderly fashion, both Dr. Gray and Magne had predicted. . . "a non-issue." If that were where things ended, one would simply ride out the storm but unfortunately . . .

Chapter Eight

Science, and by extension its discoveries, have often been heralded as ethically neutral. Should human suffering be a basis of our mortal condition? Osteoporosis, Alzheimer sufferers may disagree, but for those who choose to pay for their sins through such suffering. The Chinese government believes CRISPRing babies is a bad idea. Said statement was made on the heels of He Jiankui's claim to have made the world's first gene-edited babies, twin girls.

University of Illinois
Champaign, Illinois

"It's engineered." Bail's look and expression was emotionless, robotic Katie noted.

"But how? Why?"

"The how is easy—someone has your research paper," they were still in the lab. "The why is equally easy. Terrorism."

"Biological terrorism? I guess I always assumed such a weapon would be infectious, used against people, not the food chain."

"Let's hold off any further discussion until we get to the car." Bail was cautious to a fault. They cleaned everything up and notified campus security to come and lock up.

Katie and Bail left the building in silence and waited until they were safely traveling west on Interstate 72, Decatur, before resuming their conversation.

"Terrorist or no terrorist, I still find it impossible to believe that someone—anyone, for that matter—could duplicate my research. It's a statistical improbability. It's impossible!" Katie said before continuing. "They had to have had my research paper. But again how and who would do such a thing?"

"We discussed this before, Katie," Bail said.

"I know we did. Outside of you, there is only Joseph in Arkansas, Texas A&M, Marshall, and Amged." Katie sat there. Silent. Bail drove down the interstate. They were virtually alone on the highway. Nary a car in sight but for those sitting idle next to the occasional farmhouse dotting the flat Central Illinois landscape.

Katie smiled and almost laughed. She remembered trying to describe to her Rutgers friends traffic situations in and around Forsyth. At any given hour, any road, there was a traffic jam in New Jersey. Yet here, now, or at any hour there was not a car in sight. Perfect *as if* scenario, they built the interstate just for her. Bail broke the solitary feeling, when he invaded her nostalgic thought with present-day reminders.

"I trust the unending tracks of farmland have not lulled you into a hypnotic state."

"No, I was just remembering what it was like to grow up here, fond childhood memories. Life was simple. Uncomplicated. Now when we try and move two steps forward, there are those taking us ten steps backwards. Why? What possible reason?" Katie continued to look at the farmland and farmhouses. Snow began to fall. No answer forthcoming.

"Anger and hatred are likely emotions that drive such people. I can't believe it is limited to self-righteous indignation born out of religious beliefs. In short, I think all terrorists and their entire families should be dealt with in the severest sort of way regardless of what is deemed to be humane treatment. It may sound cold and dispassionate but innocent people die. And for what? No, it's has to stop."

Bail clearly has strong feelings on this subject. But he has to deal with them later in life, Katie thought while she pondered Brad's likely opinion. She was obviously against terrorism but thought the family comment a bit excessive. "I'll pull the trigger if no one else will," Bail finished saying having reached the exit for Forsyth. A few minutes later they were pulling into the Pendleton driveway.

"So what did we decide?" Katie asked.

"We decided to think further what authorities to contact and for you to get some sleep."

"How about you?"

"I'll stop by my office and call Dr. Montero before sending her an email. Afterwards, I will head home to take a much-needed nap." Katie exited the car. Mike was at the door. He and Bail exchanged a wave.

~~~

Bail made his way to his office choosing stairs over the elevator. *Might as well begin working off future effects of the muffin now.* He walked into his office and sat down. While he logged into his computer, he sent a text message to Celeste letting her know where he was. Next he dialed Dr. Montero's number. She answered on the third ring.

~~~

"Hello, Bail," Dr. Montero's voice sounded fresh, relaxed.

"Angelina, how are you this morning?"

"Fine, thank you. I received your text. Good news bad news, I'll take them in that order," she said, getting straight down to business now that the pleasantries were exchanged.

Bail exhaled. "I will be sending you another email with attachments. We have determined gene sequencing used for the spore from the sample provided. That's the good news."

"And the bad news?" she interjected.

"And the bad news, Angelina, is that the spore is engineered and likely an act of terrorism," Bail responded. His tone matter-of-fact.

"Terrorism? Biological terrorism . . . and against us?" initial beliefs fulfilled. "Who? Why? What for?" She spoke rapidly, not really expecting an answer. It was more of a knee-jerk reaction. Bail remained calm and silent. After a long pause, she finally asked, "What now?"

"Well, I've been thinking about that. From our standpoint, we will continue research for a fungicide. From an authority standpoint, we will notify the Secretary of Department of Agriculture, who will contact Homeland Security. I would suggest you discuss this with Jesus and Fernando before contacting the appropriate branches of your government."

"Bail, thank you for your help. I know this was not your problem and I appreciate what you have done."

"Don't mention it. I only wish there was more I could have done," he said before adding, "Anything on the super-seed?"

"Nothing negative so far. I understand it was planted quickly, We should know something soon."

"Angelina, if you could keep me up-to-date on this. I am interested in how this plays out."

"I will, and again, thank you."

Bail completed his telephone call with an email to Dr. Montero, sending a blind cc to Katie. It was late and he was tired. He accidentally used Katie's work email address at Feldman & Company Biotech. A small mistake one normally might not make were they not tired. Having completed his task, he left his office for home, a nap, and hopefully a warm bed.

Chapter Nine

Since 2008, the top 10 American farm subsidy recipients received on average $1.8 million per year. That's $150k per month, or $35k per week while the average taxpayer's salary is $52,500 per year. Farm subsidies have evolved.

Buenos Aires, Argentina

The Delta flight arrived Buenos Aires International at 7:27 p.m. Larry's flight was on time. He was met by his contact at the baggage claim outside customs. This being a low-profile information-gathering mission, Larry was traveling light (i.e. unarmed).

Melina Mendez was five feet, eight inches tall, black hair with eyes to match. She was athletically attractive by most people's standards, Larry's included. She approached Larry with a warm friendly greeting. No code words required.

"*Buenas tardes, Señor Larry.*"

"*Señorita, buenas tardes.*"

"How was your flight?"

"Long, nine hours, direct." Larry stretched while his two pieces of luggage traveled the carousel.

"This way, please," Melina lead them through the airport and to her car. She was parked outside the terminal gate, short-term lot. They approached her car, a Ford Fiesta. She popped the trunk with her remote. Larry placed his luggage inside. He then closed the trunk and they both entered her car.

Larry was staying at the Hilton Hotel in Buenos Aires, which was where Melina dropped him off. "I'll wait in the bar while you check in and get cleaned up," she said. Twenty minutes later, Larry joined her at the bar.

"CC and Coke, please," the bartender stared in response.

"Canadian Club . . . *sí*," Larry confirmed.

"*Sí*," the bartender located the bottle and mixed Larry's drink placing it in front of him. Larry turned to Melina . . . "Cheers," he said with a smile. "Happy hunting," Melina responded clinking their glasses together.

"I have a Jeep Wrangler outside for you. Soft top, fully insured." Melina handed Larry the keys.

"How long have you worked for us?" Larry asked.

"Seven years. I was recruited while I was on vacation in New York. I thought I was in love. It happens," she said matter-of-factly before adding, "And you?"

"College. I wanted to be that double-naught spy everyone sees in the movies but a motorcycle accident left me with some permanent injuries. My childhood dream no longer a reality. I'm here now because no one else saw this but me." He ordered another round of drinks, both having finished their first.

They talked for a while longer about their individual lives. Both seemed happy with where they were individually. "It could always be better," Larry said. Melina agreed offering a clinked glass in response, "to happier times." They smiled, each taking a sip.

"So what is your plan?" Melina asked.

"Based upon cell phone activity, we have located the cities used. Because of the rural nature of much of Argentina, it was fairly easy." Larry thought for a moment, the best they could do was Central Illinois for the United States. Roughly five thousand square miles of possibilities. Argentina was so much easier.

Larry's facial expression must've changed. Melina looked closely at him. "What?" Larry asked.

"You were thinking something...related to this case? What was it?"

"We think . . . I really . . . my boss is now covering his bases."

Melina did not understand the reference. "Sorry, bases is a reference to baseball . . . anyway," Larry continued with a wave of his hand, "I was thinking cell phone calls were easier to trace here versus those between the United States and Saudi Arabia."

Melina sat quietly for a while before asking, "What cities?"

"General Acha, Cornel Pringles, Tunuyán, Villaguay, Veda, Balcarce, and Chascoműs. The only other piece of evidence I have is the photo we intercepted." Larry retrieved the photo from his phone and showed it to Melina. She took it and stared at it for a while.

"I know this area. This section of the Piedmont Mountain Range is near Tunuyán."

"How can you tell?"

"Because that is where I grew up. I'm from Tunuyán."

Larry took a drink and motioned the bartender over. He ordered bar food. Empanadas, assorted pastries filled with beef, cheese, vegetables, et cetera. They continued talking until the food arrived. Larry ordered a third round and invited Melina to sit at a table. "Sure," they moved to a high-top table. They had a nice view of the bar and television, which was showing the soccer game.

"I have to be in town for a couple of days before I visit these cities. Would you consider making the drive with me to Tunuyán?"

"Yes. I can use the time off from my work anyway."

"Great. I'll cover all expenses obviously."

"That's fine. Will you be going to the university in Rosario to speak with Dr. Montero and her staff?"

"I am planning on it but I need to think how to approach her. Remember, I'm not supposed to be overly active in my search for answers. Dr. Montero is in contact with your president and the Minister of Agroindustry, who are in contact with my president and the Secretary of the Department of Agriculture, so I may simply rely upon that flow of information. However, anything you might be able to add to that would definitely be of help."

"I'll see what I can find out tomorrow and call you."

The food arrived so they both took some time from the business portion of the meeting to discuss other things. *Nothing stops failure but a try*, Larry thought.

~~~

Fayetteville, Arkansas

Joseph had spent the holidays reviewing work for Marshall's group. That was how he learned to think of it. If he thought of it as Katie's group, his mind drifted to fanciful thoughts of things a fancy. "It happens," she said. He was thinking while he stared at the computer model of the super-spore.

Joseph knew enough not to question how he'd come to be in possession of the super-spore or who had sent it to him. It had simply arrived at his office. Private carrier. No signature required. Unannounced. With a private note.

The instructions were simple: *What is it? Can you defeat it?* Joseph always assumed it had been Marshall. Marshall never denied it when confronted, which wasn't exactly an admission or a confession. But it created a rebuttable presumption.

~~~

There's a certain beauty to an organism, any organism. A symmetry that belies its true nature. This one was no different, Joseph thought. He looked at it. He had been staring at it for hours. A side-by-side comparison with other known spores. Some he had even tested against the super-seed. Some spores were hybrids that he had tried to create . . . failed attempts, yes, but attempts nonetheless.

He returned to his stool, which sat in front of the computer screen, and resumed his vigil. He sat there sipping and thinking about his coffee, black, steaming hot, straight, no additives . . . *Just like my women.* He found himself laughing, age-old punch line to a joke.

And there it was. *At times it's impossible to see even the forest, let alone the trees, standing this close*, Joseph mumbled more to himself than to anyone within earshot. He had been so close but now he saw it. He instantly understood why the spore was so powerful and almost impossible to kill. The creator had to be both a genius and a madman. Joseph sat there for a few more moments using a multiple split-screen approach for comparison purposes. Finally he dialed Katie's number. Again, he relied on memory and dialed her office number. Direct dial.

Katie was not in her office, given the holidays. She also failed to have her calls forwarded, which may have benefited the overall situation. However, she did not, so, we will never know. But what we do know is that Joseph left a message . . . *Katie, it's Joseph. I discovered something about the spore I'm certain everyone's overlooked. It's important that you call me. We're all in danger. You have my numbers.*

~~~

Buenos Aires, Argentina

It was midday when Larry received this text from Melina: *Dinner 8:30 p.m. La Rodeo.*

He replied: *Sí. Drinks at 8 p.m.*

:-).

Such is the language of a developed society. Brevity.

~~~

The day had been spent productively. Larry worked out an approach prior to arriving in Buenos Aires. The cities used by the terrorists, Larry's internal decision, were independent of each other. That is to say there was no hub-and-spoke arrangement. Each city was relatively remote in location and small in population (12,000 to less than 50,000 inhabitants per city). Each city was equipped with an airport and close to the main areas affected. With profile in hand, Larry drove to Balcarce first.

Balcarce has a population of 45,000 Argentineans. It is remote in location yet relatively close to the Pampas Region from the coastal side.

It is approximately 440 kilometers southeast of the Pampas Region and 75 kilometers west of the South Atlantic Ocean. It has a small airport used primarily for crop dusting and hobbyists. There are no commercial flights.

Larry's approach was direct. He drove straight there. He parked in the parking lot. He got out of his Jeep Wrangler and walked around until he found someone to help him out. Trial and error. With seven cities, he knew he would get help at some point.

Balcarce was a bust. All errors. Larry spoke with five individuals before being provided with the name of the airport manager. Unfortunately, he received no useful information once he spoke with Mr. Rodriguez. However, Larry learned two things from the experience. First, they did use crop dusting planes. Some were visible. Second, start at the top first and be pushy. Third (three things actually), flight log books are used in rural airports. Larry noticed several being completed by mechanics. While leaving the airport for Chascoműs, he noticed a fuel truck labeled PETROL. Petrol is the national fuel company of Argentina. On a whim, Larry drove over to the truck. He exited the Jeep and spoke with the driver.

The driver stared at Larry as he approached. "*Hola*," Larry said. A hand wave and smile were added for effect. The driver nodded. Larry pressed onward. "I'm trying to locate a crop-dusting company that operated in this area once or twice over the past two, maybe three months. Are you familiar with any?" The gentleman said nothing vocal just a shake of the head in a side-to-side fashion. *No.*

"I'm curious if you have had any new accounts over that same period of time. Or if you had any delinquent accounts. I see you have a 'pay at the pump' setup."

Again, a nonverbal response . . . *No.* It was clear the driver did not want to speak to a perfect stranger, no less an American. And one asking questions. It was not a good combination. Understandable, yes. However, this was and is important.

"Listen, I am not with the Argentinean government. However, I am trying to help them and local farmers. Your cooperation would go a long way in helping me help them, were you or anyone so inclined to speak with me." The driver stood there and looked at Larry.

Although he said nothing, the wheels were turning. Larry shook his head, he reached into the coffee cup holder on the passenger side of the Jeep for a pen and paper he had placed there. He jotted down his cell phone number and handed it to the driver. The driver took it without looking and continued to stare at him. With nothing else to say or be said, Larry got back into the Jeep and drove off toward his second destination. Thankfully it was a nice day. The Jeep was a good call, better than a convertible.

The drive to Chascoműs was a little over three hours. It was sunny and midday so Larry drove along the coast. It was during the drive he received a text from Melina. The text reminded him of his invitation to her for the drive to Tunuyán. He wasn't certain why he'd invited her other than it simply felt right. The fact that she was from the town could have been it but it wasn't. It just felt right. Her invitation to dinner this evening and smiley face response to drinks seemed to make the air smell fresher. Larry laughed to himself . . . maybe he was a double-naught spy after all. "Seabreeze, Larry Seabreeze, CC and Coke . . . shaken, not stirred," he laughed while driving past signs listing the town of Chascoműs and airport, 5 kilometers.

~~~

Chascoműs has a population of 30,000. A commuter town given the absence of major industry. It had a close proximity to the ocean yet it was not a resort or tourist town. The airport was located on the east side of town opposite the Atlantic Ocean. Upon approach to the airport, Larry noticed there were six hangars and three runways. There was no control tower, but there did appear to be an administration-type building. Larry drove up to it and parked. He took a deep breath, exhaled, got out, and walked inside.

The building was basically empty. There were some booths set up with various charter service names posted above each booth. Twenty-five folding-style chairs were set in what was obviously the passenger
~~~

waiting area. Customary men's and women's designated bathroom included within the structure. One desk set behind a partitioned wall. The partitioned wall was only four feet high. The individual sitting at the desk was on the phone. He looked over at Larry and returned to his phone call. Larry stood there looking around the room until the call terminated. He turned back to the individual behind the desk, but noticed he was already walking toward him. Larry stood there until the individual was only a couple of feet away before he looked to say something.

The difference between dismay, shock, and surprise at times can be measured in seconds. The individual walking toward Larry was of approximately the same height; however, he looked to be much more physically imposing than Larry. Given his prior overall negative experience in Balcarce, Larry became less confident. This confidence was further shaken by two additional men approaching from across the building through doors that led outside. Larry thought quickly of a retreat *but for* the individual approaching from behind him. Larry's mind literally went blank when the individual walking toward him removed his hand from his pant pocket and extended it in a form of greeting.

"Mr. Seabreeze, Juan Valez, let's step into my office." The other three men sat in chairs provided in the waiting area. Each of them turned the chairs toward the office. Juan led Larry to the office and they both sat down by the desk.

"Juan, the phone call?"

"*Sí.* It was the airport manager in Balcarce. It was likely that you would be coming here. He apologizes for not answering any of your questions but hopes you understand."

Larry nodded his head in response, "*Sí.*"

"So what can we do for you?" Juan asked. Larry looked at the three individuals. It was then he noticed each was carrying a logbook. Larry sat there and smiled.

Larry reviewed the logbooks provided. There was one company that had leased hangar space for two months. Prepaid and unused but for one flight in and out. The place was occupied for less than one week.

Fuel was purchased and paid for without incident. Juan provided copies of everything requested. Records, receipts, leases, plane identification number and a tour of the hangar. Larry also received a description of the pilot and a copy of his pilot's license. The information most likely on the license was fake but they all swore to the photo. Facial recognition could be of assistance. Live in hope; die in despair.

"Thank you for everything. This information has been very helpful," Larry said before adding "these are the cities used. I believe each one has a similar airport they flew from. I am staying at the Hilton in Buenos Aires. Here is my telephone number and name. I will be there for at least ten days. Can you get me the same information from each of the remaining six airports?"

Juan looked at Larry and nodded his head. "*Sí.* I can get you this information. Give me a few days. I'll call you when I get it."

"Thank you," Larry said.

"No, it is we who thank you."

Larry left the airport administration building. He looked at the sky and time. If there was no traffic, he would be able to run and work out before drinks. Things were looking up on a Tuesday.

~~~

Larry returned to the hotel in time to run and work out. He checked his email and scanned a copy of the pilot's license for purposes of facial recognition. *Others to follow* he typed. He turned the computer off and walked to the restaurant. La Rodeo was only a mile away; the night was cool. He would have driven but he wanted time to organize his thoughts. He was early but so was Melina, driving by she honked. She drove into the parking lot while Larry waited at the door. His decision was rewarded. Melina gave him a nice hug and kiss on the cheek; both lasting longer than friendship status, Larry thought. Hmmm . . .

The night was clear, cool, and crisp, they requested to sit outdoors. The view was worth any discomfort. The outdoor area had a fire pit that was lit. Its purpose was more decorative than functional.
~~~

"So how was your day?" Larry asked after ordering their drinks. CC and Coke for him, sea breeze for her.

"Good . . . but long. I overheard some of the other secretaries talking. Rumors are the fungus was likely engineered, an act of terrorism," Melina added. Their drinks arrived. Fear and anger in her voice apparent…she inquired as to his day.

"Better. Balcarce was a bust but Chascoműs worked out very well. I'm hoping the airport manager, Juan Valez, will be able to get information from other airports for me. That would be extremely helpful." Larry spent the next several minutes explaining how he struck out at Balcarce and hit possibly the mother lode at Chascoműs.

"So you won't be going to Tunuyán?" Melina asked. It was the way she asked the question that Larry heard. Disappointment in her voice.

"No, I'll still be going. I want to verify the photo." Her mood improved with that and they talked about other things.

The waiter returned for their dinner reservations inside. However, with some deliberation, they were able to dine outdoors. Asado-cooked beef was the house specialty. "When in Rome," Larry said when asked.

From their seats outdoors, they could smell the aroma of the open-air grill. The pit, called a parilla, was large enough that the juice from the different meats being cooked could be heard to sizzle over the fire. Larry was caught smiling more than once during the evening. For dessert they shared an order of *alfajores*, which consists of two cookies with dulce de leche filling (milky caramel). The evening seemed to be going by quickly with neither one of them ever at a loss for something to say. It was while they were sharing the desert that Melina asked Larry about his schedule.

"Tomorrow I'll try and verify the pilot's license and the airplane's identification number. I suspect both are fake. However, it still has to be done." Larry caught Melina looking at him. "Is there any way you can get me a current report of some kind regarding the research Dr. Montero has completed?"

"I can try. It shouldn't be that difficult."

"Perfect," Larry said before continuing. "I told Juan I'd be here for at least seven to ten days. Given that I'd like to leave for Tunuyán on

Thursday afternoon. It's roughly twelve hundred kilometers and I want to be at the airport by seven in the morning to check the photo."

"Okay. I'll ask for Thursday and Friday off," both could feel tension in the air build.

Dinner was winding down and there was work tomorrow. Larry didn't want the evening to end. He believed Melina felt the same. Unfortunately, Larry was not a double-naught spy. He was a desk analyst. He called himself a desk operative, although there was truly no difference given, he now felt awkward. Though he had been with women before, he never truly mastered the transition phase of the evening. Dinner to bed. It wasn't the notch on his belt he aspired; he actually felt something for Melina and found himself believing that she did. Kindred spirits from a previous life.

They were getting up from the table, having paid the bill, Larry took Melina by the hand in a reflex gesture. He felt her lightly squeeze his hand. Had she turned to look at him, his embarrassment at such an honest and minimal gesture would have flustered him to the point of complete incoherency. Thankfully, he regained his composure. Unfortunately, there was another transition phase. The parking lot . . . he walked, she drove.

Melina fumbled for her keys while Larry thought quickly for the perfect thing to say. Again, his rapier wit produced butcus. Nothing. Melina finally found her keys and looked over at her car before looking at Larry. It was her eyes, he thought. They had that dark sultry look to them. Before he knew it, he had taken her in his arms and was lightly kissing her on the lips. The soft feel of her lips on his added to the intoxicating feeling he experienced. The taste of her breath was more than he could handle. The kiss ended, he found himself looking into her eyes. Lost in them, but trusting to them, and the honesty, he whispered ever so lightly . . . for Melina's ears only . . . . She smiled a tear. Larry slowly wiped it away with this thumb. He kissed her again before she led them both to her car and the hotel only a mile away. At the moment it seemed like an eternity from their vantage point.

Waking the next morning, neither felt awkward. Instead, they were relaxed and conversant. They showered and started their day. Melina would have to make an extra stop at her house for a change of clothes but they both agreed to meet later for lunch.

~~~

Fayetteville, Arkansas

Joseph cradled the phone while seated on his stool. Lost in thought… at what we will never know. He stood, cleaned up what was needed and walked to the door where he outened the light and stepped into the hallway.

"Huh??? What da f@#&…it's late, the lab's closed, hey!!! What are you doing…"

~~~

St. Louis, Missouri

Feldman & Company Biotech, Inc., had used the same cleaning service for the past seven years. One simply never changed unless there was a reason. The cleaning crew was a different story. Competitive bids meant low profit margins. That translated into low wages and even lower wages, given undocumented transient work force that populated most cleaning company crews. So when Miguel joined the cleaning crew assigned to Feldman & Company, he was just another faceless name.

Miguel was a hard worker, to be sure. He was diligent and conscientious. Staff and supervisors enjoyed his work ethic and slapstick brand of humor. If asked at a later date, no one was quite certain how he was hired, when he was hired, and by whom. After only a couple of weeks, Manuel, Miguel's supervisor, began to leave him alone for an entire shift. Other employees recognized this, Manuel spent additional time supervising them, much to Miguel's delight.

Miguel was delighted by few things. The smell of morning dew marking the first day of spring did not excite him. The sound of his girlfriend saying yes to his proposal produced a mild level of excitement. Climatic excitement was when his fingertips touched a computer keyboard. He and the machine seemed to click. Miguel was an idiot savant. Not in the truest sense, but easily within its general meaning.

The profile on Katie and Marshall was thorough. It included the names of all their pets, teachers, acquaintances, children where applicable, birthdates, graduation dates, etc. The software company that maintained the LAN (Local Area Network) for Feldman & Company was top notch. Miguel should know. He worked for them during the day writing security code for several of their financial clients.

Miguel's work at the software company did not provide him with an in-depth understanding of the LAN security system used specifically by Feldman & Company. He did have a working knowledge of the basic platform being used. With that knowledge, he was able to compromise the server. The server was important because Feldman & Company's entire system was integrated, electrical, desk tops, telephones, copiers, etc. From there, Miguel was able to set up tracers and spyware directly on the server. Having accomplished that task, he proceeded to their individual offices to accomplish the same task but on their individual machines.

Most people keep security codes written down on Post-it notes, monthly blotters, on the bottoms of coffee cups, staplers, etc. They are rarely secure, and Katie and Marshall were no different. Katie's was Brad0927 (likely first day or meeting). Marshall's was RoadRunner69. Marshall's was easy. The picture of the car was on his desk. Katie's took seven tries. Thankfully Miguel's research was thorough and the server counter had been set to X (unlimited).

With security codes, Miguel was able to access individual hard drives and load both spyware and a remote access program onto their machines. Miguel's total elapsed time from start to finish was seven minutes. Not world record espionage but still respectable. Once the task was complete, Miguel notified his contact for receipt of the final payment. Easiest $15,000 he'd ever made. "Industrial espionage is such easy money."

Chapter Ten

Boys require a greater caloric intake than girls...2,900 calories. The safe limit for either gender is 1,400 calories. Carbohydrates should account for 65% of one's caloric intake. Most individuals use refined grains to meet this need.

Quinterro Farm, Argentina

Alberto Quinterro was the last farmer in Argentina to receive the super-seed. José never even asked. It was understood. Independence of fact and mind was first and foremost. Alberto practiced what he preached. Leading by example whenever possible. The larger farming families and co-ops followed his lead out of respect. They all knew odds were against the smaller farmer. Alberto had quietly been in talks with several farmers. He would add a thousand acres to the Big Q... tragedy for some was an opportunity for others. Said farmers would either work for him and earn a decent salary or move to the city. Such is the way of life.

Alberto was sitting at his breakfast table enjoying fresh melon, bran flakes, and hot coffee while reading various newspapers. He was an avid reader of the *Wall Street Journal*, the *Washington Post*, and *Clarin*. When possible and time permitted, he would read the *London Times*. World events and financial markets were his forte. He was waiting for José to arrive and overheard Consuelo on the house phone. "*Sí, treinta minutos*," she repeated. She hung-up the wall phone and walked out to the breakfast table. She was about to say something when Alberto simply said, "Traffic."

"*Sí, señor, treinta minutos,*" Consuelo said before returning to her daily duties. Alberto went back to his coffee and newspapers. He had thirty minutes to kill.

~~~

Larry and Melina discovered a need and genuine enjoyment for each other's company. One could call this a dalliance but time spent together was not frivolous. Infatuation quickly comes to mind. However, they both discussed this and believed the passion was real and not short-lived. There was a oneness, a togetherness to their affections. Melina defined it as genuine sincerity. Given that, "why fight it?" Larry said. He finished packing for Tunuyán.

He was looking forward to the drive. There would be a stop off in Rosario at the university. An appointment was scheduled. Dr. Montero had been advised of his coming but not actually who he was or what he wanted. The detour to Rosario and drive to Tunuyán added very little to time and distance.

~~~

The pilot's license and plane identification number were fakes. This had been expected. Facial recognition turned up nothing. There was hope one of the remaining six possible photographs produced a match. Assuming Juan delivered.

Larry spoke with Juan. He confirmed the requested information was being sent to his hotel. Point of entry was also discussed. Juan and the other airport managers were working on it.

Larry and Melina tossed their luggage in the Wrangler. They both caught the other's look and smiled. This clearly had the makings of something much more than a simple investigative trip.

The drive to the university in Rosario from Buenos Ares was approximately 300 kilometers. Larry planned on three hours. Morning weather was nice, sunny, and in the low eighties. They decided to drive with the top down and enjoy the breeze. Melina found a local radio station they agreed on and their adventure began.

~~~

Quinterro Farm

José arrived later than thirty minutes but it couldn't be helped. The important thing was he did, in fact, arrive. Consuelo greeted José at the door and led him to the breakfast table, where Alberto was waiting.

"José, thank you for coming, and sorry for your traveling troubles," Alberto said.

"Traffic and last-minute responsibilities," José offered by way of explanation.

"Any news on the fungus?" *Straight to business*, José thought. *He should be in the Pink House, not me.*

The Pink House was the nickname for La Casa Rosada, or Casa de Gobierno. The president and staff have their official offices there. The building faces the Plaza De Mayo and, outside of the White House, is considered by many the most awe-inspiring government building in the world.

"I spoke with Dr. Montero on the drive. She received some research from an American biologist Jesus Aguilar studied with. Jesus is working with her. In any event, research provided on the spore shows that it was engineered, an act of terrorism."

"Has anyone claimed responsibility?"

"No, no, they haven't. I was speaking with Madame President and it's our opinion we were a test. Given our growing season being now, the real strike will be in the spring."

"The United States," Alberto said, not asked. "Should they be warned?"

"They already appear to be on alert. They have an agent in country. He's visited some rural airports and is looking into a third after he speaks with Dr. Montero today."
~~~

"Are you having him followed?"

"No. Lack of resources. Besides, we are receiving immediate updates from the Americans. They agree in us being a test. We supply and export much of what we grow but nothing by comparison with the Americans. They are supplying us with grain for our wet milling plants that are U.S. owned or affiliated. With their grain reserves and grain diverted to us, we can remain operating for nine months, maybe longer," José said while he got up and poured himself a second cup of coffee. He remained standing and looked out while speaking on a more personal basis . . . the farm . . . expansion.

"Three farms," José said with a raised eyebrow, "a thousand acres plus. Not bad . . . not bad at all. Will they accept a job or that hasn't been finalized?"

"Mac will stay, the other two will leave, too young, not enough financial capital to survive. It's a shame; we need new blood." Alberto joined José at the railing overlooking the grounds. A site he had witnessed thousands upon thousands of times yet it was never tiring. They both stood there for a bit longer than warranted, neither one believing in talismans, magic, and such but, both secretly hoping against hope that the super-seed survived.

They seemed to sense rather than say it was time to go. They turned to set their coffee cups down. It was then they saw Consuelo standing in the doorway silently praying the rosary. Alberto smiled and said thank you. He and José stepped off the veranda and out toward the nearest field.

The walk was neither long nor short, yet it seemed endless. They approached the field, seeing some signs of life. *Sporadic* or *random* would be the best way to describe it. Alberto was not yet excited by the prospect of success. Growth was good. Promising even; however, it was not dispositive and they both entered the field cautiously.

Each step was carefully placed. Neither wanting to disturb the earthly spirits that occupied Quinterro land. Alberto and José were thirty to forty feet inside the field when Alberto bent down to one knee. José mimicked Alberto's position, holding his breath.

"Moment of truth," Alberto said. He reached into the soil and pulled out a seemingly healthy corn plant. The spot where they stopped contained several healthy-looking plants. Alberto shook his head. He handed the plant to José. José took it. Looked at it, "The fungus is attacking the stock on this plant." Alberto was nodding his head in agreement. He pulled up another plant, looked at it, and handed it to José.

"Same thing."

They continued to walk the fields with the same or similar success. Good news was the super-seed seemed to have a strong resistance to the damping-off disease. Alberto found very little, if any, of that. Unfortunately, what he and José did find were spots of barren soil. The seed was still in the coated shell, having never started the germination process. They uncovered root rot, but the primary disease was affecting flow of food and water up and down the xylem tissue. Even if the super-seed were resistant to the plant stock disease, the stocks would likely not mature.

"Let's check other fields," José said. He placed his hand on Alberto's shoulder. "There may be better success elsewhere."

Alberto followed José's lead but only a reflective gesture. Neither one really expected to find true success. In the end, failure was all they discovered. Alberto called his neighbors before sending out a group text. *Meeting tonight eight o'clock. Visit your fields first.*

José placed a call to the president. He informed her of the status and suggested a cabinet meeting for tomorrow afternoon. The second call was to Dr. Montero informing her of the findings and a suggestion to keep this from the Americans until after tomorrow's cabinet meeting. "I will stop by your office to discuss this first thing in the morning."

~~~

U.S. Department of Justice

The government publishes statistics on seemingly limitless and meaningless data. Violent Victimization Committed by Strangers is
~~~

one such category. Between 1993 and 2010, there was a 77% decrease in this statistic. One can consider this a plus if you were a recipient of that statistic, indirect...or direct should the fact pattern so present itself. Unfortunately, 27% of the fatalities committed during that same time period were committed by strangers unknown to the victim, decedent. A direct correlation, were you found to be in the minority.

~~~

University in Rosario
Rosario, Argentina

Larry and Melina arrived shortly after the call from José but before eleven o'clock. The drive was pleasant. Conversation during the trip was rewarding and fruitful on both a business and a personal level. They stopped for coffee and scones for the morning drive. Traffic, due to road repair, was the underlying cause of their tardiness and delay. Driver negligence or poor time management and not wanting the trip to end were a photo finish second.

Larry and Melina were led to the ante room adjacent to Dr. Montero's office on arrival. "Dr. Montero is on the phone but will be with you shortly," the receptionist said. Larry sat listening to her half of the conversation.

~~~

As a desk analyst for the NSA, Larry's training was extensive. Such training included psychological analysis on body language, tone of voice, words unspoken versus those actually spoken. Syntax was extremely important. These classes, training lessons really, were drilled into an operative/analyst whether in the field or sitting at a desk. The agency's intent was to have training become second nature. One such class dealt with listening to one-sided conversations. The acronym made no sense to Larry. He dubbed the class, A-L, Active Listening.

He and Melina sat quietly trying not to eavesdrop on Dr. Montero's conversation. Larry was actually doing just that, actively listening. He was trying to piece together a whole conversation from the half that he heard.

Larry's attention was initially drawn to the telephone conversation when Dr. Montero referred to the speaker, José. In Larry's estimation, it was clear she was speaking with José Quinterro, Minister of Agro-industry. From her body language and facial expression, it was clear things were not good. Larry was aware that the super-seed had been delivered to countries affected. He surmised that the seed's performance was less than expected. He understood her body language. Disheartened. Curious what she would say, if anything. Larry made a mental note to visit the Quinterro farm on the way back from Tunuyán. Unannounced, of course, Larry returned to his magazine.

Dr. Montero's call with José ended shortly thereafter. Bad news is never something that inspires small talk. She looked up from the phone upon cradling it. Her door had been open and she could see both Larry and a woman with him. "Mr. Seabreeze," Dr. Montero said. She walked out of her office to the waiting room. Larry and Melina stood to greet her. Introductions made, both parties got right down to business.

"Mr. Seabreeze, I understand you are here to help us?"

"Yes, yes I am, although it sounds like I'm too late." Larry glanced quickly at the telephone.

"Timing is everything," she said. "So what can I do for you?"

"My associate and I are here to try and determine what happened. We're also interested in whether or not this event was of natural cause or unnatural," Larry continued. "We're hoping you can help us." Dr. Montero exhaled before speaking. Despair was in her voice.

"I can't tell you much because there's not much to tell. But what I can tell you is that we are working extremely hard and making progress." This was substantially less than what Larry expected. People and governments were too territorial and secretive in dire moments.

"Dr. Montero, so there is no confusion, please understand we are on the same side. What happened here could happen elsewhere and actually did happen elsewhere. U.S. satellite imagery has recorded dead plant life in other areas. Areas other than those countries that have reported crop loss. I wish I could provide you with more specific data but for obvious reasons I'm not at liberty to disclose our level of satellite sophistication. Suffice it to say, this may become a world problem."

"Mr. Seabreeze, I, too, wish there was something I could tell you, but I'm also not at liberty to say much more than what I already have."

"Nothing else?"

Dr. Montero heard concern. She believed he was trying to help and would share if he could. "Here," she said...she wrote down contact information for Bail Prichard. "Call him on your return to the United States." She stood up. Meeting adjourned.

Melina looked at Larry and smiled while they walked to the car. He reached for her hand and she took his. "What are you thinking?" Melina asked.

"The super-seed wasn't very successful. I'm thinking we'll stop by Quinterro's farm on our way back from Tunuyán." Larry stopped. He thought for a moment and checked the time. "Lunch or drive?"

"Drive. There is a favorite restaurant of mine in Tunuyán and I would like to take you there." The statement came with a smile and a kiss.

"Drive it is."

Chapter Eleven

Harvard offers an 8-week online course in CRISPR: Gene-Editing. Weekly modules, flexible learning, 7-10-hour days. CRISPR is easy to use; hard to control. The intelligence community now sees CRISPR as a threat to national security and safety.

St. Louis, Missouri

The holidays were busy for everyone. Friends, families (actual and extended), traveling commitments. "Time management," Jenny remembered one of her professors in college discussing.

"Huh," she remarked…breaking the silence with a thought.

"What's that, lass . . . huh?" Mickey asked. He was setting the drinks down at their table.

"Mick, I was in college this time last year. Now I'm here with a handsome and rugged boyfriend, involved in a full relationship, two great jobs, I got you in my corner . . . I mean, this is gonna be a tough year to beat. Even Katie has a man friend . . . old . . . but still."

"Lass, I known talent. I known ya was da real deal," Mickey said. Lawrence leaned over and gave Jenny a kiss; Katie gave her the evil eye.

"So, any word on your super-seed?" Lawrence asked.

"No, not yet. I was hoping to hear something this week but I guess it'll have to wait until next week," Katie said. She remembered Joseph's voice mail message. She tried to call him back. He had good news about the spore. I guess the thought caused her to change the expression on her face to one of uncertainty, Lawrence asked, "Is everything all right?"

"What? Yeah, everything's fine . . . I guess." Katie looked perplexed.

"That's not reassuring," Jenny responded.

"Joseph called over the holidays. He left a message. . .important news on the spore." Katie looked at Brad and Lawrence. "He's a professor at Arkansas and conducted some research on cereal grains for us. Arkansas has a well-known agricultural school. We contracted with them to independently test and verify my research. When Central Illinois Corn & Soy became involved, they sent our results plus Joseph's to Texas A&M for verification. That's who they use. Everything was fine. Later I received a package from Joseph regarding research conducted on the super-seed. It was being tested against known cereal grain diseases. This isn't uncommon but for the fact that I was unaware of the research and Joseph knew that. Then there was an errant email and phone call afterwards that added unnecessary tension to the relationship."

"Relationship?" Lawrence slipped out. The table got quiet. "Sorry," Lawrence said.

"Way da play it cool, lad," Mickey said. He knew enough to break the silence.

"Hardly," Katie said. "It was impulsive and one night. I mean who hasn't." Mickey cleared his throat and got up to leave, his face turned red. Brad gave Katie a quick kiss.

"You are so much better looking than he is," Jenny added.

"Thank you, Jenny," Brad said. Jenny pulled out her cell phone. Katie gave her the look but Jenny simply said, "It vibrated so I'm checking for messages." She quickly Googled Dr. Joseph Patrick and visually scrolled through the choices without looking until she found one with his picture. She handed her phone to Lawrence, who saw the photo and could not help laughing.

"Really, Jenny? How juvenile are you?" Katie said, already knowing the answer.

"Let me see," Brad said. Katie's face turned red. Brad noticed.

"That bad?" he said. He took the phone Lawrence handed him. He looked at Katie, who nodded consent.

"It was impulsive. It just happened."

"Yeah, Bunsen burners, burettes, and beakers have that effect on me, too," Jenny commented.

Brad had two ways to go with the photo . . . high road or low road. He chose the high road. He looked at the picture and handed the phone to Katie. "He looks like a nice guy, Katie. He was lucky to have met you." Katie took the phone without looking at the picture and minimized the screen.

She briefly noticed the various articles that were displayed, realizing instantly why Jenny chose this picture. It had the University of Arkansas name along with Old Main, the oldest building on campus. She started to hand the phone back to her when she stopped mid-stream. Jenny was reaching for the phone and stopped at the same time Katie did. The table got quiet, the air got still, and a hush seemed to fill the room, everything began to move in slow motion for Katie.

Katie was frozen in time and space. She knew what she saw. She just couldn't believe it. The mind is an amazing piece of equipment when you consider all the things that it can accomplish in the blink of an eye. For within that fraction of one tenth of one second, Katie saw what everyone missed. Katie realized what they didn't. Katie recognized what no one could. The first article was an obituary. Joseph Patrick, Springdale, Arkansas, decedent.

When Katie's mind began to return her to the present sense, she noticed the sounds of the room winding back up like a juke box being restored power. The air had a feel to it and the table was questioning her, the phone still in her hand. She didn't read the obituary; she simply handed the phone to Brad, who looked at it and saw what Katie had seen. He read what she hadn't but it was of no use. Cause of death "unknown," he heard himself say. He handed the phone to Jenny and gave Katie a hug, "I'm sorry, sweetheart."

Jenny saw the first article and also looked at it while handing the phone to Lawrence, who read the entire obituary. Campus police and local homicide detectives were conducting the investigation. The state police were also involved. No leads reported.

"We were just talking about him," Katie said in a hollow-sounding voice.

"Let's go home, Katie," Brad said. They got up to leave.

"Katie, I'm sorry," Jenny added.

"Me, too," Lawrence responded. Jenny and Lawrence remained seated while Katie and Brad left the tavern.

"How weird is that? I mean we were just talking about him."

"Yeah, but how weird is it that he just happens to call her a day or two before he ends up dead. *'Cause of death unknown'*?" Lawrence responded.

"Coincidence?" Jenny said. Lawrence and she looked at each other before resuming their evening. They were looking to kill an easy hour before returning to the condo. "I'll call her a little later to be sure she's all right."

~~~

Tunuyán, Argentina

The drive from Rosario to Tunuyán was uneventful. At times Larry found himself lost in thought. Melina didn't say anything. She knew there was work to be done. But every now and then she found herself looking at Larry and smiling or reaching out for his hand. He was different than most men she had been attracted to and yet he was so much more. She found herself smiling at that exact thought when he reached out and touched her cheek.

Larry began to slow down, the exit less than three kilometers away. To be safe, he had booked the room under Mr. and Mrs. Seabreeze. She laughed when he told her that. It was a good laugh. They checked in, unpacked, and relaxed before dressing and heading out to dinner.

~~~

Tunuyán is an old town. It's a rural town with a population of 50,000. The town itself is small enough so that they could walk from the hotel to the restaurant. Reservations were not required but they made them anyway.

The view of the Andes and Piedmont Mountains to the east was amazingly beautiful. It was easy to see how Melina remembered the view and instantly made the connection with the photograph. Larry was thinking that very thought when he overheard the faintest sound of music being carried by the breeze. Instinctively he began tapping his free hand against his leg. They walked toward the restaurant. The music increased in sound. They continued their approach to the restaurant. A few blocks away, they came upon a block party.

Several mixed-use buildings with apartments on top and restaurants on the bottom had closed the road for dancing, entertainment, and dining. Tables were set picnic style. There were roughly one hundred-plus people who were walking from restaurant to restaurant, table to table. The music was good, easy to follow, and the people were having a great time. Without thinking, Larry found himself in the street dancing salsa style with Melina.

When he was a child, Larry's mother owned and operated a dance school. The dances looked better if there was a boy dancing among the girls. Larry was always that boy from the time he could walk. Musical talent he had. Tango, salsa, hip-hop, waltz . . . Larry could dance them all and dance them well. The key to a good couple's dance is if there's a strong leader. So when Larry and Melina hit the street and started to salsa, the evening took a turn neither one of them ever expected. Reservations were quickly forgotten. They made new friends, Larry heard stories and they took a seat toward the end of a picnic table and shared a gourd filled with maté.

~~~

The morning wake was an extension of the good night kiss. After all, they were Mr. and Mrs. Seabreeze. Having checked out of the hotel, they walked to a coffee shop, where they ordered a local coffee favorite and breakfast sandwich before driving to the airport ten minutes away. By 7:08 a.m., they were standing outside a small hangar looking off toward the mountains with cell phones in hand. Larry and Melina were not taking pictures of the mountains yet to be painted with a beautiful
~~~

sunrise. On the contrary, they were confirming Melina's memory, which appeared to be correct, as observed by the naked eye.

"What now?" Melina said to Larry after they'd stood there for several minutes. Larry turned to answer. And he would have had it not been for the gentleman walking toward them. Melina turned to look; Larry nodded to her.

"*Buenos días*," the man said. "My name is Felipe. I own and operate this airport. Juan called and said you would be coming." Larry and Melina introduced themselves and offered a pleasant good morning.

"So what did Juan tell you?" Larry asked.

"What I always thought. There was something wrong with the guy but he paid in advance, he paid cash. So when I heard about the farmers, I knew that someone would be by to ask questions."

"Am I the first?"

"*Sí.*"

"So what can you tell us?" Melina asked. These were her people. Larry was not upset that she asked the question.

"I can tell you that he stood right where you are, at the exact same time, and took a picture of the mountains. It was the only normal thing he did. He was not friendly," Felipe said. "Come let's go sit in my office, I have some things for you." Melina and Larry followed Felipe toward his office.

"It's so quiet here. Peaceful. Serene, there's an otherworldly feel to it," Larry found himself saying.

"Ahhh. It is much different from the city, is it not?" Felipe said. They entered the small building that held the office and administration building. There was a package sitting there.

"For me?" Larry asked. Felipe nodded yes. He poured three cups of coffee while Larry emptied the package contents onto the desk. There was a lease, receipt for payment, photo identification, copy of a passport, plane identification number, and two separate photos, which brought a huge smile to Larry's face. He handed the photos to Melina while he looked at Felipe.

"Eh, I am not a very trusting person," Felipe said with a shrug of his shoulders.

"Can I have these?"

"*Sí.* They are for you."

They talked for a while longer before Larry asked, "Did Juan say anything else?"

"No. We are still looking for the points of entry. I would guess that they flew in from Paraguay. Bolivia or Uruguay are possibilities. Our borders are open. But that is just a guess. We will find out. Do not worry."

"Chile?" Larry asked.

"No. The mountains are too high for such a small plane."

Larry and Melina finished the coffee, offered their thanks, and left. Larry left his cell phone number and email address should Felipe remember anything else.

"What now?" Melina asked. They climbed into the Jeep.

"Quinterro's farm," Larry answered.

~~~

Quinterro's Farm

Alberto and José's Thursday evening was less than fun filled. The hall was packed. Several farmers brought their sons, spouses, or extended family members with them. The doors to the hall were open so the sound could carry. There were easily 1,500 to 2,000 people for a venue designed to hold 480. With a functioning sound system, they began the meeting.

"Can everybody hear me?" Alberto asked. The main room, two corridors, and the foyer came to a hush. "So that we all can hear what there is to be said, let's please keep the talking amongst each other to a minimum. We do not want to inconvenience your neighbor standing next to you. José and I will be here until after everyone has left. I have asked other individuals to stay and assist in answering everyone's questions. This is not the time to be bashful. If you have something to ask, tonight is the time to ask. Please do not leave here until your
~~~

questions are answered to your satisfaction." And with that for an introduction, Alberto spoke for forty minutes. He provided everyone with an understanding of the effectiveness of the super-seed on his fields. "Fifteen percent growth. Half of which will likely not mature. The half that matures, I'll let die off and plow under for next season."

The room and surrounding area were filled with murmurs. Some had better luck (success if one can call it that). Others the same, some worse. In the end, they were still in the same sad shape. No harvest.

José spoke longer. He'd been provided with some good news for the farmers. The ripple effect was worse for them yet an integral part of the economy and labor force. Banking, equipment purchases, basic needs, and necessities. They were all a huge percentage for the country's well-being. "Provided there are no additional acts of terrorism, we will survive and so will you. The president does not foresee any reason why everyone in this room cannot keep their farms."

There were no shouts of joy, applause, or confetti thrown. Everyone knew that José and the president meant well but the pressure was not on them. It was on the people in the room. It was on the family living day to day, paycheck to paycheck. The couple that just got married was in the same dire straits with the one's that recently retired.

"Money is like paint, it hides all sins," Alberto overheard a small farmer say. Alberto did not know the individual but he knew what he meant. And he was right.

It was 3 a.m. by the time Alberto and José left the hall. Those asked to stay left a little earlier. Most people's level of confidence was reasonable high. *Overly optimistic* might be a better term. Some had asked to see Alberto privately. He consented and was sure the others did. Sellers always found buyers when there was a fire and the price was right. This being no different. In the end it was business. It always is.

When they returned to the Quinterro Farm, Consuelo was still up. "Coffee? Breakfast?" she asked. Both Alberto and José consented. José would nap before the drive to Dr. Montero's. The cabinet meeting was scheduled for Saturday. He had time.

Alberto remained awake after breakfast. He showered, dressed, and returned to the business side of farming. "The best way to make a peso is not to spend one," his father had always told him. "But when you do spend, spend wisely," he said.

Alberto was at his desk and reviewing properties of farmers that had requested a private conference. With today's technology, he was able to take a virtual tour of those properties and get an accurate assessment of their value. Those that wanted to stay and become either an employee or sharecropper/renter would receive a price structure different than those that simply sold and left farming to Alberto. Early birds would also be better served than those that arrived late. Even then Quinterro holdings would increase by 15 to 30 percent, making this one of the larger family-owned farms in the country.

Alberto was completing another evaluation when he heard the sound of tires on gravel. He looked up from his pad and paper, old school. A Jeep with a man and a woman stopped in the turnabout. An American and an Argentinean woman. Alberto called Consuelo and asked her to get José up while he saw to the visitors. They would be sitting out on the veranda. "Light drinks and empanadas, please." He heard footsteps at the door.

Larry reached out to knock when Alberto opened the door. Startled by the timing of the action, Larry recovered nicely. "*Buenos días*," Larry said while offering his hand, a friendly tone, and a smile. "My name is Larry Seabreeze," he began. "I am an American assisting the Argentinean government in determining the cause of the crop loss that directly affected your country and those of your neighbors. If you have time, my associate, Melina"—Larry introduced her without breaking eye contact with Alberto—"and I would like to discuss the situation with you."

Alberto looked at Larry, then his associate . . . Melina? Alberto then turned back to Larry. "Have you stopped at any other farms?" Alberto asked.

"No, sir. Just yours," Larry said before he added, "Can we sit down? It is to our mutual benefit." Alberto looked at the man and understood.

He showed them to the breakfast table. Consuelo provided cups and plates, coffee, tea, and juices. Four saucers and cups, Larry counted. Not three. Who would be joining them? Larry looked back at the turnabout and noticed the car. Too nice for a farmer. Even a wealthy one. Government, he guessed. Alberto was staring at him when his attention returned to the table. "José?" Larry asked.

"*Sí*. Let us wait for him to join us," Alberto said. "Until then, please help yourself to some light refreshments and snacks. Melina, would you care to freshen up after your trip? Consuelo can show you to the wash room." Melina nodded, excused herself, and found Consuelo standing near the door. She showed her to the wash room. Upon her return, she found Alberto and Larry in conversation talking about the countryside. Larry excused himself for the wash room. Melina's facial expression changed for a split second when she saw he poured a cup of coffee for her.

Alberto was not staring at her. He said nothing. When Larry returned to the table, he found it silent, not tense. A third individual, José, had joined the table. He stood and introduced himself when Larry walked up.

Larry passed on the small talk. He was the initiator of the meeting. Tempo and objective were his responsibility to dictate. The short conversation he'd previously had with Alberto established common interest. Protection of the countryside and its beauty. With that in mind, he began immediately.

"I wish that I were surprised to see José but honestly I'm not. Melina and I drove here from Tunuyán this morning. We were visiting the local airport. I have visited three separate airports. There were seven used. Information on all of the airports in question is being gathered. Airport managers will forward said information to my attention. This information will include photo IDs of the pilots," Larry said. He produced photographs just obtained. He handed them to José, who looked at them and passed them to Alberto.

"I have submitted other photographs for facial recognition. Unfortunately, the quality is poor and there was no match. The photos we received today I have higher hopes for. Don't bother asking about the information on the pilot's license, et cetera, it's fake. I was unsuccessful in verifying any of it," Larry said while pausing to take a sip of coffee.

His hope was that, by providing José with some information, José would reciprocate.

"Larry, I honestly wish that I could help you. On your drive here, you obviously passed several farms. What you saw is more than I know. This farm alone was devastated. Fifteen percent survival rate, Alberto estimates, of that, maybe half will reach maturity. Not enough to harvest even if it were all in one field. Other farms are the same. The super-seed is good, but the spore is better," José said.

"Anything from the research?" Larry asked.

"Dr. Montero provided you with a name and telephone number, I understand. This Dr. Prichard knows more than we do. I will tell you that we have contracted with several fungicide companies over the past thirty days but we have learned nothing of yet," José answered.

"And the president?" Larry asked.

José looked at Larry then Alberto. Alberto nodded slightly to José, who responded.

"There is a cabinet meeting tomorrow. I expect the president will address the nation. She will try and reassure the general populace but that will not be possible. Her presidency is over," José added reluctantly. It happens. It happened on her watch. She will be to blame. Such is life. Such is politics.

"I would appreciate it if you'd contact me after the cabinet meeting," Larry said. "Here is my cell phone number. I am staying at the Hilton. I have their telephone number and my room number on the back of my card." Larry physically handed cards to both José and Alberto. He wanted to look them both in the eye. "I will obviously make sure that you are provided with any information we uncover from the facial recognition program," Larry said. He stood up to leave. Melina sensed the end and stood with Larry.

"Alberto, José, thank you for your time and sorry for the intrusion," Larry said.

Alberto and José stood and walked Larry and Melina to the turnabout. They drove off. "What do you think?"

"I think we should tell him everything we know. Otherwise we may all be in trouble," Alberto said. José agreed. Unfortunately, they did not know much.

~~~

The drive back to the hotel was uneventful. Traffic was light, and they made good time. Along the way, Larry called Juan to thank him for the call to Felipe. The call provided Larry an opportunity to personally thank Juan for being so helpful. Maybe this was how real double-naught spies operated. The common man or woman is the true unsung hero. The call provided Larry with a forum to inquiry on the status of the other four cities and the *ponto de entrada* (point of entry).

"Information from the remaining airports will be delivered to you Monday. Two more owners were concerned. I understand they have pictures of the pilots and their planes. I'm sorry to say that other owners are like me and not proactive when we should be. The *ponto de entrada* is proving more elusive, but I should have that information Monday."

"Juan, I could not have accomplished this task without your assistance. Thank you. I really mean that."

"I'll see you Monday," Juan said. He liked the American and his honesty.

It was late afternoon when Larry and Melina arrived at the hotel. Larry parked the Jeep and grabbed the luggage, tossing both bags over his shoulder. With his free hand, he reached for Melina's hand and led them inside the hotel. Nothing had been said. Larry seemed preoccupied on the drive back. Melina had decided to let him work, resigning herself to a phone call later. Apparently, he had other ideas. She relented to his wishes, which were thankfully equal to her desires. Young love is, after all, one of life's more potent aphrodisiacs.
~~~

Chapter Twelve

In 2017, 12 members of the United States Congress received farm subsidies. The largest amount paid to a Congressional representative was $637,000.00. Many of our Congressional faithful are also drafters of the various farm subsidy bills. Query: Who among us wouldn't have their cake and eat it too?

Cabinet Meeting

José met with Madame President prior to the scheduled cabinet meeting. They discussed the status of the fields. It was substantially worse than expected. "We may not survive this tragedy, my friend. Certainly, I won't," she added.

"Madame President, I'm certain a fungicide will be developed that will counter the effects of this engineered spore," José said. "Let us remain positive."

"Sí, José, we will be positive," she looked out the window at the obelisk standing in the middle of the plaza. "Anything from Dr. Montero?"

"The American, Dr. Prichard, has been more successful than we have. I think that there is more to that story than we are being told," José noticed Madame President turn and look at him.

"The timing bothers me is all. This Prichard was alerted by someone at least familiar with their super-seed and strangely worried about its viability against disease. A normal process to be sure, but still one that makes me think there is a rat in America." José noticed the president had returned to gazing outside.

"But at least they have their angels." Madame President turned and looked at her watch. The cabinet meeting was due to begin. She already looked exhausted. Beaten.

So, this is what defeat looks like, José thought. He remained seated.

"Madame President, we have one more matter to discuss."

The president looked at him, pleading for the news to be good. "Madame President, the U.S. intelligence officer visited Alberto yesterday. The visit was unannounced. I happened to be there, given the hour at which the meeting with the farmers ended."

"Alberto saw him, I presume."

"Yes, Alberto did. He had me awakened to join him with the American. The American's name is Larry Seabreeze. He is a desk analyst. An egg head, they call them."

"What was he doing in so remote an area of the Pampas Region?"

"He is looking for the *ponto de entrada* of the seven crop-dusting airplanes. He has the rural airports used and the help of their owners in supplying him with the pilot and plane information. He assures me that he will cooperate fully and asked that I do the same . . . that we do. Alberto believes we should and so do I, Madame President."

"I agree," she replied while shaking her head. "What choice do we have?" She was looking more for support than an actual answer.

"The American seems to be your angel, Madame President," José said while still sitting.

"Something else on your mind, José? Please, speak."

"Madame President, this American was not alone. He was with a woman. A woman from inside this building. Melina Mendez, Madame President. She works in the secretarial pool. They appeared to have been traveling together, I saw luggage in the car they were driving."

"It may be that we are already cooperating fully with Mr. Seabreeze," the president said, not a disparaging remark but simply reaffirming a point of fact. "Say nothing to her and let's not watch her either. Let us work with Mr. Seabreeze and see what happens first."

"Very good, Madame President."

"Well, José, unless you have something else to add, I believe we are already late to my cabinet meeting." They walked out of her office and down the hall to what she was certain would be a long afternoon.

~~~

Washington, D.C.

The president was receiving his daily (think early-morning) security briefing from Matthew Scheffield. He respected Scheffield's advice and opinion. Unfortunately, he had grown not to like the man as a person. *It happens*, he thought. He listened to him drone on about various issues effecting the world. Where it not for coffee, he believed his head would be bobbing if not the appearance of outright drool hanging from his mouth. If he had a gun, he would probably shoot himself first and then Scheffield to save others from such a slow, monotonous, and painful death. Death by a thousand briefings, they should call this. The man lacked passion. He may be a brilliant analyst, but he lacked passion.

"Matthew, the technical aspects of this analysis I can readily see. China has at least two dozen dredging platforms working day and night creating a man-made island out of virtually nothing. I understand from a technological standpoint we would build it differently and more advanced; however, they *are* building it. I also understand that the runway section will be large enough to land even their biggest military aircraft. This is clearly a military installation regardless of what the Chinese are telling us," the president remarked. Matthew tried to interject two points in his agency's defense.

"Mr. President, the Chinese claim the island is for fishing use and not military."

"And you believe them?"

"Frankly, sir, our analysts are still undecided."

"Matthew, your analysts are undecided on the fall of the Berlin Wall and that happened twenty-six years ago."

"Yes, sir."
~~~

"It's military. You know it, I know it, and here's a heads-up . . . the Chinese know it. Give me some options at our next briefing," the president said before adding, "What's next?"

"North Korea, Mr. President. They are planning a joint exercise with China while we have our annually scheduled military and naval exercise with South Korea."

"It will be interesting to see what use they make of their new island," the president said before adding, "That will give us some idea of their true intentions. Make a note for the joint chiefs to schedule this year's war games to include the man-made islands in some aspect thereof."

"Understood, Mr. President."

"How have their relations with China been? I presume they have increased of recent," the president added.

"Yes, sir, they have. China has increased their supply of grain to North Korea, covering our shortage." The president thought about that and then simply passed on any comment or question. Non-issue was the right call.

"Speaking of cereal grains, what is the current situation?"

"On that note, we have some interesting news. Our analyst that we sent out has made some positive progress. He has sent us two photo IDs and a separate photograph. The IDs are fakes. One of the photos was not sufficient for facial recognition; however, the separate photograph has produced a match. Omar Salah. He is a Yemen-born dissident who is linked to a bombing in London and some suspected kidnappings. He is considered a middleman only and not a leader. We haven't seen him in a while...most of his group has either been caught or killed. Status of his previous group is being determined, curious if this may be the remnants."

"Other cities?"

"He should have that information for us by Monday. He's also hoping to have the point of entry by Monday," Matthew said while shaking his head.

"This individual has turned out to be a true asset," the president commented.

"He has, Mr. President."

"Now a question for you, Matthew. What are your beliefs on China calling in our marker?"

"Destabilizing, sir. I think it is posturing only given our push at the South China Sea; were we to relax that position, they would likely relax the debt issue."

"I hope you're right, Matthew," the president said. He stood up, signifying the end of their meeting.

The president walked with Matthew to the door but stopped just short of it. Matthew did so. "Yes, Mr. President."

"Matthew, what is the likelihood of a terrorist act similar to the one in Argentina happening here? Farmers go into the fields in six to eight weeks. We need some assurance. That's just as important as the other issues . . ." the president paused. "And to think the world thought Brexit was a big deal."

"I'll look into it and have something for you middle of the week, Mr. President."

"Thank you, Matthew."

~~~

St. Louis, Missouri

Devastated would not be the word to describe how Katie felt about Joseph's death. *Devastated* was clearly too strong a word. She notified Marshall personally and Amged via email. Both expressed their condolences and inquired where to send a card or floral arrangement. Speaking with Marshall about Joseph helped but that wasn't it.

"He's the first person you've known who's died, Katie," Jenny said. "Plus you slept with him so there is a pseudo further attachment albeit tenuous at best."

There was a momentary pause while Katie processed Jenny's statement.

"Jenny, I believe you may be right. It may have something to do with my 'pseudo albeit tenuous attachment at best,'" Katie said while making
~~~

a disbelieving face. "However, I do believe you may have something on the first person I know being dead reason. I mean it could happen to any of us at any moment."

"Makes you want to live life in the moment and for the moment."

Katie and Jenny were hanging out at the condo. Brad was busy at work. Tax season, he called it. Lawrence was up against a deadline, so they were simply condo chill'n. They decided to make dinner at home and clean. Jenny was being accommodating, it helped Katie focus her attention on something other than Joseph's death. Nothing had been determined and the investigation was still being labeled "RAV," random act of violence.

Imagine how Mrs. Patrick feels and all the little Patrick's when informed, "Sorry, Mrs. Patrick, your husband, and your father, little Patrick's, will not be coming home tonight or any other night for that matter. He was RAVed this evening at 7:06 p.m."

Katie knew Jenny was right. *Tomorrow she would be less affected then she was today. Two days from now she would be even less affected. In time, Joseph would become a distant memory. Such is life and priorities,* Katie thought. Jenny finished scrubbing the kitchen floor. She had been relegated to cleaning the kitchen. Katie would vacuum; Jenny would dust.

A movie and a glass of wine when things were done sounded good. Katie called Brad.

~~~

Katie woke earlier than normal. Time management was how she looked at it. Brad didn't argue. Not now, not last night when she called. He was more than willing. Just like now, Katie thought. She secretly smiled.

Katie was in her office and at her desk when Johnny walked in. He had the latest research reports on three more cereal grains . . . soybeans, oats, and barley. She reached for their individual folders and noticed that they were not where they should be. Where they are supposed to be. She looked around her office and found them. She must have had a certain look on her face.
~~~

"Everyone is experiencing the same situation. Things seem just a little out of place. Offices don't seem to be clean. General disarray although not terribly."

"What's going on? New cleaning company?" Katie asked.

"No. Same company just different people. From what I understand, the guy that was responsible for cleaning our offices was killed in a botched robbery," Johnny said. Katie stared in utter disbelief. Two deaths in less than a week. Coincidence? Maybe, but Katie did not believe in them. Pendleton trait?

"What was his name?" Katie asked.

"Who? What name?" Johnny asked, answering a question with a question.

"The cleaning guy," Katie said before adding, "What was his name?"

"I don't know," Johnny made a face. "Ask Melissa," Katie pressed Melissa's extension.

"Yes, Katie."

"Melissa, I'm sitting here with Johnny—"

"Hey, Johnny," she interrupted.

"Lissa, whad-up?" Katie shook her head. It would've been easier to walk out to her desk and ask but now . . .

"Melissa, I need the name of the cleaning guy that was recently killed."

"What?" Melissa asked.

"Johnny said that the guy that routinely cleaned our offices was recently killed in a botched robbery attempt. Do you know his name? If so, I need it. If not, can you get it for me?"

There was dead air. Katie was not utilizing the pregnant pause negotiating technique. Melissa was just likely asking herself why.

"Melissa, are you there?"

"Yes. Katie, I don't have his name, but if something was taken from your office, there are contractual procedures that we must follow."

"Melissa, I just need his full name. First, last, and middle name. Call me when you have it. Preferably today," Katie said. She disconnected the call.

"Okay. Johnny, thank you for the report and update. I'll let you know my questions after reviewing these documents." Johnny got up to leave.

Before turning to review the reports, Katie called Brad and told him about the death of the office cleaning guy. "That is strange," Brad agreed.

"You don't think I'm being paranoid, do you?" Katie asked.

"No. Not at all. It could simply be a coincidence, but even that would require a leap of faith. When you get a name, give it to me, I have a client that's a PI. He may be able to help."

"Okay. See you tonight," Katie used the office phone. No reason not to.

She returned to the reports and the research. Coincidence or not, connected or not, there was work to be done. Thankfully she had the ability to compartmentalize. If not, it was likely she wouldn't have been in a position to get anything accomplished. Even now she found recent events invading her conscious thoughts.

Chapter Thirteen

In 2017, there were 15,657 murders reported nationwide. Thirty-eight-point-four percent went unsolved. The FBI considers a case cleared when a person is arrested, charged and turned over to the courts.

St. Louis, Missouri

The hypothesis on soybeans, barley, and oats was essentially the same for corn and wheat. The altered gene sequencing would produce a faster growth rate and crop yield. Computer simulations substantiated this. Computer simulations were sufficient for the patent application and reliable to fruition. Actual experiments conducted on corn and wheat validated said simulations. The applicants were using a greenhouse for the experiments, leaving nothing to chance. Seed production was off the chart.

Katie reviewed the research reports against her notes, observations, discussions, et cetera. She reconciled the results obtained from the computer simulation against those discussed in the hypothesis. She conducted the same reconciling exercise with every cereal grain. The hypothesis was 92.9 percent accurate when compared against the computer simulation. The actual greenhouse experiments were 99.3 percent accurate when compared against the hypothesis. The group was expecting wheat to fall within the same parameters. The deviation from hypothesis to computer simulation to actual experiment conducted in a greenhouse was generally easy to explain under the guise of conservative estimates versus ideal conditions. Deviation for soybeans, barley, and oats was considerably less than corn and wheat. This was to be expected. A true up.

Katie was impressed that her understanding of the process was evolving. The deviation from hypothesis to computer simulation had decreased from a –7.1% to a –2.83%. With the reports, research, and hypothesis to computer simulation reconciliation true up, Katie sent out an email to Marshall, Amged, and Patrick. A brief discussion followed. At the end of her email, she went old school with the post script . . . *P.S. What is the status of the super-seed's effectiveness against the spore in Argentina?*

After Katie sent the email, she noticed one from Melissa. Subject line was: *Name.* She opened it: *Miguel Martinez Rodriguez.* Katie sent out two additional emails, one to Brad . . . *Please forward to your client the private investigator. Our cleaning company's name is We Clean for You. See you tonight.* The second email was to Jenny: *Can you find the obituary on Miguel Martinez Rodriguez and anything else you might think of? Thanks.*

Katie had grown a little careless, she decided to send a third email. This one to Bail. She used the same email sent out to "The Group," just deleting the email addresses and typing in Bail's name. His email address popped up. Katie stared at the address for several moments before hitting Send. A thought was just on the edge of consciousness, evading her grasp. *Oh well…*the knock on her door brought her back to the present.

Marshall walked in. "Good work on the true up reconciliation, Katie. Patrick forwarded that along with the computer simulation to the patent attorneys. It saves us from an actual greenhouse test." He sat down. Katie had grown more comfortable with Marshall. The relationship seemed to have renewed itself.

"The super-seed," Katie said.

"Yes. Preliminary reports are not overly encouraging. Fifteen to twenty percent effectiveness in the affected areas. Sporadic at best…."

"Wow," was all Katie could say. "Have they uncovered anything at all?"

"It's still too early to tell but initial thoughts are terrorism . . .

obviously," Marshall added with a shoulder shrug and head tilt. "Outside of that, Dr. Montero's team has uncovered the gene sequencing used for damping off-disease. Unfortunately, a fungicide now needs to be developed. She believes there may be more than one fungi engineered into the spore. If that's the case, this will take longer." Marshall paused. "Someone has been working on this for quite a while."

"How about I take a look at it? Can you have a sample sent here?" Katie didn't want to be denied.

"Believe me, I offered your name up to Jonathan on a few occasions but to no avail. The best minds in America are currently working on this, I was assured." Katie did not feel overly enthusiastic about what Jonathan had to say. Marshall wasn't either.

"Can you get me a sample from a current field planted using our seed?" Katie asked.

"How many samples?" Marshall asked. He believed Katie was likely the best mind to have on this project.

"A cross section of dirt twelve inches deep by twenty-four inches long and twenty-four inches wide. One sample where the super-seed was effective, one sample where it was partially effective, and one sample where it was completely ineffective. For the partially effective area, if it looks like multiple disease, damping off, xylem stock damage, rust, or root rot, then send more samples. One farm should be enough."

"Okay. To avoid quarantine, I'll have to go through Jonathan via Patrick. I'll do it now."

"Okay. Let me know ASAP so I can schedule time at Wash U."

"You need any help?"

"When was the last time you were in a lab, Marshall?" They both laughed. It had been that long.

Katie looked at her watch—6:30 p.m. Too late to start something else so she cleaned up and left the office. She would stop on the way home and cook this evening. Something light . . . fish. She sent a text to Jenny inviting her and Lawrence, plans permitting.

Katie was walking into the condo at 7:30-ish. Jenny and Lawrence would pick up package liquor from Mickey's. Nine o'clock was dinner reservations. Yet another elegant dinner night out. Katie did the prep work and got everything started before she showered and changed for the evening.

She emerged from her room showered and dressed when Jenny, Lawrence, and Brad entered the condo.

"So what type of rabbit food did you make?" Jenny asked.

"Heart-healthy, Jenny," Katie said.

"Ya mean Mickey's disco fries aren't?" she responded while munching on a toasted pecan.

"So what do we have?" Brad asked.

"I made a butter lettuce salad with pickled grapes, toasted pecans, and soft feta cheese over Chilean sea bass." Katie took the Chilean sea bass from the warmer, laid one on each plate, and handed them to Brad, Lawrence, and Jenny while carrying her plate. The salad was in the bowl, and ready to be served. Jenny opened a bottle of Predator wine and poured everyone a glass. With everything out and set, "Bon appétit," Katie said.

Conversation was good and flowing. Each talking about their day. Jenny was discussing her most recent assignment regarding racial tension.

"Anything on Miguel?" Katie asked. "Not to change the subject but it sounded like you were done."

"I did find his obit. We didn't run it. One of the smaller papers did. So I called them and the funeral home that provided the information. I wrote everything down for you so remind me later."

Brad looked over at Katie. "Just trying to get some answers."

"Why, what's up?" Jenny asked, not knowing any details but curious why Katie wanted an obit.

"The decedent cleaned our offices. Now he's dead. Victim of a botched robbery. Joseph is dead. Another victim of a crime gone bad. Both within less than a week. A few days actually. Both random, both requiring an act of some sort, both violent and both apparently unrelated. I just find it to be more than random," Katie said.

"Murder? Do you think they're related?" Lawrence asked.

"It's like one of those dinnertime murder mystery games we played in college over pizza and beer," Jenny remarked.

"Except these are real, Jenny," Katie said.

"Just trying to lighten the mood, sis."

"It's a strange coincidence," Brad said. "I called my client, Tim Black. He'll stop by the office tomorrow. If you'd like to meet with us, we can go together. I can bring you back here, drop you at your office and pick you up later, or you can do some work for me."

"Okay to any or all of the above." Dinner was finished, table cleared, dishes rinsed, and put in the dishwasher.

"Hey, any word on the success of your seed?" Lawrence asked. He opened a second bottle of wine while everyone moved to the living room. Hockey season. St. Louis Blues were respectable again.

"We should go to a game," Jenny commented.

"I'll get tickets for next weekend if they're home; otherwise the weekend after that," Lawrence said. Everyone took a seat and got comfortable.

"The seed's success was less than stellar. Fifteen to twenty percent. The spore was engineered, though, so any success is a positive. I just wish I knew what Joseph meant with his message: *I discovered something that I'm certain everyone has overlooked.* I'm paraphrasing but still." The room got quiet except for the sports announcer. Slowly everyone turned their attention to the TV. Katie simply laid her head on Brad's lap, stretched out, and watched the game. Conversation was sporadic after that. The mood never really did lighten up. Death does that.

~~~

Buenos Aires, Argentina

The cabinet meeting lasted longer than expected. Issues were tangible and unsettling. Each member recognized their current livelihood rested on every member within the room. There were no exceptions. The president was in trouble for no other reason than because…it happened during her watch.

José sat quietly and listened. Juan Carlos Fábrega spoke. He was not
~~~

university educated, but with forty-five years of banking experience, he was well respected and admired worldwide. He was also president of the Central Bank of Argentina. His transitional appointment was a result of the 2008 financial crisis Argentina experienced. He approached the job with vigor and professionalism. After all, Argentina was his country under attack.

"Inflation, hyperinflation at that, is a real concern. Food products could easily quadruple overnight. Even if America keeps our factories running and supplied, we have the added cost of that expense, however minimal it may be. It will be something. Another cost for the consumer to bear," Fábrega said. His voice tailed off. *Despair* was the word that quickly came to José's mind.

"Can't we freeze prices?" one cabinet member asked.

"Freezing prices is a short-term solution. Now would be premature. Since the act of terrorism became grapevine public knowledge, food prices have risen 4 percent. Yet, factories are still running at or near capacity. It is easier to avoid the mob if one raises prices slowly versus overnight. People will start reducing quantity purchases on their own. If a grain shipment becomes delayed, the ports get crowded, truck and rail service accidents happen . . . then we will freeze prices. Then we may consider other steps. We need to start planning for those other steps now, not after it happens. Unfortunately, we all know that *it* will happen."

There was a lull after Fábrega spoke. Everyone absorbing what he had said. Would food rationing be the *other* step?

Fábrega did not particularly like his job, head governor of the BCRA. However, when asked, he simply could not refuse. A patriot.

"Then plan we shall. It's now a priority. We'll establish a website and publish procedures. We'll print pamphlets. Discipline and order will be required. Use of the Armed Forces and martial law will be contingency plans. Curfew should be included in any plan. Remember, this is only a plan of action if needed. No one says anything to anyone. Are we clear on this point?" Madame President looked at each cabinet member, each nodded their understanding. "The last thing any of us want is panic."

She got up from the table and refilled her coffee cup. Not that she needed the caffeine to stay awake; the job provided enough of an adrenaline rush for that. She simply needed the few seconds of silence to sort through everything. When she returned to the table she continued, "Questions? Comments?"

The Minister of Industry, Giorgi, voiced her thoughts regarding any contingency plans. "I would agree we need to plan now. Hopefully it will not come to martial law. Prior to that, I suggest we have the wet milling plants slowly reduce production. Maybe go to a seven- or six-hour workday schedule. I understand that that may accelerate inflation, but won't that have the added benefit of delaying use of more aggressive measures?"

"No, it won't. One might think that prudent, logical, but it's not. We are dealing with psychology here. The best way to stop a speeding bullet is not to stand in front of it. Reducing a laborer's workday from eight to seven to six is effectively telling them that supplies are short now. They won't believe that we are stockpiling an inventory of product to keep plants open longer. Even if they see the product supplies growing, they still won't believe what they're eyes see. They will horde food items now to stop the future sound of a crying baby. Everything the president has asked us to plan for would become a necessity now. I like your thought process and the message you are sending is a good one. However, it is the recipient of that message we must concern ourselves with. The recipient thinks of food on the table. They look at their neighbors and wonder what they are stockpiling. Watch, we will have a run on staple products— likely grain related—even though we may survive this six months from now. The more information we provide to the public, the more stable the country will be in the long term. Remember the Americans didn't start to lose interest in Vietnam until the news agencies published daily death toll. It was then that public opinion changed. We need to let the people know that food is available. Not overtly but enough to keep people calm. Maybe we can put some pressure on the food chain restaurants," Fábrega said. He looked at the Minister of Industry.

"I'll have them in next week individually. I'll explain that we would like their cooperation. What we need and hope to accomplish. Less promotional items, et cetera," she said.

"Okay," the president said. "Let's expect to meet weekly." The members slowly began to gather their belongings, stood up, and moved for the door.

"José, if you could stay for a few minutes," the president asked.

"Certainly, Madame President."

"So what do you think?" she asked after the room had emptied out.

"I think we will do everything we can to keep the people safe and informed. I think that the plans will all be for naught should the winds of fortune blow against us."

"That old adage yet again: *Es mejor tener suerte que bien.* It is better to be lucky than good."

They sat in silence for several minutes. Neither one was truly looking forward to the future yet to come.

"Full disclosure," she said. José nodded consent. He stood up to leave while she swirled around in her chair to look out at the Plaza and watch the people. *Maybe one last time...*she thought.

Chapter Fourteen

China is a major buyer of foreign arable land. Thirty percent of Argentina's arable land is foreign owned.

Tabuk, Saudi Arabia

The plan was simple. The bare minimum number of moving parts ensured the greatest chance of success. The planes had been purchased. Each one was in the respective countries. Purchases were brokered through a family friend with family friends of their own. That is the nice thing about money; it buys friends, loyalty.

Sherrief relied upon that friendship and loyalty. The planes were purchased through shell corporations. Each one had been established with a specific purpose in mind. A stated function, it was termed. Charter Service was one. Weather research another. Skydiving a third. China and the United States were the more formal countries. Vietnam and India were porous from a border country standpoint. Planes flying through Vietnam would be based in Laos. Four cities had been selected in Laos and India.

Operatives began infiltrating the respective countries. Vietnam and India, were less of a problem to gain entry. China and the United States were more of a challenge. Tour groups were the easiest way to gain access. Once inside the host country, one simply became detached from the group. Lost now in the crowd, never to be found.

Student visas were also a source. Dissidents were never in short supply. Every campus student union was full of individuals disenfranchised by the establishment. Jihadist recruitment was at an all-time high. Sherrief was not flattered that some of the individuals were enthusiastic toward his cause. They were a means to an end.

~~~

Amged was the contact person in America. He rented properties for the operatives. They were located near airports used by hobbyists, charter service companies, skydiving companies, and the like. The properties were fully furnished, stocked with food, car provided, spending money, and a Go-Phone for use. Each operative that became detached from their tour group knew where to go. Properties within the United States were single-family residences. Less exposure. Purpose for the rental, employment relocation.

Amged began receiving calls on his Go-Phone. Operatives called when they checked in to the individual properties. He provided each person he spoke to with minimal instruction beyond stay out of sight and stick to the plan. He would begin visiting the operatives when time permitted.

Amged had confidence in the plan, its details, its objective, and its purpose and likelihood for success. Sherrief was brilliant in his design of the spore and Jericho. Amged trusted to that brilliance. What Sherrief and, by extension of that misguided trust, Amged were not aware of was NSA surveillance sophistication.

The NSA had Amged's Go-Phone under surveillance. Whenever Amged received a call or whenever a call was sent while using that Go-Phone, NSA was able to capture the call. The word capture is accurate. Unfortunately they were not able to know what was said due to the encryption. Location triangulation was less than accurate, again encryption.

Everyone is likely familiar with cell phone towers and triangulation of cell phone users from said towers. Triangulation is of moderate accuracy. It is more accurate than cell identification and less accurate than advanced forward link trilateration. Cell phones send out a radio roaming signal. That signal is always searching for the nearest cell
~~~

phone tower. The normal cell phone does not have to be active to roam. A Go-Phone does have to be active to roam. The roaming cell phone searches for a cell tower until it finds one. The Global System for Mobile Communication measures the cell phones signal strength . . . location to the tower.

Triangulation requires three cell phone towers. The cell phone tower that the user just left, the one the user is now using, and the one the user will be handed off to. Rural areas have fewer towers than urban areas. Triangulation is therefore more difficult unless unobstructed. Go-Phones inhibit the receivers, the cell phone towers, that they are using. This further reduces the likelihood of triangulation. It is a reduction only. The listeners know of the general area.

~~~

Larry was still in Argentina when the calls began to increase in number and frequency. The calls were recorded and logged. The problem was the calls were internal; within the United States. Location was difficult to triangulate. The United States is big and mostly rural. The land around Decatur and Central Illinois in general is flat. Hills exist but rarely taller than one hundred feet. Residents often joke that they can see St. Louis on a clear day looking to the southwest and Chicago when they look to the north. Lack of obstruction equates to lack of required cell phone towers. Content of the call was unknown due to the encryption.

As with the evolution of the super-seed and the super-spore, terrorism communication was also evolving. Go-Phones were simply one alternative. Gaming was another.

Each of the rental properties was supplied with a seventy-inch flat screen television for gaming and a PlayStation complete with instructions. Further communication would be through the "chat" section of the game. The chat allowed gamers to speak separately with each other or multiple others of the game being played. Such conversation was not monitored or recorded. Technology is a beautiful thing. It is even more beautiful when you can use the infidel's own technology against them.

Currently six operatives were in country. Several more expected.
~~~

Four of the six operatives were students. The fifth and sixth were misplaced tourists. They were not considered a priority for either the Tour Company or Homeland Security. Even after 9/11, manpower does not exist to track down every missing Middle Easterner.

~~~

The Chinese portion of the operation was proceeding as planned. China was much stricter with dissidents than the United States. Once they were apprehended. But, first they had to be caught. Ashraff was the Chinese handler. Amged's cousin. He knew the location of the DC-9s. He had already obtained the extra fuel tanks and tanks for the atomizer solution. The atomizer itself was in route. Six operatives had checked in, twelve to go.

Plotting coverage of the Central States of America was substantially easier than plotting coverage of the Chinese agricultural region. Farmable land in China was spread over a much larger geographical area.

The Chinese southern upland region was too hilly for farming. The central and northern upland regions were primarily wheat fields with rice patties to the south. The Sichuan Basin was the main agricultural region. The fields were terraced with corn, soybeans, and wheat fields. Terraced farming was required due to the contour of the land. The eastern lowlands represented China's best agricultural fields.

The area was primarily rural, few or no metropolitan areas. The airports were small, rural, grass. Thankfully the planes purchased for use were already registered. Flight plans filed in previous years provided examples of what would be acceptable. Sherrief, Amged, and Ashraff had researched the flight plans and purposes. They were comfortable that theirs would be accepted. No detail had been overlooked. They were truly prepared.

~~~

Washington, D.C.

The Chinese representative had missed close to a dozen Treasury auctions. That wasn't dispositive of their belief in the U.S. economy's future. What may be taken for a clear understanding of the Chinese government's position was the lack of any response to questions regarding their absence. Complete silence.

The U.S. economy is diverse and fully mature in every sector. However, business leaders, economist, planners all understand that *mature* is a relative word based on a world economy that is in a constant state of evolution. The operative word being *constant.*

Each economy in the world, all 193 individual country economies, is always evolving. There are regional economies, regions within regions, seasonal, et cetera. Fluid. For the U.S. economy to remain mature and número uno, it has to continue to evolve, continue to remain fluid. This understanding helped absorb the shock when the Chinese state-run newspaper's lead headline story, their Sunday edition, read: *Debt Called Due, Will U.S. Answer?* There had been no warning. Matthew Scheffield and Magne Powell received little warning when called to the White House for a meeting with the president.

The Sunday edition of the Xinhua News Agency paper was sitting on the table when Matthew and Magne both arrived. The topic for the meeting was understood if not previously guessed by one or both. The president would determine who guessed the purpose of the meeting.

"I trust I did not interrupt anybody's evening. If I did, you can blame Xi Jinping. In any event, let's get started. Magne, what effect will this have on us? Short-term and long-term considerations, please."

"No effect at all, Mr. President…short-term or long-term. The markets will likely react in a negative fashion and then correct almost immediately. This news has most likely been factored in, this reaction, given China's recent absence from the auctions. We discussed this at our last three weekly meetings. Dr. Gray first posited the question. His research has been flawless. Their reaction, effect on the market was predicted. I recommend we respond through Dr. Gray; have him on *Market Watch* Monday morning, eight o'clock."

"Matthew?"

"Mr. President, I believe Magne's response is likely going to be more accurate than any I could postulate." Matthew realized his credibility with the president and this administration was now over. The Berlin Wall comment reverberated in his ear. *I just hope he doesn't ask about the South China Sea, his analyst still had nothing.*

The president was quiet for a while. He did everything but shake his head in disgust. He couldn't afford to lose Matthew, not now. The flipside of the coin was he couldn't afford to keep him either. He would have to speak with Jurgensen in the morning. His chief of staff would be able to start the process rolling to ensure a smooth transition.

"Matthew, I need a work-up on my desk first thing in the morning. Magne, I trust your judgment. Can you stay a little longer, I would like to speak with Dr. Gray," Matthew got up and left.

The call to Dr. Gray lasted close to twenty minutes. It was Dr. Gray who expressed the need to end the call. "If we want to make tomorrow's deadline, I need to place some calls now."

"Understood," the president said before adding, "I would like to see the story before it runs."

"Certainly, Mr. President. However, given the timeframe, you may not be in a position to make any changes."

"Duly noted," the president said. "Thank you for your honesty."

"Daniel, if you need anything, I will be available on my cell phone."

"Thank you, Magne. I will have a copy emailed to you." Dr. Gray ended one call only to begin another.

~~~

St. Louis, Missouri

"What did the PI have to say?"

"After telling him my tale of woe, he agreed that it was an unusual coincidence and that the details are likely connected."
~~~

"Is he going *to the authorities*?" Lawrence asked with a little more enthusiasm than necessary.

"After he's had an opportunity to perform a preliminary investigation, yes," Katie said.

"Who pays for this?" Jenny asked.

"I do initially. However, if they're homicides, I can seek full, partial, or no reimbursement of the cost. If they're joint, then I have a greater chance of reimbursement."

"How much?" Lawrence asked.

"Twenty-five hundred was the retainer asked plus five hundred for expenses." Lawrence took one of the hundreds left on the table and handed it to Katie. She smiled and accepted the gesture in good faith.

"This is a story in itself," Jenny said. "A real whodunit!"

~~~

Buenos Aires, Argentina

Larry received a phone message *Breakfast 10 A.M.* Prior to confirming said meeting, he phoned Juan to confirm their appointment at seven o'clock. Two breakfasts. *Such is the life of a double-naught spy*, he thought while he finished his fourth mile. He'd lifted for an hour prior to giving himself just enough time to wake Melina up, shower, and make it to the café.

"*Buenos días*," Larry said. He and Melina walked to the café. Juan had been sitting outside sipping his coffee. Larry and Melina were late. From their look, it was easy to see why. He almost wished they didn't come . . . young love.

"*Buenos días, señor, señorita.* Please be seated. Join me in a cup of coffee and a morning pastry," Juan said. Melina and Larry accepted the invitation and sat down.

The package Juan brought with him was quite thick. Larry tried not to look excited, but it was difficult not to glance. Christmas doesn't always fall on the 25th day of December.
~~~

"How was your meeting with José and Alberto?" Juan asked. Larry didn't flinch; however, Melina looked at him.

"*Sí*, I know. You are a good man, and an honest man, Larry. It is because of that that we are helping you help us."

"Our meeting went well. We're meeting with José later this morning. Ten o'clock," Larry said.

"Let's not delay," Juan said. "Here's the information you seek. I have also provided you with the *punto de entrada*, General Güemes and Tartagal. General Güemes is another rural community of twenty-eight thousand people. It's within five hundred kilometers of the Bolivian border. Tartagal is a larger city of fifty-seven thousand people. There are two airports. One is for hobbyists and crop dusters. It's closer to the Bolivian border. I believe the planes were purchased, retrofitted, and painted in Villazón, which has a population of five hundred thousand people. I will have more information for you by the time you get to General Güemes."

"The contact person in both airports is in the package. Looks like you will be taking another trip, Señor Larry." Juan slid the package across the table. Larry did not open it directly.

He simply said, "*Gracias* . . . thank you."

Another trip. Northern Argentina and southern Bolivia. He looked over at Melina briefly. Juan was watching him. What was he thinking? Larry wondered. They joined Juan in a coffee and pastry. Juan provided some additional information and then they left.

"*Buena suerte*, *Señor* Larry, *Señorita* Melina."

"Thank you Juan. For everything," Larry said. Juan smiled and left Larry and Melina.

They paid the check and returned to the hotel, where they scanned and emailed the five pilot licenses and three separate photographs. Larry asked Matthew to call him and discuss the case. It was thirty minutes before Larry received a call from the assistant director, Robert Reynolds. During that period of time, Larry asked Melina to go with him to Villazón and elsewhere should his travels take him there.

"And if they don't, Larry . . . what would you have of me then?"

"Then I would have of you what you would give to me."

"My heart and soul are yours for the taking." Melina was standing in the middle of the room staring at him. He knew that she would let him use her simply because she was in love with him like no other. It was because of that that he knew he couldn't leave her. Larry walked up to Melina, taking her into his arms he whispered, "Stay with me forever." He heard himself say it to the sound of her tears.

The phone rang. Larry hesitated but finally answered.

"Hello," Larry said on the fourth ring.

"Did I interrupt you?" Assistant Director Reynolds asked.

"No, sir, I was simply focused on the matter at hand," Larry said. He had yet to let go of Melina.

"Understood. What can I do for you? Director Scheffield asked that I return your call."

"Sir, I am in Buenos Aires, regarding the South American terrorist incident. I have just scanned and emailed documents for facial recognition. I was hoping for a quick turnaround."

"I'll give them a priority. Anything else?"

"Yes, sir. I'm meeting with the Minister of Agro-industry in ninety minutes, I'll email you and the director the results of the meeting. Also, I have the point of entry and the airport used. I need your authorization to cross into Bolivia. I need to travel to Villazón, Bolivia, population twelve thousand five hundred, and Villamontes, population six thousand seven hundred."

There was a pause. Reynolds knew that this was a priority. The hope was that they could find and locate the creator of the spore. That would lead to the creation of a fungicide. The fear was another attack…the United States.

Crop dusting was no longer an accepted method of farming in the United States. Fungus and pest control eradication and treatment was dispersed with the seed, time released. Local airports were required to report all crop-dusting activity thirty days beforehand for flight approval; plane, equipment, pilot, company, and fungicide and/or insecticide required approval prior to flight. Restrictions were prohibitive for a reason. Environmentalists. Reynolds approved Seabreeze's activities. He was currently being productive, and he had won the assistance of the

Argentinean people and government. The agency needed more people like Larry.

Larry sat the phone down and looked at Melina. "We have time to kill."

~~~

José was not a man to wait. He was on the verge of getting annoyed when he saw the American and his "associate" turn the corner. Youth, he thought to himself. At least they had the good sense not to bc holding hands and giggling.

"*Buenos días, Señor* José. My apologies for being late. I was in touch with my office on some facial recognition. I was hoping to have something for you now, but I will have something for you by day's end."

"No problem. Please sit down and join me in a coffee and morning pastry." The waitress returned and gave both Larry and Melina a double take. José looked confused.

"We met Juan from Chascomús earlier this morning at this very same café, same table, same waitress." Larry looked at the waitress and ordered coffee for him and Melina along with a morning pastry.

"Same order," José smiled.

"So how was your cabinet meeting?" Larry asked.

"Like you expected. We have more researchers working on this project. Dr. Montero is supervising it with the aid of her American friend, Dr. Prichard. Still it is a struggle. Financially we are fairly solid but how long that will last is another story entirely. If we can resolve this before the factories become idle, we will survive," José said.

"Where are you off to, might I ask?"

"I believe we have the *punto de entrada*...it's General Güemes and Tartagal. From there we will look to see if the planes were painted and retrofitted at a local shop. From the photo I showed you previously, the plane appeared new and the paint reflective of the sun. If one plane was painted, they all were painted."

"Do you require any assistance?" José asked. "I have been authorized to help you in any reasonable way possible."
~~~

"Not at this time, but I have your number and you mine, so I will call you with updates," Larry said.

They continued to talk for a while longer about the stability of Argentina, the region, and the possible short-term and long-term effects. The U.S. needs Argentina, a stable trading partner within the region. Brazil, too, although they had escaped the brunt of the terrorist act. Brazil survived with enough arable land to maintain viability of its people and factories.

After an hour it was time to end the meeting and resume the day's activity. Larry had a second thought and he handed José a copy of the pilot's license and plane identification numbers for verification. "I received these this morning from Juan. I sent them for facial recognition. However, your database may include photos other than ours." José looked at him, smiled, and nodded his head before confirming.

"I will see what I can do for you," José said.

"*Gracias,*" Larry said.

"*Buena suerte, Señor* Larry, *Señorita* Melina," José said. He extended his hand in friendship.

Larry and Melina finished their coffee and left after José. They paid yet again before walking back to the hotel. They would pack and leave for General Güemes within the hour.

Chapter Fifteen

In 2011, Senator Coburn issued a report listing government funded celebrity farmers that included Scottie Pippen, Ted Turner, Bruce Springsteen, and Jon Bon Jovi. Minnesota Timberwolves owner Glen Taylor received $116,502 in farm subsidies for his egg and dairy farm in Iowa. At the time, Mr. Taylor was number 350 on the Fortune 400 list. The Timberwolves were 26-40 that same year.

St. Louis, Missouri

The markets were fine and closed the day in positive territory. The pre-morning interview had market futures down over 2,500 points. Post-morning interview futures were down roughly 100 points. The climactic point occurred when Richard showed Dr. Gray that *The Rag* ran the story front page above the fold and the *Dispatch* ran the story front page business section below the fold.

"First off, how did *The Rag* get this article and why wasn't it front-page news for the *St. Louis Post-Dispatch*?" Richard asked, clearly befuddled how Dr. Gray won the interview and would be able to quiet the markets.

"Richard, the title of the article is appropriate: *Prank Call, Such Yuksters*. The Chinese government tried to destabilize the market and overplayed their hand. Truth be known, the president was against any article . . . any reference...any response. The Chinese absence is a non-issue. The owners of *The Rag* simply prove my point. They ran the story front page above the fold. You mention it on your show and now the owner will sell more papers, fulfilling his capitalistic dream. Gutsy move. And to the first point of your question, believe you me, we will get to the bottom, how *The Rag* pirated this article remains a mystery."

"Thank you, Jenny and Daniel," Mack said. He was now assured of selling the remaining papers. The president also said thank you, his approval rating went up two points. Most likely Dr. Gray's comment on this being a non-issue. Unfortunately for the president, there were still real issues that needed to be addressed and his momentary feeling of success was short-lived. He had a security briefing to attend.

~~~

Oval Office
Washington, D.C.

"Good morning, Mr. President," Matthew said. He walked into the Oval Office. He could already feel the tension. *My days are numbered*, he thought. *I just don't know the number.*

"Matthew, did you happen to catch *Market Watch* this morning? Did you happen to read the article? Note the placement of the article?" the president asked.

Which to answer first? Matthew wondered.

"Yes, sir, to all three."

"What did you think?"

"Mr. President, I thought the interview went well. The market must also believe what was said. It is only down a little over one hundred and fifteen points. Your strategy worked."

"How would you have treated it, Matthew? How would you and your analyst have done it? This is what I need to affectively navigate the waters. I trust in Magne. She, in turn, trusts Dr. Gray. Dr. Gray trust this young woman, Ms. Pendleton, whom I don't even know."

"Would you like us to check her out?"

"No, Matthew, I would not. What I would like for you to do is tell me what is going on in the world. What are the Chinese thinking?
~~~

What terrorist group struck South America and why hasn't anyone claimed responsibility for it? Where are they intending to strike next and when? That is what I need to effectively do my job. Do you have any of that in your folder today, Matthew?"

Or I could simply quit, Matthew thought. He opened his folder and began his daily briefing, world issues as he and his analysts saw them.

The briefing took fifty minutes. When it was done, Matthew looked at the president. "We don't have the simple luxury of getting to respond to a front-page article. We don't have the assets that we once had. We don't always know what each government knows and thinks. We rely to an extremely large percent upon communication captured by technology. From that captured technology, we look for trends, anomalies, and from that we determine threat levels and assign probabilities to those potential threats. Sometimes we are fortunate enough to gain a victory or two. While other times we have to sit back and ask ourselves how we missed that. When we miss, people die. When we miss, the market loses thousands of points."

The president sat there and listened to Matthew. It sounded like an excuse for failure. He just didn't get it. He was a brilliant analyst and should have remained one. The Peter Principle in real life.

"Matthew, economics is the real power today . . . you know that. Government stability second. Military might a distant third. Fortunes and lives are dependent upon the first two and not so much on the third. However, there needs to be a proper balance of the three. You are correct—we do rely to a large extent on technology to gather our information. Maybe we have lost that human element . . . that balance. Your desk analyst, Larry Seabreeze, is proving that very point. He's being tremendously effective to a very large extent because he is in country. If you believe you need more operatives, then let me know and together we can go to the Hill and asked for more money. Until that time we are stuck with what we have and there are only so many Jenny Pendleton's and Larry Seabreeze's in the world," the president said. Matthew got up to leave.

"Thank you, Mr. President," Matthew felt better about himself and his job than ever before.

~~~

National Security Office Headquarters

Assistant Director Reynolds sent the scanned documents for immediate facial recognition. The software was used on the pilot licenses and photographs provided. It was a priority. The three photographs were easier than the five pilot licenses received. The computer software could determine photograph distance based upon size differential. The pilot's license indicated height. With the pilot's known height in the picture, the distance from the camera lens could be calculated. This was necessary for the computer to correctly enhance the photograph.

The pilot licenses were much more difficult. The photography was of considerably lower quality than that of the still photograph. The computer enhancement program was utilized, which added considerably to the turnaround time. By noon D.C. time, the three separate photographs had been completed and there were two positive hits and one negative. Dossiers were provided on the two positive suspects. The negative was assigned an alias and a file was opened. He was listed as ABT.CY:107. ABT.CY:107 meant AliBaba Terrorist, Current Year, number 107 unidentified. The dossiers provided were not overly extensive and useful. Much of the information was old, eighteen months old.

Such was the life of a terrorist. Their transient beliefs and lifestyle were fickle, akin to the lifestyle of the American hobo. Here today, gone tomorrow.

It was highly unlikely that the two identified individuals were "between jobs" or gainfully employed. It was more likely than not that they were lost in the foothills of Afghanistan fighting in a never ending civil war. It was this transient behavior that increased the level of difficulty experienced by the intelligence agencies around the world. The shift to satellites and interception of cell phone activity was the
~~~

primary means of gathering information and the easiest way to infiltrate rural regions of the world.

Reynolds reviewed the dossiers of both individuals and their known associates. There was no true common denominator. The transient lifestyle also translated into a variable hodge-podge terrorist farm system akin to vagabonds living underneath bridges and somehow freely moving from town to town. It was next to impossible to understand how an individual could be involved in a bombing one week and a separate bombing eighteen months later. Where were they? What were they doing? These were questions that were seldom answered satisfactorily. However, Reynolds included the known associates in the information emailed to Larry.

With one project complete (in a manner of speaking), Reynolds resumed his oversight on operation Hecatoncheires. He was working with Major Reismann, Whiteman Air Force Base. Major Reismann was responsible for coordinating aerial coverage of the *bread basket states.* Several local Air National Guard units were providing support and actual human coverage. Matthew had communicated the president's personal belief that human intelligence was necessary.

~~~

Larry and Melina were still on the road by the time Reynolds sent his email. General Güemes was less than an hour away. This provided Larry sufficient time to decide what he would share with José. Melina had found a bed-and-breakfast. She had extended her vacation, which Larry was hoping would be a permanent one. They were getting along quite well, traveling down the highway hand-in-hand.

They checked into the bed-and-breakfast upon arrival in General Güemes. Melina used Mr. and Mrs. Seabreeze for reservation. The plan was a late dinner and an early visit to the airport. Juan had confirmed with Joseph that Larry and Melina would be by to discuss the pilot. Full cooperation was expected. Larry would contact José later, after his and Melina's nap.

~~~

Larry and Melina woke refreshed. One gets a certain level of unused energy after a long drive. What better way to release that energy than with the person you are growing close to? Larry and Melina did just that before their nap. When they both woke, Melina first, Larry feeling he were having a childhood dream, they looked at each other and smiled. Lost were the feelings of slight discomfort. They were replaced with feelings of satisfaction and wonder. Larry looked at his phone to check the time. One missed call—José—and one unread email.

~~~

The email was from Reynolds. *The pilot licenses are fraudulent however there was one positive hit and four more misses. The photos were of better quality and less grainy. There were two hits, one miss. Dossiers have been opened and provided. The hit on the photo was of a player named Omar Habib Barack. Omar is an Islamic Imam of a far leftist sect. Yet another splinter group. He is of Iranian descent and suspected of involvement in several recent European terrorist acts. He is considered highly dangerous and extremely intelligent. The likelihood of the South American act being a one and done is zero. You are to use discretion in the use and dissemination of this information. I will alert Interpol and corresponding agencies both domestic and foreign. Currently, we do not share information like this with our South American brethren. I will defer to your discretion. Keep in touch.*

The email was encrypted which elicited a chuckle from Larry. The likelihood was no one was looking to intercept Larry's emails or calls. Priority, threat level for Larry was zero. He was considering his options when Melina emerged from the bathroom. She caught him looking at her. She could feel his eyes traveling over her body, caressing her, touching her as his hands and mouth had just done. She felt her entire body tingle with warmth. She looked at Larry remembering how she had taken him. The explosion of their love, the throbbing release of energy was still on his mind…his boyish smile betrayed him. Thankfully, the day was young.

~~~

"*Buenas noches*," Larry said. José greeted him warmly.

"How was your trip?"

"The drive was uneventful. We arrived later than expected and will visit the airport in the morning before moving on to Tartagal, where we are also expected."

"Did you have any luck with the facial recognition?" José asked. He wanted to give madame president some positive news.

"Yes, we did run into some luck. The pilot license photos were grainy and returned nothing of consequence but for one. That one was Omar Habib Barack. He is suspected of several organized bombings in Europe and is a noted Islamic extremist," Larry said.

"Good. At least we got something positive from the day. The license and plane identification numbers were all fake. We will be issuing stricter regulations on both but what is that famous American expression: *Close the door after the animals don't come inside*," José said. Larry laughed.

"There are several variations, but it is more along the lines of: *Why bother to close the barn door once the cows have left*."

"Oh. That sounds better still," José said.

"José, do you have any field operatives working in the Middle East?"

"I do not believe so. Our intelligence budget and department are much smaller than yours. I will check."

"I would appreciate anything you can do. I will be sending you what I have. It won't be encrypted."

"Understood. I will see what I can do for you."

~~~

Larry and Melina woke refreshed and joined the other patrons for a continental breakfast. There were some looks (stares really) but otherwise they enjoyed the breakfast before the drive to the airport and their meeting with Joseph. Larry knew that the meeting would be pointless, but he had positive hopes.

~~~

Larry and Melina pulled into the parking lot. There were seven corrugated steel and aluminum buildings and one block structure. Larry drove in the direction of the block structure with the shortwave radio antenna attached thereto. The Jeep pulled to a stop, the door opened, and a man appeared in the doorway expecting them.

"*Buenos días*," the man said.

"Joseph," Larry said. The man nodded. "*Buenos días*," Larry said in finishing his greeting. Larry then introduced Melina.

"*Buenos días, señorita.*"

"*Buenos días, señor*," Melina responded. Joseph stepped aside. He extended his arm, inviting both Larry and Melina into his office.

~~~

The airport operations building was similar to the one in Chascomús. There were booths for charter flights, skydiving, and flight schools. There were chairs set up in the middle, which were for airport patrons. There were partitioned-off offices and restrooms. The only difference was instead of two additional guys seated, there were five.

Larry looked around. He was not concerned for their safety. He was looking to see if any of the booths were occupied. He may have missed something. "Please come this way," Joseph said. Larry and Melina followed him to his office. They walked by. The gentlemen seated became quiet where previously there had been conversation. They looked at Larry and Melina, each exchanging glances with the others. There were a few nods.

Joseph produced a package containing four sets of pilot licenses. Daily lease agreements and plane identification numbers were also available. He handed them to Larry. Larry took his time reviewing them one by one. When finished, he slid the copies over to Melina for her perusal. She looked at the documents before handing them back to Larry. Larry had his cell phone out and the email open. He slowly went through the information provided. He checked the package information with the email sent and received from Reynolds. Larry was purposefully taking his time. He did not want to rush through this one. Omar had
~~~

been in the package provided. He had been here. *What do I do?* was the thought that echoed in his head.

Larry looked at Joseph. "These guys, who are they?"

"These are the mechanics and painters that worked on the planes." Larry's face lit up. He pulled Omar's pilot license from the group.

"Do you remember this man?" Larry asked. He showed Omar's picture to Joseph and the group.

"*Sí*," came the concerted response.

"What can you tell me about him?" Larry asked. One by one, they each spoke. The man in question, Omar, was not overly vocal. He was within earshot of most conversations but that was all. The names used were the same one's listed on the pilot's license. "No! My friends, that is not true. Do you remember when the two who looked like brothers were fighting and the one called the other Hassan," one of the men said.

"*Sí*. I remember now. This man pulled him aside and he admonished them but not before first calling them brothers, Hassan, Hazim, I remember him saying." Larry showed the man the pictures and he identified the two brothers.

Further conversation centered on the painting of the planes. Joseph had the painter present and he brought his records with him. Larry tried not to get overly excited. He took the records being handed to him and looked up at Melina. She smiled at him. He turned his focus back to the files. He was looking for a manufacturer's serial number. These planes had been purchased from someone. *That someone did not pay cash for seven planes,* Larry thought. When previously asked how payment was made, the answer was *dinero en efectivo*. "Cash," Larry shook his head.

There it was. "Bingo," Larry slapped the paper. Two of the guys jumped; startled by Larry's sudden show of emotion. "Sorry," he pointed and looked at the painter.

"You needed the manufacturer's serial number for the paint, correct?" Larry asked.

"*Sí, señor*, to mix the proper paint color so it would last."

"The plane has a history. I'm hoping I can find the guy that sold the planes. Can you help me locate a broker for the sale and purchase of seven planes similar to these?" Larry asked. They all looked from one to the other, nodding their heads yes.

"*Sí, Señor* Larry. Give us *dos días*." Larry looked at Melina. "Two days. That will give us time to visit Tartagal and return. *Gracias*," Larry and Melina smiled and left the group. From the parking lot, Larry called Matthew, even though it was six thirty in the morning, Washington time.

"Matthew here."

"Matthew, Larry Seabreeze, sorry for the early call."

"Son, you know this line is not secure."

"Yes, sir, I am aware of that. I have made some fairly significant progress on the planes and possibly the broker that sold them. I am leaving now and heading to the other destination. I will call you or Reynolds in a few days."

"Understood. Keep us both informed via email at your earliest convenience," Matthew said and terminated the call.

Larry quickly sent an email to Matthew and Reynolds, providing an update on his conversation with José and the airport personnel. He included the make, model, and serial numbers of the plane's fuselage and engine. He and Melina then left the airport for the bed-and-breakfast. They gathered up their belongings, checked out, and made reservations for two days from today. Prior to leaving, Larry provided the owner with the name of the four pilots. "Can you see where they stayed in September or October of this past year? There is five hundred dollars for the information," Larry tore the five hundred's in half and gave one half to the owner with the promise of the second half should he secure the information.

Melina was laughing when they got into the Jeep. "I can't believe you tore the money in half."

"Incentive," Larry remarked before they drove to Tartagal.

Chapter Sixteen

The size of the underemployment elephant in the United States is directly related to student debt when looked at from the viewpoint of a graduating collegiate. Forty-eight percent of college graduates work in a job where a college degree is not required.

St. Louis, Missouri

Tim Black completed a preliminary analysis on both murders. His PI license provided him an opportunity to obtain data from various local, state and federal agency databanks. What he found on Miguel was surprising and definitive in his mind. The botched robbery was staged. A front to cover up what Miguel was truly doing, spying on employees of Feldman & Company Biotech, Inc. For who, would take some additional work.

Tim knew Miguel worked for We Clean for You, Inc., an office cleaning company. Missouri Department of Labor and Workforce Development listed Miguel as an employee of We Clean for You, Inc., and Office Solutions, LLC, a computer software consulting company. Miguel was employed by the software company for over fifteen years. He worked sporadically for other companies during that same period of time. Most were cleaning companies where transient labor was the norm. Miguel had a double life. Being Hispanic has its advantages.

Tim pocketed the information and placed a call to Office Solutions. He asked to speak with Human Resources.

"Ruth speaking."

"Ruth, my name is Tim Black. I'm a private investigator. I am looking into the death of Miguel Martinez Rodriguez."

"Tragic incident. But why would a private investigator be looking into Miguel's death; furthermore, why are you calling Human Resources?"

"Ruth, I would prefer to have this discussion in your office rather than over the phone. I also would not object to your company's counsel being present should you so desire. How does ten o'clock tomorrow morning sound?" Tim asked.

"I will need to confirm that with the owner and counsel. If I don't call you back, please consider the appointment confirmed," she said. Tim gave her his number and terminated the call. He did some further preliminary work before assigning the job to a junior associate. There were still tax records to search, a preliminary title search, corporate records, and a bank search. Miguel had been up to no good and had paid the ultimate price; of that, Tim was certain.

~~~

Campus Security and the Arkansas State Police had very little to go on regarding the death of Dr. Joseph Patrick. Video surveillance worked but there appeared to be incomplete surveillance coverage of the area in question. Tim contacted both groups to see what progress had been made. He received some professional courtesies after he dropped a few names of friends that worked for the Arkansas State Police. They provided him with the name of the lead investigator, Randolph Jones. Tim called Randolph.

"Jones here."

"Randolph Jones, my name is Tim Black. I am a private investigator in Missouri. I have been asked to investigate the death of a seemingly unrelated individual, Miguel Martinez Rodriguez, and Dr. Joseph Patrick. One is an apparent botched robbery the other *unknown*. The botched robbery is going to be a murder in my estimation. If it is, then I believe Patrick's will be." Tim waited. Randolph's turn to share if he was so inclined. Tim could hear papers being shuffled but that was it. Finally…mumbling.
~~~

". . . murd'r, huh," Randolph said matter-of-factly. "We have an internal belief that the death was more than *unknown*. Unfortunately, we can't prove more than that."

"How'd he die?" Tim asked.

"Blunt-force trauma to the head. He was found on some stairs, shoe untied, files spewed forth. Initial presumption is a falling man trying to regain his balance," Randolph said.

"Front, back, or side of the head?"

"Side of the head."

"Any defensive wounds? Any sign of a struggle? Anything taken, reported lost, misplaced, out of place?" There was a grunt on the other end of the phone. "Lost, misplaced, or out of place?" Tim repeated.

"His cell phone is missing."

"Has it been used?"

"No. The number hasn't been activated since his death. However, it's possible for someone with capabilities to download content and access usage."

"Have you obtained the records, transcripts, usage?"

"Not yet."

"Let me give you my number. Call me when you get the information. Particularly if the last few calls involve Katie Pendleton."

"Your client, I presume?"

"Yeah . . . my client." Tim disconnected the call and considered this case. From his computer he accessed the Internet. *St. Louis Post-Dispatch*, World News, Recent Articles. He selected Jenny Pendleton's article involving the super-seed and its use in South America. Could this all be related? He reread the article. Before leaving the website, he printed out select articles and placed them in the file.

~~~
~~~

Chat-room Posting

Success is like investing, past performance does not translate into present or future success. However, it often can be an indication thereof. Another job posting was accepted. Criteria for employment provided including time commitment. This contract was local.

~~~

Decatur, Illinois

From a secure Internet account, Amged contacted three of the five individuals currently occupying safe houses. Of the fifteen individuals, nine were currently in country. A time, date, and game had been established for contact. The game was another popular one involving aliens and earthlings battling for control of another outer world with design for future terraforming. It was an age-old battle for supremacy being played out in the ethereal fantasy land and here on earth. Real time. Real life. *Jericho will clearly prevail, and we will be the New World Order*, Amged believed. His cousin Ashraff was working with the same timeline. Same belief . . . *We cannot lose.*

~~~

On average there are over 6,250,000 traffic accidents per year. That is over 17,100 traffic accidents per day and over 700 traffic accidents per hour. Of those 700 traffic accidents per hour, 6 result in death. A relatively low percentage of less than 1 percent. In hindsight, Bail was thankful he was in the majority percentage of that last factoid.

~~~

Bail could walk to work easier than drive. He lived less than six tenths of a mile from his office. He had Googled the distance on several occasions, particularly when his common-law spouse, Celeste, of twenty years
~~~

reminded him of his weight. However, it was snowing this morning, Bail drove.

Bail left his driveway turning north down Park Place. Every town has one. He turned right on a nameless one-way road that exits Fairview Park. He would turn right on to N. Fairview Avenue and take the first left into the parking lot and campus of Millikin University. The roads were slick with new falling snow, but they were not slippery. So when the pickup truck approached Bail, he was not overly concerned. That is, of course, until he felt the slight bump.

"F*&%!" Bail said before he looked into his rearview mirror. He shook his head, unbuckled his seat belt, and began to slowly open his car door when he felt his vehicle surge forward. Bail had just enough time to pull his foot back inside the car when he sensed, more than felt or saw, the car hit his vehicle broadside.

The driver traveling southbound on Fairview Avenue was driving fast for road conditions—however, not at a speed one would consider reckless. He was a seasoned all-weather driver familiar with road conditions. He was not, unfortunately, gifted with catlike reflexes that would allow him to avoid the impending accident.

Bail's car lurched forward into his lane of traffic. He did all that he could do, which is to say nothing. His vehicle collided with Bail's car, striking it just behind the left front fender well and before the firewall/ driver side door jam. It was only during the moment of impact that he noticed several things happening in slow motion.

The driver of the car entering his lane of traffic appeared to be trying to exit his vehicle. The impact caused the driver to be thrown from the driver side of the vehicle to the passenger side. A second vehicle entered the accident behind the one just struck. The momentum caused all three vehicles to cross over into the northbound traffic.

The first car traveling north on Fairview Avenue was able to avoid all three oncoming vehicles; however, the second and third cars were less fortunate. The second car struck Bail's vehicle broadside, sending him back into the driver side compartment. The third vehicle tried to avoid the accident completely and ended up hitting the right rear quarter panel of Bail's vehicle, careening off that, and side-swiping the driver's side of the pickup truck that had caused the accident.

All four vehicles came to rest while the pickup truck sped away.

~~~

Fraternity houses line the street facing campus. East. Several members of the various houses were up and walking toward their early morning classes. Police were provided with a number of eyewitness accounts. Each witness was able to provide the police with a description of the vehicle that left the scene of the accident, including the license plate number. Early investigation provided evidence of bumper-on-bumper scraping, indicative of one vehicle pushing another from behind. The vehicle described to police and the license plate number given met the description of a vehicle previously reported stolen.

~~~

Celeste left for work after Bail. She exited the driveway and drove south. She turned east onto West Main Street and drove to the Civic Center, City Hall's location. Celeste was the city clerk, eighteen years. She would not learn of the accident for another three hours.

~~~

Bail was rushed to Decatur Memorial Hospital. His injuries were deemed life-threatening, given his absence of a seat belt. In the long run, that may have saved his life and use of his legs. Surgery lasted several hours before it was determined that he would survive and recover fully with all fingers and toes intact. Celeste notified family members of Bail's status. It was only later when colleagues started to inquire that Celeste remembered Katie. She was aware that they were working on something . . . what, however, she did not know.

~~~

St. Louis, Missouri

Katie was sitting with Brad, Tim, Lawrence, and Jenny at Mickey's Place when she received Celeste's text message. Dinner and drinks. Katie read the message not once, not twice, but three times. She found each reading more disbelieving than the previous.

Brad noticed Katie's look first. Recent activity. He knew the news was bad. "Katie, what's up?"

"This project is jinxed." Brad reached for Katie's cell phone. He pressed the screen and it illuminated. Celeste's message revealed. *Katie, Bail is in the hospital. Victim of a hit-and-run this morning. I will keep you and Jenny abreast of the situation. Surgery went well, Love, Aunt Celeste.*

Brad read the message several times before handing the phone to Jenny. She read it before passing the phone to Lawrence. Lawrence read the message and handed the phone to Tim. Tim read the message before looking at Jenny and asking the obvious question: "Who's Bail?"

"Bail Prichard is a PhD in biology. He teaches at Millikin University in Decatur. He has been working on the super-spore that was used in South America. This spore is responsible for the devastation of the cereal grain crops there. Bail identified one strain of the spore and has been working with Dr. Montero's team in Argentina. He's been assisting them in identifying the entire genome of the spore," Katie said.

"Two dead and one near death. I'd say someone is ensuring that the spore genome stay unidentified," Tim remarked.

"Are you saying that these three incidents are all related?" Jenny asked.

"Yes. I believe they are. I presume that you communicated with Dr. Patrick and Dr. Prichard while at work?" Tim asked Katie.

"Yes," Katie said.

"Through business email and telephone."

"Yes."

"So all of this would have been part of the network you use while at work."

"Yes again."

"Office Solutions, Inc., handles your network, do they not?"

"Yes, they do."

"Miguel Martinez Rodriguez worked for Office Solutions, Inc. He was a financial security programmer. At night he worked on the office cleaning crew that cleaned your offices."

"Industrial espionage?" Jenny blurted out.

"No. Murder," Tim replied. He let the table get quiet. Nobody said anything for several minutes but they were about to when the food arrived. Unfortunately, everyone had experienced a sudden loss of appetite.

Katie reached for her phone and started typing.

"What are you doing?" I asked.

"Asking Aunt Celeste who is handling Bail's accident investigation. Tim should speak with them," Katie said. "What else do you know?" she asked Tim after typing and sending the text message.

"Not much yet. It sounds like a lot of information and progress, but it isn't. I haven't answered the truly difficult questions…what information was Miguel after? Was he working for himself or someone else? Was he murdered or was it truly a botched robbery? Are these three related, or are they separate? I have a meeting tomorrow at Office Solutions. I am hoping that that will answer some questions. I'll still need to look at financial records, which should answer other questions. In the end, though, it may simply add a layer of confusion and circumstantial evidence without actually identifying the killer or what Miguel was up to. Bail's accident is a perfect example of how easy we believe in conspiracies." Tim took a sip of his beer. He looked at Katie and continued. "Simply because he was working on something with you, doesn't mean he was a target. If that were the case, why haven't you been a target?"

"Oh no," Jenny stammered. The table got quiet, food cold, beer warm. Mickey happened upon the table while Jenny mumbled *your hit and run*. She was looking at Katie.

"Ya's aren't eat'n? What's da matt'r with da food 'n drink? And who got hit and run'd?"

It was several minutes before anyone responded but it was not to Mickey; it was to Katie. "Just be careful and take normal precautions.

We only know enough to create ghosts. Give me the information on your accident and I'll add it to my investigation." Tim was confident Katie was not in any danger. He winked at Brad. But he also had to be thorough.

"When you consider the facts involving each individual and yourself," Tim said calmly. Not to say it without emotion, but to simply say it. "…one could create a connection where it may not exist."

"We are likely getting ahead of ourselves. I'm not saying that your life is in any more danger than before, but I am suggesting that you be careful," Tim said.

"I'm sorry, but there are no *'your life's in danger' take-backs*," Jenny said.

"Let's eat...but be careful," Tim joked while he reached for a French fry. Lawrence followed while Brad joined the movement. Jenny understood Tim's point. She smiled at Katie.

Jenny took a bite of her bacon double cheeseburger. Slowly, ever so slowly, they ate some of their meal. Just enough, but not a lot. Mickey left their table at some point. They dropped some money on the table and left the crowded bar, saying a few hellos on the way out or maybe not.

~~~

It was 9:45 a.m. when Tim found himself sitting in Office Solutions reception area. He checked with the reception desk. Ruth was notified that her 10 o'clock appointment arrived. Coffee was offered and accepted. A meeting of the minds, Tim thought. At 9:55, a second gentleman presented himself. Elderly, clean-cut, professional-looking, the attorney, Tim decided. He was not offered coffee, which Tim understood to mean Ruth was on her way. Before Tim could finish his thought, Ruth arrived and introduced herself to the attorney first (only after speaking with the receptionist) before turning to Tim, "Mr. Black, good morning. Please follow me."

Ruth looked like she could have been attractive with a little work and care. Unfortunately, things had deteriorated. She was five feet seven
~~~

inches tall and weighed a buck seventy-five, mid-forties, graying hair, no real personality Tim guessed. One of those women whom life had passed by; likely no regrets now, she was everybody's favorite aunt.

Ruth showed them to a conference room. She and the attorney took a seat on one side, Tim the other. "Mr. Bailey will be joining us shortly. We will begin then." Ruth laid some papers on the conference room table.

Tim had a habit of failing to write things down or remember every piece of valuable information mentioned. Since many people objected to a recording, Tim had a microphone sewn into the fabric of his saddle bag briefcase. He set it on the top of the conference table. He recorded every conversation. Even if the other party or parties were recording the conversation, Tim did. . . and he never disclosed that he was.

There was no conversation during the first few minutes while everyone was forced to wait. Finally, Mr. Bailey joined them. "Sorry for the delay," Mr. Bailey said upon entering. He looked at Ruth and smiled. "Ronald," he said to the attorney before he turned to Tim. "Mr. Black."

"Mr. Bailey."

Mr. Bailey took his seat then looked at Tim and said, "Murder? Really?" He snorted a derisive laugh. Tim said nothing, which caught Bailey by surprise. Tim generally carried a poker face with him to such meetings.

Mr. Riley, the attorney, took over for Mr. Bailey. "Mr. Black, have you gone to the police with your theory?"

"No, sir, I have not," Tim said, noticing that the attorney was slightly nodding his head in an up-and-down motion, he understood why.

"Then tell us why you believe Mr. Rodriguez, the decedent, was murdered."

"The decedent, one Miguel Martinez Rodriguez, was employed by Office Solutions, Inc., for the past fifteen-plus years. Correct?" There was silence. "Listen, this is very easy. I have been hired to do a job and I will do it. I'm giving you an opportunity to find out something about a former employee…activity you were likely unaware of. Here's the problem. If you make my job more difficult than it already is, things

I uncover may slip out to the public. This could have serious financial repercussions and consequences for you and your company."

"Are you threatening me, Mr. Black? Let me tell you something, you sanctimonious—"

"Gentlemen, gentlemen, please. Edwin, please sit down. Mr. Black very carefully and intentionally used the phrase 'may slip out,' not would." Mr. Riley said in an effort to control his client.

Mr. Riley brought Mr. Bailey under control. He also provided confirmation information regarding the decedent. "Yes, Mr. Rodriguez worked for Office Solutions for over fifteen years."

"As a programmer, I presume."

"Yes, a programmer and system design engineer," Ruth said, Mr. Riley nodded to her.

"System design engineer . . . sounds impressive. What was the pay?"

"Mr. Rodriguez made eighty-seven thousand five hundred dollars."

"Bi-monthly?"

"Yes."

"Can I get a copy of his last direct deposit receipt?" Tim asked.

"Why?" Mr. Bailey questioned.

"Call it good faith," Tim stared at Bailey just as hard.

"Let's move on," Mr. Riley said.

"I am requesting a copy of Mr. Rodriguez's' bi-monthly pay stub so I can definitively confirm that *other* bank deposits are, in fact, from his employment."

"We'll provide you with bi-monthly deposits," Mr. Riley said before adding, "You still haven't told us what this is about, so I must tell you, I am growing weary of this charade."

"True. Mr. Rodriguez moonlighted periodically for cleaning companies. He's been moonlighting for fifteen years. Several of the cleaning company clients are clients of Office Solutions. Feldman & Company is one such client. My client is not Feldman & Company although they work with them. My client believes two seemingly unrelated events are the result of Mr. Rodriguez, the decedent's activities. Either industrial espionage or something more criminal in nature," Tim said.

"I was asked to investigate." There was silence.

Tim had had cases similar to this. In actuality, all cases were similar. There was always an injured party believing that a grave injustice had been done against them. The other party was appalled that such an accusation could be left at their doorstep. Then there was the true injured party. The true victim. The one who wondered how they ever got caught up in something that would likely cost them everything even if they were found innocent, non-culpable. Too bad. When the dust settles, their name is no longer a good one.

Mr. Riley broke the silence. "Each employee of the firm signs a hold harmless agreement which includes indemnification provisions."

"I understand. However, once Office Solutions' name is bandied about, let me know how those agreements work out for you." Tim was not trying to be confrontational. Everyone had a hold harmless and indemnification agreement for everything. Mr. Bailey almost exploded at Tim after his comment, but Mr. Riley raised his hand to silence him.

"What is it you're looking for, Mr. Black?" Mr. Riley asked. He recognized that Mr. Black was arguing from a stronger position than that of his client. Mr. Riley had taken a damage control approach to this conversation.

"I'm looking for payroll records for the past thirty-six months. I'm also interested in the system diagnostics for Feldman & Company. I work with a solo practitioner who will review their system and individual desktop stations. You obviously will be responsible for the fee. You can call it whatever you want. I presume you would like to keep this quiet."

"How much can I expect this to cost me?" Mr. Bailey asked reluctantly.

"Whatever he charges you will be far less than what you would likely lose. I have no control over that." Having said that, Tim simply looked at the individuals in the room for questions. Knowing that there would be none, he looked at Mr. Riley, who again nodded his head in agreement.

"We can have the information for you by the end of the day," Mr. Riley said.

"Great. I will have Charles Freyski contact you regarding system configuration and diagnostics."

"What's your cut in this?" Mr. Bailey asked. It always happens. The victim lashes out at the bearer of bad news.

"Listen and listen well, Mr. Bailey, this is not a threat, it's a promise. Mr. Rodriguez's death is tied to your firm and his longstanding moonlighting activity. There is a likely connection to a death in Arkansas and an attempt in Illinois. You are only permitted the continued pleasure of your pompous existence because of my benevolence, which in your case is hanging by a thread..." Tim exhaled and tossed his card at Bailey, "unless you want the information to become public, you have one hour or else." Tim got up and left. He sent Charles a text message, asking him to meet him at his office.

Forty-seven minutes later, Tim's computer pinged. The email was from Office Solutions.

Perfect timing. Charles just arrived.

The over under was fifty-two minutes. Charles took the under and bought it down to minus seven. Tim took the over thinking Bailey would push the envelope. "We're degenerates," Charles said. Tim tossed him a finski and laughed.

~~~

Charles was provided the system configuration and diagnostics. He reviewed them before emailing Bailey his engagement letter which outlined each party's responsibilities. The fee was $27,000 for one week's worth of work. Tim received nothing, although gift cards and tickets would arrive periodically. They both knew how the game was played. Charles would begin upon receipt of payment—full payment.
~~~

Chapter Seventeen

From 2007-2017, the Argentinean government expanded credit to small and medium scale farmers. The budget was $80 million dollars and established programs to support exports and new subsidized interest rates to offset unfavorable international contingencies.

General Güemes, Argentina

Larry and Melina were returning from Tartagal. The trip was a loose end that needed to be tied off. That was all it was. Joseph and Juan had spoken with Manuel. He was *helpful* in a technical definition but that was the extent. His records were shoddy. The painter had also done this *en el lado* (on the side). He hadn't bothered to identify plane type or fuselage serial number. Manuel provided what information he could, to include a description of what he remembered, but in the end, he was a self-proclaimed *hombre ocupado*, a busy man. Larry and Melina struck out, but that was to be expected. Their success rate so far had been rather high.

They were an hour from General Güemes, midafternoon on a beautiful summer day. "Detour to a small reservoir and a quick mountain swim?" Melina asked Larry.

"*Sí.* Just point the way," Larry said. Melina remembered an old secluded camping area. Now if she could only find it.

They finally located the area. Without the Jeep, they never would have made it. Mules would have had trouble and likely would have turned back. Yet when they exited the Jeep next to the pool at the bottom of a waterfall, Larry knew the trip had been worth it.

They both walked over to the water and tested it. Larry with his hand, Melina with her big toe. Larry stood up contemplating water temperature and warm mountain air when he noticed he was standing alone. He turned to look for Melina. He found her standing by the mud-covered Jeep completely naked and ready for a swim. He laughed . . . but not at her.

"What an advertising commercial for Jeep you would make," Larry said. He was smiling from ear to ear. "They couldn't make enough Jeeps to keep up with demand."

Melina smiled and whispered, "Last one in has to do all the work."

Larry was interrupted by the splash. *Even when I lose, I win,* he undressed to join Melina.

~~~

They arrived in General Güemes several hours later. It was close to dusk. The manager of the bed-and-breakfast smiled when Larry and Melina walked in. He reached under the desk and withdrew a piece of paper, which he handed to Larry in exchange for five halves of a whole.

"Bingo," Larry and Melina walked up to the room for a warm bath. It was late, the manager brought them a complimentary wine, cheese, and cracker tray. They had an early morning tomorrow; otherwise, the night may never have ended.

~~~

Larry and Melina arrived at the airport by 7:30 a.m. Joseph was waiting with fresh coffee and morning pastries. They were alone when they spoke about Tartagal and worthlessness of the trip. "Manuel is a difficult man even under ideal conditions," Joseph said. "His people are like he is."

"Yeah, we struck out," Larry said before realizing that Joseph likely did not understand the euphemism. "...a wasted trip," he said.

"Ah . . . but it was necessary anyway." Joseph got up to walk around outside. Larry and Melina followed. They were not on the clock and Joseph wanted to talk. Friendship was how Larry felt. So they walked and listened while Joseph spoke. Larry did not look at Melina; he just knew she understood Joseph's need to talk. Two people he considered friends . . . ones he would never see again.

"The manager of the bed-and-breakfast you are staying at came to me. He had the information you seek but wanted to know if you could be trusted. I told him you are a good man and you a good woman and you both can be trusted. He gave you the information . . . yes?"

"*Sí.* He gave us the information."

"And you gave him the other halves . . . yes?"

"*Sí.* He told you that?"

"*Sí,*" Joseph said while shaking his head. "I have not laughed so hard since I was a young boy. Thank you for that, my friend," Joseph added. He looked out at the mountains. The lower Piedmont Mountains. "They will speak with you when you go there. Here is the name of the broker in Bolivia that sold the airplanes. He is in Villazón. He knows you're coming and can be trusted." Joseph paused and looked at Melina and Larry. "This is where we part company, my American friend. Good luck to you both," Joseph said. He embraced them. Standing outside he watched them climb back into the Jeep and drive off. "Godspeed to you, my friends," Joseph whispered. They drove off down the dirt-covered road. He stood there until the last dust settled. One last look . . . but they were gone.

~~~

Larry drove while Melina navigated. The hotel that Omar and his cohorts stayed at was in town. They'd both seen it but failed to pay attention. They drove up to the door marked office, stepped out of the jeep and walked inside. The manager was standing behind the counter doing paperwork. He looked up and immediately knew that it was the American. He put down his paperwork and closed the ledger. They both walked up to the counter. "*Buenos días,*" Larry said.

"*Hola, señor, señorita.* My name is Pablo. I understand you have
~~~

some questions regarding the four *extranjeros* who stayed with us several weeks ago."

"*Sí*," Larry said. "Anything you can tell us would be helpful. Where they ate, did they talk to anyone, see anyone, call anyone, have any visitors?" Pablo looked at them both. They seemed to be a nice-looking couple and he immediately understood why Joseph said they could be trusted.

"They only stayed with me for three nights. They saw no one and only used their cell phones. They paid cash and stayed inside. When the cleaning lady cleaned the rooms, she saw some writing. She looked. You know how people are. She said it was a map with X's marked. She could not read the writing. I am sorry," Pablo said.

"Was the map of Argentina?" Larry asked.

"No. Other countries."

"Is the cleaning lady here?"

"*Sí*, she is my wife," Pablo said with a smile.

"Can I speak with her?" Larry asked. He tried but he could not fully hide his excitement. Another possible break.

"*Sí*," Pablo said. He reached for the walkie-talkie. "Juanita, please come to the office."

"*Sí . . . diez minutos*," Juanita replied.

Juanita walked in from a back entrance. She joined them at the counter. "This is the American I was talking about. He wants to ask you some questions." Pablo turned to Larry.

"Juanita, Pablo says that you saw a map while cleaning the room of the man I am trying to locate." Juanita blushed and looked at Pablo, who nodded. "Do you remember what countries had the X's marked?"

Juanita shook her head slowly before answering. "No. I did not understand the writing."

"If I showed you a map, do you think you would remember?" Larry asked. The tone of his voice was pleading for her to say yes.

"Maybe," she said. "I can try."

"Is there a bookstore around here? Or do you have Internet access?" Larry asked Pablo.

"*Sí*, we have Internet." Pablo turned to the computer laptop stored underneath the counter.

Larry was uncertain whether it was cable or dial-up at first until he noticed that it operated off Pablo's cell phone. A hotspot. *Where would we be without technology?* he thought.

They Googled world maps. Under the belief that bad news doesn't get better with age, Larry searched for North America. The United States, Canada, and parts of Mexico were shown.

"Does this look familiar?" Larry asked.

"No," Juanita said.

"Okay. Let's try Asia and the Pacific," Larry said. China, India, Southeast Asia, Taiwan, Philippines, Japan all showed up.

"How about this? Does this look familiar?" Larry asked. Juanita smiled and nodded her head.

"*Sí*. There were many X's," she said. Larry felt he was getting somewhere.

"Do you think you can remember where those X's were specifically? Were there any dates?" But Larry knew the answer. He watched Juanita's smile fade.

Larry continued, but the rest of the nations of the world turned up blank. Not one hit other than China and parts of Southeast Asia. "I am sorry. I did not get a better look and my memory is not so good," Juanita said.

"No, you did fine. What you gave us is a big help. Thank you very much, Juanita." She perked back up and smiled. Pablo smiled. He placed his arm around Juanita. Melina looked at Larry and winked.

It was helpful to be sure. Yet, it just didn't make sense. Larry thanked Pablo and Juanita for their help. He and Melina started to leave. Melina stopped at the door and turned back. Larry hesitated but followed her lead. Trust.

Melina looked at Larry, "we never asked about the writing." Larry understood Melina's need for confirmation. She took the laptop and typed in Arabic abjad.

"*Sí,*" Juanita's smile returned. Larry and Melina said thanks and left.

Very little was said on the drive back to the bed-and-breakfast. Larry parked in the gravel lot, climbed out of the Jeep, and took Melina by the hand. He led her up the stairs and to the porch, where he stopped. He turned and led her off to the hanging porch swing. They both sat down. Melina leaned up against Larry while he rocked the swing back-and-forth. He was contemplating his next move when the owner came out to say hello. It was a nice evening and relatively early. Larry asked if a bottle of wine and a cheese plate were available.

"*Sí*. I will set something up for you in the flower garden. It is beautiful this time of year." She went back inside for the wine and cheese plate. Melina purred ever so seductively whispering in Larry's ear just enough to cause his heart to skip a few beats.

Larry placed a call to José. He provided him with an update. "China is a large exporter of cereal grains, second only to the United States in most categories."

"The operatives were clearly Middle Eastern. It is more likely that Juanita saw only a portion of a map." Larry included Juanita's confirmation of the language. Arabic writing being distinctive.

"I would agree," José said before adding something to the relationship . . . quid pro quo. "We don't have the resources to run operations, but the head of our intelligence department, Gabriel, is close with several countries that do operate in parts of Africa and the Middle East. He is quietly asking around. Give him some time."

"Agreed. We will leave for Villazón, Bolivia, tomorrow or the day after. There are still some things I want to check out. Tartagal was a bust. Poor records and memories."

"Should I investigate for you?" José asked.

"No. You could add very little, if anything."

"The woman, she is still with you?"

"Yes. It has helped out quite a bit. People feel more at ease." Larry looked at Melina. She smiled.

"You like her, don't you?" José asked before quickly retracting his statement. "Sorry, that was very rude of me. Please forgive me." Larry's personality simply made it easy for people to offer up statements and ask friendly questions.

"Nothing to ask forgiveness for. Call if you hear anything from Gabriel. If you have a close government contact in Bolivia, maybe you could text me their name and number and let them know I may call them."

"I do. Good luck, my friend," José said. A couple of minutes later Larry received José's text message.

~~~

The garden was not large, but it had been given a tremendous amount of thought. In the middle of the garden was a free-flowing water garden koi pond stocked with nishikigoi's. Surrounding the fishpond were seven separate floral arrangements—two included fountains while one had a birdbath. In the center of each floral arrangement was a table and chair set. Some had two chairs, others four, still others had chairs, benches, and love seats.

While enjoying the wine and cheese plate, Larry and Melina talked about the investigation and other things, in particular each other. They had discussed it before and felt more comfortable now than previous conversations. The end was near. After Bolivia, there would be the trip back to Buenos Aires and then what? Besides which Melina felt she was pregnant. She had not said anything. If it didn't work out, she would make the choice on her own.

"Sweetheart, we have already discussed this. You are coming home with me. It's what I want and I thought you did," a tear rolled down his cheek and hers. Discussion over; minds made up. They enjoyed a second bottle of wine together and watched while the sun set behind the mountains. The lights built into the landscape came on and provided them with an otherworldly atmosphere. Larry used the music app on his cell phone, romantic sounds filled the night air, Puccini's *La Bohème*. He and Melina danced the night away. They would leave for Bolivia day after tomorrow. He would email Matthew and Reynolds in the morning.

~~~

Larry felt he had two positive aspects to the job that most other operatives stumbled over—language and English writing skills. Larry believed his writing style was similar to that of the *New York Times* best-selling author L.A. Jaworski, whose books and realistic storylines entertained millions and had been made into major motion pictures. After a brief morning telephone conversation with Matthew, Larry sent off a secure email to both Matthew and Reynolds. He provided them with an update on his activities and opinions.

Much like Jaworski's writing style, Larry's email narrative was succinct. He mentioned and provided the serial numbers from the planes that had landed in General Güemes. He requested that status be provided ASAP. He mentioned the wasted trip to Tartagal and his conversation with José Quinterro, who offered to send in the Federales. He mentioned his conversation with Pablo and Juanita. It was here that Larry would later catch the attention of the president.

Larry discussed Juanita's recollection of seeing a map of China and Southeast Asia. When showed maps of other countries, Juanita did not recall seeing anything. It was only China and Southeast Asia that had a map with multiple X's and Arabic writing and numbers.

Personally, Larry believed the writing indicated locations and the numbers were dates. That much was a guess but Larry assessed Juanita's recollection at a high percentage. Above 70 percent. *Query: Given the current situation in the South China Sea and other tangent issues, e.g. calling the U.S. debt due, do we notify the Chinese? If so, when? An early notification could mean an interruption in the plan. Juanita saw only one map and Joseph witnessed an argument later that same day at the airport in which Omar let slip the names of the two brothers. I believe other locations exist yet, we do not know the when and where. Gabriel, the Argentinean intelligence director, is making subtle inquiries. I will be leaving for Villazón, Bolivia, tomorrow.*

~~~
~~~

Washington, D.C.

"Now this is the type of field operative we need," the president said. "This is what we need from all of our operatives. Unfortunately, you can't teach instinct and intuition, and I agree, Matthew, that a computer could not capture either. I like the man's threat assessment and . . . what did he call it . . . *query*." The president was clearly impressed.

"Yes sir, I agree." The president handed the email back.

"Do we work with Argentina much? Do you know this Gabriel?"

"No on both accounts. I suggest holding off on contacting Gabriel. Larry already seems to have that covered. Why get signals crossed?"

"No, I agree with you. Let the boy run with this. If he succeeds, then we're all winners." The unspoken or negative implication was also understood . . . swim as a team or sink alone.

"China, sir?" Matthew asked. He could see the president considering this one.

"Let's hold off for now. After all, we don't know the when and where either." The president's lips turned up slightly at the corners.

Chapter Eighteen

Decatur, Illinois was referred to as the soybean capital of the world for most of the 1900's. A.E. Staley Manufacturing Company and Archer Daniels Midland Company headquarters were located in Decatur. At one point, one third of all soybeans grown in the world were processed in Decatur.

Decatur, Illinois

Amged was not a gamer and thankfully neither were the others. The online meeting they held lasted well over two hours. Everything had been finalized. The planes had been delivered. Omar was in country and had personally verified his plane as had other pilots. The extra fuel tanks had been installed. The planes were completely stripped to their original green state. The "bladder" would hold both the silver iodide spore solution and the potassium chloride spore solution. It would be delivered within a few days along with the atomizer. The operatives had been trained on how to install both. They would not be using outside labor.

From a piloting standpoint, the excess weight would affect the plane's trim. Although the added weight still placed the plane within the manufacturer's suggested tolerable weight limits, there was still the aspect of flight during inclement weather. For this, the pilots all trained using computer flight simulators. Sherrief was confident that each pilot would be able to handle his plane.

~~~
~~~

Argentina was not alone in having rural airports used by hobbyists, charter companies, et cetera. The United States has many rural airports. It was a coin toss, rural airport with less people, less chance of overt detection but greater chance of nosy neighbor detection, or a large airport and hide in plain sight. The team chose the rural airport and utilized the aspect of luck to their advantage.

The nosy neighbor had been won over with kindness. The operatives' English was flawless. Most had nary a trace of an accent. Those with a heavy accent were relegated to tasks that required less chance of outside involvement. In the end, the operatives were where they needed to be when they needed to be there. They would begin operations the third to fourth week in February. There may be one last snowfall but temperatures of freezing or below would not affect the spore's effectiveness.

Amged spoke with Ashraff after he conducted his meeting with his operatives. It had been a productive meeting. Ashraff agreed that things were progressing. "Our meeting and plane preparedness have gone according to the plan. It's almost going too well." They both agreed to speak again after they physically visited each operative location.

~~~

St. Louis, Missouri

Tim received the information requested within the period of time suggested. A potential conflict avoided. Charles had also begun his review of Feldman & Company Local Area Network. He received his retainer agreement, paid in full. Charles had provided Tim with copies of Miguel's banking information, which coincided with his Social Security Number. With information provided by Office Solutions, Tim assigned the task of ticking and tying payroll direct deposits to bank statements to a junior associate. Differences, if sizable, would require further investigation. In the meantime, Tim returned the call from Elijah Uhl, Investigator, Decatur Police Department.
~~~

"Eli speaking."

"Elijah, Tim Black returning your call. How are you?"

"Fine, Tim. I was asked by the city clerk, Celeste Raych, to contact you regarding Bail Prichard's accident." It was the way he pronounced the word *accident* that Tim recognized he did not believe there had been a true accident.

"So what can you tell me, Elijah?"

"Please, call me Eli. Everyone does."

"Fine . . . Eli, what can you tell me? Were there any witnesses? Cameras? Cell phone coverage?"

"Tim, there were several witnesses. The accident occurred outside of a fraternity house. Their statements are all consistent and there was a picture. We have the vehicle and license plate number," Eli said. He went into greater detail on the four vehicles disabled at the scene.

"The truck was one of the big Ford heavy-duty ones, dual back axle, four back tires. It pushed Bail's vehicle into the line of oncoming traffic." Tim was waiting for the other shoe to drop.

"Sounds too good to be true," Tim finally offered.

"That's because it is, I'm afraid."

"The vehicle had been reported stolen that morning. The owner went out to go to work and his truck was gone. He remembered driving it home and parking it the night before."

"Did you find the truck?"

"Yes, we did. It was abandoned in an apartment complex parking lot on the other side of town. Security cameras show a man pulling up and parking. He is in the truck several minutes. Likely wiping it down before exiting the vehicle and proceeding into the back of the complex, which is wooded and out of camera coverage."

"Sounds like he knew the area."

"That's what we believe. If so, we may find him later rather than sooner," Eli said although both parties knew the chances were slim to none at best. Unless somebody snitched, the driver of the stolen truck was long gone.

"If you don't mind me asking, what is Bail Prichard to a private investigator in St. Louis?" Eli asked. His turn to try and discover something.

"Did you hear about the crop devastation in South America?"

"Yeah. Argentina, Brazil, and a few other countries. Central Illinois Corn & Soy is working to help them out with some sort of super-seed or some such."

"Essentially, that is correct. Bail Prichard was working with a biologist in Argentina to try and develop a fungicide. I am working for the individual responsible for development of the super-seed," Tim said before continuing. "There have been a series of seemingly unrelated events due to geography. My client is a common denominator in all three events, your's being the third. I have one St. Louis robbery gone bad. That ended in death. I have a professor in Fayetteville, Arkansas, slip and fall down a flight of stairs. That ended in death. Now I have your auto accident." Brief pause. "My apologies, I just realized I forgot to ask, how is Mr. Prichard doing?"

"I've spoken with the doctors, I understand he's doing well. He's still in ICU but that's more for precaution. I've been assured I can speak with him within forty-eight hours," Eli responded.

"Eli, after you speak with Bail, or if something materializes, I'd appreciate it if you let me know. If I hear something, I'll reciprocate."

"Agreed and understood," Eli said.

The call ended and both individuals analyzed it the same way. An accident that was greater than its appearance. An attempted murder. There was little chance of finding the driver, whether local or otherwise. Bail would likely add very little, if anything actually, to the investigation. However, questioning Bail was a loose end Eli had to wrap up.

Tim set the phone down and knew he had a difficult case. It would be difficult to solve, but if not him, then who? He checked his emails, cell phone for calls and messages. He made a list for both. He prioritized the list before calling Randolph regarding Dr. Joseph Patrick.

"Jones here."

"Randolph, Tim Black returning your call."

"Tim, how are you today?"

"Much better if you solved your case."

"No. Sorry. However, I did receive our decedent's cell phone activity. Your client, Katie Pendleton, was his last call. From the looks of it, he called her at her office and left a message, given length of call time."

"Any unusual calls?"

"No. He did research for several companies. We're checking into all of them but I don't expect to find anything there."

"How about text messages or emails?" Tim asked with a noticeable sense of urgency in his voice.

"Nothing yet, but we're still looking. Bank records too. Give me another week. If you don't hear from me, feel free to call," Randolph said.

Tim recognized that he was being sloughed off. Responsibility was his. Both knew the case would be a dead end. "Will do," Tim responded.

The call was no more productive than expected. Katie was Joseph's last call. He must've found something out and was killed because of it. So what was the message that he gave Katie? Tim asked himself. He added it to his case to-do list. Another open item that would have to be cleared. He reached for the phone…

"What's up, Tim?"

"Charles, how's it going?"

"Well. I have only been at this for a handful of hours but Office Solutions is robbing these guys blind. I could do so much more, for half the cost." Charles had a habit of soapbox rambling that, if wasn't nipped in the bud early, could get out of control quickly.

"Chas, focus."

"What . . . sorry. It's going. I found the outgoing spyware link. Fairly well hidden and sophisticated. They are running through a gatekeeper in Las Vegas, from there likely accessing the virtual highway and dark web."

"Can you trace it back to an IP address?"

"Maybe. Like I said, they're old school. So what's up? You're bugg'n me out early."

"The murder victim in a related case placed his last call to my client. He left a voicemail on her phone. It's likely been deleted; however, I need you to retrieve it for me."

"Voicemail? We may be in luck. They run everything through their servers. I'll let you know. Chaz out."

Tim was laughing and shaking his head when his associate entered. *Charles is his own person; that much for sure.* Tim looked up and refocused, "What have you found?"

"I finished the analysis of the bank statements," Carol began. "There were eighteen deposits unaccounted for. All were substantial, totaling two hundred and thirty-five thousand dollars. I emailed you the spreadsheet and provided you one attached to the bank statements. I also drafted an email to Charles for review, requesting his assistance in obtaining the sender of the wires. It would appear that Miguel was a very busy man."

"You don't believe we have an ethical responsibility and duty to turn this over to the prosecutor?" Tim asked his associate.

"At some point, yes. If we turn it over to the prosecutor now, we run the risk of not being able to meet the needs of our client. It's an ethical dilemma; however, other crimes have been committed and are likely stale whereas ours is an active case, a solvable case. The prosecutor would slow us down, allowing this case to grow stale. I say we solve our case," Carol said.

Tim read the email to Charles, making only a few minor language changes. Liking what was said, he sent the email. Tim knew that he would have to pay for this one. Office Solutions would only take him so far under the quid pro quo scenario.

"Good work, Carol. Here's the name and number of an investigator in Decatur, Illinois. Call him in a couple of days and request a police report on a traffic accident involving Bail Prichard. Also call Randolph Jones. He's with the Arkansas State Police. Tell him you're following up on Joseph Patrick's murder. Ask him for a copy of the telephone and email activity. He should give it to you."

"All part of the same case?" Carol asked.

"Yeah . . . same case."

~~~
~~~

Tim and Charles met for a drink after work. They chose a local bar down by the river. "I got your email regarding the wire transfers. It shouldn't be a problem although I'll have to charge you something," Charles said with a grin.

"I know. Just be gentle. My clients aren't rich like yours."

"I tried to tell you, security, not PI, is the wave of the future. People will pay."

"I'm too old," Tim said. He changed the subject. "So what was the last message?" Tim asked. Charles produced a piece of paper with a date, time, and message stamp . . . *Katie, it's Joseph. I discovered something about the spore I'm certain everyone's overlooked. It's important that you call me. We're all in danger. You have my numbers.*

Tim read it twice just to be certain. "It's not overly cryptic."

"No, but I take it that this has to do with South America?"

"You take it correct."

"Their crop loss was substantial, was it not?" Charles asked.

"Right again. Plus, my client's super-seed was less than successful," Tim said. They continued to drink their beer and enjoy the scenery.

~~~

Katie confirmed with Marshall the status of her request for a spore sample. She'd been CC'd on the email request and would now follow up directly. Marshall had no objection. Katie retrieved Patrick Jackson's telephone number and placed the call.

"Patrick here."

"Patrick, Katie Pendleton, how are you?"

"Fine, Katie. Both domestic and foreign sales for our seed have exceeded expectations so I cannot complain." Katie did not respond immediately with glee. Patrick remembered the request for the spore sample and continued . . . "But you are likely calling about the spore sample, are you not?"

"Yes. Yes, I am although that is good news about sales."

"Let's call Jonathan together. Please hold, Katie, while I conference him." Katie heard the beep and then the easy listening music to occupy
~~~

the dead air. She placed the call on speaker and cradled the receiver. She turned to answer an email while Kenny G played in the background. She made a mental note to download some of his music. Timeless, after all.

The call to Jonathan started to ring, Patrick included Katie. She was humming along with Kenny G when she heard Patrick clear his throat. She realized the music had stopped. "Oh . . . sorry. I guess I was mesmerized by your TDM," Katie said, not knowing if it had been one ring or five.

"Not to worry, Katie. You have a lovely humming voice."

"Thank you," Katie said, a little embarrassed. Patrick was about to say something when the phone was answered.

"Mr. Livingston's office."

"Yes, Alice, Patrick Jackson, and Katie Pendleton for Jonathan."

"Mr. Jackson, how nice to hear from you. Please hold for a moment, Jonathan is just finishing a meeting," Alice said. She placed them on hold. Patrick began to chuckle.

"What's so funny?" Katie asked.

"I once asked Jonathan about that phrase *just finishing up a meeting.* Alice seems to say that rather frequently. You see, Secretary of Agriculture historically was a very prestigious position. It still is, except to those in the know."

"I wasn't aware that it no longer held the same reverence," Katie said.

"Jonathan is the sixth cabinet member and eighth in line overall for presidential succession. That sounds rather impressive but since the sixties most cabinet positions have lost power, the president is more concerned about monetary policy and national security."

"I guess that makes economic and global evolutionary sense," Katie said. "But still that doesn't provide any insight into the meaning of the phrase," Katie continued, not fully understanding why Patrick chuckled.

"He's going to the bathroom, Katie," Patrick said. "But now a question for you . . . what is TDM?"

"TDM stands for Time Distraction Music. All the fancy places have it so one doesn't quite remember how long they were left on hold," Katie finished with a pause. "It's what I call it at least."

Patrick chuckled again. "TDM. I like that. I'll have to use it sometime if you don't mind." Katie was about to add a punch line regarding proprietary use when Jonathan joined the call.

"Patrick, Katie, sorry to keep you waiting," Jonathan said. Katie noticed a chuckle in his voice. *The inside joke*, Katie thought.

"If I were a betting man, I would bet that you are both calling to find out the status of the spore sample."

"That's exactly why we're calling, Jonathan. What can you tell us?" Patrick asked.

"I had to ensure a smooth entry, so I cleared this with Customs and Homeland Security. With the potential destructive power of the spore, I wouldn't want any undue complications for Katie, or any of us."

"Thank you. I never considered the possible complications." Katie hadn't either. For her, it begged the question, though: how did Bail get the spore? No one seemed to be aware he was working on it? They must've just mailed it, trusting to luck, and chance.

"We should have the sample to you, Katie, by early next week. I've obtained them from José Quinterro directly," Jonathan said. That concluded the conversation for her. There appeared a momentary pause so Katie excused herself from the call, thanking both Patrick and Jonathan and she resumed her day.

She had a trip planned to Decatur, check on Bail. She had cleared the trip with Marshall . . . sick Uncle. She obviously felt responsible. However, now it became a necessity. She would need his samples and research. Katie called Brad to discuss this.

"Be careful," Brad said. After they disconnected, Brad called Tim and discussed Katie's actions with him. He agreed with Brad's concern and provided Brad with Eli's cell phone number and suggested that he forward it to Katie. He asked that she call Eli and request to view the accident scene.

Katie was just leaving when Charles walked in and introduced himself. They chatted for a while before Katie excused herself. She found

Charles engaging and funny. "Enjoy your trip to bean town." Charles remained in her office at her computer.

"Bean town," Katie mumbled to herself. She left the building for the parking garage. It was then that she started to laugh . . . bean town . . . soybeans . . . Dah!

~~~

Jenny was not going. Knee-deep into another exposé for the *St. Louis Post-Dispatch* and *The Rag*. "Cutting-edge," was how she described it when Lawrence asked.

Katie was leaving St. Louis when she received the text message from Brad. *Eli's number . . . good luck . . . call him, I should have thought to mention.*

"Thank you, luv," Katie responded.
~~~

Chapter Nineteen

In 2011, the Internal Revenue Service reported that $1.1 billion dollars was paid to 172,801 deceased farmers over a six-year period.

Decatur Memorial Hospital
Decatur, Illinois

Bail had been moved from ICU to the fifth floor. He was still under frequent doctor's care and visits, but he was considered *out of the woods*. Stable was what the chart said. Visitors were permitted.

Celeste was all the family Bail had left. She walked onto the floor; stopping at the nurses' station to confirm his room assignment. Celeste had been to the hospital enough times to be annoyed by that one person who seemed to think they knew which room their friend or family member was in, only to find out later, they were discharged the week before. She knocked before entering and walked in.

If possible, Bail looked worse than when she had last seen him. Swelling had gone down some but the blacks and blues, yellows and purples and reds, all had a richer, fuller color to them. In short, Bail looked a mess. He saw Celeste standing in the doorway and tried to smile.

Celeste tried to return his smile, confidence really. She finally walked into the room, up to the bed, where she took Bail's hand, felt a squeeze of his grip, and smiled. Relieved, she sat down and started to talk. Before she knew it, she felt like they were both home talking over coffee.

It was during the conversation with Bail that Celeste informed him that Katie was in town. "She's planning on visiting you." Bail shook his head. He understood what Katie would want. "She and I will come visit you tonight or tomorrow, but I'll definitely see you tonight," she gave Bail a kiss.

~~~

Katie arrived in Forsyth a little after dinnertime. She went straight to the family's house without any detours. She thought about mentioning something to Patrick or emailing Amged but decided against it. *What's the point?* she thought. It was 6:30 p.m. when she walked through the door. Aunt Celeste was there. She stopped after leaving Hickory Point Mall. There was a brief awkward moment that passed quickly.

"I am going to the hospital now for a quick visit with your mother if you'd like to join us," Celeste said.

"Sure. Give me ten minutes." Katie put her travel bag in the bedroom, went to the bathroom to freshen up before joining her mother and aunt in the living room.

They were walking into Room 523 ten minutes later. "Remember, he looks worse than he feels," Celeste said before they entered the room, bringing flowers from the gift shop. Bail was resting a little bit higher in the bed than earlier. *Feeling stronger*, Celeste thought. Katie was prepared for the worst but felt horrible when she actually saw him. She almost dropped the floral arrangement.

"That bad, huh?" Bail said to Katie. His voice sounded relatively strong.

"Bail, I'm sorry. I feel responsible. Everything. South America, this, Joseph, Miguel . . . everything," Katie said, not meaning to be so inclusive.

"Who's Joseph and Miguel?" Fran asked.

"Joseph is a professor at the University of Arkansas who conducted research for us. Miguel worked at a software systems company and moonlighted as an office cleaner. The software system company maintains our network. Miguel worked for the cleaning company that
~~~

cleaned our offices. My office in particular. They're both dead. Both deaths unsolved. Common denominator is me. Bail too." The room got silent.

"Have you gone to the police?" Aunt Celeste asked.

"No. Brad has a client who's a private investigator. He spoke with the Arkansas State Police, St. Louis Police, and Elijah Uhl. No one has anything more than what Elijah has on Bail," Katie said while sitting on one side of Bail with her mother. Aunt Celeste was on the other side holding Bail's hand.

"Have the police been in to interview you?" Katie asked.

"Tomorrow at ten, Investigator Uhl will stop by to ask what I remember. Which is not much, I'm afraid to say." Bail's voice cracked once. Dry. Celeste filled a glass of water for him and helped him drink some.

"Mind if I stop by again?" Katie asked.

"No, not at all. I don't think Uhl will mind either," Bail said. Katie stood up, followed by Fran, to leave.

"We're going to wait outside. When you guys are done, I just need a minute alone with Bail," Katie said.

"Sure." Celeste nodded while Fran and Katie left.

They waited in the overflow room in silence. Katie flipped through a magazine while Fran sat there in silence wondering how her daughter's life had become so complicated. Was she in danger or wasn't she?

Celeste joined them a short time later. Visiting hours were almost at an end. She nodded at Katie. Katie stood up and went to speak with Bail.

"Bail . . . first off, I'm sorry that I got you involved in all of this." Katie tossed her hands up and shook her head from side to side.

"Don't worry about it," Bail said. "There is no way either one of us could have predicted this outcome."

"Bail, I need your research. I am having spore samples sent in and I need to see where you left off. What you have discovered. Joseph left a message on my office voice mail. There was something hidden within the spore."

Bail had always believed that the spore itself was more complicated than complex. The combined gene sequencing was decades ahead of where it should be. In hindsight, he would have approached the problem differently. "My research is stored on the network server. File name is *Montero-spore*. My username is *Bail*. Password is *sunset*. The samples that I have are locked away. Celeste can help you retrieve them and gain access to my office."

"Thanks, Bail. Get well soon and again I'm sorry that I got you involved," Katie left the room and rejoined Celeste and her mother in the waiting room.

"Off to the university?" Fran asked since she was driving.

"Yeah . . . Bail's office."

The drive was another ten minutes. Decatur traffic was light. Fran pulled into Bail's parking space. She, Celeste, and Katie got out. They walked to the door. Celeste used her card key to activate the door lock. They proceeded into the building and up the stairs to Bail's office.

With the information Katie had, she sat in Bail's chair and accessed his computer. She typed in his username and password. She laughed when the homepage/screen background was displayed. "What's so funny?" Aunt Celeste asked.

"Bail's background is a picture of you and him at your sixtieth birthday party," Katie said.

"Well, it is a nice picture."

"I never said it wasn't," Katie responded while she searched for and copied the research files. They were extensive. Bail had been a busy boy. That was a good thing. Katie knew Bail was thorough. Anything he did would have been done correctly and to perfection. Katie checked Bail's emails to ensure nothing was missed. Once everything was copied, she deleted the data from the server per Charles's instructions. It was only a matter of time before somebody looked.

The next step was to find the spore samples that Bail was working with. Again, Katie followed Celeste. Fran walked in confused silence.

They retrieved the samples from the lab and left the building for the parking lot. The driver of the car that had been watching the building activity simply noted the time and number of individuals. He also noted the direction in which the vehicle arrived and departed.

Thankfully the individual had not been paid to think. His instructions were clear. Notify us if a woman driving a Volkswagen Passat enters the building and leaves the building with a package and heads toward Park Place. Fran drove a Ford Edge and did not leave the parking lot with a package. Neither did she head toward Park Place. On the way to Forsyth, it was decided that it would have made more sense to take two cars versus one. It was also determined that it would be a good idea to stop for a beer at the Roadhouse on the way home and catch up on the rest of life's events. *Quae fortuna cessit* . . . fortune favors those who are lucky!

~~~

Katie was back at the hospital by ten o'clock. She arrived early in case Bail had any questions about the evening's adventures, which he did. Having satisfied his curiosity, he and Katie discussed how best to approach the spore research. "As I mentioned, in hindsight I would have attacked this problem in a much more six-dimensional approach."

"I was thinking one-dimensional. Head on, blunt force analysis, which would have worked but for the fact that the spore is more than one dimension. I knew that, by the way, yet I proceeded onward against my better judgment . . . believing that I would save time . . . not lose it."

"Define the problem in arriving at the solution," Katie said. "Don't let the problem define you."

"Research 101. I begin every lecture with that statement. I'm impressed you still remember."

"I'm surprised you didn't," Katie said. Bail smiled.

"I think that whoever designed the spore knew something about multi-gene sequencing. The coincidence is just too high for it to be ignored. Somehow, they have your research papers." Bail paused for a moment while he looked at Katie. "Aside from that, I believe there're only two things to—" Bail's thought was interrupted when Investigator Uhl walked in.

"Mr. Prichard, Investigator Uhl, Elijah Uhl. This must be your daughter."
~~~

"Niece, Katie Pendleton on my spouse's side," Bail offered.

"Katie, Elijah Uhl, I am investigating your uncle's accident."

"Any ideas, any leads?" Katie asked.

"Unfortunately, no, there are none. The vehicle used was reported stolen earlier that morning. When we finally located it later the same day, it'd been wiped clean of fingerprints. Even those of the owner."

"A professional job?" Katie asked.

"It would appear so. We're hoping your uncle will know something that may shed light on the accident. Otherwise we have very little to go on."

"Eyewitnesses? Other drivers? Security cameras from the campus?" Katie inquired.

"There are plenty of eyewitnesses from the fraternity houses. That's how we got the information for the vehicle. Unfortunately, the driver was wearing a ski mask. So there're no descriptions. The other drivers remember things happening very quickly. Glimpses at most. Camera coverage provides partials but not enough to aid in the investigation," Elijah said.

"Any chance I can get a copy of the file including the camera coverage?" Katie asked.

"For what purpose?"

"Prosperity. It's within my right," Katie said.

"Are you an attorney?" Elijah asked.

"I don't need to be one to obtain the records. Would you like for me to engage one?"

"No. I'll give you the records."

"Great. I'll stop by around one o'clock," Elijah looked at Katie before beginning his questioning of Bail.

In the end, though, Bail didn't remember much. The initial shock of the bumper tap was pretty much the extent of it. There were no disgruntled students or jilted lovers. No unresolved faculty quarrels or recent conflicts. No outside research projects that had produced results in conflict with what was promised or desired.

"So this is a case of mistaken identity or a simple random act of violence?" It was Elijah's tone Bail and Katie questioned. "Statistically speaking, both answers are highly unlikely," Elijah looked at Bail and Katie, not believing either one. Call it professional instinct.

"After a number of years, every investigator develops a sixth sense regarding people and their honesty. You two are not being completely honest with me. You both know something and are not saying what. I cannot force you to tell me something that you choose not to. I can only say that it makes my job more difficult when the people I am working with are not being honest with me. I'll have copies of everything and will leave them with your aunt. Here's my card should you remember anything or decide to speak more freely with me." Elijah handed both Bail and Katie his business card. Neither one saying anything other than thank you.

"Don't you think we should've said something?" Bail asked Katie.

"Like what?" Katie asked. Honestly, they both knew there was very little they could say within reason.

"I guess you're right. You can't very well tell someone this may be part of a worldwide terrorist plot involving a biology professor who works at a small Midwestern liberal arts university in a relatively secluded town. It appeals more to the *Penthouse Forum* crowd versus international intrigue." Bail caught Katie looking at him. "You're too young. Print media plus you're a woman," he said while shaking his head.

"I've read *Penthouse Forums.* I just assumed everyone knew they were fake."

Katie visited a little while longer with Bail, discussing research strategy, but when the doctor arrived, Katie excused herself. She stopped at the scene of the accident and looked around, watching traffic flows, before driving to the Civic Center for a copy of the file. She said good-bye to Aunt Celeste before beginning the drive to St. Louis. Traffic permitting, she would have time to visit the gym before dinner and drinks with Brad.

Chapter Twenty

Through the Conservation Reserve Program, signed into law in 1985, farmers are paid not to farm their land. Such contracts are for 10-15 years and the "annual rental payments" are not deemed rental income for federal tax purposes.

Mickey's Place
St. Louis, Missouri

There'd been a change in plans. A romantic dinner for two was replaced by smothered chili cheese fries, cold beer, college basketball, hockey, and cheers every time the Blues had a shot on goal against the Devils. "So how's *the fam?*" Jenny asked.

Mickey's Place, Jenny had been busy doing her own thing. Not everyone can ride the wave of international intrigue and mystery. Some people are destined to be concerned with the mundane. Stock market woes, money supply issues, South China Sea, Russia's Putin, Jenny thought, *how did this world survive?*

"Mom and Dad are fine. Michelle's Michelle. Aunt Celeste was upset, and Bail was a facial rainbow of colors. He's well on his way to being Bail," Katie finished. The room chose that moment to erupt.

"You okay, babe?" Brad asked.

"I was thinking just the two of us," Katie said.

"Still haven't figured us out yet, have you, Brad?" Jenny said. Lawrence and Tim walked in. Mickey chose that moment to stop by and say hello.

"Helllooo," Mickey bellowed. There being one combined hello for the five of them.

"Mick, how are ya?" Jenny asked.

"I'm doing well, lass," Mickey joined their table to talk sports with everyone. SLU was having another good year and looking to make a meaningful tournament run. When the conversation ended, Mickey left everyone to their entrées, which were quality black Angus beef served medium rare. Mickey's famous twice-baked potato, sautéed broccoli with almond slices, and crisp snow peas were the sides. They opted for the garden salad versus the minestrone soup. Everything was served family style.

Tim was not joining them for dinner, but he was included in the beer and conversation. "Katie, thank you for the copy of Bail's accident report and campus video. I'll follow up, but I don't expect anything to come of this from the police standpoint."

"How about Joseph? Anything further on that?" Katie asked.

Tim started to shake his head no. He'd read some of the initial emails and text messages provided by Randolph and knew that there'd been a fling. *It happens,* Tim thought. He wasn't judging. "No, Katie, no new developments. They're likely won't be either. I'll follow up with Randolph and Eli," Tim looked at his watch. "Thanks for the beer. Let's meet in your office Sunday ten o'clock. Charles will be done by then, okay?"

"Yea, ten's good," Katie said. She looked at Brad, who nodded.

Tim left. Jenny looked over at Katie and noticed how tired she looked. Stress does that to a person. Her next exposé.

~~~

Villazón, Bolivia

The drive from General Güemes, Argentina to Villazón, Bolivia took close to fifteen hours. It was a very scenic route. The countryside was nothing short of beautiful. Larry was thankful he was in a Jeep. Some
~~~

of the roads were less than passable. Prior to their leaving, José had couriered a couple of unregistered handguns. A note was attached: *Even though my counterpart Manuel Dominquez has been advised of your presence, some of the locals may still find you objectionable. Sorry!*

Larry accepted the handguns in the manner in which they were given . . . a gift of safety. Although he was *rated* in small arms fire, Larry was not a marksman by any stretch of the imagination. He showed Melina the basics—safety, chamber, point/aim, shoot. Trusting that self-defense would not be required.

Crossing the border was a nonevent. There were no checkpoints for passports. There were no signs at all. Larry was curious how a Bolivian would feel about driving through the cement jungles of American cities, the great expanse and openness of the Midwest, or the subterranean transportation networks in the larger cities. Would they wonder and question "how do these people do this?" He knew that it was a lifestyle. A heritage. It was not something easily acquired.

Larry was curious when he came to Argentina. He had not traveled much as a child or young adult. What would the accommodations be like? Food? Water? Honestly it was no different than America. Even the smaller, rural communities were modern. He'd given Villazón very little thought along those lines.

The city of Villazón has a population of 37,000. Larry was easy to spot even with his tan skin. Melina too. Her soft appearance and features profiled her a foreigner, not a local. Larry drove through town spotting the bed-and-breakfast. But first, they would check in with the local police, Manuel's suggestion. "This way the police chief can get the word out that you're a friend and not to be bothered."

Larry felt like an outlaw riding into town on his horse. He stopped at the sheriff's office . . . *Just pass'n through, Sheriff. I'm not look'n fur any trouble.*

When they stopped in front of the police station, Larry wasn't overly surprised to see three sets of eyes on him and Melina.

"Chief Martinez?" Larry said.

Two men continued looking straight ahead but the junior-looking officer betrayed the chief's trust. A stern lesson in "chicken" was in order. Knowing that he was busted by his own deputy, Martinez spoke up. Larry responded and asked to go inside. Martinez hesitated, but relented.

"What can I do for you?" Martinez casually asked. Larry produced his cell phone and hit Send. Manuel answered on the third ring. Larry spoke flawless Spanish Bolivian, already becoming familiar with the local accent. After a short conversation he handed the phone to Martinez, who reluctantly accepted it.

As Minister of Rural Development and Land, Manuel Dominguez was used to people doing what he asked of them. He anticipated that his conversation with Martinez would be short. It was. Martinez's demeanor and overall posture changed immediately. He simply handed the phone back to Larry after contributing maybe two words to a three-minute conversation. Larry said, "Thank you, Manuel," and ended the telephone call.

Martinez looked at Larry, nodded, got up, and walked out of the police station with Larry and Melina in tow. He looked at his deputies and told them in no uncertain terms, "*Estos dos deben ser dejados solos y no molestados. Proporcionarles siempre cortesía preguntó.*" (These two are to be left alone and not bothered. Provide them every courtesy asked.) Martinez looked at Larry and nodded. Larry thanked Martinez and extended his hand, a gesture of goodwill. Martinez accepted it graciously.

Before leaving the police station, Larry inquired to the quality of the bed-and-breakfast and he asked about the broker Paulo Perez. Martinez informed Larry that Paulo could be found at the airport day and night. Larry and Melina got into the Jeep and drove the three blocks to the bed-and-breakfast. They grabbed their belongings from the Jeep and walked inside.

The owner was on the telephone when they entered. *Martinez,* thought Larry. The señorita was looking right at him. They casually walked up to the front desk. Larry completed the folio handed to him by the desk clerk. The phone call and folio were completed at the exact same time. She took the folio and accepted payment. Larry booked the room for three nights, Mr. and Mrs. Seabreeze.

The room was relatively large and nicely furnished. In the States, such decoration with folk art would be considered rustic. In Bolivia, this was clearly the honeymoon suite. Larry and Melina showered prior to dinner.

"When are we ever going to be back in Bolivia again?" Larry said. Melina laughed. They toured the town and surrounding area. There were some nice shops that they visited. A local clothing store had some attractive local apparel that one would never find on the runways of New York, Paris, or Milan. Larry convinced Melina to try on several of the dresses and tops. He particularly liked the dresses and purchased two. They found a top that they both liked. It was really more of a shawl. Both the dress and top were traditional clothing for Bolivian women. "Wear one," Larry asked.

"If you help me change, I will," Melina said playfully. Playfully or not, Larry prided himself on never having to be asked twice.

~~~

The evening went well. Dinner was good. They shared a small pot of chuño, which is a dried potato stew, and salteñas, meat turnovers. Both delicious. The drinks were refreshing, and the dancing was exciting. A prelude to nighttime maneuvers.

It was obvious from the looks that everyone in town had been warned to leave them alone. Larry was thankful for Manuel's involvement.

~~~

Morning came and the sunrise over the countryside was breathtaking. Larry and Melina woke early and were downstairs for coffee and a traditional Bolivian breakfast, a local cereal grain—quinoa. After finishing, they returned to the room to freshen up before driving to the airport to meet with Paulo. The police captain had left a message confirming that Paulo would be available.

~~~
~~~

Bolivia is a land-locked country bordered by five separate countries. It is hilly if not mountainous. Villazón is located in the southern portion of the country just north of the Argentinean border. The Valles, a local nickname, is a relatively flat section of Bolivia, encompassing an area of gentle rolling hills and broad valleys filled with grassland and farms. It provides its own beauty with clear blue skies intermixed with rugged mountains and lush green grasslands.

The airport was three miles outside of town. On the drive, Larry and Melina watched a falcon soaring freely on top of the thermals. At points in time, the bird of prey appeared to be hovering above a particular spot . . . had it spotted its prey?

Reaching the airport, Larry approached the least dilapidated-looking building. His first thought was of government stability. One may not like the current regime but at least there was stability. Melina caught the look on his face . . . "What are you thinking, honey?"

"Just about things I have taken for granted," Larry said. He smiled at Melina and squeezed her hand. "C'mon," they hopped out of the Jeep and walked to the office.

The inside was a little nicer. The furnishings were comfortable in appearance. They were old but well preserved and maintained. The furniture consisted of a desk, chairs, and tables. In most other countries these would be considered antiques. Valuable items to the right buyer. Here it was furniture that served a purpose. Functional. Not feng shui.

The standing fans and ceiling fans were designed to circulate the air so that it did not get stale. The fact that the temperature felt cool was strictly a bonus. There was the occasional flypaper hanging from the ceiling. Some had been there so long, Larry noticed that they had become decorations. Looking around the room, he finally settled his gaze on a gentleman he assumed was Paulo.

Paulo was sitting in the chair behind the desk, watching both Larry and Melina. He surveyed the room. He'd expected someone to enter his office asking questions . . . just not these two someone's. After the story broke, it was only a matter of time. They didn't look imposing, yet Martinez was quite clear: "Help them out . . . or else." In all of Paulo's years of service, he had never once heard Martinez utter a threat.

Larry and Melina approached the only other person in the building. They walked over while Larry casually looked for exit signs and doors. Curious if they would be joined by others. Seeing none, he walked up and introduced himself and Melina.

"Paulo Perez, my name is Larry Seabreeze, this is my associate, Melina Mendez," Larry said. "Mr. Martinez said you might be able to help us."

"*Sí*, I can help you. What is it you wish to know?" Larry looked at Melina and smiled.

"May we sit down?"

"*Sí* . . . please sit."

"Paulo, I am interested in some planes you recently sold. It may have been five to six months ago. You sold between four to seven planes . . . crop dusters. I am interested in who you sold them to," Larry asked.

"It was seven. I brokered the whole deal. Four here and three through my brother in Villa Montes. The buyer was Middle Eastern. A Saudi Arabian named Ibn Saud."

"Did you have dealings with him before or after this transaction?" Larry asked.

Paulo understood why Martinez liked this guy. He seemed to be a good man, unassuming, nonthreatening; though he had a sense of urgency. You could feel it in the air around him.

"No," Paulo said while shaking his head. "That was the only time that I had what he wanted . . . what he needed."

Larry frowned and looked down at the floor underneath his feet. No way a Saudi would come here, Larry thought. "The only time? There have been other times when you have had opportunities?"

"Some, not many."

"Have there been any opportunities since the sale of the seven planes?" Larry asked. Paulo hesitated . . . the moment of truth.

Larry understood people and their body language. Paulo would tell Larry anything and everything he wanted to know, provided he asked the right questions.

"*Sí*. There has been one time. Three months ago Saud contacted me. His client was looking for larger planes. He asked me, but I think it was only a courtesy."

"Larger planes? How large?" Larry asked.

"DC-9s, 737s."

"How many?" Larry asked, trying to remember anything he could about the DC-9 and 737. One might have been a turboprop, the other a jet. Both approximately the same size.

"Saud was looking for three or four. But others were also looking for similar planes about the same time."

"Multiple brokers to hide the actual number being purchased," Melina said.

"That would be my guess," Larry glanced at her.

"Paulo, would you know if the order was filled?"

"*Sí*, I believe it was. It got quiet."

"Can you confirm that for me? Can you contact Saud and tell him you have four DC-9s if he's still interested?" It was clearly a request and Paulo was going to do it. That much was a certainty.

"*Sí*. It may take a day or two," Paulo said while Larry's eyes looked around the room a little more closely.

"How do you contact Saud?" Larry asked. They were literally out in the middle of nowhere. *Carrier pigeons*, Larry thought, almost laughing to himself.

"Satellite. I'll send an email," Paulo produced a laptop. His cell phone was next to it.

"Would you know who the ultimate buyer is?" Larry asked. Paulo didn't answer but only shook his head from side to side while he sent the email.

"Will he suspect anything?" Melina asked.

"No. Sometimes the merchandise is not to the buyer's liking so they need others. We will find out when he answers."

"Where do you normally find such planes?" Melina asked. She realized people love to talk and show what they know.

"They are in old rundown airports like mine," Paulo said before adding, "Come. Let's take a walk." He stood up and led them out of the building through the backdoor Larry'd missed.

It was not until they were outside that both Larry and Melina noticed how dark it had been inside. No lights. Windows only. Larry shielded his eyes and squinted until his pupils dilated. Melina donned a pair of sunglasses. Paulo simply laughed.

They walked down the grass runway past one hangar after another. Four in total. The physical structures were in desperate need of repair yet would likely survive the next few storm seasons simply because they had to . . . needed to . . . the owners could not afford to repair them.

Each of the four hangars held small single-engine airplanes. Some in better shape than others. There was a class system within Bolivia. The elite class owned the better planes clearly. The cholo's shared their planes with others to help defray the overall expense.

Larry noticed a plane in the last hangar that was sitting low to the ground. He looked at Paulo then up to the sky, where he saw several birds soaring ever so freely. He smiled and walked toward the hangar. He passed Paulo and mumbled, "A Glide-Mor out here?"

Paulo and Melina followed Larry into the hangar. The glider was well-maintained. Easily the best-maintained plane Larry had seen since landing in South America.

"You fly?" Paulo asked.

"Yea," Larry said with a smile. "My grandfather lived in a small town outside of St. Louis, Missouri . . . Highland, Illinois. Highland is a traditional small rural town. He lived in a brick house on Zschokke Street past the town's water tower. There was a local airport outside of town with a grass runway similar to yours. I believe it was called Highland-Winet Airport." There was a simple pause. "They had a glider club. I spent a summer there and my grandfather took me to the airport once," Larry chuckled slightly.

The smile on Larry's face was apparent while he walked down memory lane. It was priceless, Melina thought. She noticed that Paulo felt the same joy that Larry did about flying. Paulo was walking down his own memory lane as Larry told his story.

"Anyway," Larry continued with a wave of his hand, "my grandfather had some business or some such to take care of. He repaired antique clocks. While my grandfather conducted his business with the owner of the airport, one of the guys took me for a flight. I had such a good time I got my license before the end of the summer."

"You still fly?" Paulo asked.

"Yes," Larry produced his license.

"Please . . . take her up," Paulo said, pointing to both Melina and the glider.

"Are you serious?" Larry asked.

"I insist," Paulo said.

Larry looked at Melina. "I can't explain it, babe, so you're gonna have to trust me. It's the closest thing to that—Larry pointed at the falcons circling overhead—as one can get."

~~~

Melina looked afraid but shook her head and said, "Okay." Thirty minutes later the tether from the pull plane was released and Larry and Melina were gliding. Melina was up front and had the view of her lifetime. They circled, climbed, banked, rolled, and looped before landing. Larry was certain Melina's yells were of joy and not screams of fear and terror. They landed after a good two hours of glide time.

Paulo met them at the runway. Larry landed and coasted to the last hangar. They were both standing next to the glider when Paulo showed up. All three of them pushed the glider back into the hangar, where Larry did his post-flight inspection of the glider with Paulo's oversight. When completed, both Larry and Melina thanked Paulo.

They were walking toward the parking lot in relative silence when Larry spoke. "When we were landing, I noticed some abandon planes sitting out back."

"Yes, our boneyard."

"Are any of those planes the one's previously sold to Saud?" Larry asked.

Paulo looked at Larry, over toward the abandoned planes, down at the ground before looking back. He was embarrassed because he liked Larry and Melina. He was embarrassed even though he wasn't privy to Jericho. He was embarrassed because he always had that suspicion—that
~~~

sixth sense and feeling of distrust—but a dollar is a dollar in any country. He looked Larry in the eye, "*Sí*, two are."

"Where are the other five?" Melina asked.

"Destroyed, I believe. These two I kept."

"Why?" Larry asked.

"Greed . . . to sell them again."

"Can we see them?" Melina inquired. Paulo extended his hand toward the boneyard, "Sure."

They walked over to the boneyard. Some of the planes were well past their functional years and appeared to have been cannibalized for parts. However, the two planes in question were under a tarp, removed from the elements. Larry looked at the plane and asked, "Have they been dusted for prints?"

"No. Never even considered," Paulo answered. Larry was walking away from the plane. He checked his watch for the time and called Reynolds, Matthew would be at the reception.

"Reynolds."

"Robert, Larry here."

"Larry, you understand that this line is not secure."

"Understood. Sir, I have in my possession two of the seven planes I believe were used in the incident. I need to dust them for prints. What is your recommendation?" There was a very slight hesitation.

"I would agree. The likelihood is we'll retrieve nothing; however, if we don't dust, there will be a veritable treasure trove of information lost to Murphy's Law. I'll send you a kit. Good work, Larry. Field work becomes you," Reynolds disconnected the call, recognizing like Matthew's that Larry was a natural.

Larry rejoined Paulo and Melina. "We will be back in a couple of days after I receive the necessary equipment," Larry looked at Paulo. "Care to join us for dinner tonight?"

"Ah . . . tonight is the festival. We will all be dining tonight. I invite you to sit at my table. It will be in front of the dress shop, maybe you have seen it?" Paulo asked. Larry and Melina both blushed.

"*Sí*, I think I know which one," Larry answered.

"What is the festival?" Melina inquired. Curious if she should wear one of the more traditional dresses Larry had purchased for her.

"It is Alasitas . . . Bolivia's festival of small wishes." Paulo began. "The entire town will be dancing tonight. We celebrate together. The festival is religious and one that includes local Andes tradition."

Bolivian's celebrate Alasitas annually. Each town may celebrate it on a different day but most towns will conduct their individual celebration between the third week in January to the second week in February. Villazón celebrated Alasitas in February.

Franciscans focus on the Virgin while the *yatiris* (local shamans) focus on the Andean God Ekeko. The typical Bolivian cares about both equally.

The festival involves one's dreams. You buy or create a reasonable facsimile of your dream. This facsimile is blessed by a local priest and offered to the God of Plenty, Ekeko, with the hope that your dream will come true. El Mercado de las Brujas, the Witches' Market, is where one goes to buy their dream. Stalls and shops are filled with miniature items, cars, cameras, toys, euro notes, dollars, versus the local bolivianos currency. The key to this tradition is that someone, a particular someone, should purchase Ekeko for you. One should not buy their own Ekeko statue. Melina and Larry left the airport hoping to have enough time to visit the Witches' Market.

~~~

The main dish served this evening was *mondongo*, which was a spicy pork dish with rice, potatoes, and corn (*choclo*). The traditional drink served was *chicha*, a fermented drink made from corn. Larry had three, given the drink was served in a scooped-out pineapple. Melina found the *singani* more to her liking. The white grape crop was particularly good this year.

The entire festival was enjoyable. Melina shared her pictures and video with the group. Paulo was amazed. He had never performed a loop in a glider nor was he familiar with anyone who had. He was
~~~

equally amazed at how Larry was able to fly inverted. He asked if Larry could show him, which was understood.

Paulo's daughter flashed both Larry and Melina a discerning glance regarding their earlier afternoon shopping habits. The look was a reflection more of their obvious feelings toward each other rather than a questioning one of morality. In the end, all had a pleasant and enjoyable festival. When the evening transformed to dancing and music, Melina and Larry sat back and watched for a while before joining the group. The festival continued into the wee hours. Larry and Melina shared their dreams with each other later that night . . . a miniature plastic baby girl and a ring. Another festival in the making, it would appear.

~~~

The adage that time flies when you're having fun is true. The festival and the glider instructions were enjoyable and seemed like ancient history. The DHL package was promised, delivered, and on time. Melina and Larry found themselves back at the airport by midday. Three days in a row. With the portable fingerprint kit in hand, Larry went to work on obtaining the latent fingerprints.

There were two things Larry expected—either a treasure trove of fingerprints or a complete wipe-down. Unfortunately, Larry would have to dust the entire plane, inside and out. Doors, handles, wing handles, fuel caps, headsets, tanks, controls, seats . . . everything would be dusted for perspiration and body oil from individual fingertips. Larry was hoping the individuals would not have been using gloves, although that was a dangerous hope. *Live in hope, die in despair*, Larry mumbled to himself. He did not realize that Melina was standing behind him . . . "Is everything okay, honey?" she asked.

"Sorry, sweetheart, I was talking to myself. "*Vivir en la esperanza, morir en la desesperación*, is an American adage."

Dusting for fingerprints makes the perspiration and finger oils become visible. With an adhesive, the chemical used to "dust" for prints aids in helping to lift the fingerprint from the contact point.

When dusting for fingerprints, one is looking for matches . . .
~~~

minutiae. The lifted finger print hopefully will contain ridge lines within the lifted print. Breaks. Ends. The identified fingerprints are compared to rolled prints in a forensic exercise that hopefully will result in a correct identification. In this case . . . of the terrorist.

"How's it going?" Melina asked.

"Not like I would have thought. I've retrieved some fingerprints from key parts of the plane. Three separate prints from the gas cap; one from the wing handhold; four from the interior."

"Is that good?" Melina asked.

"It's eight more than I expected. Once complete, I'll send these back to Washington with the plane identification number. The fingerprints will be compared against those currently on file. Hopefully we'll match a name to the print," Larry added a smile. He wished there were something Melina could do versus sit and wait.

It took over seven hours to dust both planes for fingerprints. The task was tedious, persnickety given my novice status. One an expert would have completed the in substantially less time. Larry was thorough but lacked experience, which simply added to the time. In the end, the task was completed, and twenty-two separate prints were obtained. The individual who had cleaned the second plane was less than thorough. Larry and Melina said good-bye to Paulo. They would not be going to Villa Montes. They would leave in the morning after DHL arrived for the package. Larry would send an email to Matthew and Reynolds, alerting them of the package's ETA.

"Still no word from Saud?" Melina asked Paolo. Phew! Larry knew he was forgetting something.

"No. Nothing. Not to worry, he'll respond." Paulo commented as they exchanged good-byes.

Melina drove back to the bed-and-breakfast. Larry's eyes hurt from squinting. She had no problem driving a manual transmission. Clutch, shift, release; it was just like her father taught her. "It's seems easier than when I first learned how."

Melina parked in the dirt and gravel parking lot of the bed-and-breakfast. She and Larry went inside and placed the package in their room. There was nothing to do between now and noon tomorrow except say good-bye to Martinez and enjoy the day, evening, and morning, which they did.

~~~

The DHL driver was there at exactly twelve o'clock. Larry handed the driver the package and received his receipt. "It's a beautiful thing," Larry said. Matthew and Reynolds had both responded positively with his success. Now it was a simple return trip to Argentina with a stop at the Quinterro's ranch, the University of Rosario, and then Buenas Aries, where he planned on relaxing for a few days before the return flight to the States.

Larry and Melina passed the police station where they waved their final good-byes to the chief and deputies when a red pickup truck skidded to a halt directly in their path. They came to an abrupt stop just shy of an accident. Dust billowed from the skid. Paulo jumped out of his vehicle. Martinez stood at the site of Paulo's truck. He stepped down off the porch and walked over to the two vehicles.

With paper in hand, Paulo was excited. He slowed down when he saw Larry. "My friend . . . Saud responded," Paulo handed the paper to Larry. Larry took the paper and looked over at Martinez and then at Melina. He smiled. He read the email to everyone present.

"This is great news. Saud needs two planes," Larry handed the email back to Paulo. They stood there for a moment. Dust settling. The email had been read. Understood. Digested. Silence. Eyes fell on Larry.

Time was critical. Two planes were needed. *They must be ready for a long flight. Extra fuel tanks a must,* the email said. Paulo needed to respond today for pick-up the day after tomorrow. Larry reached for his phone and called Matthew.

"Matthew here."

"Matthew, Larry here, listen, we got a big break. Paulo, the broker of the first set of planes, sent out an email to the buyer, Ibn Saud. Saud had been looking for larger planes a few months ago. On a whim, I asked Paulo to confirm that the order was filled. Saud responded that he needs two more planes day after tomorrow with extra fuel tanks. Sir, I
~~~

believe China is their next target. Can we supply Paulo with two DC-9s stripped down to their green state and outfitted with fuel tanks?" Larry asked. Matthew paused, still amazed that Larry had succeeded so well.

"I'll check here and suggest you do the same. Call me back in an hour." Larry didn't hesitate. He called José and explained the same thing.

"*Sí*, I can get you those two planes and land them there tomorrow," José said.

"Done," Larry didn't wait the hour and called Matthew back immediately.

"We're going with José Quinterro. He'll have the planes here tomorrow," Larry looked at Melina and smiled. "We're staying!" They drove back to the bed-and-breakfast and extended their stay three more days.

~~~

Two planes landed. The pilots taxied to the boneyard. Larry, Melina, and Paulo walked over to the boneyard and met the pilot and copilot of both planes. They were all talking when a third plane landed and stopped next to the fuel truck. The pilot got out and walked over to the group.

"José," Larry extended his hand.

"You have been productive, my friend," José said.

"Your boss, Sheffield, is ecstatic at what you have accomplished in the field. He said for me to tell you that you are a natural."

"Well, thank you, but let's get this case averted before we start celebrating," Larry said.

"I see you've met Gabriel and Edwin."

"Yes. We were just talking about what they've done to the planes when you landed." They both turned back to the DC-9s. Gabriel instructed Paulo on what he believed he would need to know. Paulo was a quick study and felt comfortable with the planes. When that was done, they returned to Paulo's office.

"So what are you thinking, Larry?" Gabriel asked.
~~~

"I presume you are all leaving."

"Like you, we do not look Bolivian and would be hard to explain," Gabriel answered.

"Did you bring what I asked?" Larry looked at José.

"*Sí*. It's in the airplane."

"Perfect. They are supposed to be here at ten o'clock. I was going to have Paulo take Melina and me up in his glider. From there, we'll provide additional surveillance. Rolling hills and such would make for too little ground cover. I was planning on setting up the motion-sensitive cameras where they can provide head and facial photographs. Paulo will have three armed men with him as before. I think that that should work. What are your thoughts?" Larry looked to Gabriel and Edwin and then back again to Gabriel.

"I think that would be sufficient. Let's set up the cameras and show you how to use them. Paulo, I would have five armed men this time. They will not be surprised by the three." Paulo nodded. Everyone got up and walked over to José's plane and took out the equipment. Gabriel and Edwin went about the task of setting up the cameras. They set them inside steel drums and placed them back so that they could not be seen. Three more were placed by the last hangar and the plane closest to the DC-9s.

"There is nothing to do but collect the chip after the planes have left. The hardware you can keep. The batteries will last several years. They're solar charged," Gabriel said.

José instructed Larry and Melina on the use and power of the camera that he had for them. It was a Canon Powershot SX50SH. Unfortunately neither were shutterbugs. Thankfully the camera was fully automatic. Literally point and shoot. There were three lenses provided. Two telescopic lenses and one standard. "Practice today, tomorrow . . . tonight," José said with a smile.

"You'll be taking the photographs, Melina," Larry said.

"I guess we'll practice today, tomorrow . . . tonight," she said.

José also had some intimidating firearms for Paulo and his friends. He produced two M16A4 rifles. He also had one Kar-98 sniper rifle. Paulo graciously accepted them. The job being complete on their part, José, Gabriel, and Edwin wished everyone good luck before they returned to the air and Argentina.

Once everything was set up, there was nothing else to do but hurry up and wait. They discussed everything over dinner. Paulo, Martinez, Melina, Larry, and five deputies all had their assignments. They were not anticipating trouble; however, they were prepared to prevent it from happening should the buyer feel the need. "Better to show force and not need it than need it and not have it," Martinez commented before they ended the evening and parted ways.

Chapter Twenty-one

A quarter of U.S. jobs will be severely disrupted as artificial intelligence, AI, accelerates.

St. Louis, Missouri

Sunday at 9:30 a.m. Katie entered her office. She and Brad had stopped for bagels, cream cheese, and a white fish spread. Katie was thankful that St. Louis had a large Jewish community. Decatur didn't and people in Forsyth likely couldn't spell the word *Jewish.* Not a sin in and of itself but it did translate into poor if not sub-par bagels.

"Hard crust on the outside, soft hot tender middle inside, is an art-form that people of the Jewish persuasion have imbedded into their DNA. Not to stereotype . . . just stating a fact," Katie smothered her plain bagel with whitefish spread. French roast hazelnut coffee to complement. Brad chose a plain bagel, cream cheese, and coffee black.

Tim and Charles had been waved through security. "A-list," Charles said when he passed the guard, who laughed. Arriving at the floor for Feldman & Company, they walked into Katie's office and joined Brad and her for bagels and coffee.

Good mornings exchanged, bagels offered, coffee provided. They sat and talked for a bit before getting down to the purpose of the meeting.

"I would estimate three to four weeks," Charles started off the conversation. "Your emails and telephone calls have been monitored."

"By whom? Do you know?" Katie asked.

"No, we don't," Tim said. "But let's hold off any questions until the end. Charles, you need to organize your thoughts and explanation of the facts, hold the dramatics until after we're done. Can you?" Charles tried to look hurt but couldn't quite pull it off.

"Okay," he said. "What I did was review the system configuration for deviations. None were noted, but that does not mean there are none. I did the analysis on the server and individual desktops. I also looked at the communication between the server and the desk tops, electronic speed. I found no known discrepancies." Charles took a sip of coffee before continuing. Katie seemed to be smiling slightly, Charles noted.

"So then I actually looked for discrepancies, I found several." The smiles turned to confused-looking frowns, Charles noted. "The difference is the hidden spyware programs on the server, your desktop, and Marshall's. These guys are good. Their spyware runs with its own platform. Inferior spyware utilizes the hosts existing platform. If you have laptops or a smartphone, it's likely on those." Charles noticed that Katie jumped at the suggestion of spyware.

"Katie, I noticed your desktop is on. Can you go to the C Drive for me, please?" Charles nodded Katie acquiesced. "Look down the list of folders for one titled *Notify Me*. Do you see it?"

"No," Katie said.

"That's because it is hidden. If you could, search for *Notify Me*." While she did so, Charles took a bite of his poppy seed bagel with chive cream cheese. Katie waited until Charles was done before saying, "Found it." She swiveled her monitor for everyone to see.

"Now if you could . . ."

Charles got up and walked around Katie's desk. He moved to the keyboard. Katie surmised his intention and moved out of the way. He typed quickly on the keyboard and the screen popped up 7 hidden folders and 328 hidden files. He returned to his seat and sat down.

"Marshall's desktop is the same. Did you bring your laptop?"

"Yes." Katie handed it to Charles. "The server has twelve folders that are hidden. The additional ones are for remote access, primary access, administration, and the other two I believe are for communication for other nonprimary users." Charles flipped the laptop around so Katie could see that it had also been infected. Charles returned to his coffee and said nothing.

"That's it?" Katie said after several moments of silence. Charles feigned indignation at Katie's comment.

"What, were you expecting . . . show tunes?"

"Well, no. Honestly I'm not certain what I was expecting."

"Good. Then I have performed my job admirably and have met or exceeded all of your objectives and expectations," Charles said. Again there was silence.

"If I were bidding on the job, I would tell you that the system installed is adequate for your needs. The company, Office Solutions, is doing an adequate job. They are, however, charging twice what you are getting. I could do this job for half and still be overcharging you. Yet I could give you more bells and whistles than you are currently getting." Again there was a pause. "Was that more of what you were expecting? By the way, I could even bore you with details . . . but I won't."

"No . . . I'm sorry . . . I just . . . I just don't know what I was thinking . . . expecting," Katie said.

"So wait a minute," Brad said. "You haven't deleted the spyware program?"

"Yeah, that's right! Why are they still there?" Katie leaned forward in her chair. She felt the pinch in her neck and waist and almost laughed. *Old age*, she thought. She was easily the youngest person in the room by half.

"I thought that that was what we were here to discuss," Charles said. His deadpan poker face caused Tim to laugh and Katie and Brad to fall farther down the rabbit hole, lost in confusion.

"What?" Katie asked.

"That's why we're here," Charles said.

"Katie, Brad, we need to discuss our options regarding the spyware," Tim looked at both parties before continuing to resuscitate their thought process.

"If we remove the programs, the recipient would know that we discovered their existence and assume we notified the police. That would ensure they get away unharmed or alternatively move Katie up the ladder and risk assessment food chain," Tim said.

"Agreed?" he asked.

Katie and Brad had both recovered nicely. Benefit to age and experience. "The other alternative is to feed them false information and try and flush them out. That is risky because we are not equipped to respond to anything overt."

Tim refilled his coffee and grabbed another bagel with cream cheese versus butter this time. He was fortunate in that he didn't seem to gain weight. When he sat back down, he added a third option. "We could just do nothing and see if they try and determine what's what."

"That could also be risky," Brad said.

"Maybe not so. They likely expect dormancy since Joseph and Miguel are dead and Bail's injured," Katie offered, all eyes were on her. She went to take a sip of coffee before realizing what was unspoken. The cup made it to her lips before returning to her desk. "That just leaves me."

"Yea," Tim said while shaking his head.

"Wait a minute," Brad began. "You can't use Katie to flush out some terrorist, she's not bait."

"It's already been done by Katie," Charles responded.

"What do you . . ." Katie stopped, she understood. "The samples . . ." Her voice trailed off.

"Yes again, Katie. The request for samples. It's likely they deem you a threat. We don't know so please be careful," Tim added.

"Can't we trace them?" Brad turned to look at Katie. She mumbled something barely audible.

"What was that babe?" Brad asked. Quietly Katie looked up. Her face was void of color.

"…my h-i-t and-nd run..." she stammered.

"Yes" Tim quickly said having remembered his open item list. He handed her a fresh cup of coffee…hot…black. Katie took a sip, reflex.

"A few weeks ago, my drive to work, someone hit the left front of my car. I was forced into the other lane of traffic." Katie's began to rethink the incident for what it may have been.

"The truck in the lane adjacent to mine had room so they were able to avoid hitting me. I filed a police report but no one got the license plate number of the car. Insurance fixed the damage…I thought nothing more of it…rush hour..." Katie finished feeling more shaken than before.

"I'll check with the local and State Police on the accident report," Tim said to a quiet room. He looked at Charles and nodded. Charles began with hopefully mood changing news.

"As a courtesy to Tim, I installed a trailer program to monitor outgoing data dumps and remote access usage. I'll be alerted if and when it's activated. I've tried to adjust my trailer to mirror that of the lead in the hope it will penetrate the firewalls of the gatekeeper and dark web virtual highway they're using," Charles said.

"There's another option," Tim said. "Find another researcher and set them up with proper protection." The look from the room said it all NWM . . . *no way, man.*

"When will you get the samples?" Brad asked. His voice sounded concerned. Tim was happy for his friend. Too bad about the age difference.

"Early this week," Katie said. Meeting ending.

"Think about your options," Tim and Charles left first. Katie and Brad sat in silence before leaving.

~~~

Katie returned to the condo looking more stressed than ever. "Katie, what's wrong" Jenny asked. She and Brad sat down.

"What? Oh nothing. I'm all right," Katie said. "We may want to keep the curtains and blinds closed to provide the shooter with less of a target. Or should I just wear red with a bull's-eye painted on my shirt." Katie and Brad both tried to laugh. Jenny stared blankly at them.

"I'm sorry, Jenny. I'm being melodramatic."

"Meeting with Charles and Tim didn't go well, I take it?"

"No, it went well. I just thought that it would end there or solve something."
~~~

“Neither,” Jenny questioned?

“You are correct, Jenny,” Brad brought out two coffee cups and a fresh pot of coffee.

“So what’s the verdict?” Jenny asked.

“Charles found seven hidden spyware programs on my computer and Marshall’s. There are several more on the company server. He hasn’t deleted them in case we want to notify the authorities or try and flush out the terrorist,” Katie said nonchalantly.

“Flush out? Who are you now, Nancy Drew?” Jenny questioned. “Why not just delete the programs and be done with it?” Silence.

Brad finally spoke . . . “that’s an option and one we obviously discussed. Unfortunately, that would close the book on Miguel and Joseph’s murders plus the attempt on Bail. Is that what we want?”

“No. Of course not, but I don’t want my sister added to the list,” Jenny said, knowing full well she’d painted herself into a corner with no window or door in sight.

“There has to be a way to accomplish both,” she continued.

“How?” Katie asked. “Besides, I’m likely already on their list… remember the hit and run?”

Jenny hesitated before responding. She looked at Katie. The seemingly innocent incident returned to memory.

“You aren’t seriously thinking of playing the target . . . are you? The hit and run was your only break.”

“I’m not really thinking anything right now, but I’ll let you know.” Katie got up and walked to her room. “I’m tired. I think I’ll lie down.” She left the door open. Brad joined her.

Jenny sat there before going to work. “You better let me know,” she mumbled.

~~~
~~~

Villazón, Bolivia

They arrived at the airport early. Larry brought thermoses filled with strong coffee. Martinez brought quinoa. After everyone was ready and awake, Larry, Martinez, and Paulo walked around the hangars and planes. They'd worked out a reasonable plan. Everyone was informed of their individual responsibility.

Hector was carrying the KAR 98 sniper rifle. He was the best shot and would be hiding in the hills and low underbrush. He attached a high-powered scope to the rifle.

Martinez would stand with Paulo. He would be armed with a pump-action shotgun and a handgun. Melina and Larry would be up in the glider. Four other hombres were stationed around the planes in relative plain sight. Two were armed with the M16A4s provided by José while the other two had early-edition AK-47s. It was the best they could do.

They were all standing, waiting. No one said much, each in their own thoughts, hoping, praying that this went smoothly. That no one got hurt. Larry was the first and only one to speak. He looked at Paulo . . ."showtime."

Paulo was tethering the Glide-Mor with Melina and Larry when they passed a small jet airplane circling to land. Saud was early. Everyone was positioned and ready to greet the guests.

The plane landed and taxied toward the boneyard. Martinez greeted Saud and his entourage. He improvised while Paulo was returning to the airport, having released the tether for the Glide-Mor.

"Business," Martinez looked at Saud. "He runs an airport and people pay to get tethered so that they can glide like a bird. You're early anyway," Martinez continued. "Go look at the planes and see if you like them."

Martinez waved toward the DC-9s. Saud and his associates, which there were seven, looked around the airfield. They saw the four men they were supposed to and they looked at Martinez. Martinez smiled and raised his right hand above his head. Behind him with a clear field of vision all persons that were supposed to see the reflective twinkle did.

Saud nodded his head and spoke something in Arabic. Martinez did not move when Paulo's plane landed and taxied over to Saud's plane. He stopped about one hundred feet in front of it. He blocked any sudden escape if things turned ugly but provided enough room for the plane to maneuver by easily if not.

"My friend, why the show of force?" Saud asked Paulo when he walked up.

"Friends I owe money to," Paulo said. "They are only protecting their interest." Paulo pointed to the two DC-9s. "Come let us look at them and finish business. Some of the cholos must return to the fields."

Saud smiled. He liked Paulo. He was a simple man and a smart one. He displayed the right amount of force and respect at the same time. He was a man you could deal with. He had underestimated him both times.

They reviewed the planes thoroughly. Both the mechanic and pilots were impressed with the level of care. Of the fifteen planes purchased, these two would fall somewhere in the middle top half of the good ones.

The inspection of the planes took two hours. Once the mechanics and pilots were satisfied with the planes' operation and performance, Saud reached for his phone and authorized the wire transfer. The mechanics and pilot used the remaining time to perform additional inspections deemed of less importance. Paulo never once looked directly at the various cameras scattered around the field. He kept moving and talking to ensure Saud did. He only looked up in the air if Saud did. "It looks so peaceful, does it not?" Paulo asked.

"Where is the sense?" Saud responded rhetorically. He looked at his watch while Paulo called his bank to confirm receipt of the wire. With that, Saud shook hands and they parted ways.

~~~

Larry and Melina had taken several pictures of the plane they arrived in. They were even successful in taking pictures of the party themselves. They remained aloft for another thirty minutes after the three planes departed just in case. Once they landed, everyone pushed the glider back into the hangar and walked to the office. Ten minutes later Martinez
~~~

and the hired hands left. Payment to be made later this evening. Larry, Melina, and Paulo retrieved the cameras placed about the field before leaving for town. They had agreed to meet for dinner.

At the bed-and-breakfast Larry sent an email to Matthew and Reynolds confirming the photographs and confirmation of the plane that Saud arrived in. Because of the likelihood that the individuals had previously scanned the planes for homing devices either while on the ground or while the planes were in the air, an AWACS (Airborne Warning and Control System) had been on station since 9:00 A.M.

Paulo's bank account was known and his wire transfer was cleared in the shortest amount of time possible without arising suspicion.

~~~

The AWACS had tracked Saud's plane from 600 miles away and at a classified altitude but one known to be in excess of 35,000 feet. While the parties were on the ground, the AWACS remained on station with a general understanding of the time the planes would be airborne.

The air controller in the AWACS, Sergeant Major Johnson, was an eleven-year veteran. He was responsible for the surveillance and had been tracking the glider and assigned targets. He was aware that the operator of the glider was an NSA agent, Larry Seabreeze. He knew Larry was maintaining surveillance and had taken photographs of the suspected terrorist plane. But Larry was pushing the glider to its limit. At one-point Johnson was overheard shouting out, "no way?" and "who is this guy, a double loop." Thankfully Johnson recorded the glider's flight activity for Seabreeze's later prosperity. Four-plus hours later the surveillance ended when the two DC-9s took off and the jet plane followed, leaving Villazón, Bolivia at approximately 1:15 that afternoon.

The AWACS was able to stay in the air for twenty-four hours. It was not preferred but it was easy to accomplish. This crew had been prepared to fly for twelve hours. The replacement crew was on board and would split the shift at six hours apiece. So two hours into the DC-9's flight, the crews switched out.

A fully fueled DC-9 could fly 1,500 nautical miles. The flight to
~~~

the airfield in Laos was the equivalent of a walk in the park with the extra fuel tanks. The Cessna Citation unfortunately did not have the same range. So when the three planes reached the coast of Africa, the Cessna was forced to land and refuel while the DC-9s remained on their course and heading.

The AWACS was able to monitor both activities without any problem. Even though the DC-9s began to deviate from their filed flight plan and turned off their squawk box, the AWACS was still able to maintain uninterrupted contact. The field the DC-9s descended to was not a marked airfield. The longitude and latitude were recorded before the AWACS returned to the coast of Africa to intercept the Cessna. The Cessna maintained course and speed and flew straight to Riyadh, Saudi Arabia. Once the plane landed, the flight was recorded and documented, the AWACS turned and headed for home.

~~~

Larry and Melina were celebrating the success as a team. *Team* would be the operative word. They shared dinner with Paulo and Martinez, who were instrumental in the affair. Larry had emailed Matthew and Reynolds his itinerary along with a downloaded copy of the photographs taken. It had been agreed that the photographs would be shared with the Argentineans, credit given. They would download the photographs and provide what support they could in trying to identify the members of Saud's group. Larry would complete his trip with stops at the Quinterro's farm, the University at Rosario, and an exit meeting with José. After that, he would help Melina pack for the States. Seabreeze's plus one at all future family and friends' functions.
~~~

Chapter Twenty-two

Average collegiate debt $37,172. Law students $122,158, medical students $166,750, physical therapist $80,000. Forty percent of college graduates take a position that does not require a degree, ten years later the percentage decreases to twenty percent. Too many people seeking too few jobs. Technology?

St. Louis, Missouri

Katie arrived at the office. She'd adjusted her arrival times and routine given the underlying circumstances. She was taking no chances where her life might be at issue.

With a fresh cup of coffee in hand, she sat in front of her computer and read through an email from Patrick Jackson via Jonathan Livingston. . . . *samples will be received tomorrow. Katie Pendleton should have them the day after* . . . Jonathan said. She needed to prepare.

Katie knew now that whoever was responsible for the terrorist act in South America was likely the one monitoring her emails and telephone calls. Miguel, Joseph, and Bail had only one common denominator: her. She understood the conscious choice she was making and taking. There were now five individuals, including her, as a common denominator.

~~~

"Dr. Montero speaking." Katie had retrieved her telephone number from the information provided in Bail's files. He was thorough. Katie read through his notes.
~~~

"Dr. Montero, Katie Pendleton." She began her tale of woe after first introducing herself. "I am the inventor of the super-seed and a colleague of Dr. Bail Prichard. How are you?" Katie was fairly confident that news of Bail's accident had not reached Dr. Montero and her group.

"I am fine, thank you. To what do I owe the pleasure of your call?" Dr. Montero asked.

"Dr. Montero, I'm informing you that Bail was involved in an automobile accident and sustained fairly extensive injuries. He's been moved from the Intensive Care Unit and is progressing nicely. I've been to see him and have retrieved his files, which included your telephone number. At this point, I'm inquiring as to the working relationship you had with Bail. Were you working separately or together?"

"Thank God. I am glad he'll be all right," Dr. Montero began. "As for a working relationship, we were working independent of each other. The damping-off discovery was based on Bail's research. We've been able to develop a fungicide that is reasonably successful in defeating the effects of the disease, provided the plant does not succumb to root rot, rust, or xylem stock damage."

"Huh," Katie said. "That would seem to follow with some of Bail's notes and conversations he and I had. It's his belief that the spore has a redundancy quality to it that would resurrect itself even after a disease had been thought destroyed."

"Wicked," Dr. Montero responded. "How would we defeat that?"

"Time release . . . and trust to the strength of the plant," Katie said. "Dr. Montero, I'm to receive a spore sample and will begin my research within the next two to three days. Can you email me an update on your research since the last update you provided Bail?" Katie made the request trusting to Charles and Tim yet in stark contrast to Brad's wishes.

Charles's instructions were clear, business as usual, trust to his trailer spyware. Don't do anything overt that might cause the terrorists to renew their potential interest in her candidacy.

"Sure . . . I don't see why not," Dr. Montero said.

"Great. I have your email address. I'll send you an email of introduction along with my contact information."

"That would be fine," Dr. Montero said.

Katie hung up the phone and sent out the email. She liked Dr. Montero and thought the telephone call went well.

The explanation of the accident provided Dr. Montero with an understanding why Bail had not responded to her previous emails and telephone calls. *It happens*, her computer pinged and she noticed a new email. Subject matter: *Introduction.*

Katie returned to Bail's research with the added information provided by Dr. Montero. She was curious what research progress Dr. Montero had made. She sat there and took some rough notes, twice breaking the lead on her pencil. "Stress," sending Jenny a text message: *When can we do the massage?*

~~~

Jenny received Katie's text message and laughed out loud. "Stress is a silent killer," Jenny said to Michael, her editor. He looked up.

"Is everything all right?" he asked, clearly concerned.

"My sister. She's overworked and has a lot on her mind. I was thinking of taking her to the Swedish stone massage. It's part of my research for the exposé."

"Okay. When did Tim want to run the article?" Michael was interested in helping Jenny.

"The first part is due this Sunday, 'Living Well' section. The second and third parts are due the following two Sundays."

"It looks like another excellent opportunity for you, Jenny. You're a natural."

"Thank you, Michael. I appreciate the compliment."

~~~

Jenny arrived at the condo shortly after Katie and Brad. It being hockey season and St. Louis enjoying a competitive season, everyone was eating in this night. Lawrence stopped for package liquor at Mickey's while the pizza and wings had been delivered from Monical's. It truly was the best thin-crust pizza made anywhere in the world. The Winterfest microbrews that Lawrence picked up would go extremely well with the pizza and wings.

They were lounging around in their usual game night sports attire. Jenny was thankful that she remembered about this evening's plans and included an extra session of cardio in her morning's routine. Her plate set, beer opened, she was ready for the Blues versus the Blackhawks. Both teams were in the hunt, but then again this being hockey, everyone was in the hunt for a playoff spot.

Everyone used the first period to fix their plate, grab a cold brew, and get comfortable in their seat. By the second period, the first period activities were completed and general conversation regarding the team's performance began. It ebbed and flowed with the game. In the end, it was agreed that the Blues had all the component parts necessary to make a deep playoff run for Lord Stanley's Cup. For this game, the puck slid their way. The third period conversation transitioned from the game to the day's events and lives.

The room was silent for a period of time until Lawrence asked Katie about her spore samples. "Have they arrived?"

"We should receive them within the next day or so," Katie said.

"Any further developments?" Lawrence followed with.

"Not much. I contacted the lead researcher in Argentina. She sent me their work. They've made some progress but the engineers built a dormant redundancy into the spore, which is likely why my super-seed had some success but not complete. That might also explain why they had trouble understanding their general lack of success. I must admit, though they have made significant progress, unfortunately the spore is far more advanced than anyone's ability to stop it."

"Hey, what happens if the courier delivering the spore gets into an accident and the spore is released into the atmosphere? Any chance of us becoming zombies?" Lawrence's question was clearly a reflection of today's appetite for drama.

"Wouldn't that be awful?" Jenny remarked. "Flesh eaters. How preposterous a concept is that . . . zombies. Talk about overdone."

"But the public eats it up?" Brad hesitated. "No pun intended."

"No. No zombies from the science experiment," Katie commented.

"Too bad," Lawrence responded. "What could be the outcome and how likely?"

"I thought we went over this before," Katie said.

"I addressed it in my article with Dr. Gray," Jenny added.

"I may not have been paying attention," Lawrence returned from the kitchen with beers for everyone.

"Well, I'll forgive you this once," Katie continued, "Cereal grains are in everything. If they were to have set their sights on one of the larger agricultural exporting countries, it could've had a much more destructive impact. Without such foods, people would be hard pressed to get the calories they need."

"Obesity would be the big loser from all of this," Jenny joked.

"Yeah, that and the old, the sick, and the young would find it difficult to remain healthy. Thankfully it was a semi-isolated strike," Katie finished with.

"Any chance of it happening here?" Lawrence asked. The room got quiet. No one was really in a position to answer; however, Brad went for it.

"I'm certain the U.S. borders are secure and Homeland Security and the FBI are doing their jobs . . . hopefully." He included yet silence enveloped the room.

~~~

Presidential Meeting
Washington, D.C.

"Anything further on the Treasury issue?" Matthew asked.

"No. None. The Chinese have yet to appear at Treasury auctions. It's not anticipated that they'll return. The economic models used by Magne show no appreciable affect due to their absence. Calling the debt due was mere grandstanding."

"How's your operative doing in South America?" the president asked. Matthew had some extremely good news on this note and was holding it for the end.
~~~

"He's been very effective. We identified two additional terrorists and have forwarded their names and fingerprints to Interpol and other agencies. He's been effective in brokering two DC-9s for use in future operations by the same terrorist group we believe is responsible for South America," Matthew's voice regained its strength.

"We tracked the DC-9s to a field in Laos and the buyer's separate plane to Saudi Arabia. It appears Laos is a staging area. Satellite imagery shows multiple DC-9s on the ground. We believe the next strike will be China," Matthew finished, adding the location of China on his own. The analysts were undecided…there simply not being enough evidence. Matthew understood the reluctance but still . . .

It was 8:45 a.m. when there was a knock at the door. The president's secretary entered. "Excuse me Mr. President, Jonathan is here." The president look confused before Matthew answered, "Show him in, please, Stacy." Stacy looked from Matthew to the president, who nodded.

"Good morning, Mr. President, Matthew," Jonathan said.

"Jonathan," Matthew said.

"Good morning, Jonathan," the president said. "What's going on?"

"Mr. President, I received a call from Jacobs in Homeland Security regarding samples of the spore that caused the devastation in South America. Jacobs informed me that Jonathan was requesting the admittance of the spore samples for research and development of a fungicide. The ultimate recipient is a woman named Katie Pendleton. She's the researcher that developed the super-seed. That seed had varying degrees of success against the spore. I contacted Jonathan to discuss the issue of admittance. It was while we were talking that Jonathan had a credible suggestion," Matthew gave the floor to Jonathan.

"Mr. President, Matthew and I spoke about the current state of affairs with China's push in the South China Sea, their man-made islands, and China being a likely terrorist target. I understand that there are several planes, DC-9s, I believe, located in Laos. Sir, China ranks first in wheat and second in corn export. They are a major exporter in the area of cereal grains."

"Aren't we?" the president asked rhetorically.

"Yes, sir, we are. The largest by far," Jonathan said.

"So, we could be a target," the president said matter-of-factly.

"Mr. President, we are a target for everything and everyone," Matthew said. "But we are better in the espionage arena than the Chinese."

The room got silent for a moment before the president asked the obvious question. "What are you proposing, Jonathan?"

"Sir, why inform the Chinese government? If this were an ally, I'd understand the sharing of information and a likely joint exercise. The Russians, yes, I understand why we would alert them. But the Chinese . . . why say anything?"

Ruthless, inhumane, was the president's initial thought. He always figured Jonathan for a spineless backstabber and coward but never like this. *Why?* It was a logical question so the president asked it.

"What is to be gained or lost by remaining silent on the issue?" Jonathan looked to Matthew to respond.

"Mr. President, Jonathan's reasoning at first may seem barbaric and inhumane, but truly it's not. I believe it's within the best interest of national security," Matthew said before being cut off by Jonathan.

"Sir, it goes without saying that if China were an ally, we would alert them and coordinate a counterstrike to thwart the terrorist act. We routinely share information of a similar nature with Russia. We do it in good faith. But the Chinese government has been reluctant to show us, or anyone for that matter, a modicum of good faith. If their crops were partially affected by the terrorist fungus, it would be an enormous opportunity for your administration to gain an advantage over the Chinese in a nonconfrontational manner. Mr. President, you would appear benevolent," Jonathan said, both impressed with what he had to say and the face time he had available to say it. Matthew looked over and nodded, the president pondered the idea.

"It has merit," the president said, "and we don't have definitive information . . . correct?"

"That's correct, Mr. President," Matthew said. "Such information must be reviewed and substantiated. We don't want to appear overly aggressive and offend a sector of the world population that's already sensitive to Western labels."

"Okay. Put something together on this so we don't look the fools and release the spores to Ms. Pendleton. Hopefully she'll have success in developing a fungicide. Matthew, tell Jacobs to beef up Homeland Security. I don't want anything to bite us in the backside on this one," the president got up and went back to his desk. Jonathan and Matthew were both at the door when the president looked up. "Good work today Matthew, Jonathan. Thanks for being on top of this."

"Thank you, Mr. President," they both said. They smiled, each had a bounce in their step, Stacy noticed.

~~~

Matthew returned to his desk and contacted Jacobs, "What exactly am I looking for?" Jacobs asked.

"Crop dusters and large aircraft are what we believe will be used in Southeast Asia . . . DC-9s to be exact. The president authorized release of the spore to Ms. Pendleton," Matthew placed a second call to Jonathan.

"Nice work this morning, Jonathan," Matthew said before Jonathan had a chance to say hello.

"Yeah, the president was very receptive. I must admit I was a little shocked that he was so quick to embrace our idea," Jonathan said.

"The Chinese have been pushing hard these past few months and this is an opportunity to push back."

"Payback's a dish best served cold," Jonathan responded to some friendly laughter.

"Listen, can you provide me with an analysis of our cereal grain reserves and an anticipated harvest of each item so I can include it in my report? What excess we might have for additional export," Matthew asked.

"Sure. Give me a few days," Jonathan terminated the call.

Matthew sent off an email to Reynolds, a follow-up to operation Hecatoncheires. He almost chuckled at the code name were it not for the fact that he had to Google it.
~~~

Chapter Twenty-three

In 2017, $13.2 billion dollars in farm subsidies were sent to 958,000 recipients...$13,779 per recipient. During the same period of time, $650 million dollars of farm subsidy overpayments was admitted to by the Department of Agriculture.

Buenos Ares, Argentina

Larry and Melina arrived at the Quintero's ranch, expected guests. Weary travelers of the road. They'd stooped in General Güemes to thank Joseph. He was happy to see two people he enjoyed yet believed he would never see again. "I'm only happy that I could be of help, my friends," parting for the last time.

~~~

Consuelo greeted Larry and Melina at the door. She smiled and invited them both inside. She showed them to the wash room, where they "freshened up," before taking them out to the veranda. Alberto was sitting down reading the newspaper. He stood up and smiled inviting Larry and Melina to join him.

Greetings and pleasantries exchanged, Alberto poured them each an iced tea and offered a fresh garden salad. Larry couldn't help noticing the newspapers on the table top.

"Anything of importance?" Larry asked, nodding to the newspapers.

"*Sí . . . mucho,*" Alberto said before continuing, "The world is a complicated and dangerous place. It's becoming more difficult to raise
~~~

a child and afford a family," Alberto's eyes moved from Larry to Melina, where they lingered. He saw something. "But I'm just an old man whose life has passed him by. Do not listen to me or the naysayers. When have we ever been right?"

Consuelo arrived with more ice tea and fresh garden salad and served them before returning to her other duties. Alberto resumed his previous thought. "So I understand you have been busy?"

"*Sí,*" Larry looked at Alberto. "We were both busy and productive in identifying some of the individuals in question." Larry briefly explained the trip to General Güemes and Villazón, Bolivia.

"Have you been able to determine what other planes of that type were brokered within the past six months?" Alberto asked, clearly interested in the issue on both a personal and professional level.

"We're quietly looking into all such transactions. I've asked Joseph and Paulo to make inquiries." Larry raised his hand to stop any rejection or reproach from Alberto before continuing . . . "I've impressed upon them the need for absolute discretion."

Alberto withhold any comment. His hands were resting on the arm handles of the chair, he leaned back. "Paulo, I do not know. Joseph, I'm aware of. He's competent."

"I am also planning on speaking with José and Gabriel. I trust they're in a position to provide something," Larry said.

Larry sat there looking comfortable. He didn't exude confidence or strength yet he clearly possessed both, Alberto thought. They continued the conversation well into the evening. Alberto was interested in Larry's opinion on various world issues. They discussed the South China Sea, the Euro, Russia, and the U.S. economy and debt issue.

"You will be my guest tonight," Alberto said. "I insist." Larry merely shook his head in acceptance and smiled. Melina sat in silent amazement at how easily Larry interacted with each of the individuals they had come in contact with. She was happy with the choice she had made.

~~~
~~~

They woke early in the morning, showered, and dressed before joining Alberto on the veranda for breakfast. They spoke about the remainder of their trip with Alberto providing important insight for their meeting with Dr. Montero and José and Gabriel. "They've all been advised to assist you to the fullest," Alberto said. "We are appreciative of your help in this most trying of times."

Leaving the house, Larry found himself caught in a time warp. The Jeep was freshly washed yet the image indelibly etched upon Larry's mind was of Melina standing next to it while at the lake. Thankfully he found himself smiling. "Is everything all right, Larry?" Alberto asked.

"As my guest, I took it upon myself to wash your Jeep. I only wish that there was more I could do." Alberto's comment only served to add to Larry's confused look and smile.

"Yes. Thank you, Alberto. The gesture is much appreciated." Larry shook hands and said good-bye. Alberto smiled at Melina before giving her a hug and kiss while wishing her good fortune.

~~~

The drive to the University at Rosario was an easy one. Thankfully it was another beautiful day. Larry and Melina arrived at eleven o'clock. Dr. Montero was there to greet them along with Doctors Jesus Aguilar and Fernando Alvarez.

"*Buenos días*," Larry said. He and Melina walked up to the three individuals waiting for them.

"Mr. Seabreeze, Ms. Mendez, it's good to see you again," Dr. Montero introduced her compatriots.

Dr. Montero remembered Larry and Melina. She had been advised by José to show them every courtesy and answer any and all questions completely and honestly. She was hoping that she could do just that. Uncertain how to proceed, she simply asked the obvious question. "What can I help you with?" offering a smile she hoped was confident and friendly.

"Dr. Montero, Mr. Aguilar, and Mr. Alvarez, Melina and I were assigned the arduous task of determining the who, what, when, where,
~~~

why, and how of this terrorist event. To that end we have been relatively successful in determining the answers to certain questions," Larry said. Melina could feel rather than sense Larry's transition into the moment. She smiled at the compliment he'd paid her: "we."

"The *who* you likely guessed . . . terrorists. More specifically, we believe that some of the terrorists may have come from Saudi Arabia. The *what*. . . the spore you are working on, which brings me to you. The *when* and *how* are answered by crop dusters. Seven to be exact. Likely a month or so after the fields were planted. *Where* is unfortunately an easy one to answer . . . *here*," Larry said with a compassionate look on his face, "Argentina. The trade winds were favorable for terrorists and unfavorable for surrounding countryside and personal properties. *Why* is more of a psychological, philosophical answer that we can all discuss at nauseam and never fully understand," Larry said before continuing. "What I would like to learn from you is what progress have you made in addressing the spore...in particular, the stumbling blocks?" Larry asked, looking directly at each of the three doctors. Larry's look made the question all the more personal.

"We've made significant progress. With hindsight, we would have addressed this problem much differently," Dr. Montero began. "We believed the spore was a super-spore similar to the seed being a super-seed."

Melina's look halted the conversation. "What super-seed?" Melina asked.

The look of disbelief on Dr. Montero's face was priceless were it not for the gravity of the situation.

"Katie Pendleton (she continued) is a bio-engineer who lives in St. Louis. She developed a super-seed for cereal grains. Someone else developed a super-spore," Dr. Montero noted Larry's hand raise at the elbow, a question.

"Dr. Montero, you are a noted biologist, correct?" Larry asked.

"*Sí*, I have published some papers that received wide recognition."

"How likely is it that two separate individuals developed competing technology of a similar nature?" Larry asked.

"Technology like this . . . not very likely," Dr. Montero said before adding, "If you're suggesting what I think that you are, then you should know Ms. Pendleton has contacted me. She has begun working on the problem."

"Only now?" Larry's incredulous stare said more than mere words could convey.

"Prior to her direct involvement, it's our belief"—she gestured to include Drs. Aguilar then Alvarez—"that Miss Pendleton was indirectly involved. On your first visit I advised you of assistance we received from an American biologist of some repute, Dr. Bail Prichard. Dr. Prichard was a previous instructor of Miss Pendleton's and a classmate of Dr. Aguilar's." Larry mumbled in response, *El mundo es pequeno.* The world is small.

"Dr. Prichard shared research with us but it was clear he had help. Although Bail is an intelligent individual, he quickly became the leader in this research because of the outside assistance. Bail was able to develop a fungicide that addressed damping-off…a portion of the spore. Unfortunately, the spore engineering has built-in redundancies. There are at least three separate fungi, we believe," Dr. Alvarez had joined in the conversation.

"What type of technology are we talking about?" Melina asked.

"CRISPR technology . . . the new word in WMDs." There was the proverbial pregnant pause before Dr. Montero turned her computer monitor so that both Larry and Melina could see it.

"Katie Pendleton's research focused on the genomic DNA of the cereal grain. Corn in this case. With her research, she was able to isolate and engineer a new strain of seed. The spore operates the same way. CRISPR is the technology that allows an individual to edit the code sequencing of any genetic DNA or RNA strand. Plant life, animal, human, bacterial, viral, anything, *everything!*" Dr. Montero added with emphasis.

"This technology is not limited to scientists either. For less than the price of a cup of coffee at your local Starbucks, a terrorist or rogue army state could purchase a kit enabling them to hold the unsuspecting world hostage to a super-plague," Dr. Alvarez interjected. The look on Melina and Larry's face was all too real.

"This is the world we live in," Jesus added while the DNA strand of the super-spore spiraled on the computer screen.

"What you are looking at is one cell of the spore used against the farmlands of Argentina. One hundred million such spores would fit onto the head of a needle. Yet its genetic combinations are far greater. Bail aided us greatly. Since then, we've uncovered a second fungus, root rot. As common a fungus as damping off, but it's the redundancy that's our concern," Dr. Fernandez commented.

Larry was silent. Thinking. Processing information that he was unfamiliar with. He, too, recognized mistakes in his investigation. Until now it hadn't cost him anything; however, he was entering a new phase of the investigation. If he wanted to continue with the same degree of success, he would have to step up his game. He had failed to contact Dr. Prichard…what was the cost?

"Dr. Montero, could you provide me with the contact information for Katie Pendleton?" Larry asked.

"Certainly. Since Bail Prichard's automobile accident, she's been our contact person," Dr. Montero provided the information requested.

"It would seem that the other side may be equally involved, Mr. Seabreeze. Please, you and Ms. Mendez, be careful," Jesus's concern was noted. Larry stood up to leave. They each thanked the other before Larry and Melina found themselves back in the Jeep and on the road, yet again.

~~~

The drive to Buenos Aires was scenic yet uneventful. Larry and Melina talked about the investigation. True progress had been made but nothing was decided, no new leads, no new points of interest. Returning to the hotel, they checked in and rested. Larry sent an email to Matthew and Reynolds. New itinerary was also provided to include St. Louis, Missouri, and Decatur, Illinois.

Larry and Melina found themselves lying on top of the bed, staring at the ceiling. Each holding the other's hand yet lost in their own thoughts. Larry was contemplating the next phase of the investigation
~~~

while Melina was thinking along more personal lines. Boys and girls are different in their independent thought process . . . hunters versus gatherers.

Later that evening they found themselves at the local restaurant for a late dinner. The weather had been nice so they walked. The manager at the front desk recommended two or three restaurants within easy walking distance. They arrived early for dinner. Larry suggested a drink at the bar. He ordered a CC and Coke with a twist of lime. Melina went with club soda and a lemon twist. Larry raised an eyebrow. He turned to Melina, smiled, and toasted, "*A nuestra buena fortuna.*" The teardrop that slowly rolled down Melina's cheek confirmed his suspicion. Larry smiled, kissed her softly. He expressed his love for her and slowly wiped away the teardrop. Larry motioned for the bartender. Handing his drink back, he ordered a club soda with a lemon twist. "*Estamos en esto juntos,*" he said to her. We are in this together.

~~~

With a one o'clock meeting, Larry and Melina left with plenty of time available to them. Larry was looking forward to their meeting with José and Gabriel. After that, it would be time to head back to the States . . . Seabreeze party of two plus.

Larry and Melina arrived at Casa Rosada twenty minutes early. They walked across the Plaza de Mayo hand-in-hand. They were admitted without question. When notified by his secretary, José wasted no time in greeting them. While they were kibitzing, Gabriel joined them. After the small talk, the conversation got down to business.

Larry spoke freely and openly about what was discovered during the investigation. He produced a flash drive containing the photographs taken and the current files on five of the seven identified operatives.

"Matthew emailed the files to me this morning and confirmed the release of the information to you. His email address and contact information are provided, should you discover anything of interest," Larry said. Gabriel accepted the information with a smile. "But now I need to ask something of you both . . ."
~~~

"Please," Gabriel said.

"The buyer of the seven planes initially used in the crop-dusting incident, Ibn Saud, purchased several DC-9s and similar-type aircraft."

"The two DC-9s we provided you . . . *sí?*" José said.

"*Sí.* Those planes were followed to an airfield in Laos and are under satellite surveillance," Larry said. "I have asked Paulo, the Bolivian broker, and Joseph, the airport owner in General Güemes, to discreetly inquire about the delivery of similar-type planes . . . green state, extra fuel tanks, and a large storage tank. I would like for you two to see what information you may be in the position to provide on the sale of similar aircraft."

José and Gabriel both looked at each other and nodded in agreement. "*Sí,*" Gabriel said while they continued to discuss the case and certain aspects thereof. By three-thirtyish they had pretty much exhausted all aspects. The meeting was ended. It was then that José asked Larry if he would excuse the three of them for a brief conversation. Larry looked at Melina and was rising out of his chair when she placed a hand on his arm and gently pushed it down. Larry obliged and remained seated. Melina looked at both José and Gabriel. She had enjoyed her time and position but knew it had come to an end.

"José, Gabriel, I have enjoyed my service to my people and my country. But I will be resigning my position effective immediately. I will be relocating to the United States with Larry." Melina found her hand held in his. José and Gabriel were silent before Gabriel started to speak. Unfortunately, he was interrupted by Larry.

"It goes without saying that I would never ask Melina about her duties while under the employ of the Argentinean government," Larry said. José and Gabriel looked at each other and smiled before they both turned in unison and offered their congratulations and support.

Larry and Melina left Casa Rosada and walked across the Plaza de Mayo. Melina stopped, turned, and looked before proceeding with Larry to the hotel. Their schedule was tight but it allowed an opportunity for her to introduce Larry to her family and friends. Larry understood this and delayed their departure for an additional few days . . . the benefit of hindsight.

Chapter Twenty-four

In 2011, Chinese companies owned an estimated 240,000 acres of U. S. farmland. In 2013, Shuanghui (a Chinese concern) purchased Smithfield Foods for $4.7 billion dollars. A by-product of this acquisition was 146,000 acres of U. S. farmland. A farm advocacy group termed such foreign ownership a "...national security concern. Once owned, they're going to keep it forever." Land ownership in China is not permitted.

Decatur, Illinois
Tabuk, Saudi Arabia

"You give the Americans too much credit," Sherrief said to Amged.

"They are no longer Admiral Yamamoto's sleeping giant," Ashraff added.

"They are an old and foolish drunken giant," Sherrief laughed at his own comment.

Amged did not dispute that; however, he did believe the Americans were no longer the paper tiger everyone suspected. He was a true Islamic believer and did not succumb to such portentous traits.

"They're no closer to solving the spore riddles, deaths, or auto accident. We would know, the spyware's still available," Sherrief added. "You worry too much, my brother." Amged could only acknowledge that he did.

The game they were playing permitted instant messaging, which was exactly what they were doing. Advancing aliens were bothersome. Jericho would stand supreme.

"We fly in one week," Sherrief, Ashraff, and Amged were of one mind.

~~~

St. Louis, Missouri

"The guy's a genius," Katie said. Howard and Johnny were equally frustrated by the spore's complexity. Unbeknownst to Katie, she had made great strides in understanding and unraveling the mystery behind the spore yet she, too, had fallen prey to its simplicity. Only Joseph had grasped the true understanding of the spore and CRISPR technology. The key to unlocking the secret was in the sequencing, yes, but was also in the . . .

Katie's thought process was interrupted by Melissa…

"Katie Pendleton speaking."

"Katie, Dr. Montero here. I have you on speakerphone. I'm here with Drs. Aguilar and Alvarez."

Good mornings were offered and exchanged by all.

"Katie, the sequencing string you identified fit perfectly with what we'd been working on. The disease is root rot. It's a common fungus spore much like damping off," Dr. Montero said. She and her team felt a sense of pride. They finally contributed something meaningful to the program. It had taken some time and effort but they were truly beginning to understand the power of CRISPR.

"Yet there's still something fundamental that we're all missing," Katie said before adding, "That's great work, everyone. If you could please send me the entire sequence so that we both will work with a current copy."

"Certainly, Katie," Dr. Montero agreed before the call ended.

"Well, that's good news," Howard said. Katie glanced at him. *He's right and he's trying to lighten the mood*, she thought. Unfortunately that still didn't help in identifying what they were missing.

~~~

"Lass, I agree," Mickey was saying, "but dat still don't mak't right."

"Mick'e, I'm juss say'n . . ." Lawrence started to laugh. Jenny looked over at him with her hands on her hips. Mickey mumbled something to the effect of "Oh, laddie."

"Whad's so fun-e?" she asked. Lawrence tried to stop his laughter.

"You. When you are arguing with Mickey, you start to sound just like him."

"Now, liss'n, laddie . . . I mean Lawrence . . ." Jenny said in defense of herself but couldn't. She, too, ended up laughing.

After a few minutes when the laughter calmed down, Mickey returned. "Ah right now, where was we, lass?"

"I think we finished, Mick," Jenny said. "I'll send out the invitations. The party is next week so we should be good."

"She'll luv it, lass."

Lawrence and Jenny left Mickey's and found themselves back in the condo and on the couch. College basketball conference tournaments. March Madness . . . preliminaries to the greatest sports tournament ever. Although Rutgers never made the tournament, Jenny did enjoy the season. She received Marielle's text message confirming their party. Michelle, Emilee, and Amged would be present. Emma would try and get free from her master's studies. Katie had also sent a text message. Jenny read it: *Will work late tonight if you want to meet Brad and me at Mickey's later.* She smiled and turned and faced Lawrence.

"Back to Mickey's."

~~~

Katie found that problem solving for her meant tireless discussions for everyone else. "What are we missing?" Katie asked yet again.

The computer was set up to a projector screen that permitted each of the individuals to see both the progress made versus that yet to be discovered. While she looked at the screen, Katie replayed in her mind Joseph's last voice mail to her . . . "*I discovered something about the spore I'm certain everyone's overlooked.*" Katie stared at the spore's DNA strand slowly rotating vertically on the screen next to the horizontal spore's
~~~

strand. Howard and Johnny did the same. Each of the three focused on the tree and not the forest. How long they were standing there with the knowledge that they would likely still be standing there were it not for Brad's wakeup call is anyone's guess. Katie answered on the fifth ring before her voicemail picked up.

"You forgot or are you working?" Brad asked with a hint of jocularity in his voice. He had come to know Katie very well.

"Sorry," she said. "Guilty of working." She looked at her watch. "You're downstairs, aren't you?"

"Yes, I am, sweetheart, but in your defense, I just pulled up."

"I'll be down in ten minutes. Let us clean up here." Katie pressed the red receiver on her cell phone to terminate the call. She then helped Howard and Johnny clean up the lab. They put the basic stuff in their lockers before taking the proprietary information with them.

"Brad and I are heading over to Mickey's if you'd like to join us?" Katie offered.

"Sure," they both said.

~~~

Everyone arrived. The bar was crowded and parking at a premium. They walked inside and received a warm greeting from Mickey. "There's my workaholic," Mickey gave Katie a hug. "Brad how 'r ya, lad?"

"Fine, Mickey. Thankfully I was able to get Katie out of the lab. Your mushroom bacon cheeseburger was a big help."

"One of me specialties," Mickey offered a greeting to Howard and Johnny. He showed everyone to the table currently occupied by Lawrence and Jenny. Mickey found an extra table and, with Johnny's help, fit everyone in comfortably.

Cold beers were served, steak fries with gravy and fried onions ordered. Everyone was deep in conversation, sports on the television, shuffleboard and general bar room banter. After several beers and hours passed, thoughts of work and responsibilities were being replaced with feelings of playfulness and thoughts a-fancy. Katie found herself feeling the weight of the world lifted from her shoulders. She was
~~~

completely relaxed. She and Brad had just won their third straight game of shuffleboard (given the hour and amount of alcohol consumed, these were non-sanctioned games) when she noticed Johnny look at his watch and place a call. On reflex, Katie did the same—it was 12:34.56 a.m. She instantly froze and looked at Johnny, who paused in mid-sentence, they looked at each other before slowly turning to Howard, who noticed. Howard stopped talking to his newest dream girl. Brad noticed the Bermuda Triangle reaction and realized three was tonight's magical number. Katie guttered on her next slide. Match lost to two up-and-comers.

"It's not random," Katie said. They were all seated at the table. Howard's young filly somehow understood tonight wasn't happening while she returned to the pasture that would be Mickey's Place.

"No, it's not," Johnny said before adding, "It recognizes a particular strand of DNA and binds to it, effectively negating it."

"So it has the super-seed DNA strand within the spore," Howard added.

"What's going on?" Lawrence asked.

"She's figured out a very major piece of the puzzle," Jenny said. "I've seen that look a thousand times before."

"Spooky the way they all seem to know what the other is thinking and going to say," Lawrence looked at Brad. Brad was smiling, "My chick's going to save the world. Not many guys can say that!"

"Chick?" Jenny commented. "We haven't been called chick since the sixties."

"So what did you figure out, babe?" Brad asked.

"If we're right, we very well may have figured out what Joseph's message was," Katie was trying to focus her thoughts before Johnny jumped in to help.

"We always believed there was a degree of randomness to the spore's DNA sequence, but there's not. In fact, it's the exact opposite." Brad, Lawrence, and Jenny all looked confused.

"It's like a snowflake," Katie began "no two are the same. That's because every section of the atmosphere may be slightly different than the adjacent section. The same can be said for ground soil. The microorganisms, rain or water disruption, fertilizer, sunlight, et cetera, may be just a little different than that of the adjacent soil and seed or the soil and seed ten feet, twenty feet away. Just pick a number. The spore is able to recognize that. It binds its specific fungus DNA strand to that of the seed, and in this case, the super-seed, thus ensuring infection and destruction of the plant. Where the soil was just right, the super-seed was able to survive and grow to maturity at a relatively high percentage." The table grew quiet either at Katie and Johnny's exclamation or the deer-in-the-headlight look Howard displayed.

"What's wrong, Howard?" concern settled in Katie's voice.

"That means they did have your research, there's a traitor in our midst," Howard looked at Katie.

"Couldn't they have figured out what you did?" Lawrence asked.

"No," Katie said.

"So what do we do?" Lawrence asked.

~~~

NSA Headquarters
Fort Meade, Maryland

Larry was amazed at the final four days spent in Argentina. Melina's family accepted him with open arms and hearts; so much so that they quickly arranged an engagement party. Larry proposed. He and Melina discussed it and it only made sense. He was still thinking about that when he walked into the office…first time in forever. *Is this how a real field operative feels?*

It was a relatively early hour. He wanted to visit his cube and make certain everything was in order before his debriefing by Matthew and Reynolds. The morning was blocked out but, it could last longer. Larry checked his emails and regular interoffice correspondence and found everything in order. He was behind on certain cases and decided to address that with Matthew and Reynolds. Larry walked down to the
~~~

cafeteria for a cup of coffee. He grabbed a second cup for the debriefing, a backup.

Larry walked upstairs and stopped at Matthew's office. He met Reynolds at the door, both admitted at once. "Good morning Larry, Robert," Matthew said. "I see you came prepared, Larry," motioning to the coffee.

"Good morning, sir," Larry responded. They walked out of the office and down to a vacant conference room. Entering the conference room, Larry noticed the credenza had a fresh supply of paper and pens displayed for use. Matthew and Reynolds each grabbed one and they all took a seat.

"We will be recording this debriefing session along with personal notes. Unlike an operation that went bad, this one has gone surprisingly, well" Matthew said. "Reynolds and I are very impressed with your thoroughness, resourcefulness, and ingenuity."

"I trust your compliment is on the record," Larry smiled while they laughed.

"Okay, let's get started. Larry debriefing sessions are conducted to ensure that all relevant knowledge and information has been obtained and communicated. They are generally conducted by a senior operative. This helps to ensure that all aspects to an investigation or operation are considered, which is why there is more than one debriefing scheduled.

Unfortunately, with your itinerary and the issue at hand, we will be circumventing that process. We'll both be asking questions that may seem similar but likely aren't, so please consider them as such," Matthew said.

"The second aspect to the debriefing is designed to lend support and shed light on areas the operative may have overlooked or not provided with enough importance. This is due to the fact that the experienced operative was not conducting the actual operation and seeing it with a fresh set of eyes and perspective. Debriefings are a critique of one's work, a constructive critique. Are we clear on this point?" Matthew asked.

"Yes, sir," Larry said.

"Okay, then, let's begin by you describing your actions starting with when we last spoke face-to-face." *Literally the beginning*, Larry thought.

Larry started at the beginning, describing everything. His approach to the case was to include what he had intended to accomplish versus what he actually did accomplish. "Self-evaluation and recognition reconciliation are the foundation upon which an operative hone their craft," Reynolds said. It was another compliment Larry understood. Larry explained Melina's involvement and that of the local airport owners whose support proved invaluable.

"That is generally the hardest thing for operatives to understand. Trust . . . when to do so and when not to," Matthew interjected . . . again a compliment.

By the time Larry reached the point he chose to speak with Alberto Quintero, it was past lunchtime. Matthew suggested that they order lunch from the cafeteria, have it delivered, and plow through. Reynolds and Larry agreed.

Larry recognized that a certain degree of his success was related to luck which again seemed to win him points. The information on Paulo, and Paulo himself, was a huge break. Larry considered identification of the broker of paramount importance and drew an end to what he deemed the first phase of the investigation.

"Query," Matthew began. "Are you the best operative for the next phase of the investigation?" *Time to build a case for myself,* Larry thought.

"Yes, sir, I am," Larry continued. He addressed the basics first simply, a starting point. He discussed the issues of continuity, familiarity with the players, irreplaceable knowledge, and the intangible *feel* of the case. But the coup de grâce of Larry's argument was his personal belief that "I can solve this. To switch operatives now would be detrimental to the overall aspect of the case."

"But can you solve it in time?" Reynolds asked.

"Yes. I believe I can," Larry responded.

"Good," added Matthew, "because I have a signed letter from the president authorizing you to continue your investigation on U.S. soil. You know, we are not permitted to operate on U.S. soil. That remains the purview of the FBI."

Matthew and Reynolds began cleaning up while Larry remained

seated. The meeting was obviously concluded. Matthew looked up. "Is there something else?"

"Yes sir, there is," Larry cleared his throat and adjusted himself in the chair.

"Sirs, while on assignment, I worked closely with an agent in Argentina, Melina Mendez. We became intimate and have decided to get married. I have asked her to relocate back to the United States. She agreed and is currently at my condo in Georgetown . . . sirs." Matthew and Reynolds both returned to their seats. They respectfully hesitated before speaking. It was Reynolds who spoke first.

"First off . . . congratulations on the relationship and honesty, what to do . . . we can discuss that upon your return from this assignment. Good luck to you, Larry."

Larry returned to his cube and placed a quick call to Melina. After having been together nonstop, he was experiencing separation anxiety. Melina was, given the sound of her voice. They spoke for a while before Larry ended the call and began to gather things for the trip. It had been a while since he walked the streets of St. Louis; however, he still had fond memories of the zoo, the Arch, and his Cardinals. They were clearly one of the perennial favorites for serious October baseball and a likely shoo-in with a big bat and a younger Ace. Wainwright had seen better seasons.

Larry completed the ticket purchase and left for home. Melina was anxiously waiting. Tonight's dinner was with the Seabreeze family. The drive to the condo was free of normal traffic, given the early afternoon hour and weekday. Larry arrived and was greeted warmly at the door. Melina was clearly experiencing several different emotions. From the look in her eye, she had the same idea. Without further ado, they walked together and aided each other in the release of stress and energy. Dinner was not for several hours. They had time.

~~~

The guest of honor arrived fashionably early. Larry and Melina were relaxed and engaging with family members, nieces, and nephews. Prior
~~~

to their arrival, Larry had had an opportunity to show Melina around the main house and the seventy-five-acre horse farm, including pool, patio, and stable area.

"Do you ride?" Mary, Larry's mother, asked. Beth, Larry's older sister by a year, also accompanied them to the stables. The Seabreeze's currently stabled twenty-three horses.

"Yes," Melina said. "I was an equestrian rider in my younger years."

"Really?" Beth said, showing interest. "Which event?"

"Steeples," Melina responded with a smile. "And you?"

"Barrels," Beth commented on the walk to the oval track.

The remainder of the evening went swimmingly. The tour of the immediate grounds and dinner complete. Melina found herself on the other end of the emotional spectrum by evening's end. On the walk to the car, Larry's mother asked the obvious question: "When will we see you again?"

"Not long this time, Mom," Larry and Melina added a smile to their good-bye.

"Take care of my daughter-in-law and future grandson," Mary said. Larry and Melina both looked startled. "I noticed neither of you were drinking." They smiled in response.

Chapter Twenty-five

Thirty-six million Americans hold jobs that will be affected by the growth of AI. Seventy percent of said jobs will be completed by machines. Evolution is not mutually exclusive...accounting and legal jobs are at risk...traditional white-collar jobs. Evolve or be displaced.

St. Louis, Missouri

The flight to St. Louis was on a standard commercial carrier. Coach. No upgrade. If they were going to speak to Bail Prichard, Larry knew that they would have to drive to Decatur, the airport there was less than transportation friendly. He had contacted the hospital, Decatur Memorial, and learned that Bail had been released. He was home resting. The university had given him a medical leave of absence.

Upon arrival at St. Louis' McDonnell Douglas International Airport, Larry and Melina rented an Xterra and checked into the downtown Hilton Hotel, thirty-five minutes away. Larry was finally earning meaningful *rewards* bonus points, he thought while checking in.

"Penny for your thoughts," Melina smiled as they entered the room.

"I'm thinking reservations at my favorite Italian restaurant on the Hill, and then I was going to invite you to take a nap and shower with me before we dine."

"They do have an oversize bathtub," Larry smiled and followed her lead.

~~~
~~~

Dinner on the Hill was superb. Appetizers, entrées, and sparkling spring water only added to the ambiance. The night young, the weather warm, the air fresh with just a trace of chill to it, Larry and Melina found themselves walking down by the Arch and waterfront. He pointed out constellations visible on what was a clear St. Louis night sky. The waters of the Mississippi flowed by. It was the perfect evening and night. They sat on a bench and talked.

The conversation turned to the investigation. "What are your plans for Katie Pendleton?" Melina asked.

"I read her file, which included work habits, personal life, et cetera. Much of this was gleaned from desk agents posing as telemarketers. That's how we get basic information on people. We actually call their friends and family. You'd be amazed how easy it is to get people to talk," Larry said.

"I know—it's a trick we learned from you. We use it," Melina said. "People love to hear themselves talk."

"I was planning on driving by the research lab at Washington University late tomorrow morning. The company she works for has rented laboratory time through the evening. I believe she'll be there. I'd like to get a look at her to decide on our approach." Melina appreciated the use of the word *our.* She felt involved anyway but still appreciated the honesty in Larry's voice. "If the position presents itself, I may approach her directly. Otherwise I was planning on stopping at their office Monday morning."

"Unannounced?"

"Yes, unannounced…one never knows whom to trust…ours is a dirty profession…remember."

~~~

They woke up early, and with coffee in hand, they parked outside the research lab. They arrived close to eleven o'clock. Relatively early, all things considered. The coffee was in styrofoam cups. The discarded wrappers of the breakfast and lunch sandwiches were on the floorboard of the seat behind them, the glamorous side to investigative espionage.
~~~

They had witnessed several people coming and going from the research center. One such individual entering the building fit the picture and profile of a Feldman & Company Biotech, Inc. coworker. A second individual returned to the parking lot to retrieve a bag. It held a laptop computer. Both individuals worked with Katie. Melina identify Johnny James and Howard Long. She had the company personnel file on her laptop and was reviewing it.

Larry and Melina were in the middle of discussing baby names when a car pulled up, parked, and the driver got out. He entered the building. Melina was not able to identify the individual. Larry was deciding what to do when the older gentleman and Katie emerged from the building and walked towards his car . . . hand in hand.

Katie briefly looked their way and Larry thought that she made eye contact but decided against it when there was no double take. She and the older gentleman drove off, Larry and Melina followed.

~~~

St. Louis is an easy town to navigate with GPS. From Washington University, Katie and her yet to be identified gentleman friend took Interstate 64 East.

"Where are they going?" Melina asked.

"I haven't a clue," Larry responded. For in all honesty he hadn't. He would not know for another ten minutes.

"Do you like hockey, sweetheart?" Larry saw the Scottrade Center, home to the St. Louis Blues.

"Hockey?" Melina asked.

"You'll love it," Larry answered. "It's soccer on ice."

~~~

Katie and Brad's conversation had gone a little differently. "Is everything all right?" Brad asked.

"Yes," Katie said. She was thinking something but couldn't quite put it into words.

They made good driving time to the stadium. Traffic was light.

Brad inquired about the research and productivity thereof. "We're on to something. After last night's revelation, we're on to something," Katie said, clearly excited by the week's prospect. "Of that I'm certain," she continued. "I sent Dr. Montero an email and changed the course of her research for this week. I need her team to focus on identifying a different strand of the spore genome," Katie said. She was not upset at attending the hockey game for their lab experiments were running. The game provided a brief respite from building pressure of ongoing research.

~~~

Brad and Katie arrived at the stadium. They had a pass for preferred parking. Larry and Melina paid for parking, twenty bucks, steep, even if it is reimbursed. Larry made a mental note of the gate Katie parked next to. The gate would provide him with an idea where their seats might be. When he and Melina purchased tickets, he would mention this to the sales person. Their tickets could then be purchased with a little more accuracy. Larry's preference was for tickets either behind Katie or alternatively directly across from her. It was Larry's belief that either would provide proper surveillance viewing.

"Why don't we simply speak with her," Melina asked. It was more of a statement than a question.

Larry looked at Melina and thought for several moments before he responded. "Sweetheart, I am doing what I believe to be the best course of action to take. I need to act slowly to reduce the mistakes I will likely make. I think this best."

~~~

The seats Larry and Melina purchased were on the opposite side of the ice rink from Katie. They were at a 145-degree viewing angle. Not ideal but it was the last two seats next to each other available. Larry bought them both a Blues souvenir hockey jersey to help them blend into the crowd but passed on the foam "WE'RE NUMBER ONE" finger/hand.

"The game should be a good one, St. Louis versus the Montreal Canadiens." In the end it was a good game if you were a Canadiens fan.

Melina located Katie, the unknown gentleman, and two other people they seemed to be with. She pointed them out to Larry. Periodically they would glance over to make certain they were still there. Otherwise the first 40 minutes were left to the game, explanation of the term *icing*, and Italian sausage with steak fries and lemonade. "We need to start working out," Larry said. Melina smiled.

Midway through the third period with the Blues losing by a score of 5 to 2, Larry and Melina left the rink for their car. On the way Melina provided Katie's home address to Larry. He input the address in his GPS and they left the parking lot. He stopped at the end of the interstate entrance ramp. Larry presumed Katie and the gentleman would be going to Katie's condo or at least in that direction. He and Melina watched for the car.

The old adage that "third time's the charm" still holds true. The first two vehicles Larry selected proved to be wrong. Thankfully Melina had the eye. She correctly identified the car Katie was in. Larry stared forward when her car drove by. "She looked," Melina said. Larry waited until their car was well into traffic and Katie was likely no longer paranoid before he joined the other vehicles on the entrance ramp and interstate.

With Melina acting navigator and lookout, Larry sliced through traffic like a stock car driver on Daytona's straightaway. "Four cars ahead, two lanes over," Melina reported.

"Got'um, sweetheart," Larry responded while he listened to Melina sing along with the radio. It was an easy listening station, she with an enjoyable voice.

The GPS alerted Larry of the exit. He changed lanes in anticipation. The lead car changed lanes in preparation of exiting the interstate. To avoid being made, Larry increased the number of cars between them, hoping one or two would exit.

No such luck!

"Batting a thousand," Larry remarked exiting the interstate one hundred or so yards behind them. He was batting a thousand when the traffic light changed to red. The lead car pulled into the left lane.

The GPS informed Larry that a right-hand turn would be required at the bottom of the exit ramp in one quarter of a mile. They were heading elsewhere . . . "Hopefully to a bar," Larry mumbled. He made a right-hand turn at the light. An inconspicuous roll through complete with breath held was the plan. Odds would be required to take that bet.

"Babe, see if you can see where they go. I'll drive down a block or two before turning around."

Three blocks farther down was Katie's gated community. Larry passed it before turning around. There being a slight hill, Melina lost sight of the car Katie was in. She noted a second car turning left. "Possibly the couple they watched the game with," Melina postulated.

"Let's hope so." Larry did a U-turn and proceeded down the road in the direction opposite of that which he had been driving. He spotted Mickey's Place and saw both vehicles. "Bingo," Melina laughed.

"What now?" she questioned.

"Let's wait a moment. Hopefully a group arrives and we can enter the tavern with them, again, inconspicuous."

They waited close to twenty minutes before a group of five guys walked up. Larry and Melina quickly got out of the car, leaving the Blues shirts behind.

~~~

Mickey's Place was your typical local neighborhood tavern. Larry and Melina walked up with music and laughter escaping into the surrounding area. It had the feel of a happy place.

Approaching from the opposite angle of the five individuals, Larry realized they were on a collision course. Three of guys noticed the same. To Larry and Melina's good fortune, they were able to enter in the middle and not either end. Who really sees seven faces in a group?

Once inside, Larry spotted a table for two just off the wall and led, Melina followed. They sat down and became acclimated to their immediate surroundings. They became part of the background fabric known as Mickey's Place. It was several minutes before Mick spotted them. He brought them place settings and menus.

"Sorry, ya two must'ta snuck'n when I wasn't look'n. I'm Mickey
~~~

an dis'ere's me place," he said. "Can I get ya someth'n da drink?" Larry noticed Melina smiling at Mickey and his accent. "Lassie, ya hav'a luv'le smile."

"Thank you," she blushed slightly.

"We'll have two club sodas with a lemon twist and an order of disco fries," Larry said. Mickey nodded and was off to the bar to get the drinks and drop off the order.

While they waited for the drink and appetizer order, Larry and Melina surveyed the room in search of Katie. Again Melina spotted her. "Back table facing me. Three rows behind you and over your left shoulder." She laughed . . . "This spy business is way cool."

They sat there and enjoyed the evening while their conversation turned to the future. The only break was when Mickey delivered the drinks and decided to sit with them. Hector brought the disco fries and an extra place setting and napkins. Mickey's was that kind of place.

Mickey finally left the table. It was then that Melina noticed Katie and her date (Melina begin to think of him) were no longer seated. "She's gone," Melina said. Larry quickly looked over his left shoulder and spotted the empty table. He may have held the stare a split-second too long, for when he turned back around, Katie was standing underneath the restroom sign staring right at him. Her gentleman friend standing directly behind her.

Situations like these clearly never last as long as one thinks. For example, if one were to ask Melina, she would've given a completely different answer than each of the other three and the same can be said for each of them. Gospel truth be told, Larry didn't flinch and neither did Katie. She walked toward him. Confrontation eminent.

"You're following me . . . Why?" Katie demanded in a stern and calculated voice. Her friend was standing with her. Both had their arms crossed. A clear display of body language. Melina didn't flinch. Larry was thankful. He looked at Katie and her friend and simply said, "Join us." Katie hesitated for a mere second before locating two chairs and sitting down on one, Brad the other.

"I am following you," Larry looked directly at Katie.

"You were in the parking lot this morning and I thought I saw you at the hockey game," Katie responded.

"Who are you? What do you want?" Brad asked.

"And you are?" Larry asked.

"Katie and I are seeing each other."

"He's my boyfriend," Katie said, using the archaic vernacular. Larry smiled but withheld an actual laugh.

"I am responsible for investigating what happened in South America. Suffice it to say I'm now acting with specific powers and within said specific powers granted to me. My name is Larry Seabreeze and this is Melina Mendez. She is Argentinean and working for her government." Katie did a double take at the mention of the country, Argentina.

"That's right," Larry said. "We're both assigned to investigate the occurrence and determine its origin…natural or not."

"And?" Katie prodded.

"We received your name and telephone number from Dr. Montero. We also received the name and telephone number of Bail Prichard. I trust he's in good health. I understand the hospital released him and the university extended him a leave of absence after his unfortunate and untimely traffic accident."

Larry sat for a moment, studying Katie. Having now met her, he realized that he wasn't quite certain what information he wanted or needed from her. He had not yet determined how integral she was to this aspect of the investigation. She was important, yes, but in a sense, he was still attempting to understand his side of the equation, let alone hers. Was he truly the man?

Katie continued to stare, saying nothing. Larry finally relented. "I'm sorry if we intruded on your personal time. I simply wanted to observe you first to determine how to question you. I can see now that I have some things to consider. You don't have lab time until tomorrow evening, why don't we stop by your office . . . ten o'clock?" Larry reached into his pocket and produced a $20 bill for the table. He and Melina began to stand. Katie and Brad remained seated.

"All I did was produce a seed that would feed the world," Katie stared at Brad and began to cry.

~~~

Larry was deep in thought when he walked over to the Xterra. He held the door open for Melina (chivalry being alive and well). He walked around to the driver side and noticed that Melina had the hotel address available for the GPS. A keeper.

"So how does she fit into our investigation?" Melina asked. Larry appreciated Melina's proprietary interest in the investigation. He was certain he could not have progressed this rapidly without her assistance.

"I'm not certain yet. I know she's important; however, I'm not entirely certain that she's an integral part. Tomorrow's meeting will be more of an open-ended discussion. Hopefully from there we'll be able to determine whom else to focus our attention on."

"How about the Saudis and Laos/China issue?"

"Matthew assigned those pieces of the puzzle to regional assets that would not appear as out of place," Larry responded.

They were not far from the hotel and returned inside of thirty minutes. A quick bath in the oversize bathtub and Melina and Larry were ready for bed. Melina caught Larry looking at her in the mirror. She could feel his eyes on her. Looking, touching, caressing, tasting. A nibble here, a kiss there, a touch. She shuddered as she imagined his strength taking them both to where she wanted them to go. She looked at Larry and smiled. She turned with her back now to the mirror. She rested against the countertop, inviting Larry. There would be time for love later.

~~~

Larry and Melina woke refreshed. They joined the other hotel guests at the continental breakfast. A glow seemed to envelop them. Were any guest brave enough to look, they would've seen it.

~~~
~~~

They arrived at the appointment ten minutes early. It was a crisp late February morning. Temperature was in the low forties with a slight breeze. Larry parked in a nearby parking garage. They walked three blocks to the office of Feldman & Company Biotech, Inc. Upon arrival and communication with the receptionist, Larry and Melina were shown to the conference room. Along the way they were offered coffee and bagels. Coffee was accepted but the demur for the bagels was unmistakable.

The conference room was of decent size. The table was a rich mahogany with twenty-four plush leather-bound chairs surrounding it. The company's name was prominently displayed on the wall opposite the entrance. Larry noted two drop-down projectors. He'd seen such type before but only once. They were required for the three-dimensional viewing.

There were matching mahogany credenzas at both ends of the conference room that appeared parts of a set rather than functional units. Larry and Melina were resting nicely in their seats when Katie joined them. She brought two individuals, neither of which looked as if they were chemical biologists.

"Good morning, Mr. Seabreeze, Miss Mendez," Katie sat opposite Larry and Melina. Their seats faced the door. "This is Charles Freyski and Timothy Black. Charles is a systems analyst with a forensic background and Tim is a licensed private investigator." Where required, identifications were provided.

~~~

Katie and Brad, along with Lawrence and Jenny's input, had discussed the possible scenarios available to her. It was believed that collectively they had been exhaustive in their thought process. Full disclosure was the proper course of action. "*Cards on the table*," it was decided, to the agreement of all. A late-night telephone call to Tim was made. "I'll make certain Charles is available," Tim confirmed.

~~~

"Larry, I have asked Charles and Tim to attend today's meeting. They may be in a position to provide you additional details necessary to complete your investigation and help us with ours," Katie said. Larry's interest was clearly piqued.

What investigation? Larry wondered. He realized, of course, that they would disclose what that investigation was.

"I have no objection to their attendance. Melina?" Larry turned to her.

"No. I am certain that it will be a benefit, although I am curious—what you are investigating?" Melina asked. Katie paused for a moment before Larry interjected, "Why don't you start at the very beginning?" So Katie did.

It is not a long narrative even going back to her first microscope and chemistry set. Which is exactly where she began. The story was new to both Larry and Melina and somewhat insightful. Larry made several mental notes. He was certain Melina did. In the end, Katie's narrative took her to the present day and time.

"You have two deaths, a likely failed attempt, potential hit-and-run, computer espionage, possible worldwide terrorist act . . . all because of a genetic breakthrough that could feed the world using half of the existing farmland currently in use. "Clearly the technical definition of *no good deed goes unpunished*," Larry said in summation of Katie's narrative.

"What can you tell us?" Tim asked.

Moment of truth, Larry thought. He looked at Melina. She gave an ever so slight nod of her head. Noticeable only to Larry even if one were so inclined to have been paying attention.

"My current assignment has been sanctioned by the highest level of our government. Melina is permitted to operate on American soil. Phase One of the investigation began with the intercept of patterned cell phone usage which was inbound. Inbound calls are those that originated from a location outside of the United States. They are generally deemed to be of interest to U.S. intelligence agencies. We were able to triangulate these calls to a location in Saudi Arabia. Specifically, the northern mountain region." At this mention Katie shifted in her seat. Charles, Tim, Melina all understood the meaning of this action.

"The recipient of the inbound calls was determined to be Central Illinois." Again the body shift. Imperceptible except to the trained professional. "Unfortunately, the exact location of the sender and recipient cannot be determined, the phones in use are encrypted disposable prepaid phones. This information led me to Argentina. With the help of the Argentinean government and Miss Mendez, we were able to locate the broker that sold seven single-engine airplanes used for crop dusting. Said broker was recently involved in the sale and purchase of several larger planes, DC-9s or their equivalent. These planes were sold to a Saudi named Ibu Saud. Delivery of two planes was to locations in Southeast Asia. It is believed that another strike is eminent. Particularly given our belief that Argentina and parts of South America were a field test for the spore."

Larry was slightly amazed that the synopsis of their endeavor took a relatively short period of time to explain, given the physical time and energy involved. Such is life for a double-naught spy.

"Melina and I came to St. Louis to discuss your part in this equation," Larry faced Katie directly . . . eye to eye. "We were initially uncertain if you were important or integral to our successful resolution. We now believe you to be integral. The question to answer is, how integral are you?"

There were several moments that passed before Charles spoke. He did not feel pressured to speak. On the contrary, he actually wanted to speak. "Your statement begs the question," Charles said. "If not Katie, then who could possibly be more integral than her?"

"Agreed," Melina responded. "But unfortunately Katie hasn't told us everything. Katie, who do you know from Saudi Arabia?"

All eyes turned their attention back to Katie. "Amged," she said quietly. "Amged Hussainsiraj. He's a chemical engineer at Central Illinois Corn & Soy. He works in the research and development department. They're a global corn and soybean processing company with a plant located in Decatur, Illinois. But he's a U.S. citizen. He can't be involved."

Katie didn't sound like she believed her own statement. Her voice didn't sound convincing even to her so how could it sound convincing to others?

"He may not be involved directly," Larry said, "however, we have to explore all avenues and possibilities. There are several things you mentioned that are of immediate interest. Two deaths plus the attempt upon Bail. The computer spyware and open access line. Your research and individuals that were provided a copy of your papers. Your belief that said research was cannibalized by the spore's engineer. Let's not forget, farmers are moving into the fields. We believe," Larry looked at Melina, "that there will be a coordinated strike on the United States and other countries."

"With modern fertilizers, crop dusting is virtually nonexistent within the United States. Particularly given farming's close proximity to populated areas and the chance for environmental issues. There may be some in select parts of California and other Western states but very little. China and Southeast Asia may be otherwise," Katie elaborated. Growing up in Forsyth, she was more than familiar with farming and its seasonal nature.

Looking at Tim, Larry asked, "Other than what Charles has uncovered, have you been able to formulate any leads of a viable nature?"

"No. Unfortunately not. I believe the two deaths plus Bail's accident are more than mere coincidences, but this is not something I can prove. There's simply not sufficient evidence, physical or otherwise," Tim said, more than a little disappointed.

The room became quiet, deathly quiet and still. Each individual understood circumstantial evidence was no evidence at all.

"Isn't the DC-9 a plane designed and manufactured by McDonnell Douglas?" Melina asked.

"Yes," Charles answered.

"Wouldn't they maintain records, ownership, transfer of such planes for warranty and recall purposes?"

Nobody answered immediately. Melina may be on to something but it would be a long shot at best, the plane's production ended in 1982. "It should be something we could easily verify," Larry looked at Tim. "Do you know anyone at McDonnell Douglas?"

"No, but I can inquire," he answered. The conversation continued on for another half hour before Charles interjected.

"What about use of the spyware tunnel?"

"A TV trap designed to 'flush out' the terrorist sleeper cell?" Larry asked; Charles laughed.

"Yeah, something like that."

"It's something to consider. Let's give it another day or so. In the interim I'll set up a background in case we decide to proceed down that avenue," Larry said.

Charles and Tim had some additional input that was discussed. It was clear the meeting was coming to a close. *Everything has a life of its own*, Larry thought. Katie showed him and Melina back to the reception area and door.

It could not have been more than two or three minutes between the time they left Feldman & Company offices and when they were walking past the security officer's desk. Larry was stopped by the officer. Looking confused at first, until he understood that there was an urgent telephone call for him. Larry answered the phone. "Larry Seabreeze."

"Larry, Katie Pendleton here. I was checking my phone messages and noticed that I received a call from Amged. Before I return the call, both Charles and Tim suggested that I speak with you."

"Hm." Larry sighed. "Can you return the call tomorrow, thus providing me with an opportunity to set up a background should someone choose to inquire?"

"Sure. Call me on my cell phone to confirm," Katie said.

~~~

Larry and Melina left the building and walked to the parking garage and car. Without thinking, Larry found himself heading in the direction of Forest Hill Park and the St. Louis Zoo. It was a nice day. Larry believed a walk and relaxation would help clear his head. He needed to formulate a plan of attack. To avoid lost time on the investigation, he contacted his office and was transferred to the appropriate section responsible for creating individual backgrounds and aliases.
~~~

Larry discussed what was needed and an associate assisted him in establishing a profile, a former classmate of Bail Prichard and Jesus Alvarez. Having accomplished that, he dictated an email to Matthew and Reynolds and sent it off. The DC-9 information should be easy enough to obtain. He was assured that his alias would be provided by day's end to include a Facebook page complete with a gmail address, photos, friends, and a list of articles coauthored. Until that time, Larry found himself holding hands with Melina and enjoying crisp outdoor air while they walked through the zoo.

Zoo animals existed within reasonable facsimiles of their natural habitats. Larry's favorite was polar bears while Melina seemed partial to Bengal tigers. *Who had it better?* Larry always wondered . . . a conversation for another day.

Chapter Twenty-six

A recent NSA memo called online gaming a "target-rich communications network" where terrorists could communicate "in plain sight."

Decatur, Illinois
Undisclosed location throughout America's Heartland

Alien Alert was a top Internet game played by men and women of all ages to include children, adults, and terrorist alike. Amged was playing it with eight associates while conducting business via the game's messaging option. Said option was difficult to trace if not impossible.

"Yes, we have received the atomizer, platforms have been installed. It's a simple attachment before takeoff," Omar Salah said.

"You are certain that the jet's engine speed and wash will not affect atomizer spray?" Omar Habib Barack was head imam, his word went a long way.

"Omar, I have told you how many times not to worry. Jet engine wash and turbulence will not affect the spray, given the low level of altitude with which we will be flying," Hazim responded.

"Hazim is correct," Amged added. "We have nothing to fear."

The instant messaging was quiet. Everyone seemed to be satisfied with the tentative schedule. Tentative, each flight was subject to unpredictable weather conditions. Clouds were needed. Preferably dark ones.

"Is everyone set to go?" Amged asked. Each individual acknowledged in the affirmative. There had been no problems with the planes themselves or other hobbyists. Amged terminated the call after confirming the next scheduled game. The game ended with the standard "Allah is great… Death to the infidels."

~~~

Whiteman Air Force Base

Major Reismann ended his call. A 15-year veteran, he considered himself a lifer. Reynolds had proven equal to the task and assurances promised. He understood. Reismann reached for the coffee mug and walked to the breakroom. He craved the excitement and thrill of planning missions. Terrorists were a bonus, cowards.

Authorization came directly from the top. Reismann had worked out a full-proof plan. Seven Air National Guard units were involved in the joint coverage. Reismann had sufficient planes at his disposal and a thirty-minute response time. He was confident in their pending success.

~~~

St. Louis, Missouri

Larry woke. Melina was still asleep in his arms. He looked at the desk clock and noted the time—5:38 a.m. He got up, carefully extricating himself from any entanglement. He sat at the desk and looked through his emails. One was expected. Nothing regarding McDonnell Douglas which earned a head shake.

Larry read through his alias's biography and committed it to memory. Matthew and Reynolds both provided encouragement and confirmed that "on-the-job training is not a preferred training method. However, all things being equal, what other choices are there?" One plane in Laos had been flown into China. Location unknown.

Larry noted an obvious omission, the Chinese government had not been notified of the plane's movement. "Some questions are above my pay grade," Larry mumbled.

"What was that, honey?" Melina asked.

"Sorry, babe. Talking to myself. I didn't mean to wake you."

"No, that's all right. I'm awake." Her head was lying on the scrunched up pillow.

"One of the planes we brokered was flown out of Laos and into China. Matthew's email doesn't mention anything about whether or not they informed the Chinese government," Larry said. Melina's initial response was a questioning stare.

"Surely they informed them." Her voice and tone was unmistakable.

"I'm not as certain as you," providing a short pause before continuing. "Think about it, we have knowledge of a terrorist act that is designed to attack the food chain. China is currently building a man-made island in the South China Sea. They're holding war games with North Korea. Add to that their unilateral withdrawal from Treasury auctions plus their attempt to call the debt due. A grandstanding ploy, I'll admit. However, if you agree that our evidence is not one hundred per cent bulletproof, one could argue we don't want to be alarmists. One could also postulate that it's not our responsibility, the Chinese government should take care of their own people before attempting to rule the world. Having said all of that, if terrorists strike, and they do attack the cereal grains, we, American we, can provide grain to the Chinese people and possibly gain valuable concessions from the Chinese government."

Melina looked at Larry and understood his logic and reasoning. She also understood his patriotism. However, she did not think that way personally and believed he did not.

"You don't really believe what you just said . . . do you, honey?" she asked while lightly biting her lower lip in a childish attempt to sway his decision her way.

"Babe, this is the world we live in. It's a macro look but that doesn't negate existing facts," he said. "I am just surmising that that is what Matthew's thought process is," Larry said. He noticed her seductive look. "But of course, I don't think that way," Larry quickly added before crawling into bed. Matthew would understand.

~~~
~~~

By ten o'clock, Larry and Melina found themselves at Feldman & Company. This time they were shown into Katie's office. It had a nice view of downtown St. Louis.

"So . . . how should I proceed?" Katie remained seated behind her desk. Larry and Melina were both sitting across from her.

"My bio has been established. An email account exists, we're friends on Facebook. I also attended the University of Illinois with Bail and Jesus," Larry said before adding, "My name is Raycek Banner."

"Raycek Banner . . ." Katie said with a snicker.

"Why? What's the joke?"

"Bail . . . Raycek . . . Banner . . . Seabreeze . . . the names sound like characters in a book, all hero spies—oh, forget it," Katie said. "Suffice it to say that whoever prepared your alias bio is intelligent, well read, and has a certain wittiness about them."

"Huh," was Larry's response.

"Okay, so what should I say to Amged, I need to return his call?"

"First off, don't offer up anything unless he asks. Provide a vague description of your research discoveries, don't offer up Raycek Banner, wait until he asks but let him know that he first contacted you at home." Katie looked quizzical.

"He would've gotten your information from either Bail or Jesus," Melina said in answer to Katie's questioning stare.

"Okay, then let's call him."

~~~

The call lasted approximately twenty minutes. Patrick and Jonathan requested that he call to follow up on the spore research and remaining cereal grains. "Research on both is going well. I have the lab for the remainder of the week, so I'll complete the next scheduled cereal grain. On the spore, we've made a couple of significant breakthroughs," Katie said. She wanted to bait Amged. Again, there was no proof one way or the other—she simply wanted to know . . . *are you or are you not a terrorist?*

"Breakthroughs . . . that's great news, Patrick and Jonathan will be
~~~

happy to hear that," Amged seemed like he wasn't going to bite. "How's Bail?"

Katie hesitated. She wasn't certain how Amged knew of Bail, but before an undue amount of time passed, she responded . . . "he's recovering nicely. The university gave him an extended leave so he should be in good shape. No pressure, which will aid in his recovery."

"Great news. Katie, we will speak soon," Amged said in ending the call.

"It's not him," Katie said. "He seemed uninterested in who *we* are."

"Nobody said that this would be easy," Larry answered.

They continued to talk for several minutes before ending the meeting. Katie had to prepare for her lab research and Larry had to figure out their next step. He and Melina left the building, Larry noted the temperature. Warm weather with signs of spring in the air. Winter was officially over, in his opinion. Women were dressing in light clothes and bright colors. Men's thoughts were turning to things *a fancy*. Rain was not in today's weather forecast; however, it was over the next week to ten days. "Typical wet and stormy Midwest weather. From one season to the next. Thunder, showers, and tornadoes will be in our forecast for the foreseeable future," the evening meteorologist had said in conclusion of the news.

~~~

Larry and Melina were sitting at a downtown coffee shop when Katie called. "Amged just contacted me via follow-up email. He said that he was thinking about our conversation and wondered who is *we*?"

"Okay," Larry said in response. "Provide him with the information and let's see what happens."

"What are your plans for the investigation?" Katie inquired. The thought of working with a spy had somehow intrigued her.

"I sent an email to my desk analyst to obtain files on Dr. Joseph Patrick and Miguel Rodriguez. To that, I will add Amged Hussainsiraj. However, unless I hear something from my office or McDonnel Douglas, I will likely drive to Decatur for a look-see," Larry said before adding,
~~~

"Wait before responding to Amged. Can you send me an email and an update on your research with general instructions? I should get involved now that he may have taken the bait."

Larry and Melina went back to enjoying their coffee and conversation, contemplating the investigations next step.

~~~

There were several options. "Our choices are not clearly defined. In Argentina it seemed easier to decide a course of action," Larry mentioned.

"I have been thinking along those same lines. Didn't you say that your grandfather lived near St. Louis?" Melina said.

"Yes, Highland, Illinois, an hour drive," Larry smiled at her remembrance. "Why? Interested in seeing the airport where I learned how to fly?"

"I am interested in you, honey," Melina said with a playful smile. Larry smiled back and added, "Yes, let's take a drive. It may relax us both."

They left the coffee shop and walked to the parking garage. On the walk over, Larry's phone beeped, alerting him to the receipt of Katie's email. His alter ego. Larry had a separate tone for that account. He checked the email and laughed at its formalness. Melina gave him a look so he handed the cell phone to her, email open. She read the email several times before handing the phone back.

"I don't see the humor," Melina said.

"It's in her writing style," Larry said. "She's so formal."

"She writes well," Melina responded while they merged into traffic.

They'd been on the road for a half hour when Larry's cell phone rang. Larry looked before answering. "Hello."

"Seabreeze, Matthew here. Where are you?"

"Chasing down a lead, sir," Larry looked at Melina, who smiled while shaking her head.

"I'll be sending you the name of an individual to contact at McDonnel Douglas. They're expecting your call."
~~~

"Thank you, sir," Larry began looking for an exit. Melina Googled the address of McDonnell Douglas and entered it into the GPS.

"Next time," she said.

When Larry was back on Interstate 70 heading east toward St. Louis, he placed a call to Jennifer Simpson, Manufacturing Warranty and Plane Transfer.

"Jennifer speaking."

"Miss Simpson, Larry Seabreeze here. I was given your number by Matthew Sheffield. How are you?"

"Fine, Mr. Seabreeze. I understand that you are interested in ownership of our DC-9s."

"Yes. I'm not certain what Mr. Sheffield may have mentioned to you but we're interested in records kept on aftermarket purchase and sale of your planes?"

"Yes, we do to the extent we're notified by either or both parties to a particular transaction," Miss Simpson answered knowing Matthew had discussed this specific issue with her. Jennifer understood government contractors are required to maintain a certain degree of transparency.

"Have you had any such transactions reported within the last year?" Larry asked. The actual time requested was greater than warranted; however, Larry was hoping to see Ibn Saud's name somewhere.

"I'm certain that we have, unfortunately I have already logged out of our system. I have a doctor's appointment that I'm late for. If you would like to stop by my office tomorrow morning, I'll be available," Miss Simpson said.

"Great," Larry said. "My associate and I will be at your office at 10:30 a.m. tomorrow morning."

"Mr. Seabreeze, I will see you tomorrow," Jennifer said while Larry confirmed the address.

~~~

The remainder of the day seemed to move at a snail's pace. Whether it was because of the differences in the type of investigation or Larry's lack of experience, it seemed they were constantly looking for directions.
~~~

Larry knew that if this kept up, they would never catch the terrorists until it was too late. It was decided that he and Melina would return to the hotel and prepare for tomorrow's meeting while reviewing the Rodriguez and Patrick murder files. The weather having changed for the worse, they felt lucky at not having driven to Highland.

Heavy dark rain clouds rolled in. The trip to Highland seemed like a distant dalliance. National Weather Service issued a Severe Thunderstorm Watch until well into the early morning hours. Tornadoes had been spotted near St. Jacobs, Illinois. Local flooding was also a concern. The weatherman commented that during this time of year, weather forecast were extremely accurate, given the built-in likelihood of rain. Something stirred in Melina, but she couldn't quite put a finger on it.

Chapter Twenty-seven

Computers will replace most blue-collar jobs. Efficiency and performance will increase while error and risk will be eliminated. SAM (Semi-Automated Mason) can lay 1200 bricks a day compared to 400 by the average human. Without John Henry to stand tall, technology wins by default.

St. Louis, Missouri

Larry and Melina were shown to Miss Simpson's office by her secretary. Coffee was offered and accepted. Larry noted the secretary carried an extra cup back with her, which was likely intended for Miss Simpson. They were shown directly into her office and motioned to sit down. She was on the phone and mouthed, "Thanks," to her secretary for the coffee. The call lasted another ten minutes or so before ending. She then buzzed her secretary and requested that further calls be answered by her.

"Sorry for the call. It came before you arrived and lasted longer than it should have. Well now, you're interested in aftermarket transfer of DC-9s for the past year. I've printed out your information. The DC-9 was one of our more popular commercial planes. Surprisingly there were thirteen reported transactions within that time period," she said while handing a copy of the printout to Larry. It was several pages long and seemed to be a history of each plane. The paper was the traditional green and white paper, 16-inch-by-24-inch, with perforated sides used by a dot-matrix printer. Larry accepted it with a smile and thanks.

"Miss. Simpson."

"Jennifer, please," Larry nodded consent.

"Jennifer, I'm interested in two things that I hope you can provide. First, do you have records concerning the name *Ibn Saud*? Second, have any of your planes had a destination point of Tabuk, Saudi Arabia?" Jennifer looked at Larry for a moment and then Melina. She was uncertain of her involvement, but it was clear to her that Larry considered her involved.

"I would have to check on both of those requests; however, before I do that, let me set you both up in an empty office," Jennifer said while she stood up. Larry and Melina stood up, taking their coffee cups and computer printouts with them.

The empty office was three doors down and sparsely furnished with two chairs and a small metal desk. The desk came with a swivel chair behind it. "Coffee is just down the hall on your right-hand side. Your search request will take approximately thirty or so minutes. If you could, please provide me with correct spelling of both requests?" Jennifer asked. Larry found a pad of paper and pen in the desk. Writing them both down, he handed the paper to her and she turned to leave.

Larry noted that Melina was smiling. "Progress," she took a seat adjacent to Larry's and they began looking through the printout together.

The printout was chronological, oldest to newest. The upper-left-hand corner had the search request "Reported DC-9 Transfers 12 Months" and results "13." "*Omen*," Larry mumbled, Melina looked at him. "Superstitious . . . black cats . . . Friday the 13th . . . omen . . . a foreboding prophetic sign. Generally deemed to be bad, not good."

As Larry and Melina looked at the first entry, they noted the headings: DATE, SERIAL NUMBER, CURRENT OWNER, REPORTED HOURS FLOWN, MAINTENANCE, EXPLANATION. EXPLANATION was a *catch-all* category requiring special request. They looked through two or three before Melina pointed out a buyer. The company was called Cloud Chasers, Inc.

"They're people that study storms for a living. Scientist of a type," Larry said.

Melina still looked confused, Larry thought. She shook her head in a slight twisting side-to-side motion, *No, that is not what I was thinking.* She had more of a *thought . . . one that is right on the tip of her tongue,* Larry realized. He hesitated before understanding that he had not been paying much attention to the various owners. He flipped back to the front page and began again.

They looked at buyers and sellers to obtain a better understanding of likely users of the plane. Early purchasers were the airlines of that era. Charter companies and large manufacturers were next. Cargo companies and other shipping concerns followed. Foreign buyers became interested in the DC-9 once the price point became more palatable. That left specialty concerns the ultimate buyer of last resort.

Storms, LLC, was the first eyebrow-raising specialty concern encountered. That transaction occurred in April, close to one year ago. There must've been a natural break in the transaction. Larry flipped back to the first transaction, which occurred in February. The buyer, Cloud Chasers, Inc., was located in St. Francis, Kansas . . . *makes sense.* Larry recalled various television programs on tornado alley and thunderstorms, Kansas being prominent in both.

They continued flipping pages when two more buyers showed up that were specialty concerns, Storms, LLC, and Tornado Alley Research, LLC. Larry looked over at Melina, who completed her thought . . . "they're evolving." Storms, LLC, was located in Oakland City, Indiana. Tornado Alley Research, LLC, was located in Elkhart, Kansas. Larry, again, flipped back to the beginning of the printout and retrieved a pad of paper and pen from the desk.

"I'm evolving," he said with a smile.

By the time they were done, Larry's schedule looked like this:

Tornado Alley Research, LLC	April	Elkhart, Kansas
Dustbowl Research, LLC	June	Kimball, Nebraska
Environmental Storm Impact, LLC	July	Madison, Iowa
Rain Dancers, Inc.	July	Hamburg, Iowa
Central States Storms, LLC	October	Highland, Illinois

Larry and Melina both looked at the completed chart. Seven entities and transfers of planes. Locations were Central States. Each location coincided with two things: entity identity and the nation's breadbasket. The Central States—Kansas, Iowa, Illinois, Indiana, Nebraska—the heartland.

"What does it all mean?" Melina asked. "They are all research companies, scientific entities involved in weather res—" Larry raised his hand interrupting Melina. He didn't mean to but she'd triggered an important thought.

"Let's assume they've evolved. Let's assume they've gone from crop dusting to cloud seeding," Larry said. "Would seven planes be enough… or are there more?"

"We need a map," Melina took Larry's laptop out of the case and turned it on. While it was booting up, Jennifer walked in. Larry had almost forgotten about her.

"Okay," she said. "Ibn Saud was involved in one transaction and that was Central States Storm, LLC."

"Oh, *nnnooo* . . . " Larry looked at Melina. He'd suddenly gone deathly pale.

"We were right there," the volume of Melina's voice trailed off.

"Right where?" Jennifer asked. "What's going on?"

~~~

Highland, Illinois

Hazim was a devoted Muslim. He was more fanatical than even the imam. He had dreams of standing on dead bodies of many infidels and their capitalistic society filled with shiny objects. He looked east and sent a photograph to Sherrief. "Again, Allah is with us this day and has joined us in battle." The picture was of a lightning bolt striking down from above. Truly prophetic when one thinks about it objectively.

~~~

St. Louis, Missouri

Larry quickly added three columns to his schedule:

Company	Date	Location	Cereal Grains		
			Corn	Soybeans	Wheat
Cloud Chasers, Inc.	February	St. Francis, Kansas	8th	N/A	2nd
Storms, LLC	April	Oakland City, Indiana	5th	4th	N/A
Tornado Alley Res., LLC	April	Elkhart, Kansas	8th	N/A	2nd
Dustbowl Research, LLC	June	Kimball, Nebraska	3rd	6th	N/A
Environ. Storm Impact, LLC	July	Madison, Iowa	1st	1st	N/A
Rain Dancers, Inc.	July	Hamburg, Iowa	1st	1st	N/A
Central States Storms, LLC	October	Highland, Illinois	2nd	2nd	N/A

Larry and Melina stared at the schedule while Larry reached for his cell phone to call Matthew. The first call went to voicemail so Larry phoned Reynolds.

"Reynolds here."

"Reynolds, Larry. Sir I believe we have an emergency situation. I'm in St. Louis at McDonnell Douglas. I've reviewed an aftermarket transaction schedule for purchase and sale of DC-9s. There were thirteen transactions. Seven of those transaction involved storm and tornado research entities. Sir, what if they are using cloud seeding to disburse the spore? Farmers are in their fields now and it's raining here," Larry went to the National Weather Service website and noticed clouds covering much of the Central States.

Reynolds listened to Larry and understood what he was saying. The idea had a certain believability to it that should be considered. "Let me make some calls and I'll get back in touch with you shortly," Reynolds ended their call.

Larry looked at Melina. She had been listening while Googling something. She turned his computer screen to face him. Highland-Winet Airport. Larry quickly looked at their airfield's grass runway length and pointed it out to Jennifer. "Yes, that would be sufficient for a DC-9," she said. Larry called the airport.

"Sanders."

"Yes, I'm trying to reach the operators of Central States Storm, LLC," Larry said.

"I'm sorry but they left early this morning, they wanted to get ahead of the storm," Sanders responded.

"Approximately what time?" Larry asked.

"I'm not certain. However, based upon the flight plan filed, they left the airport at 6:30 a.m.," Sanders answered. There was a pause. Larry was getting a sick feeling in his stomach. They had been so close, a lucky break that missed.

"For these types of flights, are flight plans required?"

"Yes and no. Yes, they are required. However, they are allowed deviations for this particular type of flight plan, given the potential for a storm to change directions." Sanders paused before he asked, "With whom am I speaking?"

Larry wasn't ignoring him; he just needed knowledge and fast. "Are flight plans a matter of public record?"

"Yes, they are. Who are you?" Sanders asked with a little more authority, but Larry had already disconnected.

Larry immediately called Reynolds, but the call went to voicemail.

Larry then dialed his number, knowing that it would be answered by the receptionist. He was shaking his head. He looked up at Melina, hoping for a lifeline but knew it wouldn't be coming. Melina had also changed. Her body language changed. Jennifer remained standing, not knowing what to do.

"Shirley," Larry said before she could answer the phone. "Shirley, this is Larry Seabreeze. I need to speak with Reynolds or Matthew *now*."

"Larry, I'm sorry but they are in a meeting and asked not to be disturbed."

"Shirley, this is an emergency. I'll accept the responsibility, but you must interrupt them." Shirley hesitated before agreeing. "Please hold." A few moments later Larry's call was placed through.

"Matthew."

"Matthew, Reynolds, Larry here. It's happening. I confirmed one plane is in the air. A flight plan was filed and I believe they are using cloud seeding to disperse the spores. I'll be emailing you a schedule of aftermarket DC-9 transfers. The schedule includes cities and states. I believe there are at least seven planes in the air. If they complete their task, we're doomed," Larry said. He attached the schedule. Matthew and Reynolds hesitated before responding.

"Larry," he heard the ding. Confirmation of email receipt. "I just received your email," Matthew said. "We're looking into flight plans filed by storm chasers and noted twenty-one filed flight plans. We'll cross-check that with your schedule and get back with you shortly."

Larry looked at Melina. Jennifer was still standing, looking confused.

"What's going on?" she asked. Larry stared at Melina.

"There's nothing more we could've done," she said.

"Yes there is," Larry responded. He quickly shut-down his computer and gathered the spreadsheet. It may be late, but they were going to Highland-Winet Airport…another loose end needing to be tied off.

~~~
~~~

Whiteman Air Force Base

"Major Reismann here."

"Reismann, Reynolds here with Matthew's in the background." Reismann could hear Matthew's. He caught bits and pieces of the other conversation, state and local police from the sound of it. He heard enough to know that this was no drill…Reynolds droned on. "Listen, we have a strong belief that *it's* happening. We need you to get your people airborne now."

"Reismann, Matthew's is requesting filed flight plans for all storm chasers filed within the past 72 hours. It's cloud seeding. Flight plans will be uploaded to the cloud." Neither laughed at the pun this time. "I just sent you a list of aftermarket DC-9 transactions within the past 12 months. Try and focus on those airports first. Once we get filed flight plans, we can narrow down possible target area." The call ended both understood the urgency.

~~~

Reismann was the consummate tactician. He'd already texted his units. By the time his own unit was in action, Reismann was in the operation's room. He reached for the speaker phone. One last review of the plan. Air National Guard members began to arrive. "Very few moving parts" Reismann said.

Good news, bad news was how Reismann always viewed this op. Bad weather was a given…inevitable delays of personnel, another given…inability to guarantee communicate, a third given…difficulty of smaller planes to operate under variable conditions, etcetera, etcetera. Yet there was good news, maybe the best news, another op was running and with it an AWACS was airborne. Reismann's odds for success improved substantially.

~~~

NSA Headquarters

Reynolds and Matthew sat silent. Neither one wanting to disturb the calm before the proverbial storm. They did not like their chances but trusted to the plan. They had contacted local and state police for twenty-one cities with filed flight plans. Determining an entities authenticity had been assigned to several desk analysts. Priority understood.

~~~

Highland-Winet Airport

Larry and Melina drove straight to the control tower. Things had changed. Larry thought surveying his surroundings. Time later for reminiscing. Melina understood.

Larry walked into the tower room and immediately produced his badge. He realized that this was the first time he had ever *flashed it. Pre and post* he thought.

"Larry Seabreeze, I need to speak with Mr. Sanders now." Authoritative tone left no doubt that this was not a request. Individuals scurried off in search of their boss.

Larry didn't stand and wait. He followed thus halving the distance. Sanders emerged from a back office.

"Sanders here. Are yo…" Larry interjected.

"Larry Seabreeze (again with the badge). Sanders, I need to see all of the records for Central State Storms, LLC. I also need to see where they stored their plane and gear." Larry's request and tone was polite, yet authoritative. Sanders briefly hesitated.

Sanders turned and spoke with a scurrier who walked off to the office area and file cabinets. Larry looked at Melina who followed.

Sanders looked at Larry and mumbled something. He turned back towards his office with Larry in tow. While Sanders pecked away at a computer for stored electronic files (Larry understood), Larry was back on the phone with Matthew and Reynolds…confirmation provided that
~~~

our planes were in the air. Larry's second call was to the local police. He advised them of the situation and the need to send a detective unit to the airport. Larry also called the local state police barracks and requested additional support. Dusting for prints was not Larry's forte.

~~~

Whiteman Air Force Base

"Major we're currently tracking three planes believed to be your targets." The AWACS operator responded. There were six onboard operators, Reismann had been tasked two.

"The others?"

"Transponders have likely been disabled sir, or their equipment may simply be older…Mode S or even earlier…sir." The operator was young and nervous. Reismann had a reputation, well-earned but still…one a young buck didn't want to cross…even though it couldn't be helped.

Reismann knew that his plan had to be fluid to succeed. Older, bigger, slower planes flying within storm clouds would be easier for pilots to maneuver than lighter, smaller planes his people were flying. For this type of operation, a flight simulator was good but not the real thing. His people had been warned.

"How soon to first intercept?"

"Fifteen minutes sir."

Reismann exhaled slow and steady, he stood over an operation's table, old school. The game was on and he could only watch from the side lines. Subtle changes would be required.

~~~

Highland-Winet Airport

Having retrieved three sets of gloves and booties from his car, *condoms?* Sanders smirked, they entered Central State's hangar and adjoining office. Local police arrived first. They had been directed to the hangar where Larry and Melina were visually surveying the area. Sanders was standing in proximity so not to be in the way. Detective Hillard approached Sanders first. Drinking buddies.

Hillard returned to his car after briefly speaking with Sanders. He placed a call to his dispatcher requesting two more units. Returning to the hangar, he approached Larry and Melina.

"Detective Hillard, Larry Seabreeze and Melina Mendez" Sanders said by way of introduction.

"Detective" Larry and Melina said including a handshake.

"So what are we looking at?" Hillard began. His look was not one of skepticism given his years on the *force*. Hillard was a realist, but this was Highland, Illinois not New York City. Two back-up units arrived. They pulled up to the hangar, Hillard was reminded that this was two units more than the town needed. State police and sheriff units arrived providing Hillard recognition required…*the world we live in*.

"Yes it is" Melina responded. They left the office hangar to pow wow with new arrivals.

~~~

Larry was in-charge (unofficially). His decision that everyone respected… special permission or not. Cover story was easy, Sanders was dropping off requested paperwork and stumbled upon questionable documents and receipts. Everything being in plain view, he forwarded photographs to his longtime friend Hillard. Probable cause decided, Hillard advised Sanders to contact state police. Together, evidence of a possible crime would be gathered…*the world we live in*…Hillard added to everyone's understanding.

"So we're all in agreement…then let's get started," Sergeant Curry stated.

Being a 15-year veteran of the Illinois State Police, Curry took control of the crime scene. With Hillard's help they had the hangar and assigned office dusted within short order. Twenty-seven separate prints/
~~~

forty-two counting partials and smudges were obtained. The place had been cleaned, but in a hurry.

"Another moment of truth" Melina joked…an attempt at levity. Local news station reported continued severe thunderstorms for much of the central states.

"Larry, we received electronic prints and documents," Matthew began. "Good work. We have assets in the air and have intercepted two planes targeted." Matthew understood mixed feelings Larry was trying to process…he had yet to develop a coldness that comes with the job.

"There have been complications but we're confident any damage will be minimal. Good work Larry, field work becomes you. I'll be in touch." Matthew disconnected while Larry sat in silence. The call had been on the speaker phone and he received some reassuring nods and pats on the back. Everyone else began to go about their day. Recognition for them would be months in coming.

Hillard remained standing. He looked at Larry and Melina. More at Melina really. He uttered one word "Argentina." Melina looked. She understood this was not even a question. Larry simply shook his head in acknowledgement. Hillard said nothing before he turned and left.

~~~

Whiteman Air Force Base

Reismann hated to lose. He especially hated to lose when he knew that he held the winning hand.

Kimble, Nebraska was a bust. Forecast of thunder showers dissipated quickly. Skies were clear and blue. Federal, state and local authorities arrived finding three Muslims of undisclosed nationality present. They were taken into custody. The DC-9 was seized for forensic investigators.

Reismann received confirmation that two of the cities and planes listed on Reynolds's list were legitimate operations. Pilots landed when approached by Air National Guard chase planes. Threats of being blown out of the sky were not warranted. Nothing to hide.
~~~

The problem was the weather…tornadoes…forty-three tornadoes were reported in the coverage area. The DC-9 was a bigger plane and better able to deal with the environmental demands structurally. Intercept planes were smaller and operated more efficiently at higher speed. Pilots understood the danger. Unfortunately, the carrot dangling before the terrorist zealots was *Ibn Kathir's sura 55 reference to 72 virgins…*how can a non-believer compete. Mindless rank and file are fodder for their master.

*We're losing the initiative…*Reismann said to an empty room. Very few moving parts. He reached for the phone and dialed Matthew. His call was answered immediately.

"Reismann, how do we stand," Matthew asked? He deplored deception but understood the need.

"Weather is an unfortunate element that we cannot compete against. Sir, I need permission to use lethal force to down any remaining planes."

This had been discussed ad nauseam. Coverage area was semi-remote however any visual effect of shooting a DC-9, let alone multiple DC-9s, from the sky was something that could also take down a sitting administration. Collateral damage. God forbid a plane crash in a populated area or worse yet, pilot error…gravity takes hold of everything.

Moment of truth Matthew thought. He almost chuckled. Reismann was a huge Alan Parsons aficionado. Eye in the Sky (AWACS codename) radioed in while Matthew was rethinking his options. He tried to listen but quality was poor. Weather.

"Anything" Matthew asked?

"Another plane has been intercepted and forced to the ground. Unfortunately, in the process we lost a chase plane due to an aerial collision. Apparent stabilizer damage. Sir smaller planes are having more trouble than anticipated given the variable nature of wind."

"The pilot?"

"He's fine. His plane crashed in a field near where the DC-9 was forced to land."

"In a field?" Reynolds blurted out.

"Yes sir…whatever and wherever were the parameters…nonlethal."

Reismann understood visualization. This could become a worldwide YouTube nightmare if they fail to contain the situation.

Silence filled the air while everyone considered multiple situations and options.

"Let's hold off on use of lethal force." Matthew's voiced lacked strength, Reismann heard resignation. He understood the call and likely would have made the same one. It wouldn't take much for a few missed shots to turn a small town into war torn Aleppo, Syria.

~~~

Highland-Winet Airport

Larry and Melina were the last to leave Central States Storms, LLC. Larry couldn't move and Melina wasn't pushing him. She simply shouldered silence with Larry. *They had become a team* she was thinking when she felt Larry's hand on her shoulder. She looked over, smiled, and stood up to leave. Walking through the hangar doors, Melina stopped. Larry looked back. Lost in his own thoughts, he had continued walking. He noticed the smile on Melina's face…looking to the sky. A rainbow was full and a double. Larry listened while Melina quoted Genesis 9:13—"I do set my bow in the cloud, and it shall be for a token of a covenant between me and the earth." Larry was about to say something when Matthew called.

"Larry, here."

"Larry, Matthew and Reynolds. Where are you?"

"Melina and I are leaving Central States. From here, I am trying to formulate our next step." Honesty, Matthew smiled. Larry might just change the profession unbeknownst.

"Larry, we need you to meet Major Reismann at Whiteman Air Force Base. Reismann is overseeing interception of planes in question. Currently, they have intercepted three planes and are tracking several others. The problem is the weather. Smaller chase planes are less stable than larger DC-9's." Larry listened and understood…yet another variable not considered.
~~~

"Understood. We are an easy three hours away. I'll advise when we arrive." Larry ended the call. He and Melina left the airport after first thanking Sanders for his assistance.

~~~

Whiteman Air Force Base

"...force them down...use of lethal force *is not authorized*." This had been discussed but still needed to be reinforced. Reismann didn't want to be responsible for someone taking matters into their own hands. Chain of command stopped with him but he understood personal nature. This attack was taking place on U.S. soil. Their neighbors and friends. Reismann listened to an exchange taking place.

"...Big Country come left and descend to 13,000 feet...make your air speed one, five, zero...copy." The AWACS controller was currently tracking nine suspected targets. Each had been assigned chase planes. His orchestra to direct.

"...copy Maestro...coming left...descending to 13,000 feet...air speed, one, five, zero." Big Country was a C-5 Galaxy "on maneuvers." It was being used to force a smaller and slower plane to the ground. Literally.

Trailing pilot used their on-board cameras to record the incident. Prosperity and training purposes.

With landing gear down, Big Country emerged from clouds directly above the DC-9. The first thud and vibration of impact likely startled pilot and associates. Second and third thuds shook the terrorists to their core. They were completely helpless. They landed within fifteen minutes of Big Country's pilot becoming involved. "Just having some fun," Big Country was overheard saying before they disengaged and left for home. Trailing chase planes followed the DC-9 and landed after they did. State and local authorities were waiting to take the terrorist into custody. Reismann congratulated those involved but knew that other DC-9's had somehow eluded him.
~~~

PART III

It happened . . . the unthinkable happened. Terrorist struck again on U.S. soil. "We never saw it coming . . ." Jenny wrote.

Matthew and Reynolds had been in contact with federal, state and local authorities covering twenty-one cities. These cities housed airports where a storm chaser company had filed a flight plan. There may have been more locations involved; however, without a filed flight plan, it was mere speculation. Of the seven cities provided by Larry, only Kimble, Nebraska was a bust. Forecast of thunder showers dissipated quickly; skies were clear and blue. Sheriffs took three Muslims of undisclosed nationality into custody. A fully fueled DC-9 was seized for forensic investigators. Six other cities were examined. Two turned out to be legitimate operations, but four were deemed terrorist cells, planes and crew never returned. One plane was forced to land in a field outside of Wapello, Iowa, another forced down by a C-5 Galaxy were not on Larry's list. Such planes had been sub-let. Another missed variable.

~~~

From the five planes recovered, with standard flight time available to a DC-9, including extra fuel tanks, investigators were able to determine ground coverage. The storage tank that carried the spore solution mixed with silver iodide in some and potassium chloride in others, using make and model of the atomizer, provided investigators with maximum coverage area. Two things were certain: The plan was ingenious and they were four planes short, based upon confirmed coverage…crop loss reported.

~~~

It is amazing what we individuals take for granted, Jenny thought. Food being a more basic item. The ability to eat anything and everything we want. When we want it.

The powers that be, had a very real dilemma. Without a falling tower and television coverage, was there really a terrorist act? Can we parade fifteen individuals in front of a camera when another thirty likely escaped…with only a vague notion who they were and where they went. Can we say we thwarted part of a plan? Claim credit for being partly correct? Spin doctors were smart enough to be vague during the initial phase of realization by the American people and those of other countries.

~~~

The goal of the terrorist act was not one-hundred percent field saturation although that may have been achieved in isolated locations. On the contrary, terrorist aim was damage, destruction, and disruption similar to that achieved in Argentina. Field and crop loss of 70-plus percent would be a total loss. The cost to maintain remaining crops would be prohibitive, given random appearance of a healthy plant. The impact was severe.

States like Iowa and Illinois rank one and two for bushels of corn and soybeans grown in the United States. Crop loss was greater than 70 percent. Indiana and Ohio ranked fourth, fifth, or sixth on both. Kansas, Wisconsin, and Missouri rounded out the top ten. Each of those states were considered a complete loss.

Wheat production was no better. Kansas was the number two grower of wheat in North America to include Canada. Kansas was a complete loss.

Foreign fields received no better treatment. Early numbers were later revised upward. Satellite imagery was used. China's 14 percent of cultivatable land was a complete loss. Central uplands contained wheat fields. Eastern lowlands maintained China's best farmland. To the south were rice paddies and Sichuan Basin terraced fields. All easily reached from airfields selected. All disrupted, damaged, and ultimately destroyed. Based upon satellite imagery, China may very well have received the deadliest of blows.

Punjab was India's breadbasket. The area was filled with large commercial farms. Satellite imagery showed no sign of a successful crop. Rice and wheat are two of India's major crops.

Vietnam was also struck. Chief agricultural product was rice. Analysts believed Vietnam was struck simply because of location.
~~~

Collateral damage occurred in neighboring countries—Laos, Japan, North Korea. Cloud seeding is known to increase storm intensity, severity, and longevity. This fact, whether known or not, was a benefit. Collateral effect only added to scenarios favoring unrest.

~~~

Seven months after the attack, government rationing in the U.S. was running smoothly. Vouchers were used for cereal grain-based products. Vouchers limited a family of four to caloric intake from cereal grain-based food items to 600 calories per individual. An added benefit was obesity. It dropped by 73 percent. Twenty-seven percent were simply too obese to be of concern.

Each country had its own rationing system but vouchers seemed to work better than use of letters, numbers, or a combination thereof.

To reduce rampant inflation, a price freeze was established. It had the effect of keeping inflation at a relatively modest 13.7 percent. The price freeze was adjusted upward every three months, which alleviated much of the pressure caused by the price freeze itself.

Jenny quoted Dr. Daniel Gray saying, "Jenny, imagine waking up and finding that a 2,400-calorie diet cost you $100 on day one and $100,000 on day two. Whatever would you do? How could you explain that to a newborn child? You simply couldn't. America can live with inflation at 13.7%. Imagine countries that cannot?"

Dr. Gray was correct. With the Internet, it was easy to see unrest in other parts of the world. Martial law and curfews were the norm. People closed their windows to avoid the sound of a crying baby. "I would imagine that hunger is a terrible way to die. To go to sleep hungry is difficult."

"If you are the crying child, yes . . . but how do you think the mother and father feel?" Dr. Gray asked.

~~~

China's domestic cereal grain food storage was far less than the United States. Corn cribs and silos used by the Chinese were not properly ventilated. Mold and other infestations creeped in. Field mice and similar rodents were a problem. Nine months of cereal grain supply was closer to four months. "It's hard to close the window on over one billion people. However, charity begins at home." Erin Brackfield quoted Jenny Pendleton on this statement several times.

The United States cereal grain food supply had been depleted with the aid to Argentina. To compensate, land reallocated for agricultural use planted the super-seed. The yield was encouraging. With reallocated land, overall farming was still down close to 50 percent. Yet at 50 percent, there was still deemed a tolerable error limit that was within reason.

India, North Korea, Vietnam, and Laos were hit hard. Japan and South Korea were thankful they were U. S. allies. Requests for cereal grain imports were answered. Pricing was agreed to and considered fair. Japanese government and her people were not trying to rule the world.

Piracy was a concern. Shipments received naval escort . . . not always visible. Each cargo ship was shadowed by U.S. submarines. Two cargo ships were attacked by pirates, but nothing came of it once submarines went to periscope depth.

China and the United States did not see eye to eye. The United States government wanted concessions from China, Russia, and India plus the usual Middle East countries. Without those concessions, there would be no delivery of the super-seed to Australia, Canada, or Brazil. The United States could guarantee its current level of commitment. Conservative calculations put suitability at ten years. More than time enough to solve the riddle of the super-spore protein.

Chinese concessions were large. Territorial and monetarily large. South China Sea Island project was to be stopped. Buildings and structures were to be dismantled and removed. Man-made island were to be returned to the sea.

Monetary cost was equally punishing. "For the United States to permit exports to China, Canada, Australia, and Brazil would need the super-seed. Otherwise their exports, along with France and Germany, would be equivalent to placing a pimple on an elephant's backside," a junior Senator stated on a popular Sunday morning program.

"That's exactly what Dr. Gray said." Lawrence and Jenny were eating bacon, egg, and cheese sandwiches on toasted bagels. Hot coffee seasoned to taste was also available. For some people, life remained good.

Katie had taken several bushels of corn and wheat super-seed to the Outpost. Phillip was grateful. A local farmer agreed to help plow one of the fields. Katie's intention was nothing more than a goodwill gesture; however, it helped feed over one hundred families the first year. More families and areas were supported over the next two years by "micro-farming."

Chapter Twenty-eight

Non-believers of overpopulation and technological unemployment put their faith in technology. The earth is not overpopulated. Technology will maximize earths known resources while discovering those yet hidden.

St. Louis, Missouri

"Realization occurs before recognition," Lawrence found Jenny awake and at her computer typing.

"It's not easy being you," Lawrence went for coffee.

"What was that, honey?" Jenny's long, slender fingers danced across the keyboard.

Lawrence sat across from her at the table. With two cups of coffee in hand, he forced Jenny to promise not to be such a workaholic. In exchange for said promise, he would provide her with her coffee seasoned to taste.

Lawrence drank his coffee while Jenny typed. There were no books of interest to him or magazines of similar ilk, *Popular Mechanics*, *Field & Stream*. Lawrence reached for a current *Maxim* and began turning pages. Based on photos and stories, life goes on.

It does! Jenny was proof. Sitting across from Lawrence, organizing her notes, with a fast-approaching deadline . . . life most definitely goes on.

~~~
~~~

Washington, D.C.

"Birth and death rates," Larry began. "Rates of birth and death are measured per one thousand people per population. Prior to the terrorist act, the number stayed relatively stable for thirty plus years. However, sirs, since the terrorist act, said numbers have changed drastically. Birth rates have dropped close to 21% two months in a row. Death rates have risen almost 26%. Sirs, we're experiencing a zero-population growth rate. Within six months, we should easily be at a negative growth rate." Larry let the data sink in.

"Numbers directly correlate to NATO countries. China, India, and Russia are likely experiencing greater shifts. It's starvation, sirs." Larry finished before Matthew interjected.

"Larry is correct, sir; underlying factor is starvation of the old and infirm...even the young. They'll always be the first to go. Sir, what Larry is not aware of is our previous discussion," Matthew added.

As with any situation that exists, there are always "what if" scenarios; this situation being no different. The "what if" scenario Matthew referred to dealt specifically with providing aid versus withholding same. Pressure points . . . when and how to provide aid versus withholding same for concessions. One was considered a sign of weakness; the other a sign of strength. Act too soon and recipients will hold you in contempt. An unnecessary delay can result in rebellious anger. That was the psychology. Practicality was somewhat similar.

President, Matthew, Jonathan, and two other cabinet members had discussed and decided upon concessions. Such concessions included debt reduction and South China Sea issues. Anything short of that would be a lost opportunity.

"We must tread lightly," the president said.

"Sir, Larry's security clearance . . ."

"...has just been raised."

"Yes, sir."

"You're hoping citizens of various countries topple their governments." Larry posited.

"Yes," the president answered. "One computer model listed civil unrest in China and India, probability more likely than not. Withholding food increases said percentage."

"Russia?" Larry asked.

"Secretly we came to an agreement with Russia over seventy-five days ago. They're giving us access to their underwater drone technology, larger rocket technology while unilaterally reducing their nuclear weapons in a manner easily verified. We need their stability in select regions of the world. They understand the MAD scenario. Our Chinese brethren believe they can survive a conventional and nuclear engagement." The president answered Larry's question, which was intended for the group.

"If I may . . ." Larry began.

"By all means," Matthew responded.

"Yes, please, speak freely," the president added.

"I understand the need to gain concessions from China; however, I'm uncertain what the logic is for India."

"We need India and China to develop a viable middle class. To do so would mean that India would have to discard aspects of the caste system. China would have to allow development of a hybrid system within the communist form of government. To an extent they have, however, we're not certain the Chinese younger generation is willing to engage in civil unrest," Matthew said.

"Stockholm syndrome," Larry mumbled.

"Something like that," Matthew agreed. There was a pause before the president looked at Larry.

"What are you thinking?"

"I was thinking about the Berlin Wall and how we, and everyone else, missed it. If you look at China now versus Russia then, there are very few comparisons. I doubt if the old Chinese guard will go quietly into the night."

The president nodded in agreement before speaking . . . "Interesting point. Larry, thank you for joining us and I appreciate your contribution to the crisis. If you could excuse Matthew and me."

"Mr. President, Matthew," Larry nodded to both and left the room.

The president looked at Matthew. "He's more of what we need."

"I agree, sir. He has proven to be very resourceful and productive. I will assign him to the China desk and have him prepare an analysis of the two countries. He may have insight that we do not, given the age difference."

"Matthew, are you suggesting that I am old?"

"Yes, sir, I am," they both chuckled.

~~~

St. Louis, Missouri

Research was progressing but at a slower pace than expected. "We have close to one hundred and fifty scientists involved; yet, we've made little progress beyond what Bail, Dr. Montero, and I originally discovered," Katie said to Brad over a beer and an onion cake appetizer. Fried onions with mustard were a delicacy at Mickey's Place. Their prices had risen but not much more than the rate of inflation. Barley production was not affected like other cereal grains. Russia and Germany being the largest growers of barley were able to meet demand of those still thirsty for spirits.

"Why not hold a symposium on the research? You could chair and lead it while providing direction," Brad suggested.

"You're not the first person to mention that. Others have. I guess I'll send out a group email tomorrow doing just that," Katie said.

"Thought'ah saw ya's. Com'n fer eh beer?" Mickey walked up. He looked the same. He still tried to impress upon people the need to relax and remain stress free.

"Just a quick one, Mickey. Voucher day tomorrow."

"Eh. Reminds me of da war."

"The war?" Brad asked. He looked at Mickey disbelievingly . . . *What war?* he was wondering.

"Yes, laddie, da war."

"But Mickey, you aren't that old," Katie bit.

"O'Reilly versus O'Reilly," Mickey said, "was a war fer da ages. Left me eat'n tomato soup fer months."
~~~

"Yeah, I can see that," Brad said out of moral support. Katie's playful slap aside.

"Are you still meeting with Charles and Tim tomorrow?" Brad asked after Mickey walked away. It had been a short exchange. People seemed a little more distant than previous. Not so much Mickey but people in general. The bar had not seen crowds since the terrorist act. Jenny had written an article that addressed this very issue. Psychologists called it PTSD (post-traumatic stress disorder).

"'People have lost their feeling of invincibility,'" Jenny quoted noted psychologist Dr. Ruth Helsinki. "There was a mild case of that with 9/11 but this is much worse given, where they struck, how they did it, and the ripple effect. Let's not forget, very few of terrorists have been apprehended," Dr. Helsinki said. "This lends itself to thoughts of a second attack."

~~~

Jenny wanted to scream. "I can't help you then if all you want to do is scream at ghosts," Lawrence said.

"It's not that . . . I know things."

"Clairvoyance, Jenny?" Lawrence said with a smile while trying not to laugh. "Really?"

Jenny had that serious look on her face. The one that meant laughter was currently dangerous to Lawrence's health. Lawrence smiled in response while Jenny continued . . . "from my research. I never divulge everything because of national security concerns. The administration knew China was a target and chose not to warn them." Lawrence's response was pragmatic.

"That's because the administration wanted to put the Chinese government in a position of vulnerability," Lawrence offered.

"I know that . . . South China Sea, debt forgiveness. I know all of that but is it morally right?" she asked while looking at Lawrence. "People are dying from starvation."

"The alternative is war, Jenny. Would you rather that be the answer in lieu of starvation? Remember the first article you wrote . . . *Displacement*
~~~

via Technology. Economist said the world is overpopulated. Maybe this was God's plan all along, the humane way of dealing with the issue."

Jenny looked at Lawrence "really" but changed her mind in mid-sentence. The best she could do was "Maybe?"

~~

"What time are you meeting with Charles and Tim?" Brad asked.

"Eleven. We'll conference in Larry; I don't know how much progress Charles has made," Katie said.

"I am surprised Larry couldn't do more than expected."

"Dark web," Katie answered with an equal amount of frustration. Which was a truthful answer. Virtual tunnels disguise servers being used. The light post Charles's tracer program used brought him inches closer; however, it was never close enough. A software breakthrough was required. Larry's individual success with the two separate murders yet likely connected was no better. He believed Joseph and Miguel's death plus Bail's accident were all related, yet "Where's the proof?" Investigator Uhl had asked.

He was right. Circumstantial evidence was extensive, but unfortunately one can't legally convict on circumstantial evidence. It can never achieve preponderance of the evidence standard or beyond a reasonable doubt. Everyone felt frustrated.

Chapter Twenty-nine

The average individual can survive seven days without water. That same average individual can survive sixty to seventy days without food.

Tabuk, Saudi Arabia

Sherrief noticed people treated him in a different light. He even felt different. No, it had not been a complete success, but yes, he had succeeded in bringing the infidels to their knees. Sherrief told Khadijah that he had had a dream. In his dream both Allah and Mohammed came to visit him. They wanted him to strike a fatal blow to the infidels after the infidels struck out at each other.

"How will you do this?" Khadijah asked. She worshiped Sherrief. Willingly offering herself to him. Pleasure, yes, but necessary. Sherrief took her in ways that proved his spiritual qualities.

"Of that I will tell you soon. Jericho is still strong. Ibn has even joined his respect to mine. He will make a good addition to our growing family of followers," Sherrief felt his excitement building. "The imam at the Mosque, elders, women, children all look at me and quietly nod. My Jericho fighters say the same. They, too, want to finish what we started. Even now the infidels have yet to understand the true nature of our power . . . my power," Sherrief's scream silenced Khadijah's. The strength of his explosion was of biblical proportion. He released the grip on her neck at just the right time. "Your life is mine when I want it," Sherrief looked down on her. He could still feel the muscles of her body gripping him, holding him, squeezing his life force from him.

"I am ashamed I have but one life to give my God," Khadijah felt Sherrief's body tremble. She would squeeze what life she could out of him until he took her again.

~~~

St. Louis, Missouri

"Good morning, Tim, Charles," Katie said.

"Katie," they both said.

"How have you been?" Tim asked.

"Good . . . frustrated by all of this but still good," Katie said. She just couldn't accept things were moving slowly. There had been a discussion that since the terrorists had attacked, there was little likelihood that the spyware door was still open and active.

Unfortunately, naysayers were proven incorrect by the light post traveling further into the rabbit hole. How they'd come to think of the virtual highway. They were being baited . . . "Catch me if you can."

"Will Larry be joining us?" Tim asked.

"Yes," Katie said. "Let me call him now."

Technology is a beautiful thing. Via the Internet, Larry was present through a remote link. Visual and audio clarity was so perfect that it was like looking at a three-dimensional photograph.

"Amazing," Katie said.

"And it will only get better," Charles added.

"Katie, Tim, Chas, how is everyone?" Larry asked.

"Hello, everyone," Melina called out.

"We are fine," Katie and Tim said.

"Larry, Melina . . . congratulations. How's Angela?" Charles looked over at Katie and Tim with his self-aware grin he affectionately referred to the Freyski curse.

"Yes, how is Angela?" Katie asked.

"Nice recovery, Katie," Larry said to laughter.

"But thank you all anyway. Both mother and child are doing fine."
~~~

"How did you know, Charles, and we did not?" Katie tried to ask quietly but the audio microphone was extremely sensitive.

"Just doing some 'contract work' for us," Larry answered. "Chas happened to be present when Melina delivered."

"Contract work?" Tim mumbled.

"What can I say?" Charles responded. "I've got skills."

"Speaking of which, have you told them?" Larry asked.

"Told us what?" Tim said more than asked.

"I've developed a software worm/detonator that will solve our dilemma. Our problem has been various protocol servers that this individual's spyware runs through. Each server is a filter. Each one more refined than the other until the return/response is clean of attachments. What I have created and have been granted permission to use is a worm that will attach itself to the spyware and detonate when and if it is filtered clean. The detonation will then send both the worm and the spyware it was attached to back to your server. With that we will have the recipient's IP address. From there I would hope Larry would be able to use his position of authority within the government to identify the culprit," Charles said.

"So let's do it," Katie said.

"We shall. Unfortunately, no one has accessed your server for the past six weeks. They have been pinging only. So we may be late, yet again," Charles said. "Other than that, how is your promotion working out?" *Have to keep the pot stirred*, Charles thought.

"What?" Katie blurted out.

"Yeah, Katie, Tim, I received a promotion. I am working the China desk. I would talk more but . . ."

"Understood," Tim said. "Congratulations."

"When will we see everyone?" Katie asked.

"Let's see what happens over the next few months. Everyone has a lot going on right now. Charles, feel free to answer any questions that you can. Everyone, good speaking with you all," good-byes exchanged.

The remaining three stayed quiet for a period of time. Each remembering a couple that they had become friends with due to a pressure situation.

"China desk," Tim said.

"Yeah. President more or less authorized it. Given his promotion and task at hand, Larry will end up running the agency," Charles said.

"Head spook . . . pretty cool," Tim commented.

"Yeah. Let's just hope he can solve our problem for us," Katie continued to discuss each other's respective lives and issues at hand.

~~~

St. Louis, Missouri

The symposium was two days away and Katie was prepared. "I just wish it were today," she said during a conference call with Bail and Dr. Montero.

"Not to worry, Katie," Dr. Montero said. "You'll do fine, believe me. No one understands the process better than you."

"That's right, Katie. But I'm glad to see you with the same devotion when you would sign up for my summer science intensive programs," Bail commented.

Bail had returned after a few months of rest and rehabilitation. There were some scars, mostly physical. The limp was permanent; the cane a necessity. It was good to have him back though, Katie thought. She needed his moral support and research experience and understanding. They worked well together.

They talked for a while longer before the call ended. Two more days of intense research and preparation were on the agenda.

~~~

Jenny was conducting research. She had Googled several pre- and post-government websites. Utilizing the same sites and topics, she was looking for the effect of the terrorist attack. Trends. She was hoping to answer her own internal hypothesis. Was this the event?

Lawrence was watching Thursday night football, Atlanta Falcons versus New Orleans Saints. He was interested in the game but not to the mutual exclusion of Jenny. He looked over and noticed that she had stopped reading. Her face and posture defeated.

"Sweetheart . . . is everything all right?"

Jenny looked up without smiling. When she spoke, it wasn't with sadness but resignation. "Honey, the U.S. is approaching a net zero population growth rate."

"Are you asking?" Lawrence said with a smile, trying to lighten the mood.

"If . . . and when . . . you'll know."

"Women always know when," Lawrence responded.

"Pig," she said with a seductive smile.

"But seriously, if the U.S. is at a net zero population growth rate, what is the rest of the world situation like?" Lawrence asked.

"Most of Europe, including Russia, is slightly negative. Africa, the Middle East, and Asia are all negative by a percentage point or two. Australia is the only nation that still has a positive population growth rate."

"What's the cause?" Lawrence asked.

"Elderly, infirm, young are dying of normal causes exacerbated by lack of a proper diet, caloric intake, nutrition . . . i.e., starvation." She paused before adding, "Birthrate drop-off is likely due to fear of a horrible and dangerous world." Jenny paused yet again before continuing, "I need to get a quote from Dr. Helsinki or someone."

"Me? I'm someone," Lawrence said. Jenny tossed a decorative couch pillow at him in response. "I'm joking. Why not ask Dr. Gray or maybe get a contact name from him?"

"Wait a minute," Lawrence snapped his fingers and continued, "How about Larry? He got promoted. Plus, he sits on the China desk, which is a hotbed of activity and contention."

"Yeah, that's not a bad idea. Wonder why I did not think of it first."

Jenny sent Larry a text message. *Larry, congrats from Lawrence and me on the birth and job promotion. Trust Melina and Angela are doing well. When will we see you all? On a side-note can I interview you for a valuable quote on a follow-up article that I am doing with Dr. Gray? Thanks/Love to all . . . Jenny and Lawrence.*

~~~
~~~

Charles arrived a little later than expected. It was unintentional and unavoidable. "Good morning, all . . . sorry, I am late . . . overslept again," he entered the conference room. Marshall and Katie had been waiting.

"Overslept?" Katie said. She was obviously irritated Charles was cavalier about his responsibility.

"Calm down, Katie," Charles said. "I was alone so I'm upset, too." He took a few minutes to set up. He would be responsible for the virtual presentation platform. Having done this before, he was, in fact, cavalier.

"Okay, let's set this up," Charles looked at Marshall and Katie. "Who has the list of email accounts?" Marshall slid the list across the table. Charles looked at the list and then Katie. Color from his face seemed to fade. "Wow . . . this is a long list."

"Stop it, Charles," Katie commanded. "I'm nervous enough."

Charles read the names of some fairly prominent individuals, include the president, Larry Seabreeze, Alan Guth, Ashoke Sen, etc. There were also the familiar names—Amged, Dr. Montero, Bail Prichard, etc. Charles started to laugh when he got to the bottom of the list. "Michelle Pendleton . . . sister, I take it?"

"Yeah, her high school science class," Katie responded.

"Okay, give me a few minutes while I input these email accounts to prompt their setup. Each recipient will be asked to download proprietary software. It doesn't matter whether they are part of a network or not. They simply agree to standard terms and conditions, check the box, and press Enter. The software is self-loading and self-executing. When the presentation has ended, and everyone has signed off, the program self-erases, leaving no cookies behind." Charles was well into loading email addresses. *This will be a breeze to monitor. Should have slept later.*

"Don't we need to test your platform to ensure its stability?" Marshall asked.

"Already done. I'll be here tomorrow to monitor platform stability while the symposium is ongoing.

"There are two hundred and seventy-one names currently signed up. Assuming another fifteen to twenty late arrivals and we're well within the parameters. I've used this platform for up to five hundred and fifty users without a hitch. Trust me, tomorrow morning will run smoothly from my end," Charles looked at Marshall and then Katie, whom he gave a quick wink to. Katie was not sure how to take that, but why should she, Charles thought.

An hour later, Charles had all email addresses input. He was sending out a group email inclusive with instructions attached. He pressed enter and was done . . . 10:18 a.m. "Done," Charles said.

"That's it?" Katie asked. She was more than a little nervous.

~~~

Melissa, Feldman & Company's office manager, arrived in the conference room followed by two additional individuals carrying several pieces of equipment. "Chas," they both said.

"Walter, Adam," Charles responded, "let's get set up. I want to test in twenty."

"You got it, boss," Walter and Adam sprang into action.

"What's all of this?" Katie asked.

"Camera equipment and a screen for your PowerPoint presentation that I anticipate you'll be using."

"Oh . . . I hadn't thought of that," Katie said.

"Thankfully I get paid to consider what you haven't," Charles said to Marshall's laugh. Seeing everything was in good hands, Marshall got up to leave.

"Charles," Marshall looked at Katie and smiled before he left.

"Once we get this set up, we can do a walk-through so that you will be comfortable. The more comfortable you are, the better you will feel. The better you feel, the better your presentation will be." They got down to business and set-up, testing, practicing the presentation, then repeating for perfection.

~~~

The symposium was at nine o'clock. Katie arrived at six. "Thanks," Katie said when she found Charles waiting for her with his own fresh cup of coffee. Katie caught a whiff of the aroma. "Sorry," Charles said, "proprietary blend."

"Let's do this," he said before Katie could respond.

Charles followed Katie into the building and office. He was set up and online in five minutes. Katie was nervous. She was in her office reviewing everything yet again. By 8:15 a.m., Charles came to get her.

"People are coming online," he said. Katie looked at her watch.

"It's only 8:15." Somewhat irritated.

"Yeah, I know. Coffee time," Charles answered.

"Coffee time?"

"Yeah 'coffee time.' The time before the lecture when people get to talk with the host."

"What?"

"Yeah . . . let's go," Charles led Katie by the arm to the conference room. The equipment was up and running when Katie walked into the room.

She was greeted with friendly "good mornings" from several people already in attendance. Katie realized she was now live. She returned all greetings with a heartfelt smile and wave.

Charles had a screen set up on the opposite wall, which showed her what everyone else would see. It would also show her who was asking a question. In this case, it displayed the current speaker. Katie took a deep breath and entered the role of symposium leader.

The conversation was light, relaxing. One by one, people popped in so that by 9:11 a.m. everyone was present.

Charles was first to speak. "Just some basic housekeeping rules. On everyone's monitor there is a telephone number. Please write that number down now. In the event that you lose connection or appear to be experiencing what you believe to be technical difficulties, please call that number. You will be speaking with Walter or Adam. Guys, please say hello . . ."

"Hello."

"They are at a remote server. They will correct any problem you believe you are having. I will be responsible for everything that happens here. But trust me, this is seamless. I believe you will all enjoy the experience. Now only two points to remember: One, these microphones are sensitive so no shouting or trying to talk over one another. Second, we have the junior and senior high school science classes from St. Teresa High School in Decatur, Illinois, with us today so no off-color remarks. Lastly, if you leave but plan to return, let us know so that we don't think there is a problem on our end or yours," Charles said before adding, "Any questions?" Proverbial pregnant pause. Hearing none, he said, "Let's get started . . . Katie," Charles sat down.

"Thank you, Charles," Katie began. "First a little background," she said. She spoke for a few minutes about the impetus of the super-seed. Her hope and dream of what it could do for mankind. She discussed her sequencing breakthrough with the advent of CRISPR technology and its uses for both good (super-seed) and evil (super-spore). There were some questions and she provided answers. This part of the of the discussion was going perfectly.

Charles was outside the conference room monitoring activity for appearance purposes, which was exactly what Charles wanted Katie to think. He wanted her to act normal. No play acting involved. Charles and Larry had discussed this ad nauseum. Both believed Katie was the weak link. So, simply remove the link from the chain to ensure its strength. Walter and Adam were running everything. They had not been briefed on anything other than "make certain nothing goes awry." Having done this before, everyone was confident of success.

Charles was viewing the presentation via a double monitor. He was listening to the presentation along with his music playlist featuring the best to Pink Floyd, Head East, REO Speedwagon, and Wishbone Ash. His retro playlist.

While jamming to tunes, Charles flipped the camera on his target and went to work. Thankfully, most of the participants were using personal laptops, which provided minimal firewall protection. Even if it were sophisticated, the software downloaded would have permitted Charles to access Amged's computer. He had designed a special spyware program. It was decided that stealth was the approach to take. Charles planted his own spyware, which was to view emails, account protocols, and anything else Charles found "interesting." Larry would be provided access after the symposium.

After two hours, they called a fifteen-minute break. Katie had completed her introduction and discussion on the super-seed sequencing with the aid of CRISPR. There had been several questions, which she confidently answered. This was still considered cutting-edge research, let alone usable technology. Thus, a need to ensure everyone was working with a proper understanding and foundation.

Katie found that she was enjoying herself. She felt the enthusiasm that comes from brainstorming. Energy, energized, were the thoughts running through her head. The break ended, and they were back at it.

The second stage was a discussion on the super-spore. What had been discovered and what hadn't. Charles watched Amged and his expressions reflect the flow of the conversation. "The spore is sophisticated maybe more than the super-seed," Bail had said. Amged smiled at the comment.

"It's comprised of a single cell as most spores are," Katie added. "We've broken down the cell wall, which Dr. Montero and her team can answer questions regarding." There were several questions asked and Dr. Montero answered them without hesitation. Katie used the time to take a mild break and prepare for the final part.

"Once we could pierce the cell wall, we discovered a nucleus with seven individual proteins," Dr. Montero said before continuing. "We've been able to isolate four of the proteins. Two were involved with damping off. Two more were involved with xylem and rust while the remaining three have proven elusive." Katie and Bail joined the discussion regarding what had been tried and considered. Participation was active and engaging. Unfortunately given the time, Charles was forced to interrupt it and suggest that they continue after a thirty-minute lunch break.

"Tradition dictates discussions continue over lunch, so please feel at ease," Charles reminded everyone.

Everyone seemed to be participating, including several of the high school students. This was a good sign. Thirty minutes came and went.

"We now come to the point in time where we all need to focus and speak freely. The remaining three question marks are of a protein structure never seen. It is this aspect of CRISPR technology that makes biological WMDs a real threat and no longer a possibility. The three remaining proteins have a side chain R of undetermined nature. To date, all experiments to determine the R variable have proven unsuccessful."

"Now four of the proteins were discovered, given our understanding what they did, i.e., damping off and disrupted xylem flow up and down the stem. But the other three we aren't certain what purpose they serve. We once thought root rot but we were wrong."

"We simply haven't been able to break the peptide bond that connects the string of amino acids together," Katie took a sip of coffee. Fourth cup today.

"Why can't you just use trial and error?" Larry asked to help jump-start any discussion.

"The human body has over 30,000 different kinds of proteins. We may know what 10 percent do. Corn has over 6,000 different kinds of proteins and we know even less. A single monocellular spore may have only a few proteins, but unless we have an idea what they do, we are looking at potential combinations of astronomical proportions," Michelle answered.

The symposium came to a halt. Walter and Adam checked equipment, which they knew to be operating properly, yet a pin could be heard to drop were one so inclined to drop a pin.

"Excellent response and one on point," Ashoke Sen said to break the ice.

"But that doesn't make any sense," the president responded.

"Human insulin contains 51 amino acids in two polypeptide chains. If one amino acids is out of sequence, we have something other than human insulin. Her response makes perfect sense. I assure you, Mr. President," Vladimir, another scientists, said. "What denaturation processes have you employed?" he asked Katie.

"The usual—heat, acids, centrifugal force, etc.," she answered.

"We can provide a list to everyone. Unfortunately, whoever created this protein has discovered a way to bypass the denaturation process," Katie said.

"So without some type of idea as to their function, we are at a loss. If I understand you," the president said.

"That is essentially correct," Katie responded. Again, the room was quiet for several moments before the discussion began anew. There were some good ideas that sparked robust debate and set the possible stage for different types of testing but nothing overly concrete and promising. Still, Katie was enthusiastic regarding the symposium's success.

"Were there any similarity to the R variable used on the other four proteins discovered?" someone asked.

"No. None," Bail said.

"One was boron, another was sodium, I think the third was krypton, and the last was barium. All relatively easy to obtain, Dr. Montero commented. "We can include this to the list of further follow-up information provided."

The discussion continued for another forty-five minutes before there was a natural ending. *Everything has a life of its own*, Katie thought. It took ten minutes for everyone to close out of the program and another thirty minutes for Walter and Adam to confirm shutdown. Charles was all smiles. He closed out of his laptop. "Nice work, Katie."

"Yeah . . . it was, wasn't it. It was fun and hopefully productive."

"Grab a beer at Mickey's?"

"No. I'm still feeling energized. Adrenaline rush maybe," Katie said. She had a look in her eye. Pensive. Wheels turning. Wood burning. She looked like she was on to something. "I'm going to call over to the lab and see if it's available. We're scheduled for tomorrow, but I feel the moment now," Charles was packing up. They said good-bye while she called the lab. Twenty minutes later she was in her lab coat and looking at the spore.

The discussion on the periodic table had her thinking. Was there a pattern or was it simply random selection? Unfortunately, ninety-plus minutes later Katie's caffeine-fueled hope came crashing down. She was burned out and frustrated. She was on her third cup of coffee (not to include the previous four she had during the symposium) and on edge. She had six more samples to test and zero energy available when she reached for the coffee and ringing cell phone without looking.

~~~
~~~

"What," she said in lieu of a more traditional greeting.

"Excuse me?"

"Sorry, Brad. I spilled my coffee . . . urh, it's in some of the petri dishes," Katie said.

"Babe, it's late. After the symposium, I thought you might want to get something to eat. Unwind," Brad said.

"You're right. I should have...I do have some pent-up frustration energy that needs to be released. How about I stop by instead?" Katie said more than asked.

"I can be persuaded to accept company. I'll start a bath," Brad answered.

"Perfect, I need to rinse these dishes out . . . give me twenty minutes." Twenty minutes later, she and Brad were enjoying bubbles, relaxation, a bath, and a release of her frustration.

~~~

By nine o'clock, Katie was back in the lab with Johnny and Howard. They had arrived at 8:30 a.m. She arrived late, but thankfully with coffee, bagels, and cream cheese. Johnny and Howard read through her notes from the night before, both having spoken with her prior to her abrupt departure. They knew where she left off and where to begin. The next six experiments were set in the petri dishes ready for viewing. After the bagels and coffee, of course.

While eating the bagels and enjoying the coffee, they discussed the symposium from the day before and what favorable comments, if any, they had heard. Katie was still talking while Johnny was finishing up the last bite of his bagel. Howard, being finished and having cleaned up, was preparing slides. He had several laid out. Without really thinking, he placed one slide on the microscope, focused, looked, refocused, and looked again. There had to be a mistake, Howard thought. He set the slide down. He picked up a second slide. Repeated the process . . . same thing. Howard turned to look at Katie and Johnny.

"What?" Katie asked.

"I don't know . . . you have to look at these two slides," Howard said.
~~~

Katie looked at the two slides then stepped aside for Johnny to see. Johnny looked and was also stunned into silence.

"What did you guys do?" Katie asked.

"Only what we had discussed last night," Johnny looked to Howard for support.

"Yeah, we looked at your notes this morning before taking the petri dishes from next to the sink," Howard responded, maybe a little too defensively. They all three had a close friendly working relationship; however, at times . . .

"What did you say?" Katie asked less sternly than it sounded. Howard didn't view it that way. He seemed reluctant to say anything, given she was looking directly at him.

"We read your notes," Howard said hesitantly.

"After that," Katie said, sounding short but again unintentionally.

"Uhhh . . . petri dishes . . . I used the petri dishes . . ." Katie was at the sink. Howard had used the petri dishes that Katie had cleaned from the night before.

She quickly walked back to the microscope and studied each remaining four slides. Five of the six slides showed a clean denaturation of the remaining three protein cells. Five out of six . . . it couldn't be a mistake.

"Okay, let's re-create what you did with six new petri dishes," Katie said. Thirty minutes later, tests came back zero for six. Complete failure! Johnny and Howard were dejected.

"Guys, that's a good thing," Katie rinsed each petri dishes off and set up a second trial. Thirty minutes later zero for six again.

"Good thing?" Johnny asked.

Katie was smiling. "Yes, Johnny that was a good thing," Katie took Johnny's coffee and poured some into each petri dishes. "Sorry, I finished mine," handing Johnny his cup back. Empty. There may have been a sip or two left. Backwash.

They left for lunch while letting any coffee sit in each petri dishes. They walked over to the student union and enjoyed a quick lunch before returning. It had been over an hour's time since they rinsed each petri dish individually. They then set up an experiment before moving on to the next one. Six for six.

Katie, Johnny, and Howard all sat there quiet. They felt that if they disturbed the moment, it might change the results somehow. Finally, Howard caved. "It has to be the caffeine."

"That would be my guess," Katie said.

"Is it a heat substitute?" Johnny asked.

"Don't I know it," Katie let slip to Johnny and Howard's laughter.

After they all had a good laugh, they sent out an email to Bail and Dr. Montero to confirm their findings before sending one out to the group. Katie then looked at her watch, noted the time before sending out a text to Jenny and Lawrence inviting them to Mickey's Place for a small celebration. She called Brad . . . "old-school." Thirty minutes later they were toasting to success.

"That's great news, lassie," Mickey joined the group in a toast. "Th's rounds on me," he announced to the sounds of glasses clinking. The bar had been reasonably busy. Nothing like days of old when it would have been three deep for a Sunday night Week 11 game. Still they had fun and toasting helped alleviate stress and shock.

~~~

Katie was not hungover when she awoke, which was a good thing. She was in the office and on the phone with Bail, Dr. Montero, and her staff. "We confirmed your research. Caffeine is the answer," Dr. Montero said.

"So how did you do it?" Bail asked.

"Saturday night after the symposium I felt energized, so I went to the lab. We had it reserved for Sunday anyway, but I wanted to get a head start."

"That's my girl." Bail laughed.

"Well, I had my petri dishes set up when my cell phone rang. I guess I was wired from coffee and I wasn't paying attention. I reach for my cell phone knocking over my coffee. Some splashed into the petri dishes," Katie said. She heard nothing but laughter.
~~~

"Yeah, but at least we solved it," Katie said.

"Yeah, that you did," Bail said although his voice was no longer jovial.

"Why? What do you mean?" Katie asked.

"Bail," Dr. Montero said.

"Katie, you solved the riddle—that much we all agree. Unfortunately, in your excitement, you may not have noticed something that Dr. Montero and I did." Bail hesitated before moving further toward dropping the other shoe. "Free radicals are attached to the protein molecule. When released into the soil, they attack the microorganisms that make the soil rich," Bail said to silence. Complete and utter silence.

"So, the cure and disease are equal?" Katie finally said.

"Looks that way," Bail said.

"So where do we go from here?" Dr. Montero asked.

"What do you guys think, send out a group email for starters?" Katie asked.

"Yeah, for starters," Bail said. Dr. Montero agreed.

"Okay. Let's look to speak in a day or two," Katie said.

"Free radicals," Katie mumbled. The "unpaired electron," she typed out the email . . .

Symposium Members.

I have good news and bad. The good news is that caffeine breaks the peptide bond on the three remaining proteins. I discovered this after working in the lab Saturday. The symposium motivated me. The motivation ended with me spilling my coffee into some nearby petri dishes. Sorry, I wish I could create a believable thought process but I can't. Once you are done laughing—it is funny—read on for the bad news.

Free radicals.

Free radicals are released when the protein bond is broken. I have checked the previous four proteins, caffeine is ineffective, and there are no free radicals. These three were the doomsday proteins.

Based upon tests performed and confirmed by Bail Prichard and Dr. Montero and her staff, the release of free radicals destroys the microorganisms in the soil. It's what makes the land black gold. Please conduct your own test and hopefully you can find something that we missed.

Thank you,
Katie

Katie pressed Enter and sent the email. She sent one to Larry and the president. On that one, she deleted the last paragraph and added a brief definition of free radicals. She also offered up some suggestion to both the president and Larry. "Heavily fertilize the fields after first plowing under coffee grinds. The coffee grinds are noninvasive and ecologically friendly to soil and environment.

"Unfortunately, I have no suggestion on the free radicals. I also don't believe there is a choice other than that suggested." Again, Katie pressed Enter and sent the email.

Chapter Thirty

Technological unemployment has been discussed since Aristotle's time. John Maynard Keynes popularized the term in the 1930's and believed it to be a maladjustment.

NSA Headquarters

"…Charles focus…you're not focusing." Matthew slammed his hand down hard on the table a third time. He was not as understanding as Reynolds or Larry. Patient either.

"Listen yet again, you are authorized to do whatever it takes. I just need absolute proof. I don't care what you think you can do, just gitt'r done…do you understand or need I explain it to you yet again…" Reynolds had never seen Matthew like this, but the stakes had never been this high.

"I understand. You have to understand what I am attempting to do has never been done before…I just want to make certain there's no blowback on me." Self-preservation…Larry understood Charles's dilemma and felt partly responsible. Matthew's head was spinning. He was on the verge of pulling the plug…

"Chas, relax…we're all on the same team…same page. You're fine…just get us what we want are we clear on that…" The statement hung out there like a balloon waiting to lose air.

"…yeah, we're cool…we're clear…" the conference call disconnected. Larry and Reynolds both showed sweat beads across their forehead.

Matthew looked like a man ready to explode. *Stress* was all Larry could think. He extricated himself from the room.

Larry walked back to his office in silence more than reflective thought. He was momentarily sidetracked by a call from Melina. She was reminding him of dinner with his parents...another forgotten obligation. "7:30...I'll be there." Larry walked into his office and called Charles. Failure was not an option.

~~~

Decatur, Illinois

Amged woke early. He greeted the morning sun the same each day. He stood there with shades drawn back, bathing himself in morning sunlight. He felt this was truly meant for him. His house had been designed and built so that his bedroom faced east. Southeast to be exact. Coordinates 22° latitude, 30° longitude, Mecca, Saudi Arabia.

The house was luxurious by anyone's standards. For Decatur, it could only be considered opulent. It was built on Lookout Point, kitty-corner to Ivy Hill Park off Lost Bridge Road. It was secluded and accessible by private driveway or boat dock. The house was located on a quiet cove.

Sliding glass doors of the master bedroom had the Crescent and Star edged into them. When the early morning sun shone on them, it cast an awe-inspiring reflection across the room.

Amged walked into the predawn morning. He had stopped at the podium and touched the Quran before stepping across the threshold that separated the bedroom from the patio. He read al-Fātihah every morning to begin his day. "Allah is great." After his prayer he showered, dressed, and left for work. "Just a little while longer," Sherrief had said. "We have one more act to complete . . . Be'er Sheva'."

Amged passed through the south gate of the plant and headed directly to his office. He saw more than noticed the two black SUVs parked in the lot. The windows were tinted but he paid little attention to
~~~

them. Homeland Security agents waited fifteen minutes before entering the building.

Amged noticed six individuals sitting around the conference room table. Someone was standing with his back to Amged. He appeared to be giving a presentation. Amged recognized no one. The gentleman in the break room was an unknown and must be part of the group. Good mornings were exchanged. Two guys in the restroom were part of Homeland Security had Amged needed to avail himself of relief.

Amged was downloading his emails when ten agents from Homeland Security entered his office unannounced. Ten minutes later he had been arrested and mirandized. It had still been a beautiful morning. Amged gave thanks to Allah for this day.

~~~

Washington, D.C.

The president was in a somber mood. Understandably so. A cabinet member and friend was involved in a terrorist act on United States' soil and against the world. Whether he was a pawn or a king, the point was moot. He was involved.

At the president's request, Larry provided him with a second copy of an email. It had been approximately one week since he had learned of the treacherous act. The investigation was almost complete. With very few emails, communication was decided to have been via cell phone. Charges were to be quietly made to prevent harm to innocent family members young and old alike.

Jonathan arrived at the office at his usual time. Coffee in hand, he said hello to Susan, his secretary, and proceeded to his office. Another typical day ahead. No longer in a position of power, Jonathan believed his future professional career had slowly been taken from him. Death by a thousand cuts was how he viewed it. He could have, should have, positioned himself a power broker after his government position ended, but he failed to maintain contacts or to play The Game required. He
~~~

had not burned any bridges, he reflected. Looking absently out of his window into the still morning Washington air. It was more the fact of not completing the construction of necessary bridges. Jonathan turned to face his desk. He noticed more than actually saw the piece of paper set in the middle; on the ink blotter.

Jonathan thought to call Susan but decided against it. Instead he looked eerily around his office, expecting to see the delivering hand hiding in a corner. Somehow, Jonathan knew what the paper was.

He was standing next to his desk when Susan notified him of his early morning appointment. Jonathan was unaware that he had an appointment and asked her to reschedule it. He was "not feeling well."

"It's the president," Susan said, somewhat embarrassed.

"Yes, of course," Jonathan said. "Please show him in."

Susan showed the president in and offered him coffee, which he respectfully declined. Not feeling comfortable herself, she quickly left for the break room and her solitude.

"Mr. President, good morning," Jonathan said.

"Good morning, Jonathan. Forgive the last-minute intrusion. I was on the Hill early and decided to stop by." The president casually noticed that the letter/email was gone and Jonathan was on edge.

"Please sit down, Mr. President." Jonathan took a seat in front of his desk…sitting next to the president.

There was silence in the air, not tension. The move was the president's, not Jonathan's. The president knew this and he also was aware that Jonathan knew this and had tactfully decided to take a chair next to him. Just two old friends involved in a friendly chat.

"Jonathan, we have been friends for over thirty years. We have worked together for most of those years. If there was a problem, why didn't you come to me?" the president asked.

Jonathan hesitated before answering. He wasn't certain how the president would address the email though it was a foregone conclusion that he was the one who placed it on his desk. How he knew? How long had he suspected? Known? All questions that he was well beyond asking. Damage control was what this conversation was about.

"To avoid public embarrassment, Mr. President, I will resign for health reasons," Jonathan said. It was at that moment that he realized this was more than damage control.

"Jonathan, this is an act of terrorism. Treason...not just against the United States but against all of mankind. How did you become involved in this?" the president asked . . . one old friend to another.

But there was no answer...how could there be.

"I would like to be able to tell Becky and the family if I could?" Jonathan asked.

He was standing again by the window, looking absently out at the monuments. He hadn't even been aware that he stood up and walked over yet he must've for he was there. The phrase a *penny for your thoughts* came to mind yet he recognized that he had none. He wasn't thinking anything he was simply standing, staring.

The president had risen from his seat. He walked to the office door, turning to Jonathan only to say, "All of your accounts have been frozen so please do what you must for Becky and the family before being at the White House, three o'clock."

Later that day while meeting with delegates from Canada and Australia, the president was informed that Jonathan Livingston had died. Cause of death: tragic accident.

The president asked to be alone and the courtesy was granted. He sat in silence looking long and hard at the Presidential Seal on the floor of the Oval Office. It was only after several minutes that he began to fully understand the true meaning of the symbol. A tear rolled down his cheek, he walked to the door and invited his guests back to the meeting. The time to lead had returned.

CPSIA information can be obtained
at www.ICGtesting.com
Printed in the USA
BVHW032144291119
565084BV00016B/46/P

9 781973 673903